CUNNING WOMEN

CUNNING WOMEN

Elizabeth Lee

WINDMILL

1 3 5 7 9 10 8 6 4 2

Windmill Books
20 Vauxhall Bridge Road
London SW1V 2SA

Windmill Books is part of the Penguin Random House group
of companies whose addresses can be found at
global.penguinrandomhouse.com

Penguin
Random House
UK

First published by Windmill Books in 2021

www.penguin.co.uk

A CIP catalogue record for this book is available from
the British Library.

ISBN HB:9781786091161
TPB: 9781786091178

Typeset in 12.5/15.5 pt Bembo Std
by Integra Software Services Pvt. Ltd, Pondicherry

Printed and bound in Great Britain by Clays Ltd, Elcograf S.p.A.

The authorised representative in the EEA is Penguin Random House
Ireland, Morrison Chambers, 32 Nassau Street, Dublin D02 YH68.

Penguin Random House is committed to a sustainable
future for our business, our readers and our planet.
This book is made from Forest Stewardship Council®
certified paper.

For my mum, Sally

An Unfamiliar Pain

Lancashire, 1620

Annie sleeps curled up on the bed we share, wet thumb fallen from her mouth. I kneel, calling and shaking her. She frowns and mutters.

'Wake up,' I say.

She pushes me off and turns her back.

'Get up. Time to search.'

Her eyes open and she sits forward, clutching my arm. 'Has he come?'

'We rang the bell, didn't we? And the ash is untouched.'

She looks to see that the thin ring around the bed shows no trace of his hoof print.

'I'm safe, then,' she says, lying back down.

'No.' I pull her to her feet. Have to know she's free for another day. Too late for me, I'm doomed to a future I cannot escape, but she may yet be saved. She's so scrawny I could carry her with one hand. Ignoring her complaints, I drag her over to the weak light of the slit in the wall, standing in the narrow space between our mat and Mam's, and begin the daily ritual. I pull the clothes over her head and she stands, naked and shivering, as I search every part of her skin.

I start with her side, where my mark lies, the rounded shape of his mouth berry-red. Her side is clear, white goose-pimpled skin stretched tight over jagged bone. I lift and turn her arms, spread her fingers to inspect the flesh between them, look behind her knees and on the underside of each foot. The flea bites she has picked are rough but the mark I pray I will never find would be flat and dark. A stain that no washing can remove, though God knows I have tried. As she bows her head I hold her hair and search the back of her neck.

She is not his yet.

I pull her into my arms and cradle her. 'Nowt.' Let out my breath at last. Every day I begin by reassuring her. Every day I begin with foreboding.

She springs from our mat through the doorway to John's empty one and back, clapping her grimy hands. 'He doesn't want me.' She smiles, wipes her nose and licks off the slime trail it leaves.

I laugh and pull the clothes on over her head before she skips away into the other room to stand in the spilled ashes from the fire and take what warmth she may.

Mam has risen from bed, blanket pulled around her as she stands in the doorway.

'No visit?' she asks, words sliding through the gaps in her teeth.

I shake my head.

'He'll come. None of your tricks can stop him.' She glances at her familiar, a hare, harmless to us but a willing carrier of curses, she says. It appears only to her, but we know its presence by her whispered words of love and plans of ruin. 'We know it, do we not, Dew-Springer?' I stare, trying to see its footprints in the ash or glimpse it shifting around her feet. Nothing.

Squeezing past John's mat and the table to reach the fire, she waves Annie away, and pokes the lifeless ashes, dust rising and coating the mould on the wall. The blanket falls from her shoulders, showing the ridge of her backbone, and her own mark.

'Firewood,' she says.

'I'll go to the shore, fetch some driftwood. Perhaps find some clams.'

'Help me wipe her first?'

I dip a rag into the bucket and Mam catches Annie before she can run. She cries out and struggles as I scrub her dirty face and hands, but hasn't the strength to escape. We gave her the last of the bread two days ago.

'Dolts,' she shouts, fists clenched and teeth bared. Mam and I try to control our laughter at her angry face, damp hair sprouting out. 'Gormless.'

The door bangs against the wall and we stare at John as he stands with legs apart, hands behind his back and elbows out, trying to bulk his thin frame.

'You'll never guess what I got,' he says.

'A bird,' Annie says. 'A spadger, a little brown one?'

John rolls his eyes. 'Why would I bring a bird, squirrel?'

'Be more use than you,' I say.

Annie wipes her nose on her sleeve and shrugs. 'No matter, there's spadgers in the woods. I'll get my own.'

'No, guess properly. Guess what I got.'

'A clout is what you'll get if you don't tell us,' Mam says.

A toothless threat. She has never raised a hand to us. Only once I've seen her driven to violence. A swift and deep fury, rising to protect her own.

John swings a fist round from behind his back, puffing up as though he has a chest of gold. Mam gasps.

From his hand dangles the body of a lamb. Blood drips on to the floor, a steady pat, pat, pat.

Mam staggers over and gathers him into her arms, lamb and all. The back of his tunic is stained red. 'Oh, John. You're quite the man. We're saved.'

She is right. Without this we have nothing but scraps from shore and hedgerow to eat. The steady drip is mesmerising, beat of it against the floor, spreading puddle at his feet. A trail up the hill, and through the abandoned shell of a hamlet sur-rounding us, that will lead straight to our house.

John flushes and shakes her off. 'It's only a little 'un.'

She takes it from him, turning and examining its limp body, holding a bowl to catch the precious blood. 'Makes the meat all the sweeter. Plenty here for us.'

'And I know where there's turnips.'

'Then go, lad. We'll have a feast. Annie wipe the table, Sarah fetch my knife.'

John runs out of the door and I bring the knife, but Annie stays where she is.

'It's so small,' she says.

'Big enough to feed us all,' I reply.

'It's a babby.'

I stop and look at her. She is watching Mam split and strip the skin, the white wool now stained crimson. Tears stand in her eyes. She wipes the back of her hand across her mouth, lips wet.

I kneel in front of her, take her bony shoulders in my hands. 'He killed it quickly. It didn't feel a thing.'

She stares past me at the lamb, now no more than a lump of meat on our table.

'Come with me, little cub,' I say. 'We'll collect seaweed to have with it and wood to build the fire.'

I take her hand and walk her out of the door.

We eat long before the sun has reached its peak. A feast the like of which we can't remember, one that should be saved for evening but we cannot wait. John fetches turnips, Annie and I find a little seaweed, and they are cooked in the pot together with the lamb. A meal richer than we are used to, meat full of flavour as it falls apart in the mouth.

Once the food is in front of him John digs in with his fingers, shoving turnips into his mouth so that pieces fall and stick to his chin, tearing into the meat with his teeth.

Mam, Annie and I are only a little more controlled, eating without pause. We neither speak nor look up from the bowls until they're bare.

I lean back in my seat, sigh, clutch my tight belly. There is an unfamiliar pain there. The pain of greed. John looks around at us, a king who has fed his people.

'You did well, son. There'll be more to come too. Broth from the bones. The blood I can use for curses and the money will buy us more food.'

John lets out a long, loud belch. Annie laughs and even Mam smiles.

'How did you come by the lamb?' I ask.

Silence for a moment. Mam rises and begins to gather the bowls, her movements swift and jarring.

John shifts in his seat, looks down at the back of his hand and scratches it. 'Took one of the Taylors', didn't I? Out on the path, anybody's to keep.'

'Stolen.'

'Of course stole, did you think I'd found fairies' gold to pay for it?'

'Didn't work for it, then?'

'It was on the track, free for the taking,' Mam says.

'Not free, stolen. He could hang for this.'

'They won't hang John,' Annie says, chewing on a grimy nail. 'We'll never let them, Mammy will curse their eyes to fall out and I'll feed them to the birds in the woods so they'll not find him. They won't hang you, will they, John?'

'No need, little squirrel. Lamb was out of the field, could've been wild for all I knew. Won't be missed, unless Sarah's wretched conscience gets the better of her.'

'If you worked ...'

'There's no one'll have me, I've banged on every door asking for every task and not a soul will give me one.'

'It makes a truth of all they say about us.'

Mam slams the bowls back on to the table. 'They say it and we must be it. Would you have me choose the other?' She holds my gaze until I look away.

'Besides,' she says. 'That Matt Taylor has plenty, he won't miss a little lamb. And he's a gudgeon if ever there was one, him and that mewling son of his.'

I sit at the still-cluttered table as John sharpens his knife on a stone and shadow creeps in from the walls. Mam has set the lamb's head to boil, having saved the eyes. When the skull is clean and white we'll take it to the village and someone shall be pleased to have it buried in their home as a charm to protect from evil spirits. The stench fills the house.

'Mammy?' Annie says around her thumb. 'Tell me how I began?'

The scrape of the knife stops. Mam leaves her pot and sits with Annie. Sometimes she pushes her away when this question is asked, sometimes tells stories of sunny days.

'Your beginning was like no other. You were a gift, sprung from the ground, filled with enchantment.'

Annie nestles against her. 'Filled of magic, aren't I, Mammy? But Sarah and John had a daddy.' Her mouth droops. 'I wish I'd a daddy.'

'He was a good man.'

A memory comes upon me, so swiftly here and gone that I barely feel its presence, of his warm hand resting upon my head, of the scent of salt-soaked clothes.

In the gathering gloom Mam's expression is hidden, but the way she tips her head tells me that she's losing herself into the past. I try to catch John's eye but he is busy smoothing his sharpening stone on the cloth of his tunic.

'He was tall,' Mam says. 'High as a tree with arms thick as branches.'

I hold myself tight, knowing she skims her memories and chooses the brightest to share now. Others may come later.

John snorts. The knife scrapes again. He was five when our father died, the age Annie is now. There cannot be much he remembers.

'That's just his look,' Annie says. 'What was he like?'

'His hair was curly, black and shiny like a pebble wet with seawater, and his eyes were the colour of the sea itself.'

Mam's face is turned away from Annie now. 'He called me beautiful. My skin was the prettiest ever seen, he said. Smooth and fair as fresh-churned cream.'

Annie's thumb leaves her mouth with a pop. 'But what was he like, Mammy? You're not hearing.'

'She's tired,' I say, standing. This nonsense must stop. 'And so are you. Bed. I'll fetch the bell.'

'I don't want to.' Annie crosses her arms, dips her chin into her chest.

John taps his knife against the rock, holding it close to his eyes so that he may see it in the fading light. He does not look up.

'Darkening out,' he says. 'Night's come. And you know who comes with it, looking for new blood.'

I smack my palm across the back of his head. 'Stop that, goffy.'

Annie is across the room instantly, little hand slipping into my own, and John sits back, eyebrows raised, feet on the table.

Mam stays on the bed, arms about her knees. Annie and I take the bell, her hand over mine. Three rings in each of the eight corners of the house, then we place it back on the floor by the fire.

'There,' I say. 'Safe now.'

'Will you lie with me?'

I glance at Mam. Her body stays as before, her mind trapped in memory.

'All right,' I say.

We study the ring around the bed before lying down. Unbroken. Tomorrow I shall sweep it away and make a fresh one as I always do, trickling ash from the fire through my closed fist, steadily, so the loop remains constant. It is all I can do to keep her safe, and this is all I wish for. It is there to protect Annie, not me, for he does not make return visits, I'm told.

She curls up next to me and I pull the blanket over us both. Her arms hot around my neck, breath sour with the food. The stink of the lamb's head hangs in the air.

I've no memory of the night he came, marked my skin and drank from me. Choosing me for a purpose I have yet to discover. The dark red patch on my side has been there for as long as I remember. Mam didn't tell me what it meant until I was twelve and before this I had thought nothing of the stain I carried, finding no more significance in it than my blue eyes or unruly hair. She ignored my tears, as the possible lives I had dreamed for myself shrank to one. They remain for Annie, though.

She sucks her thumb and winds my hair around her fingers. All I can hear is John's knife scraping against his toenails, his chewing as he lifts the shavings to his mouth. Of course he does not carry the mark, and I used to envy such freedom to choose a skill and carve his own path. But now I look to the lives John may have and see nothing but this one he already lives.

'People will pay for the blood.'

I start as Mam's voice cuts across the room. Annie's eyes open, the steady sucking on her thumb stops.

'Shh,' I say to them both.

'Good for curses. A death mark in blood, that'll satisfy. Then they may pay for the cure too.'

'You've woken Annie.' Irritation makes me bold, so that my words surprise even myself. Mam does not respond.

'And the eyes,' she says. 'Everyone wants an eye kept on their enemies. You've fed us for a week with this, John. Next time fetch a bigger one.'

I sit up and the hair Annie clutches in her sticky fingers is pulled from my head. 'There'll be no next time.'

'Then what should we live on?' The quietness of Mam's voice suggests as much anger as if it were raised.

'We can manage.'

'And what form of managing do you think I should take up next, if your brother's not to help me? What choices are left me since your father's gone?'

Annie wriggles and whimpers. It's the same every time. Mam's thoughts of my father begin sweet as nectar and end bitter as wormwood.

She turns her back but speaks clearly enough. 'You're a woman now. There are ways other than begging that you can be of use.'

No more to be spoken. The only sounds are Annie's slow breaths and the shuffling of Mam and John as they prepare for bed, the rustle of mice nesting in our mats. I lie awake, seething with thoughts of what my life might have been had I freedom to choose, and what it must be knowing I do not. But I will not give up all command over myself. If Mam thinks to dress and paint me and let me be used by the village men, I will maim them one by one before earning a single coin. If it's witchcraft she speaks of I'll have none. His dark power is in me, I have felt it, waiting to be unlocked. I am marked, my fate to one day conjure my own familiar and spin curses as Mam does. But not this day.

Lying in the darkness, I listen to the creaking of door and roof, the shifting of branches in wind. Feel his prowling presence, reaching to the anger that twists in me, calling upon me to embrace it, and become my true self.

Flesh and Blood and Bones

It was the noise that drew Daniel's attention, a desperate and pathetic bleating coming from the hedge. He turned towards it, stumbling over the rough grass, milk spilling from his pail. Stopping to listen, he heard scuffling and muttered swearing.

Someone was stealing a sheep and were Father here he would rip their arms off rather than allow his property to be taken. But it was only the animal's terror that moved Daniel, prompted him to let go of the pail, run over to the hedge and call out.

'L-leave that creature be. Leave it at—' His voice escaped him.

Daniel was staring into the filthy, angry face of the Devil-boy from the old plague hill. All thought left him. He stepped back, reaching a hand to steady himself against the prickly hedge as the world tipped then righted itself, all the while unable to look away.

The boy smiled slowly and, without dropping his gaze from Daniel's face, lifted the lamb and drew a knife across its neck.

Blood poured from the wound and the animal kicked and shuddered. A small sound escaped Daniel, an expression of fear and pity that prompted mocking laughter from the boy.

He leaned over the hedge. 'Dust know me?'

Daniel nodded. Heart clattering, mouth dry. Terrified now of what curse this boy would lay on him.

'Bring hell on you if you spake a word,' the boy said. He swung the lamb over his narrow shoulder and strolled down the track.

Daniel watched the lamb's blood spreading down the boy's back. He felt the warm, sticky liquid on his own skin, smelled metal, tasted salt. Blinking, he saw everything through a sheet of red.

The beat of his heart ran faster, the rhythm jarring and irregular. He tried to breathe deeply, steadily, but no matter how he gasped no air would come. Falling to his knees he felt a dread that his father would discover him in this most humiliating position, as he pitched face forward and the redness before his eyes became darkness.

Daniel grew aware, slowly, of the scent and chafe of grass. It pressed into his eyelids, bristled between his lips. He licked and spat, rolled on to his back, opened his eyes. Staring into the clear wash of sky, he could not at first remember how he came to be lying there.

The bleat of lambs brought it back to him, the slice of knife and rush of blood. Black smile of the Haworth boy.

He lurched upwards, staggering to his feet and lifting the bucket, focusing on the sting as the skin on his knuckles cracked and bled, and listening to Father's sharp calls to the oxen. Milk threatened to slop over the side as Daniel walked, pail pulling on his arm. He wanted to hold it with both hands out in front of him, but he had been caught doing that once by Gabriel, the farmhand.

'Shall I call my little sister for you, Danny?' Gabriel had said. 'She could carry that pail with her fingers, she's used to women's work. But there, so's you.'

He had walked away, laughing and shaking his head, and Daniel had sworn he would never again endure such ridicule. His arm might rip from his shoulder, but he would carry the bucket with one hand.

Daniel strove to keep his mind empty, but could think only of the boy's twisted lips as he spoke. There were stories of the Haworth hag and her warped brood; that the youngest brat was found stealing teeth from the graveyard, that Tobias Barton's three children died one after another when he chased the eldest girl off his land for begging, that the boy had demons in his power.

He had never seen one of them up close before, and the experience had been every bit as foul and wretched as he had feared. They knew of him now, he had tried to thwart the boy, and sure as night would fall there would be a price to pay. Daniel could not imagine what witchcraft would be done with the flesh and blood and bones of a month-old lamb.

The words still whispered in his ear.

'Hell on you.' And Daniel shivered.

Wet Boots and Fresh Fish

Mam clasps a poppet in her hands, sewn from a piece of cloth that was once part of my father's tunic. Made in his image, some strands of his hair attached.

The doll is ragged now, scorched where she has burned it, scarred where she's sliced then stitched it. Her weapon tonight is thorns, pulled from the brambles that clog Matt Taylor's hedgerows, and stained with her own blood.

I crouch beside her, against the wall of the house, but she doesn't falter. She presses a thorn, slowly so that I hear the material tear, into the leg of the doll. 'For sailing out into a storm,' she says. Tears run down her face into her mouth and the words are wet, slippery and bitter.

The next thorn goes into his cheek. 'For letting the sea swallow you.'

Another and another and another into his chest, his back, wherever she can fit them. 'For leaving us, for leaving me to become this, for abandoning the childer to a life of hunger and cold ...'

I reach out, put my hand over hers, stop her. No good ever comes of this, the poppet only feeds her pain, and I cannot bear to see her with it again. She hesitates, fingers still hovering above the doll, then looks up into the distance, past my shoulder, and rubs her face. A smear is left on her cheek.

'Remember?' she says, still looking past me.

'Father?'

'Life as it was.'

I search for an answer that will not hurt her. 'Sometimes.'

I've tried to hold my memories, keep them like the moth caught in the bubble of hard yellow sap that clings to the ash trunk, but they will not stay. There have been more years since he passed than we ever had together.

Once in a while a picture comes, a scent brings him back. The lift of his brows and creases in the corners of his eyes as he smiled down at me past the great stretch of his legs and body, the rush of air as he swung me high on to his shoulders. Those are real, I'm sure. The smell of wet boots and fresh fish. His hands, hard-skinned yet gentle, as they softly pinched the plump bed of my thumb. Mam's laughter, soft and sweet, like the sounds of shells shaken in a small fist. That woman was taken too.

'It all went with him,' she says. 'The food on the table, the cloth in the windows, the wood in the fire. You used to play in the fields with that farm lad, they even let you feed a lamb once. We went to dances. I used to call Alice Turner a friend, now she'll spit as soon as look at me.'

Her tears have dried, leaving clear tracks through the grime on her face. She sighs, pulls the thorns out gently, laying them aside for next time.

'Jonathon,' she whispers, stroking the strands of hair that remain. 'Come back to me, in any form, I'll not fear you. Just come back.'

She cradles the doll in her palm, holds it against her cheek, presses it to her nose. I put my arms around her and she looks at me for the first time, shakes her head.

She grabs my hand. 'Should you choose a life with another, that life will be shattered and the one you love will suffer most cruel. Keep true to the one that's chose you.'

I ease my hand from her grip. This warning has fallen from her lips so often that I can't remember a time when I ever thought a life of love and happiness with another would be mine. It does not stop me dreaming of it, though. I lick my lip, glance past her shoulder.

'Who is this?'

The man is almost upon us before we see him, his feet scattering pebbles as he walks up the path to where we sit by the house. Black cloth billowing, soft hat held to his head in defiance of the wind that beats in from the sea. We wait, still crouched against the wall, watching him.

He could have remained hidden, walking through the woods that run up our hill at the edge of what once was the hamlet from the river below. But night is enough cover, and he has chosen the quicker route of the path. Picking his way through the tumbling silhouettes of the handful of dwellings surrounding ours, once homes to those long ago taken by plague, many still furnished with fallen and broken chairs or shattered plates, now slowly succumbing to the invasion of root and branch. Annie scours them, untroubled by the spirits of those still bound there, returning with pieces plucked from the leavings. Some of those doors still attached show the remains of the cross they were marked with, though most have fallen and rot into the ground with their owners.

The moon is bright, sky speckled with stars that gleam like flecks of ice, lighting the trail of dark splashes of lamb's blood up the path. I notice them for the first time, distracted as I was by Mam. We need rain to wash away our guilt, but there'll be none tonight.

Mam wipes her face and stands. 'Inside,' she says, and I'm happy to obey. He is a regular visitor, not one I fear, with a changeable countenance but never angry. Tonight he's slowed by melancholy so that I give him a smile, since it's all I have to offer. He returns it and hands me two radishes, still grainy with mud.

'Thank you.'

'Next time I will bring you bread.' His voice strains to shed the weight of his misery.

'You are in need of a potion,' Mam says as I turn away.

His voice lowers and I linger in the doorway to hear. 'If only I could resist, a man of my position should be stronger. But I fear without it I—'

'A man of any sort needs comfort, Seth,' Mam says.

The door closes and I am in the murk, feeling for the table to lay the radishes on, taking a few steps with a hand along the wall until my foot knocks against the pile of findings Annie keeps by our mat: stones, and her favourite shell from the beach, flat and smooth. The pieces she has brought from the deserted dwellings that surround us: parts of bowls, usually, broken into jagged, muddy shards. I crawl in next to her, refusing to let myself think of what they once contained, of the hands that held them.

There are few who come to our door and Seth is the sweetest of them all, always bringing a gift of some kind, and if he is cheerful, swinging Annie round by the arms until she laughs and hiccups. Though if we see him in the village we are to treat him as a stranger, for they know him by a different name there.

I am especially glad of his arrival tonight; the company and coin he brings will lead Mam away from sorrow. He was not a perfect man, my father, and even now she knows it as well as I, telling stories of his drinking and flirting with a light in her eyes. She forgives him every time. She forgives him everything, except dying.

The lamb allows us to live as others do, as Mam, John and I once did, for two days. By the third morning we're left with only broth, and Annie has licked the bones clean. As I finish searching her for marks, Mam turns to me.

'We must go to the village.' She catches Annie as she tries to run to the woods. 'And you, lass. There's work to be done. Come, Dew-Springer.'

Mam takes her familiar on every trip to the village or the cottages that line the seashore, for protection. She has often warned us of the need to guard our knowledge from outsiders. We must always keep a gulf between their lives and ours. I wonder what form my familiar will take, when the time comes, and whether it will bring a feeling of safety.

We walk with Mam as far as the edge of the village, the path still marked by the lamb's blood, though we don't speak of it. Next time I fetch water I shall try to wash it away, for we can't afford to provoke anger. Most endure us without much complaint, for they make use of Mam's herb-knowledge when they need, though there will always be some that suspect us of more. Of worse. And it is true that Mam, if angered, is not beyond calling upon dark forces to bring about suffering. Matt Taylor is one that does not look kindly on us, and would take little convincing of our guilt.

Mam breaks off from us towards the fishermen's cottages that line the harbour, for John has brought tell of a woman there whose hen broods and will not lay. It is likely cursed and she'll ask Mam to divine who this enemy is and punish them, as well as rid it of the enchantment. Mam carries the lamb's eyes and what remains of the blood, for both might have a use here. We skirt the village and pass to the other side, and I am glad that she yet expects no more of me than begging and gathering herbs. The time comes, I know, when she will insist I learn the cunning ways, and all that means: herbs and healing but also curses and retributions. Sometimes she asks me, but always I resist, feared of the stirring within myself: the call to anger, the lust to harm. The will of he that claimed me.

It is Sunday, and the good people are on their way to church. A day with almost as much meaning for us as it has for them, for we must live by the pattern of their days if we're to know when to catch them to our advantage. The villagers are dressed in their best to meet God, though I've never understood why. Surely He sees straight through the clothes to their blackened souls beneath. No pretty flower will hide the look that's an invitation to another's husband, no scrubbing of a hand will remove the bruise it left on a wife's face the night before.

Annie and I are used to keeping unseen, skulking round corners and lurking in shadows. We have learned to step silently. Over the hedge we see hats and caps bob along the path. When we step on to the road they scatter as though a stone has been thrown among them. The ladies drop their eyes and move aside, the men raise their chins and glare. Mam has taught us which villagers will never show kindness and which are happy to buy from her, though none are inclined to give and get nowt in return, as we well know.

The first stone hits Annie on the back, and she cries out, a combination of pain and bewilderment. I know from the sound that she's not badly hurt, but clutch her to me and spin around to see a lad and lass, not much older than she, laughing as they let fly some more. I'm caught on the shoulder and arm that protects Annie, a sting and spread of heat that is not strong but angers me.

'Plague-sore,' they call. 'Basket-scrambler.'

I almost throw Annie to the ground. 'Wait there,' I say, marching towards the children.

Their expressions of amusement slip into fear as I bear down upon them, something burning through me. I've not thought what I shall do when I catch them. They turn and run into the arms of a woman who rushes towards them, gathers them behind her and meets my eye with a sickened look.

'Sorry,' she says. 'I'm sorry. They're just babbies, they mean no harm.'

'They were throwing rocks. They hurt my sister.'

'I – I know, I'm sorry. I'll thrash them, I promise, just please don't – please don't curse an illness upon them.'

Tears brim in her eyes. The children hide behind her shabby petticoats, that are patched and worn. I embrace the growing fury, a throbbing of anger that draws me up tall and brings the whisper of black words to the edge of my tongue. The woman cowers before me as though I were the one throwing stones.

I lift my chin and hold out my hand. Wait. She closes her eyes, drops her head and then fumbles in her petticoat to produce her pocket. Holds it out to me, shaking so that she struggles to open it, but there's no need. I can see the thin, soft material holds no coin.

'Please,' she says. 'I'll come to your mam and spend all that we can spare. My – my husband ails and cannot recover, she perhaps has some tonic that will …' Her voice trails off, and I drop my arm, drop my gaze from her stricken expression. Turn away from any sympathy that rises in me for her situation, her sadness, her despair. When they treat us this way I become the very creature they fear me to be.

I walk back towards Annie and, as the woman scuttles past with her children, we approach Samuel Finch, the netter, and his wife Nelly. They are young, newly wed and without children yet. Not ones that Mam has mentioned either way, and I decide to try our chances.

Annie widens her eyes and droops her mouth. She's filthy, face smeared with dirt, leaves caught in the clump of her hair. I pull her finger from her ear.

'Excuse us, sir,' I say, reaching out to touch his arm. The cloth under my hand is thick and warm.

They stop and turn towards us. He shakes me off and I know that my optimism was a mistake. Still, we must try.

I hold Annie in front of me. 'My sister's hungry and we've nowt to feed her. It's been days and she's just a little lass, so sweet and never marding.'

He glances around. She looks at Annie, her eyes big and gentle.

'I wouldn't ask but she's weak and hungry and if we could only beg a small kindness from you good people, we'd be—'

Nelly smiles at Annie, begins to play with the folds of her petticoat, where her pocket lies. Weighted with coins for church, no doubt. Surely God would not begrudge one given to feed a hungry child, she's thinking. I know the kind of soft, motherly woman who will respond, and today my knowledge will furnish us with a coin to take home.

But soft, motherly women do not control purse strings. He reaches out and bats her hand away. A bracelet of fading bruises circles her wrist.

'Oh, Samuel,' she whispers. 'Could we not …?'

'No. You want to consort with heathens? On the way to church?'

He turns, pushing the small of her back as they walk away so swiftly that she stumbles a little.

'For God's sake, Nell,' he says. 'Step firm.'

She looks over her shoulder at us. I offer a smile, for her kindness is rare. Though a coin would be better.

The throngs dwindle and we've no success. I sit with Annie at the side of the road as the familiar clawing of hunger returns, imagining the tables these church-goers will return to, laden with meats and cheeses and bread, fragrant and fresh-baked. Annie wriggles her dusty toes, legs stretched in front of her.

One last villager makes his way to church, sauntering up the path, unafraid to appear late before God. Matt Taylor's farm-hand, Gabriel. Last summer I saw him spike a squirrel with a pitchfork and leave it to die in the heat. I think of the lamb, and look away, willing him to walk past.

'Excuse us, sir,' Annie says.

I turn too late to stop her. She is wearing her saddest face. I swear she's managed a tear.

'I'm hungry and there's nowt to feed me,' she says. 'I'm a good girl, never mard—'

'And here's me thinking you just theft what you need.' A shadow falls over us as he looms above, blocking the sun.

I catch his eye. Shall Annie and I be made to pay for the work of our foolhardy brother, now? My mouth dries, heart thumps.

'Are you banished from church, sinners?' he says.

I stand up. My head barely reaches his chin and he is broad, his wide shoulders leaning in to me. 'Are you?' I ask.

Annie's upturned face looks from me to him. She does not fear village men, not even this brute, but is inquisitive about them as she is with the animals in the woods, as though they're a different breed of person. Tall and bearded, clothed in doublets. She does not see such creatures at home.

'If we could beg a kindness from you ...' The word 'good' has stuck on her lip.

There is laughter in his eyes now, cruel and powerful. 'Kindness, is it? That's all you ask for?'

'Not from you.'

He takes a step towards me. I do not move. A mistake.

'Now why's that?' he says, his voice quiet. 'I might give a kindness.' He dips his head close to mine so that I can see flecks of green in his eyes, feel his breath on my skin. The smell of him reminds me of the boiling lamb's head. 'But what would come to me in return?'

He wipes his hand across my cheek, rubs his thumb over my mouth and, without giving myself the chance to think of what will result, I look him in the eye and growl, as I've heard the wild dogs at night, snap at his thumb. Sink my teeth in, taste blood. He leaps back, yelling, then slams his fist into my face. A blast of pain sends me spinning to the ground, the taste of my own blood mingling with his.

I hear screams and Annie launches herself at him, battering his leg with her fists. He kicks her off, swearing and sucking on his bleeding thumb. She crawls over to me and I sit up, wiping my face clean and holding her tight.

He crouches over me, breathing heavy and fast. 'You'll pay for this, you little whore.'

Lifting his cap and smoothing his hair down, he straightens up and walks to church, no quicker than before. I watch him, stroking Annie's head and trying to steady my breathing.

Anger feeds my lust for his suffering. I feel again the thud of stone against my shoulder, see Annie's wide, uncomprehending eyes and the jeering faces of children, smell the sickly-meat odour of the farmhand. Fury beats through me, scorching under my skin, filling my mouth, driving me to my feet so that Annie falls to the ground.

'A curse upon you.'

The words break through my lips, grainy and tainted with the farmhand's blood. Voice low and jagged. Not my own. Not loud. He turns anyway.

'I curse you break into sores that weep and burn, that torment you with pain and repulse any that lay eye on you.'

He stands, stricken, then laughs and continues on his way. But his laughter struck false and I feel his fear. I remain standing, as the power burning through me rises to meet the terror that bloats within him.

At last I become aware, as my heartbeat steadies, that Annie cowers at my feet, whimpering and covering her face. I scoop her into my arms, once more her sister. Once more nothing but a ragged, empty-bellied girl, smarting where hand and stone have struck me. We turn back towards the cursed hill.

Spires and Beams

Daniel joined Father in the kitchen just as Bett was chopping some of last autumn's parsnips and adding them to the pottage that would cook until they were ready for it that evening. A fire glowed in the grate, throwing a sheen on to the gleaming surface of the table that stood next to it, and the room smelled of baking bread and the bubbling grain and beans.

'Are you ill? Looks like there's a fever on you.'

She laid her hand on his forehead. A touch that was efficient if not loving.

'No,' she said, shrugging and turning back to the pot. His good health rendered him unworthy of attention.

Father grunted. ''Tis idleness not illness that delays him. Come, lie-a-bed, Bett needs to away and we must go to church.' His mood was unusually sour, and blood seeped from his nostril. Daniel feared he could guess the cause.

'Y-you, ah – you have a …' He tapped under his own nose.

Father scowled and wiped the blood away as they stepped through the door. 'There's a damned lamb missing,' he said.

Daniel shuddered. 'Keep an eye out. It's escaped through the hedge, no doubt, and must be found. I cannot abide to lose a thing of value.'

Daniel trudged behind him, grateful that he'd had the presence of mind to wash the blood from the path by the field the day the lamb was taken. All the while, the Devil-boy's voice seethed through his mind, as it shadowed his dreams and left him afraid of darkness. Glad he had again been spared to see dawn, Daniel did not allow himself to feel guilt at burning through so many lights and waking to a pile of ash on the floor. He made them himself, pulling and stripping the rushes, dipping them in mutton fat. A job that left him retching from the stink. A job for a woman, in any other house.

He jumped at a rustle in the hedgerow; at the sound of a whisper, surely, from that direction – 'Bring hell on you.'

Blonde tendrils of hair escaped Molly Matthews's hat, grazing the back of her neck. Daniel tried to concentrate on the image of Christ and the words of the parson. Kept his eyes open until they burned, for when he blinked the boy's face taunted him.

If he leaned forward in his pew he would be able to smell Molly's skin, newly scrubbed for church.

Daniel was weighed down by the sleepless night. Church was surely the safest place to be, yet he could not be rid of the fear that the Haworth boy would appear, reaching a filthy hand from under the pew to grab him, or transforming the serene features of Christ into his own rotting smile. The faint but constant smell of fish, always present when the village gathered together, churned his guts.

At the back of the church the door creaked and swung. Daniel gripped the pew in front – the boy had come for him, even the house of God could not keep such wickedness at bay, and Daniel would be cursed or killed right here as he worshipped.

Every head turned, filling the building with the sound of rustling, though Parson Walsh did not pause in his descriptions of damnation. He thumped his hands together and glared round at the congregation, raising his voice to demand attention.

Daniel looked to see Gabriel enter, head bent towards the floor, frowning. Watched by all, he simply found a space and sat. A collective sigh of disappointment washed through the crowd; the interruption had not met expectations. Gabriel lived with his young sister and frail mother, tending to their every need, and he was often late for church. The only task he never complained about, carrying out with a care that left Daniel bewildered as to how one man could be both so gentle and so brutish.

Daniel closed his eyes, swayed. Breathed again, and turned back to the parson and his spittle-flecked warnings of the fires of hell, but found himself looking straight into Molly's smiling face.

He blinked. Her eyes were too light, the colour of pale green apples; her lips too laden with mischief, curved into a smile that should not be worn to church. His eyes narrowed as if dazzled.

She leaned towards him. An aroma of smoke and iron, somehow out of place against the delicately coloured cloth of her petticoat.

'What's kept him from church?' she whispered.

Daniel suppressed the urge to hush her. Opened his mouth, waited for the words to come. No easier at the sight of a pretty face than that of the demon-boy.

'A fight?' he managed at last. Also a cause that often delayed Gabriel, though usually after the tavern.

She leaned closer, resting her hand on the back of her pew. 'Or a lover.'

The smile spread over her face at the same speed as the blush over Daniel's, until she turned away at last.

He looked to the parson, but her face was all he saw. If God gazed down into Daniel's mind through the spires and beams, the coifs and hats and freshly combed hair, He would not find what He should. All Daniel could think of was the flavour of Molly's lips.

After the service people gathered in small groups. Boys picked and offered bunches of wild flowers: girls blushed, pretending coyness. Sunday was the most entertaining day of the week.

Daniel followed Father to join Mr Matthews and some fishermen, Bett's husband Nathaniel amongst them, as they stood talking under the oak, its branches beginning to bear a cover of light green leaves. They all nodded at Father and fell silent, waiting for him to speak.

'Good service,' Father said. 'Bit of gumption this week.'

The men murmured agreement.

'Though your farmhand near set the parson to forgetting his thoughts,' Mr Matthews said.

A rustling of leaves, surely. Daniel willed himself not to glance around. The Haworth boy's demons could change form at will, it was said, and might be creeping between gravestones, stalking Daniel even as he stood. He forced himself to focus on the conversation.

'He is not under my bidding at church.' A reprimand, for Mr Matthews rarely showed the deference Father was used to receiving from village men.

Nathaniel looked past Daniel's shoulder, and frowned. 'See those two huddled together?' He indicated Sam Finch and a man named Turner. 'Doesn't sit right.'

They all glanced over. 'That money changing hands too?' Daniel asked.

'Don't look too close, son, or speak too loud,' Father said. 'Wherever you turn there'll be someone buying another's silence. You keep your innocence and look away.'

'Just as the magistrate does, though 'tis not innocence that blinds him,' Nathaniel said.

'And let's be thankful for that,' Mr Matthews said, shading his face against the sun. 'Sharp eyes can bring profit. I shan't say who supplies my fish, but all I pay for it is a half what others do and a promise not to tell whose wife it is that he beds. Besides his own.'

Father frowned and Daniel knew that Mr Matthews had once again misjudged. His parents' marriage had been brief but happy, and Father did not look kindly on such betrayals.

'Put your sharp eyes to better use, and keep them looking out for my lamb,' Father said. 'One's been lost, and I cannot track it down.'

'You thinking it's been stolen?' Nathaniel asked.

Daniel breathed deep to calm the quickened beat of his blood, dipped his head to hide the guilt that was surely written there. 'It's perhaps just escaped through the hedge,' he said.

'More likely stolen,' Father said. 'Keep an ear to the ground, lads?'

Daniel remained still, waiting for someone to say they had seen the Devil-boy carrying the lamb, but no one spoke. He sensed a shifting behind him, a breath at his neck, that set him lunging a little to the side and almost into Nathaniel. The demon was upon him. When he glanced back there was nothing to be seen.

He barely felt the humiliation of Father's frown and Mr Matthews's smirk. All were aware of the role he played on the farm. He was no man, and all knew it. This day it was a dread of worse than ridicule that drove him away. Daniel pretended a need to speak to Gabriel and left Father to seek out the family grave, as always. As he trudged towards the gate, glancing side to side in fear of some malevolent presence, a pair of polished brown shoes stood in his path and he almost walked into the owner of them.

'You look so serious.' Molly's voice sang with laughter.

'Do I?' He did not have the temperament to entertain silly girls. Even one with such ripe lips.

'And why do you find it so hard to look at me? Is my face disagreeable to you?'

'Of course not.'

'Then why must you look at your feet?'

She reached out a hand and tipped his chin so that his eyes met hers. He was determined enough to hold her gaze, but powerless to stop the blush spreading over his face.

'Perhaps you'll be less serious on May Day,' she said, releasing him. 'I have new clothes to wear and I hope you'll be able to look at me then. Will you ask me to dance?'

He would rather dress the sow in a petticoat and gambol with her down the village street. 'I'd be delighted,' he lied.

His mistake, this day, was clumsiness. Often after church he made some error and Father, having given all his goodness to God and his affection to a headstone, combusted into rage.

Coming in, skittish with dread, he swung the door too hard and knocked over that day's milk.

'Oaf,' Father yelled, as Daniel knelt by the puddle and mopped it up. 'You know what you've just lost me? Know what that's worth?'

Daniel kept his head to the ground.

'Never mind the stink it'll leave.'

Daniel stood to take the soaked rag outside.

'You listening to me?'

He raised his eyes in time to see a fist, feel the blow slam into his face and send him spinning, door handle cracking into his forehead.

Daniel folded to his knees, milk soaking through his breeches. No blood this time. Through his fingers he saw Father's legs step in front of him, his chest then face as he knelt.

'Son,' he said. 'Why must you always goad me so? You know I anger swift.' With gentle touch now he pulled Daniel's hands free, peered at his face. 'Not hurt, not too much. Here, let me help you.'

He lifted Daniel to his feet, sat him at the table near the fire. Reached out a hand that hovered over Daniel's head then withdrew.

'Bite to eat, perhaps?'

Daniel nodded and forced a smile. Father heated a pan to make sops and dripping, as Daniel knew he would, as he always did. He was sick to the stomach, a feeling worsened by the scent of the warming milk. One he would always associate with pain, and his father's regret.

Summer Sky

The well, like all that once made up our hamlet, is tainted by death.

It still stands, twined in ivy and clogged with mud. Even if we could draw the water, we dare not, feared that poison spreads from the flesh rotted underground. We can never be sure where the dead are buried. It's said there were so many and they passed so swiftly, no time was left for the dignity of a church service. Whole families lie, one upon the other, in the tiny gardens where animals once grazed and food was grown, furrowing the land around our home.

I walk down the hill to the well on the green, passing Matt Taylor's farm on the way, almost tripping over one of his sheep out on the path. The empty pail knocks against my leg. She blarts as though she can tell I'm imagining the taste of her cooked flesh. No better than my brother.

Beyond, I hear the cry of a horse, wild surely to be pounding and calling so. I place the bucket at my feet and push through a gap in the hedge, scratching against my skin and snatching at my hair. There's a hushing noise too, a soothing murmur. The sounds come from the next field and I approach steadily. Through the clouds a shaft of sunlight falls thick as butter. I don't know why I must see but I cannot turn back, though I hear clear in my mind Mam's voice. Her warnings to keep away from the villagers, of what may befall us should they choose to take trade elsewhere.

The horse is night-black and gleaming, ears back, eyes rolling. Shrieking and kicking, galloping round and round the field. Bad to the core, anyone can see, a disposition that can only be cured by Mam's skill at freeing her from the curse that she clearly bears. No right-minded body would go near her.

Matt Taylor's son stands not two paces away from where she's stopped. Hand reaching out, eyes fixed on her. Bigger than I remember him, standing tall and straight. Neither of them sees me.

I know of the farmer's son. A timid thing, I would not have thought he'd the courage to face this creature.

He stares her down without a flinch. There's a stillness about him that is entrancing. The beat of my heart slows as I watch.

The mare skips, ready to run off or kick out, as he edges forward. She's held in his gaze, unable to look away. As am I. The fine hairs on his outstretched arm are driftwood-white.

She bares her teeth, chewing and licking, drops her head. The farmer's lad turns his back, walks off. Just as I think she'll surely attack, she follows, head dipped, calm now.

He runs his hand over her forehead, whispers to her, rests his cheek against her muzzle. She stands as though she were a pet kitten.

Under his spell just as the mare is, I forget myself. Forget that I'm the girl from the family up the hill who is mocked or feared but never spoken to. Let myself imagine I'm released from the burden and promise of the power I carry within.

I step forward. 'How did you do that? She should've killed you.'

He starts and turns towards me, a deep flush spreading over his face. The horse whinnies and he reaches a hand to comfort her, eyes still on me. He focuses briefly on the skin on my cheek, broken by the farmhand's knuckles, then drops his gaze.

'Oh, I …' He looks behind, confused.

''Tis a gift.'

'Oh no, it's just … It's nothing.'

'I've never seen owt like it.' There's a rare gentleness about him, a self-doubt. 'Can I stroke her?'

He hesitates, nods. 'Carefully.'

The mare darts back, showing the whites of her eyes and snorting as I walk towards her.

'Don't look at her,' he says. 'Just – keep your head down. That's right.'

I move towards them, looking down. Slowly. Slowly. The mare shifts a little. He keeps a hand on her neck. She will not hurt me, I know. He won't let her.

'Good,' he says.

I reach out a hand and he guides my fingers to the mare's forehead.

'Here,' he says. 'Like this.' Together we stroke her with round movements. She blows softly.

'See,' he says. 'She likes you.'

His words are like summer sky, I could lie underneath them and be warmed. The sun, breaking through weighty cloud, catches his every freckle and blond eyelash. A bruise shadows his eye, swollen and fresh.

'How did you learn it?' I ask.

'I just – I don't know. I'm no good at anything.' He laughs, uncertain. Shrugs. 'I like animals, I watch them. It's easy.'

'You're good at this.' I stroke the mare and she nuzzles my hand. 'It's like you bewitched her.'

As I speak the words, he recognises me. I see it in his eyes, a flash of fear. He is suddenly still and clutches the horse's back. She cries in response. I don't realise I'm smiling until I stop. The unfamiliar sensation leaves me and I am once more just a thin crust of person with nothing inside. The sweet solid warmth of being another was brief, but its absence burns like the sores I cursed upon the farmhand.

He stumbles back, tripping over his own feet, gasping like a stranded fish. Face white as the sky above us is dark. I hate him for the kindness he has shown then taken away more than I've ever hated the brutes that taunt and beat me.

The mare begins to stamp and toss her mane. I try to will her hoof into his skull but I cannot, the gentleness of his voice stays with me. Instead I leave, flitting back over the rough grass, tearing through the hedge that rips my skin, lifting the bucket and slamming it into the bruises it has left on my leg as I run to the well.

Clouds heave and flex, lightning splits the air and rain falls fat and cold. And I'm glad of it, glad of the pounding thunder and black skies and wet clothes that chill me through. Soon it will be all I can feel.

Sound of the Storm

Daniel waited as her words settled into him, the realisation of who she was and why she had come. She was the witch-girl. The Devil-boy's sister. He stood, the mare shifting at his side, as the sky above darkened and then split with lightning. Was this her work? Was this a warning?

He watched her go, both relieved that she left and immediately wishing her back. She had come only to harm him, surely. And yet. Her smile, so soothing, and given solely for him. Like a warm hearth, the comfort of which he could not resist. Her absence left him chilled.

Her words slithered round his head. Voice sweet and clear as a spring raindrop, pretty little face full of light. He could not find the night in her. Those eyes. Every colour of the sea in there.

It was witchcraft that made her appear so, for sure.

Bewitched. The word carried a weight she must have been aware of. To let him know who she was, to demonstrate the power of their unhallowed ways. To remind him of the punishment that was his due. He wished that she had cursed him, and he now writhed in whatever suffering was his due. He could not bear the waiting, the fear of the inevitable torment to come.

Daniel turned and vomited on the grass, just missing the mare's hind leg. She did not flinch, leaning into him when another blast of lightning ripped through the clouds above them.

He led her to the barn. Still shaky, the ground heaving under his boots. The mare followed willingly. Father and Gabriel sat in the corner, drinking ale and eating bread and cold eggs, while rain hammered the roof.

Father pointed to the horse. 'What's this?'

'Tamed the mare.'

Daniel was certain an expression of satisfaction flickered across Father's face. He would be judging his son's achievement by its weight in coins. 'Stable her, then,' he said.

As Daniel moved away, Gabriel spoke around the bread he chewed, 'Could've broken that horse myself.'

Daniel had witnessed this process. It left him sick and biting through his lip to stop the protests escaping. Broken was the word. Gabriel tied the animal at head and foot, beating until all spirit was gone. Every time Daniel saw it he swore he would not stand by and watch again.

'Nathaniel says you've not found that lamb and I was thinking today that it must've been stole, else we'd have it by now,' Gabriel said.

Daniel stopped. Father grunted.

'And I was thinking on the way to church, sure as anything it was that family that lives in the plague village that's took it.' He scratched the side of his head, frantically, so that his cap slid back and forth. Daniel's grip on the mare tightened, and she gave him a baleful look. 'It'll be that little whore that lives up the hill.'

Father frowned. 'They're a bunch of black-hearts, for sure. But I doubt it'd be the lass, more likely the son if any.'

The boy's face rose in Daniel's mind: the sneer, the threat. The blood.

Gabriel scratched harder. 'We should gather some men, go and find what they's at. Tonight. I'll find her, the—'

'What, that little lass?' Father asked.

Gabriel snatched his hand from his head, flushed. 'No. Just – they all, I meant.'

'When I find the culprit I'll choose the punishment,' Father said.

'Lamb drowned,' Daniel said. Without forethought and surprising even himself. 'Saw it in the stream.' He was in too much turmoil over the Haworths to fear uttering this deception. Worse hid in the shadows than his father's temper.

Father blew out an irritated sigh. 'That falls on you, Gabriel. You need to check and block the hedges better. I'll dock your wage.'

Daniel left the sound of Gabriel's protests, the mare following him now with a trust in her eyes that reminded him for a moment of the Haworth girl, the open expression she carried as she stepped forward.

She appeared harmless as any animal on the farm. Beaten, afraid and ready to run, her fear all that made her a danger. An enchantment. No more.

Those That Know Me

The hill is slippery with mud and sodden grass. A shot of pain as my foot lands on a stone. I cry out and stagger, losing balance and falling to the ground.

I lie, thinking of the look on the boy's face, of all Mam's warnings that we must remain separate from the village. The knowledge we carry, passed on from her grandmother and guarded by each chosen member of the family, must remain ours alone. And here am I, speaking with him as though we are the same kind. Happen he tricked me, just as he lulled the horse, into trusting him. His show of fear a deceit, and he had known me all along.

Scrambling up, I shake out my dripping petticoat, glare down the hill to the farm and village. To the places I shall never belong. I was chosen by another, for a fate I do not yet know, but I am ready to accept it. Exhausted now with resisting it.

Clamber up the hill. Hands and knees where I must. I need to be among those that know me.

I throw myself at the door and stagger into the house. At the sight of Mam bending over the fire my anger thins and spreads to nothing. I'm worn down. Like a child Annie's age I walk to her, resting my head against her shoulder.

She folds her arms around me, sits me on a stool and fetches the cloth. Wipes my face with slow strokes. When I'm clean she turns away. I reach for her arm.

'I want you to teach me.'

We start with healing and protective charms.

'Let's begin sweet,' she says. 'Much of our trade satisfies a want for revenge or a wish to cause suffering, of necessity for that's the nature we serve, but there's purity to this side that suits you well. 'Tis good you embrace it. You've not the choices of other lasses.'

Her voice falters as she speaks, and I know she means I've not the chance of a husband. I think briefly of the fear in the farm lad's eyes, then draw myself up strong. What use would a husband be to me, anyway? No. I shall stay with Mam and John and Annie. I shall learn the skills of our kind.

I've often wished I was born to that other life of food on the table and warm clothes. A husband, a family. A life of laundry in the stream with other women and church on Sundays. Mam tried to give us that life, but he that we serve conjured the storm that ripped it from us, took our father and all else besides.

We are not made for that life. I must turn my mind to cunning ways now. This part of our gift has always called to me, the easing of suffering and healing of hurts. It's a kindly skill. As I work I imagine a time, not far from now, when the village sees us as only benevolent. When we're welcomed and our lives may mingle. In this time, if one morning I wake and discover a mark on Annie's skin, it won't carry such dread. She will remain safe. Soon I'll have the power to show them the good in what we do, to take away their fear. For though she's wrought of magic, it's of a different, gentler kind than that we serve.

There's much I know already from watching Mam, and I could tell anyone which herbs will cure a bellyache or calm a rash. Many a time I've gathered plants for her. Now she goes about teaching me the skill of transforming them to salves or tinctures, of learning charms to find lost goods or release curses.

Today I mash the mallow leaves and stems we've gathered until they become a thick, sticky paste that fills the room with its fresh scent. Mam guides me as I add a little water and stir, making a tonic that, taken by the spoonful, will soothe a sickened stomach.

John sits, watching. There's a hunger in his expression as he takes in Mam's hand guiding mine, her soft laugh as I fail to mash the mixture smooth. He twitches his leg, taps the point of his knife against the table, waiting until she snaps at him to stop. She does not, and he scrapes his stool back, leaving without a word.

I remember John's face when he heard Mam explain what my mark meant. He was but a lad of ten years, watching wide-eyed. The next morning he stripped and searched his own skin for a mark, running to Mam in excitement when he found a small dark stain on his chest.

She barely glanced his way. 'That is not his mark, son,' she said, bending to lift an infant Annie from her basket. 'You are not chosen nor ever shall be, for yours is not the kind of soul he seeks.' She jiggled Annie with one arm and placed the other hand on John's bare shoulder. 'You're man of the house. Your job is to work. Provide.'

She turned from him. He pulled his tunic on and ran down the hill to the village. The first time he sought work and his first taste of the cruelty and skitting of the folk that refused him.

She does not comment now on his leaving, but watches me and pats my hand. 'You've your great-grandmother's blood,' she says. 'Now you shall come to the village and help me sell.'

I shake off the sadness I feel for John, swallow down the thrill of unease her words bring. I am cunning folk, and can be no other.

Mam and I wander from house to house, the shore at our backs and the breeze brackish with the scent of fish, coating our mouths and crusting our hair. This part of the beach is long, the sand smooth and, as the weather softens, the sea lilting gently. It's busy with people: men in boats and hauling catches, women wading to find clams. This is not the part Annie and I come to, nor have I ever wished to.

Apart from Taylors' farm, the village houses cluster down by the sea. Dew-Springer seeks out any that might need our skills and today leads us here, according to Mam. Door after door closes against us, though most have used Mam's cures at some point and she saw many of the children into the world. I learn what John endures when he seeks work.

One woman stands back and folds her arms when she sees us. 'You know that cunning woman from across the river came by not days since, and I've all I need from her.'

Mam stiffens, barely breathing, and I feel the fury spark in her. 'That hag,' she says. 'She's a trickster and a devil besides, her wares are nothing but water and black magic.'

The woman remains unperturbed. 'Her wares cost me less than yours. So.'

She shuts the door on us, and we move on to be turned away again and again, Mam muttering the whole while about how her rival is no more than a fraud and a dealer of foul doings. I do not point out that she is not beyond the use of a curse when it suits her.

'No matter,' she says. 'We shall set Dew-Springer to act upon her.'

When at last Robert Turner opens his cottage door, we're called in. We wait in the dim room, where a basket of fish sits in a corner and his boots dry by the fire.

'It's Alice,' he says. 'She's taken with a malady and lies a-bed but cannot sleep.'

We follow to where she rests, eyes open wide and fingers clasping at nothing.

I watch as Mam takes in the sight of the woman she once knew. Alice sits up, throws off her blanket and rises to her feet, staggering.

'What's she doing in my house?' She looks wildly from Mam to her husband. 'Get her out. Leave me be, you sorcer-ess.' She lunges towards Mam, hand raised, but Mam steps away and Robert clasps Alice, holds her still. She weeps and moans into his shoulder. 'Can you see it?' she whispers. 'It's here, do you see?'

He shakes his head. 'You know I cannot, my love. Ruth is here to help you. Lie down and let her go about her work.'

Mam sits on the edge of Alice's bed, takes her hand. She waits for a moment, silent, looking upon this woman, once her friend, with both compassion and contempt. 'Tell me,' she says.

'It's dark,' Alice flutters her hands. 'Moving, in the shadows and, and – winged, like a bird. And it whispers, I hear it, can you hear it?' She looks wildly at Robert and Mam. 'Such things it speaks of, tells me I should do, terrible things.' She presses her hands to mouth. 'Hurts, it wants me to cause hurts, to others, to my own self. Whenever I try to sleep it is upon me. I am cursed, yes?'

Mam brings Alice's hands down and pats them. ''Tis just a sprite, they're known for mischief but no great harm. We shall have you soon free of it.'

Alice grabs Mam's fingers and presses them to her lips, lies back down. In the other room, Mam shows Robert how to fill a witch jar, cutting a chunk of Alice's hair and some of her fingernail shavings to put in.

We go down to the sea for water and Mam instructs him to add a handful of sand and some stones. I watch some men haul a boat ashore, heads bowed and hands busy. They show no interest in us, but I'm mithered by their presence. I prefer the solitude on the scrappy part of the shore Annie and I visit when we must. When the jar is done Mam presses it into Robert's hands.

'Bury it in the furthest corner of your land,' she says. 'I'll return with a poppy elixir. She will soon be cured.'

He nods. Mam holds out her palm for his coin. 'The elixir will cost more,' she says.

We turn back towards the green and the hill. Mam is silent until we reach our door.

'I called her friend, once,' she says.

I say nothing, for the loss is scored on to her face. But I try to imagine what friend means, what it looks and feels like. I remember children from before, when my father still lived and we dwelled by the sea. I remember scrambling over wet rocks and peering into the little pools, dipping our hands in to catch the tiny fishes that were trapped there. I don't think this is what friend means when you are grown, though, when you are a wife, a mother. What it would mean for me now, stranded as I am between child and mother. Perhaps only ever to be one of these.

Mam chats to Dew-Springer in whispers that shiver with malicious intent while I pick up the pot of salve we're taking, for we have been asked to treat a pox.

'Why dust have to go?' Annie asks, sitting at the table and swinging her legs as she chews on dandelion leaves. She is just returned from exploring the ruins, her knees and hands smeared with mud. 'There's babby foxes in the woods and they're all starting to crawl and jump around now and I want to show you. And I found another piece for us to play with.'

She places a small wooden thing on the table, shaped like an acorn, flat at the top and coming to a rounded point at the bottom. It is speckled with dirt and mould, and I can see it crumbles at the edges. Annie looks at Mam expectantly.

'Show her tomorrow,' Mam says. 'Take John. He'll play with you and visit babby foxes.'

Still rolled in his blanket, John sits up, with his hair askew and expression indignant.

'Unless you've plans to join us and ask for labour?' Mam asks.

He grunts and lies back down.

'But what is it, Mammy?' Annie asks. 'My piece?'

I can't take my eyes from it. Useless now, softened with age and decay, but I can imagine the little hands setting it to spin on the ground, small voices ringing with laughter.

Mam glances at the treasure. 'It's a top. For childer, they would've spun it.'

Annie's mouth pops open as she stares and twists, but it falls over immediately.

'Put it with the others,' I say, only so I may stop thinking of the little hands mouldering under the soil, of the voices now silenced.

She slides from the stool and places it carefully with her collection, jumping on John on the way back. He groans and complains, but I know he'll not resist her for long.

'Oh come, John, come and see,' Annie says. 'I'll show you where the foxes hide, but you must be silent else you'll scare the mammy.'

'Leave me be, Squirrel,' he says, burrowing under the blanket. I know he'll be up and off to the woods with her as we step through the door. His affection for Annie runs as fierce and protective as mine, though he feigns disinterest in front of me and Mam, should we think him weak and incapable as our protector. I do, but it's his softness, his inability to resist anything Annie asks of him, that thaws my feelings towards him.

Mam turns from the path that leads down to the green and cottages at the shore, heading left towards the Taylors' farm. She nods to a girl who waves.

'Sweet lass, that Phyllis,' she says.

I stop. 'You said the village.'

'Farm is part of the village. Step on, lass.'

I grip the bowl of salve, remembering the lad as he coaxed the mare, the gentleness of his voice, sunlight catching his eyes. How fear froze him when he realised who I was. 'Who is the salve for?'

'Farmhand. Suffering a rash of cow pox or the like.'

'Oh.' I begin walking again. It's not the lad we seek, at least, and I imagine he must be busy with tasks. I remember the farmhand's fist against my face and the fury beating through me as I cursed him. Happen my powers have ripened and his pox is my doing. I should be feared of what I've done, but the memory only brings back my anger, and I'm more inclined to witness his suffering than to bring a salve to heal it. Happy to take his coin, though.

We've barely stepped into the yard when I see the lad, carrying a basket of eggs. He blanches at the sight of me, looks behind as though willing someone to come to his aid. We both falter, and eggs roll inside the basket. A task for a woman, I always thought, though perhaps am mistaken. Mam frowns at me and then turns to him.

'Good morning, young man. We're called to see to your farmhand's affliction?' She gives him a gap-toothed smile.

His gaze darts from her to me and back again. 'C-called?'

'Yes, by the housemaid. Bett, is that not her name?' Mam does not appear ill at ease, though I don't know how much is pretence. 'We've brought a healing salve.'

He eyes the pot in my hands, still keeping his distance. 'How – how does it work?'

I try to hate him, but the memory of his kindness, however fleeting, undoes me. Mam glances at me, her expression bewildered. I doubt any villager has asked such a question of her before.

'I – well, it's the garlic,' I say.

'Garlic?' He places the basket on the ground, steps towards me a little. 'The – that grows in the woods? The flowers?'

'Aye, though it's the root we use. Soothes the skin.'

He peers into the pot. 'I didn't know.'

'Not many do,' says Mam, sending a frown my way.

I remind myself how he changed when he knew me. But he knows me now, there's no hiding that I am the cunning woman's daughter, and yet he remains gentle. And only a little feared, I think.

'It's also good for a belly-wart and easing a weakness of breath,' I say.

Curious, he steps closer. 'Oh? But – so, how do you …?'

'Hush, lass.' Mam laughs but her look is a warning. 'Do not be giving away all our knowledge, we've need of—'

'How's the mare?' I ask. Hold my breath. His reply will show the truth of what he feels about me, my family.

His eyes lighten. An unfamiliar warmth comes upon me. 'She's well, thank you,' he says. 'She's—'

A holler from behind cuts him off.

'You.'

The farmhand, pointing straight at me. The boy steps back.

'You,' he shouts again. 'You did this, with your witchery and curses, and now you dare step foot on this land?'

He barges past the boy, knocking him so that he staggers, stops in front of me. Jaw working, chest heaving.

'Make it stop.' He is a desperate sight, scowling and missing patches of hair where he's scratched his scalp raw. I fight laughter. 'Uncurse me,' he says.

At this both Mam and the lad turn to stare. He steps away, eyes fearful again.

'Nay,' I say, speaking only to him. 'I didn't—'

I ignore Mam's sharp glance, look past the farmhand to the lad. I must show him my innocence.

'This isn't – I'm only learning to heal.'

He remains silent and gives me no sense that he under-stands. The farmhand roars accusations, Mam speaks soothing words, but I care nothing about either.

'Accept this,' Mam says, taking the bowl from me and bend-ing to place it at the farmhand's feet. 'It will ease your suffering. Please, we're healers. No more. No cost to you, sir.'

She reaches for my hand and pulls me away. I do not want to go. The understanding that my powers run true, that my curse upon the farmhand came to be, jolts through me. It is too much. What injury might I cause next time I anger? What peril might I bring upon my family? All this I feel and yet, more than it all, I think of the lad. That moment of fleeting warmth, vanishing so quickly. For now, I do not want to be me. I wish to be the girl who watched him tame the mare, and nothing more. He stands stricken, as though it were he I cursed.

We're halfway up the hill before Mam speaks. 'What have you done?' She stands with hands on hips, breath coming fast. 'You must tell me all of these mares and curses. Haven't I warned you to keep away? We don't go a-meddling in their lives and they leave us be, that's how it must stay.'

'He hit me and I was angry. It was supposed to be sores.'

''Tis the friendly talk of mares that I fear more than the curse.'

'I didn't think I had the power.'

'Of course you do. You are marked. You've the gift, have I not told you so all these years?' She grips my hands in hers. 'But wield it with care, lass, do not go blasting out your fury and letting all know it was you. They fear it.' Dropping my hands, she steps back and I feel her struggle to contain her anger, feel her urge to slap the words into me. 'What more must I do to make you take heed? Would you put us all, put your sister, at risk?' She looks behind, drops her voice, though no one but we venture so close to the plague village. 'I've warned often enough of the fates of those that were doomed for no more than we do now.'

Though I don't wish to think of it, the story of those that lived not so very far from here looms over us. The one Mam tells, when she fears we may be tempted by the comforts of village life to wander there unguarded, of a man that hunted our kind. How they were condemned by law and church. How friend turned against neighbour, daughter against mother, until they were strung from a noose. I can almost feel the rope tight around my own neck.

Beautiful Wretches

Daniel knelt in the vegetable garden, careful not to crush the seedlings, breathing in the scent of fresh soil as he shook it from the roots of the radishes and spring cabbage he gathered at Bett's instruction.

He sat back, listening to the trill of the blackbird and watching woodlice scuttle into hiding. Trying to free his mind from thoughts of the witch-girl, the tempestuous dance of her hair as her mother pulled her away. The sun rose, breaking through the branches of the apple trees, newly tipped with blossom. As if God Himself were smiling down, though Daniel was certain that God had no interest in his feeble existence. He tarried a while, watching the blackbird dip down to collect the goose feathers he had left at the foot of the tree for its nest. But he must be gone. Preparations must begin if the pea crop was to be sown.

Sighing, he gathered the plants and walked to where Bett busied herself bundling linen in the kitchen.

'Ah,' she said, peering into the basket he placed on the table. 'Good, you've chose well. And saved me a task, thank you.'

Daniel eyed the laundry. A thought occurred to him. 'Washday?'

'Aye.'

'Shall I – would you like me to come with you?'

She cast him a perplexed look, and he felt his cheeks redden. 'To the river? With all the women?' she asked.

'It's only – I heard that those from the hill, the girl, she uses the river too and lately I've thought – you know, after Gabriel and the … the … I should accompany you. For – for protection.' His face smarted.

Bett stared for a moment, then chuckled and went back to sorting her bundle. 'Well you're a kindly soul and it warms my cockles to know the care you have, but there's no need. And have you not tasks to be about?'

Daniel started and made towards the door, picturing Father's anger at his tardiness.

'I've never feared they Haworths anyway, and besides,' Bett said, voice muffled by her turned back, 'they'll not venture to that stretch of river.'

Daniel stopped in the doorway. 'Oh?'

'Nay. I've heard tell they use the scrub patch where it's rocky and the trees grow thick.' She glanced up, his idle presence distracting her. 'So I'm quite safe.'

He remained fixed, her words curling into his mind.

He knew the part she spoke of. Might find himself wandering there later.

★

Screaming, a sound to stop the heart and freeze the blood. Someone was in trouble. Daniel ran, afraid of what he would find but determined to save the poor creature that suffered so.

The noise came towards him at full pelt, inside a tiny frame, all flying limbs and flapping hair. She crashed into him with surprising force and strength, knocking him to the ground. He caught the creature, held on though it was like trying to grasp an eel.

'Shh. It's all right, you're safe now.'

'Let go,' the child yelled, struggling harder.

'Settle down,' he said. 'You're—' The little fingers grabbed his hair and yanked. 'Ow, wait …'

Daniel loosened his grip and the child ran into the arms of the Haworth girl, who stood over him. His stomach gave an unpleasant lurch. He wasn't sure whether with anticipation or trepidation.

'What are you doing to my sister?' she asked.

He sat up, rubbing his stinging scalp. Fought the urge to run. He regretted now whatever demented impulse had led him here. Searching for courage, though the blood beat through him so fast that he felt it roaring under his skin, he found his tongue at last. 'Y-you're better to ask what she's doing to me.'

'Were you stealing her?'

He could not tell whether it was sunlight or witchery that lit her eyes. He stood, scrambled to his feet, ready to run if need be. 'I thought she was hurt, the poor thing. She – I was trying to help.'

The poor thing snarled at him from the protection of her sister's arms. He held up his palms.

'My mistake.'

'Not your first.'

'Certainly not.'

She watched him over the top of the child's tangled head, her eyes startling dark blue, bright against her dirt-smudged skin. The wind snatched the untamed tangle of her hair from her face. There was an unexpected sweetness to the curve of her jaw, a slant to her lips that might have been mocking or friendly.

'Well. I'll leave you be.' He meant to walk away, but did not move. She seemed no more than a girl, but they were about some heathen ritual, perhaps. He had heard such stories of the family.

'She ran because I tried to wash her.'

'Oh?'

'Aye. She's teeming. Lops.'

'L— what?'

'You know.' She imitated scratching her hair.

'Oh.' Perhaps a more earthly reason than witchcraft after all. He remembered once again her smile as he tamed the mare.

The contempt the girl wore was a thin shell, which barely hid a depth filled with fear. His instinct, as with any creature that attacked because it was afraid, was to calm it.

The brother's face drifted through his mind. Was she a demon like he? Had she willed Daniel to seek her out, for he could not fathom why he had? He should go.

He wanted to flee now. Every part of him poised to leave. The child was slight, hair dirty and matted, the girl's eyes a storm of defiance and doubt. They needed help, not fear. Just as in his attempt to protect the lamb from her brother, and against every warning crying out within, moved once again by another's pain he stepped forward when he should have stepped away.

Daniel crouched so that he was level with the child's filthy face. 'Don't you like the river?'

She bared her teeth.

'You know there are fishes in there the colour of the moon.'

She unfolded her arms.

'And shells that whisper the sound of the sea.'

She inclined her head.

Daniel stood and shrugged. 'Still. If you don't want to see, we'll leave them.'

The child looked up at her sister, tugging on her arm. 'We could just look,' the older girl said. 'If you like.'

They all walked to the water's edge. Daniel unlaced his boots and took off his socks, picking his way through the rocks to paddle in the shallows, head bent to the water. A glance showed them lingering at the bank.

'Quick,' he said. 'A fish. Come, see. Take a step in, just cover your toes.'

'I'm going to,' the girl said, leaving the child and walking in.

Daniel touched her arm, and she glanced at him, startled, expression guarded. He pointed to the little fish swimming near her ankle. She peered down with delight, as though he had shown her the actual moon. 'You've seen them before?' he asked.

She shook her head. 'We don't like the water.'

He did not question. The sea and river both sustained and destroyed, providing food and taking its pay in the lives of the men that sailed it, the women that washed clothes in it. Most could not swim, and even he only did so in the calmer waters of the river. 'You're safe here,' he said.

Her smile was sudden and bright. Surely there could be no deceit in it. 'Come on, Annie,' she said. 'Come, sken.'

The child paddled in, petticoat dangling in the water.

'Here,' Daniel said, crouching, reaching down to the muddy bed. 'Look.'

As he cupped his hand and caught the fish she came closer, bending so that her hair spread and floated in the gentle sway. He opened his palm and showed her the creature as it jerked and twisted.

'You found one,' she said. 'Is it a moon fish?'

He laughed. 'It's – well yes. As good a name as any. We have to put it back now. Help me find another? Look closely.'

She turned slowly, hands and arms in the river, face almost touching the surface. Daniel looked at the girl, standing behind the child.

'Her hair's already wet,' he said.

She began to cup water and pour it over her sister's hair. The child frowned and batted the girl away.

'There's one,' Daniel said. 'See? Want to hold it?'

The child spat out the rivulets that trickled down her face and held her hands out. Daniel gave her the fish, smiling as she gasped. She could not have looked happier if he'd filled her arms with honey cake.

'Done?' he asked the sister. She nodded. He took the child's hands and placed them in the water so that the fish was freed. She was shivering now.

'Well,' he said. 'Enough for today perhaps?' He pinched her chin softly.

They waded out, the girls holding hands, legs shining wet. Ragged clothes fanning out in the water, damp matted hair gleaming in the sun. Beautiful wretches. Daniel retrieved his boots and socks.

The girl jerked her hand out towards him, a pebble resting on her palm. 'To thank you,' she said.

He took it from her, studying the smooth grey stone, still wet from the river.

'Mammy will be cross,' the child whispered, gasping.

'Not if we don't tell.'

'Oh that's nice,' he said. 'With the hole in.'

She looked at him as though he was an idiot. 'Aye, it's a hag stone. Brings protection from curses and such, haven't you one on the farm to keep the milk from souring?'

He shook his head. 'My father does not hold with—'

The child hopped from foot to foot. 'And if you look through the hole you might see a fairy, or put it in the river and see a water sprite.'

Daniel turned the stone in his hand. 'A great gift. I shall treasure it.'

'Aye,' the girl said. 'You should.' She shook the child's arm gently. 'What dust say to the lad?'

'Daniel,' he said.

The child had her thumb in her mouth. 'Thank you,' she said around it, then looked up at her sister. 'But I didn't get the whispering shell.'

He laughed. 'Another time.' He began walking away, then turned back. 'What's your name?'

A look of suspicion scudded across her face. 'Why?'

He flushed, confused. 'I – it's just – what people do.'

'Oh.' She frowned, drawing back, as though suspecting him of some trickery.

'So?' Talking to her was like travelling somewhere new without knowing the route.

She hesitated, watching him. He waited. 'Sarah,' she said.

He spoke without thinking. 'That's pretty.'

She started, scowling as though he had insulted her. 'You needn't look so surprised.'

'No, no. I'm not, of course, it's just, it suits you.' He took a breath. Too late now to be cautious. For once, he wanted to be bold. 'It's – well, it's pretty.'

Daniel bent his head to hide the blush, hurrying back over the mud, pebbles and grass in his bare feet. He pressed the stone into his palm, wondering at the strength of its powers; could it protect him from his own desire to see her again? Would it shelter them from the accusing eyes of the village if he could not resist?

At last preparations were done and the land ready for sowing. The days in the smoking fields setting the roots to smoulder were ones Daniel had not enjoyed. His eyes stung and streamed, his throat burned and the stench clung to his clothes for what felt like weeks after the task was done. By the time May Day arrived, he relished the entertainment it offered.

Father provided the horse and cart for the May Queen. The village women, the ones past eyeing up the May Crown or the boys, had been busy decorating it since daybreak, chatting as they worked. Now it stood, old Boris their steadiest horse waiting stoically at the front, festooned with ribbons, while the cart itself was decked with cow parsley, bluebells and crack willow.

The village green was a-buzz with voices and laughter; children squealed and stampeded unreprimanded through groups of cheerful adults. The communal meal – and abundance of wine and ale that came with it – would not take place till later, but many had indulged in a drink already. More than one, by the look of the red faces and rolling feet.

Gabriel strode over to where Daniel stood with Bett, leaving his mother and little sister to their own devices for a moment. His hair was all but regrown, his scratching almost stopped, and he considered his shaking off the curse as testament to his strength. Bett attributed his recovery to the cunning woman's salve.

'This isn't even the best bit,' he said, slapping Daniel on the back. 'Know what the best bit is, Danny?'

They had this conversation every year. 'The dancing,' he replied.

Gabriel grinned, cupping his hands in front of his chest and bouncing them up and down. 'The dancing,' he said, prancing around. 'Oh, the dancing.'

Daniel caught Bett's eye, suppressed a smile as he saw her expression.

'Look at you, capering like a constipated hog,' she said, and Gabriel skidded to a stop, flushing.

'You know 'tis the one day you can shake off that frown, shan't break you to do it,' he said.

Molly pushed past Bett, ignoring the glare she earned, pulling out her petticoats and twirling.

'Pretty,' Gabriel said.

'Did I not tell you I'd have new clothes, Daniel?' she asked.

He glanced at the three faces surrounding him. Bett wore an expression of amusement, Gabriel one of confused irritation and Molly one of – admiration. Could it be?

'Well,' she said. 'What do you think?'

Her eyes shone, only for him, and he was a confused brew of unease and pleasure that was strengthened by the knowledge that she ignored Gabriel and chose to speak to him.

'It's – it's …' The cloth was light, in both colour and substance, unlike the grey woollen petticoats usually worn. He understood her pleasure in it. 'Very nice.'

Bett laughed and he flushed, aware that his response was insufficient. Molly did not seem to mind, dipping her head and looking up at him. She began to speak but was distracted by the call for those girls hoping to be picked as May Queen to gather.

'Wish me luck,' she said, grasping his arm briefly before running to join the others.

'Good luck,' he called, catching Gabriel's eye and allowing himself, just once, to enjoy his sour expression.

'Ah,' Bett said, a playful ring to her voice. 'May Day and love blossoms already.'

Daniel basked in both her words and Gabriel's scowl as they all turned to watch the choosing of the May Queen. The girls lined up in front of the ribboned well, giggling and jostling, licking their lips and slapping their cheeks. Young Phyllis Ross, old enough this year to be included for the first time, clapped her hands in excitement and pulled faces to make her little cousins laugh. Molly waved. Through the pocket of his breeches, Daniel felt the stone Sarah had given him.

Magistrate Thompson had flowers threaded into the band of his hat, as always for the judging of the May parade. One of the rare tasks he showed eagerness for, walking up and down the line of girls, stopping to flick a curl or caress a cheek, asking whether they were in need of a position in service, for he had an opening for a maid. Again.

The magistrate made a show of inspecting every girl, tipping the chin to observe each face, commanding them to twirl and display the sweep of breast, waist and hip. It was a difficult task to choose a winner, he declared. This year as every other. But a decision was made.

When her name was called, Molly squealed, covering her mouth with her hands and turning triumphant eyes on the friends standing in line beside her. A group of boys, Gabriel at the head of them, rushed to lift her on to the cart. She clasped her hat and kicked her feet so that her white stockings showed. Though she looked right at him, Daniel turned away. Glanced at the cursed hill, beyond the green and path. Could not help himself.

'You should go and wish her well,' Bett said. 'She wants you to.'

'What do you know of the Haworths?' he asked.

Bett frowned at the turn of conversation. She shrugged. 'Cunning folk. Herb-knowledge and the like. The mam, she's a skill for sure, but I've heard stories of the lad that'd chill your blood.'

'And the girl?'

She shaded her eyes from the sun. Behind her there was laughter and shouting from the crowds around Molly. 'Why do you ask?'

'Oh – I only …'

She squeezed his arm. 'Don't fret of the Haworths today.'

'But what if – what if I'm not fretting? What if I'm—' Drawn. He could not speak it.

Bett narrowed her eyes. 'Trouble that way, lad. They're to be called on by those in need, and none other. Molly's took a shine to you, and though I grant it's hard to find a sillier lass, she's a pretty one, surely?'

Her words made sense. Yet he could not heed them.

She wagged her finger once, and left to find her husband.

The smack of Gabriel's hand on his shoulder sent him staggering. 'Didn't get your hopes set that the May Queen will choose a whelp like you for courting tomorrow, did you, Danny?'

'What?'

''Tis me she's her eye on, and it's long past time some good came my way. No more toiling that's left unnoticed, no more cursing by filthy whores. A sweet summer of shaking the tree, eh?' He winked. 'You know I had hold of her. Felt the warm of her through her clothes.'

Daniel stepped past him, made his way to the path. 'I have to be somewhere.'

He walked away from the sunny green, where everyone he knew had gathered. From the pretty girl on the cart, from the parade down the street, children throwing flowers ahead of the May Queen as the whole village followed.

From the shadow of the cursed hill, where the remnants of the plague hamlet squatted, ground tainted by the poisoned flesh that rested there, the laments of the spirits that still lingered drifting through the air. Where the girl with the stormy eyes and sharp tongue lived. The girl who saw in him what others did not.

He had never been master of his own destiny. What difference did it make to hand himself over to her? At least he was choosing who wielded power over him. There was a wildness to the thought, a freedom, that set him alight as much as it chilled him to the core.

Teeth

John crouches in the shadows at the corner of the room next to his mat, a plank of wood in his hand, the bones of his shoulders pressing through the worn cloth of his tunic. He waits to catch the mice that make their beds in ours. This is his habit only when in the vilest of moods.

'Thought you were looking for work,' I say, heaving the bucket to the wall, stained with soot and turning to mould at the top where the roof leaks. Bending over, I press my hand to my side, catch my breath. I might as well throw mutton fat on to smouldering embers. I see well enough in the dim light to notice Mam falter as she sits at the table, mashing worms and purple flowers for her May Day love potions.

'I looked, I asked, I begged as no man should be made to. Not one'll have me. All I got was a split lip.'

'Brawling?'

He remains hunched over, eyes focused on the mat and voice low so as not to scare away the mice, but there is venom in each word. 'I knocked on every door and asked to fix the roof or chop wood or even fetch water, though it's a job for a woman. And after I'd borne every insult from rogue to loiter, that dolt-headed netter said he'd not stink his dwelling by letting me through the door if I was to pay him and threw a pot of water over me. So yes I took my fee in blood and teeth. Beat him until he sniffled worse than Annie. His sneer'll not look so pretty now.'

'He's dead?' I ask, words sticking in my throat, mind tumbling with what will happen to us if this is true.

John snorts. 'Would he was, but nay. He'll live to skit me another day.'

I think of John's humiliation, knowing how every insult cuts him. How he feels his duty to replace Father, and his failure to do so keenly. I remember John, not long after Mam had told me what my mark meant and began teaching me about plants. His thin arm outstretched as he pointed to the ground. 'My familiar is a brock, a big one, and it'll punish any that harm me with its teeth and claws.'

Mam swept past with an armful of poppies, ready to strip the seeds. 'Nowt there, John. 'Tis not your fate, I've told you.'

He looked at me, tears running down his face.

'Why am I not chose?' he asked.

I swallow down my sympathy, for I cannot afford to feel John's pain. It will weaken me. It is my anger that gives me the strength I need.

Mam stands, wiping her hands down the front of her petticoat. 'Did you bring them?'

'What?' John asks.

'The teeth.'

'You're asking if after I'd beaten them from his head and he lay hollering on the ground in a puddle of blood, and I standing with it dripping from my fists – did I bend and pick his teeth up?'

'Aye.'

'I didn't.'

'What use are you? Returning empty-handed to this house when you know I can use a tooth for a curse or to sell.'

There is a crack as the plank of wood smacks down, crunch as the mouse meets its end.

'And you, lass? What have you brought?'

I think of the hag stone I gave to the farm lad, that she could have sold. 'Water.'

She crosses her arms, lifts her chin. 'Last us a day, two perhaps. Won't feed us.'

'I meant to bring nettles but—'

'Meant to is no good to me. Teeth left on the ground, no good. Nowt comes through that door that doesn't have a use, that's how we live, and yet here are you two, not a thing to offer between you.'

John swings the flattened and bloodied mouse by its tail. 'This for your pot if you like it.'

'Any more and I'll pull that clever tongue from your head. Your wit won't feed us, John.'

'I'll bring nettles,' I say.

'We need more than nettles from you. You asked to be taught the ways you're born to. It's time you used the gift you've been given.'

Her words fall through me like stones. The weight of them holds me still.

Mam does not take her eyes off me. Her voice is soft but tipped with ice. 'Nay? Then you must be what use you can.

Villagers are busy with feasting and drinking, you can fetch the teeth I'm owed.'

There is no arguing with her. And I would rather endure this punishment than face what she asks of me. But I don't do it willingly.

'What about John?'

'It's May Day, folks won't be so watchful. John can see what's been left for the taking.' She meets my eye and holds it, daring me to challenge. 'A lamb left wandering, say.'

I keep myself still so I do not fling myself at her, fling words of accusation that she makes us what they claim we are, that what she speaks of is theft, no better, and we all know the punishment John risks. She knows my objections. Speaking them will make no difference.

'You fetch nettles now and when night comes go to the village and bring what I need,' she says. 'Make sure you're not seen.'

I know the netter's house well enough but I hate to be in the village. Would she had me foraging hedgerows or even seashore over this. I am angry at her foolhardy plans for John, angry at my own silence in the face of them. Mam is lucky I do not yet fully embrace my power, which now calls to me with images not of reconciliation, but of those I despise bending to my will, cringing in fear. Every child that's hurled a stone or spoke a cruelty, every person that's turned away from Annie when she begged for food, will kneel and weep and beg as I mete out fit sufferings. And I imagine, just for a moment, that Mam is among them.

Gather and Stalk

Daniel stood in a corner talking to Bett and watching those dancing to the fiddle music. She drained her wine and leaned unsteadily towards him, reaching out to her husband to balance herself.

'Come, heart-root,' Nathaniel said. 'Leave this poor lad be and dance with me.'

She frowned up at him. 'He likes my company.'

Daniel laughed. 'True.'

'We all do, my love. But there's other lasses he should be entertaining tonight.' He jerked his head towards the dancers.

'Aye, and one in particular,' Bett said over her shoulder as Nathaniel pulled her away gently.

Daniel glanced over just as Molly looked in his direction. Yellow curls framed her flushed cheeks. He drained his drink. Her apple-eyes did not hold him the way the crashing colours of the witch-girl's did. She was bonny, though, and all the lads craved to court her. Perhaps Bett was right. One dance would not hurt.

As he stepped towards Molly, a wailing and hollering, unmistakeably female, cut through the merry chaos and the music stuttered to a halt, the dancers stumbling and turning towards the sound. Daniel felt it like a fist in the stomach. He thought once again of the witch-girl's eyes. She had been dragged there by Gabriel, perhaps, in his conviction that she had cursed him and stolen the lamb, that he might punish her in front of the whole village.

The taste of ale soured on his lips. He shoved and elbowed through the gathering crowd, past the tree decked with ribbons for the dance, to the edge of the green where the sound came from, standing uncomprehending when he came upon the sight.

It was not her, but Nelly Finch, the netter's wife, shrieking and sobbing. Blood smeared across the front of her best clothes, though Daniel could see no injury on her. Not Sarah. Relief swept through him, though why he cared so deeply he could not say. He began to walk away. There were plenty others coming to Nelly's aid, Father and Gabriel among them. She was calming enough to form words.

'Come quick and help, my Samuel's hurt,' she said, clinging to the parson's sleeve. 'That devil. One of those devils from up the hill half-killed him.'

Her words set the world turning. Daniel willed himself to keep a clear head. He had seen the blaze in Sarah's eyes when she felt threatened. Perhaps Sam had taunted her, or worse, and she attacked him in response. The village would not stand for this. They would hurt her. It was just the chance Gabriel was looking for.

The crowd stirred, moving with the sudden activity of a disturbed bees' nest, and some of that noise too; hollering in anger that a being so low should dare to hurt one of their own, shouting of the revenge they would exact, the burning of the home and beating like for like, prowling to gather lights. Each man shouting louder than his neighbour of his own courage in the face of such cowardly evil and warning the women to stay behind, they marched in a ragged line. They were on the hunt. She needed him now. He must find courage, for she had no other protector. The farm was between the green and the foot of the cursed hill. He would pass it on the way.

The mare had never been ridden and would be on an unfamiliar path in fading light. It was a risk he would never take. And his only chance.

The mare did not bend to his will in an instant. She reared and kicked, almost pitching him to the ground. He wound his fingers through her sweat-dampened mane and forced his voice to be soft, steady. She calmed a little, still pacing but more slowly, blowing into the cooling air. His plan was almost certainly doomed to fail – the horse was wild still, and he one voice against many. But he must try.

He remembered the village gathering and stalking like this once before, to chase out a pedlar who had bedded another's wife. Daniel was a child then, and recalled only vague images of great, loud men shouting in the night, faces lit by flame and fury, the odour of smoke and sweat. Father among them. He had imagined the terror of the man pursued by such a crowd, but was too small to offer protection. No longer.

Their lights flickered now between trees, marking the progress of the village men. He could not take the path up the hill. Were they to reach her first she would be pulped beneath their fists. Or worse. Daniel pulled on the horse's mane and pressed her sides. She jerked and kicked, swinging her head, resisting his attempt to exert his will. Desperate, he yelled and thrust his heels into her side until at last she succumbed. There was no time to be gentle. He knew exactly what to do; he would go through the woods.

The mare pranced and rolled her eyes at a fox slinking through, the crack of branches underfoot, swoop of a bat above her head. Daniel leaned forward and urged her on. The chanting of the crowd beat through the night. They were ahead of him. The horse's hooves pounded the ground and Daniel clung to her mane as the air raced past. All the while he pictured Sarah at the hands of the villagers, stoked as they were by anger and ale. One look and she had possessed him, fool that he was, charging ahead now on a treacherous mission that might see him killed, would certainly leave him regarded with even more suspicion by the village. And yet he did not think to stop.

He kept to the edge of the thicket, hidden, but close enough to see flames ahead. To his right a thatch of twisted trunk and undergrowth blending to shadow, to his left the empty path. He had not reached them, could not pass them. They would be upon her.

Every pounding of hoof, lift and fall of branch ahead, flicker of path through the trees brought him closer. Scent of wild garlic and bracken broken beneath the galloping horse.

At last, lights on the path. Through the black web of branches he glimpsed faces as he passed, disjointed; a bearded cheek, a bobbing hat. Flicker of fire and shadow revealing expressions that burned with a brutal hunger. Daniel hunkered to the mare's neck. Surely they must see him. Surely they must hear.

A sound to his right, no more than a whimper, and turning he saw, a flash that was gone, the soft white back of Magistrate Thompson in his flower-strewn hat and behind him, against a tree, the pale face of little Phyllis Ross. It was not unusual to find couples in the woods on May Day, but he knew immediately she had not chosen this. Her eyes met his briefly. Tears. A cub in need, and he knew he should stop, any other time would not hesitate to, but he must choose and, in the brief moment it took, he chose Sarah. Phyllis must have another rescuer this night.

A branch cracked him on the eyebrow, a sting that stole his breath and snapped his head back, sending his hat spinning to the ground. He passed the last of the villagers, finally pulling ahead. Daniel raced on until he reached the ruined hamlet, searching for a house that might be hers. Blinking blood from his eye, he searched in the darkness.

He had never seen the house up close. There was only one with roof still intact, cowering against the hillside, a battered shack keeling into the ground, surrounded by ten or so crumbling remains. No animals. Nothing to show it a home. The hill below aflame with lights. Ignoring his fear of the spirits that surely drifted through the empty doorways and rose from ground furrowed where bodies lay, he dismounted and ran across the scrub, beating on the door, praying this was the place. It opened to reveal a slight, female shape. A sibilant, cracked voice took him by surprise.

'Not often we have a gentleman riding up on horseback. A fine creature, sir. After an amatory? I've a potion that will make a honey-sop of any girl.' She looked him up and down. 'Or boy.' She held out a bowl of grey paste that stank bittersweet and writhed slowly.

'Where's Sarah?'

She stepped out and Daniel realised that this straggle-headed, sunken-faced woman was Sarah's mother. The same blustery eyes stared at him. 'You'll have no potion for my Sarah.'

'I – no, they're coming for her.'

'Coming why? Who?'

'People, they're angry, she attacked Sam Finch. Look.'

He turned to point out the lights snaking up the hill, but she had already seen.

'Fool lad, it's John they want not Sarah,' she said, dropping the bowl at her feet and yanking the flimsy door closed.

Daniel could not take in her words. Was Sarah safe? 'Where is she?'

The mother was already heading for the woods. Scent of smoke carried on the sea breeze.

'In the village, but first you keep those men and their torches from my door.'

'What if she comes back?'

'It won't matter. Because you'll have turned the pack away.' She gasped and ran towards the trees. 'Oh – Annie!'

The crowd gained, their yells and the pounding of their feet reaching him clearly now. Almost every village man there, all had either taunted or ignored him. He could leave, now, before he was seen. Run to the village, find Sarah. Hope she had a home to return to later.

Daniel rested his face against the warm, damp neck of the mare, stepped on a small tumble of wall that he thought had once housed a family's pig, and climbed on to her again. He dared not turn to look, fancying he felt the stare of the spirits whose home he had just trod upon at his back. Rode slowly to face the mob.

★

The smell of burning fat and smoke overwhelmed the salt air. Faced with the jeering crowd and dancing lights, the mare snorted and reared, almost sending Daniel plunging to the ground. He clung on, hushing and soothing. The pack cowered and staggered back from her flailing hooves. He had their attention, at least.

Daniel drew himself up. Opened his mouth. Prayed the words would come. 'The house is empty.' His own voice, louder and deeper than expected, rang with an unfamiliar authority.

'What, milksop such like you rode up to the witch house?' Gabriel asked.

Daniel looked down at him, strong with the truth. 'I did. It's empty.'

Gabriel scowled. Crackle and hiss of flames, disgruntled muttering. This was not the reckoning they had hoped for. His father in the crowd. Expressions buffeting across his face like a wheat field in the wind.

'Don't believe him,' Gabriel shouted. 'We'll search it ourselves.'

'Waste of time. Why would I lie?'

Muttered dissent. It took all Daniel's strength to sit tall, to hold fast to the mare and hide his fear that any moment she would panic and pitch him off. Only the knowledge that it was Sarah's home he protected put stop to his shaking.

'There's justice to be done,' a voice called. 'Poor Sam could be lying dead, for all we know.'

'Could be murdered.'

Voices raised in a drunken, savage cacophony. He held tight to the mare as she flattened her ears and skittered.

'Justice,' he shouted. Desperate, no idea where he was going with this. Surprised as they quietened for him. 'The man you need to bring your justice is Magistrate Thompson. Then you'll have proper penalty.'

'Proper penalty for a beating is a beating,' Gabriel said.

Daniel's heart battered against his chest. There was no reasoning with them. They began to move forward.

'Wait.'

A voice from the back, not loud but somehow laden with authority. Over the heads of the crowd Daniel saw Parson Walsh.

'Master Taylor is right. Justice of the law is the way of the righteous, not justice by blows.'

Gabriel the only one to challenge. 'An eye for an eye, isn't that what God says?'

'Do you believe yourself a greater authority than the magistrate?' the parson asked.

Gabriel opened his mouth but Daniel spoke over him. 'I know where he is, I passed him not long ago in the woods.'

Heads lifted in interest as though the scent of scandal was borne on the air. There was only one reason to be in the woods on May Day. A tradition usually favoured by the young, and the magistrate had celebrated his sixtieth birthday in memorable fashion not two months before. Daniel prayed they would go and find him, rescue Phyllis before harm was done. More harm was done.

Parson Walsh caught his eye. 'Then reason has won. Lead the way, young man.'

His tightening grip on the mare caused her to skip in a circle. Helpfully. 'I must take the horse back, parson. But if you pass into the woods here and head towards the village, you will find him.'

The parson tapped his hat and led the crowd. Daniel dug his knees into the horse's side and she galloped down the hill, air racing past so fast it stole his breath and chilled his skin, clinging so hard his fingers and arms burned. The house was saved. He would find Sarah before the villagers returned. If he survived the ride. And the wrath of the village should they discover his warning, and turn their rage and torches upon him.

Soft-skinned, Soft-hearted

I know they're all drinking and dancing at the green, but still I quicken my steps. Curse John and his eager fist.

Empty street, silent but for the cry of gulls. The sea a vast black bulk, white waves gleaming in the moonlight; boats rest quiet in the harbour, creaking in the breeze.

The blood is black and drying. Teeth gone. I have looked, I'm free to leave.

A sound of clattering fills the night, hooves on the dirt track. I turn and see Daniel Taylor and his horse. A wild pair, his face streaked with blood and mud, her eyes rolling and mouth frothing. I cannot make sense of them.

He brings the horse up to me, so close I see and smell the sweat darkening her hair, and reaches a hand down. His fingers are stained with soil, a mark of outdoor work that no scrubbing will remove.

I don't know why he is here, nor what drives him to reach for me. Soft-skinned, soft-hearted man that knows only a simple life of work and food and sleep in a bed with cotton sheets.

The only person to know my name who does not share it.

I take his hand, unexpectedly strong as it closes around mine. He pulls and I half-slide, half-scramble up the horse's side until I sit in front of him, petticoat bunched under me, his arm tight around my waist. A solid, warm touch, the like of which I've never known.

'Hold on,' he says and I grasp the horse's mane as he does with his free hand. He kicks and we are moving. I fear I will be flung to my death. As soon as I surrender my will to his I regret it.

I am feared, though not as much as I should be. We turn from the village towards the beck and I wonder what he means to do with me there. If he lays a hand on me I shall curse him with worse than sores.

At the bank, the river lilting dark and gleaming beside us, he climbs down and holds a hand out to me. I bat him away, annoyed that he thinks I need help, and then find myself unable to follow. He offers his hand again, I refuse it again, then launch myself to the ground and fall into him. The night is cooling and he is warm. I pull away, brush down my rumpled petticoat.

'What do you think you're doing?' I ask.

'I— saving you.'

I listen as he describes how he spoke to Mam, drove the villagers from our door. Never before has anyone not of my blood shown care for me. I don't trust his kindness.

'But you are unharmed,' he says. 'So all is well.'

'What's it to you?' Fear and anger at this new turn in our dealings with the village surges through me. By standing with us he has defied them. I don't understand why.

'I cannot stand to see pain,' he says.

'Any creature's pain, I suppose. Softer than the mud bank after a week of rain.'

He is steady. 'Any creature's, yes.'

My rant is set. My path, not his. To walk as I choose and face every obstacle how I see fit – and God knows, there are many, more than he can dream up.

'But yours especially,' he says.

And I am silenced. There is a stillness about him I feel I could be sucked into. He waits.

'Well,' I say. 'That's—'

'What?'

'Meaningless.' I lift my chin, cannot quite meet his eye, heart rattles faster and faster.

A breeze stirs the grass at our feet, lifts his hair. He wears no hat, I don't know why. 'Not to me,' he says.

'You care for me no more than you would an injured foal.'

He frowns. 'You are – wounded. But that isn't what draws me. You make me feel different, as though I'm – solid, or more real. I – I don't know.'

There is desperation in his expression. Nothing that's ever happened to me has prepared me for such a conversation. I'm insulted that he sees a wound in me, hidden I thought, having trained myself to turn to fury rather than fear. Insulted that he, so clearly broken in his own ways, dares to voice it. He is fearful of any that have a low opinion of him and yet defies the village to protect my family. Feared of my kind, brave facing the wild horse. I take a step away, and he reaches out, then draws his hand back. Sweat gleams on his brow.

'I don't know if – have you conjured these feelings in me?' he asks. 'Is it – to what purpose if you do not share them?'

Something in his eyes stops me from leaving. A battle of fear and anger and hope, that I cannot bear to look upon. 'Any conjuring here has been done by you, a notion of a lass that I am not and cannot be. You mustn't be kind. I'm not used to it.'

'You deserve kindness.'

'I deserve what I get. It's what I was born to.'

Clouds roll above us, uncovering a bright moon that gleams in the black water of the river.

'Born to it how?' he asks.

'Chosen.'

He shakes his head. 'By – God?'

The laughter that comes from me is tainted. 'You don't understand a thing.' I am tempted to reach out and touch the thick cloth of his tunic, the plump flesh of his cheek. 'How can you? Leave me to my life and be grateful for the comfort of your own.'

'But you're not in it.'

His voice shakes a little. His words leave me stunned, more than any blow I've taken.

'You don't want me in it,' I say.

'What if I do?'

'Then God help you.'

I have a feeling of eyes upon me. There is a movement in the trees, and I turn sharply to see the white flash of ears and tail. The horse shifts and Daniel reaches to steady her, hushing softly. I stare at where the hare was, for surely that is the creature I saw, but there's nothing now. He looks down, scuffs the grass with his boot. 'Can I ask – what is it that you feel?'

A big question. He has filled my thoughts since the day we washed Annie's hair in the beck. The echo of his touch warms my hand at night. The thought of his idiotic, freckly face will not leave me be. I cannot name how I feel. I will not.

'Cold,' I say. Turn my back. Make to leave.

'Wait,' he says. 'Your family are safe. Stay here with me a while?'

His expression remains open. I can see no malice in him, and now I'm shamed at my ill temper after he saved us. Mam's voice rings in my mind. I must go. But I do not move.

We stand for a moment, in silence. The horse steps towards him and nudges his shoulder. He almost loses his footing, flushing and clearing his throat. 'Jealous,' he says.

She's beautiful, gleaming in the moonlight, mane lifting in the breeze. I stroke her neck and she presses into me, whinnying gently.

My tongue sticks in my mouth, empty of words, and I flail for something to say that might please him. 'She's bonny,' I say. Hardly impressive, but all I can manage.

He rests his face against hers. 'She is.'

She lifts her head and snorts. Daniel laughs. 'And she knows it. But without her I'd not have reached your house in time, so we must be grateful.'

I watch him stroking her. 'I am grateful,' I say.

'Is that – that's what we'll call her. Bonny. Shall we?'

'It's – yes. That's good.' I've never struggled so to hold a conversation. We smile, too much and without reason, each a reflection of the other.

The breeze whips the grasses at our feet, lifts sandy clods to scour our legs, brings the scent of mud and sharpness of the beck. I shiver, and he frowns.

'We could light a fire, if only I'd brought a flint,' he says. 'I'll remember next time.'

Next time? I look at him quickly and he catches my eye, flushes.

'And you bring a neckerchief to keep warm,' he says.

'I'm warm enough,' I say. Then, though I don't know why I'm drawn to tell him the humiliating truth, 'I don't have one.'

I glare, daring him to show pity or embarrassment. Nothing. A small nod is all.

This conversation is pointless. There can be no next time. Mam would drag me away by the hair if she knew I were here, and I know well enough the reasons why I cannot see him again, even if I wished to.

'I—' He reaches into his pocket, brings out the stone I gave him. 'I – we could meet here. In the – at night. I'll leave the stone, I'll tie it to this branch, see?' He points at an alder at the edge of the cluster of trees. 'If I can come that night, I'll leave it there.'

He has lost all sense. We both know this cannot be.

'And you, you come and look, and if you can meet me take the stone. Then I shall know. And I'll wait for you.'

'I shall not come.'

'I'll wait.'

I dream, briefly, of finding the stone and meeting him as the light fades. Of a fire. A different life. There is a rustle again behind me, a feeling of being watched. 'I cannot come,' I say.

I run through the door to see my family. Safe. The house is smoky and dim, save for the light of the fire, before which they all sit, crammed on the ground by the edge of the table.

'Sken,' Annie says, skipping over to me, waving something in my face.

I laugh, gather her bony warmth into my arms, nuzzle her twig-taffled hair. 'Hold it steady then, I can't see.'

'I maked it. John's helping me.' She holds out a block of wood, crudely hewn into the shape of something unrecognisable.

John looks up from where he sits, sharpening his knife. 'A squirrel for my little squirrel,' he says and Annie skips back over to him. He rests a thin arm over her shoulder, giving her the knife and guiding her hand with his as she scrapes at the wood. Her face solemn with concentration, tongue poking from her lips. I wish now that I had invited Daniel in, let him see John as the boy he is, not the demon they all fear.

'Where are those teeth?' Mam sits cross-legged, moulding a lump of clay, her bare feet leaving prints in the spilled ashes. I look to see any sign of Dew-Springer, but find none, and wonder again at the hare I saw earlier.

My happiness dries and shrivels. 'They weren't there.'

She turns, the light flickering over her sagging jaw and narrowed eyes. 'Then you'll have to fetch me some of his hair, or a bit of cloth from his tunic at least.' She goes back to the figure she's fashioning. 'He will suffer now. Brought hurt to my family. He must pay.'

Somehow, I notice now the gaps in the wooden planks of the door, the holes where the rain mizzles through our roof. This house does not feel as solid as it did when I walked into it, offering little in the way of protection.

I kneel in front of Mam, take her hands and still them. 'Don't use it,' I say. 'Please. Leave them be. We don't want more trouble.'

She shakes me off. 'If they want no trouble they should not hurt my own,' she says, continuing to mould the clay.

'That isn't what I said.'

I take a handful of the ash and sprinkle it around the mat. Ring the bell in the corners, Annie's hand in mine. I do my best to keep her safe. Would I knew an enchantment to protect her from the villagers too.

Mice Shaken from a Sack

Exhausted and reeling from the night's events, Daniel stepped through the door. Extraordinary to enter the house so late. The kitchen quiet and tidy, pans polished and hanging on the wall, fire glowing behind the grate. Scent of the bread Bett had baked that day still lingering in the air. Father, sitting at the table with a flagon of ale, looked up as he opened the door and they both hesitated.

'Son,' he said, nodding an acknowledgement of Daniel's presence. 'Drink?'

It was late and Daniel had to be up at dawn for the milking. The last thing he wanted was to make awkward conversation into the night. 'Please,' he said, and drew up a chair.

Father filled a tankard and Daniel took a gulp, then another. He was dry, he realised, and this was more welcome than he had first thought.

'So,' Father said, 'mare's coming on well.' A deliberate steering away, Daniel knew, from the roles they had both played in the events of just hours before.

'Yes.'

Father tipped his tankard and inspected the contents.

Daniel raised his drink to his lips, tried to appear casual. 'Did you find the magistrate?'

Father shrugged. 'Didn't go, I left them to it.'

Daniel was desperate to know what had become of Phyllis and clung to the hope that, in sending the crowd to find her, he had rescued her in some part. Sarah's house had still been standing when he left her there, that much he knew, but would the villagers remember their cause and return another night?

His mind bustled with questions that could not be asked, just as Father did not question why he was at the home of those they considered villains or worse, nor why he turned the crowd away. Silence stretched, broken only by the faint lowing of oxen.

'Always work to be done,' Father said. 'You know.'

Daniel nodded. The space between them taut and empty.

The sound of heavy steps on the yard outside had them both looking at the door before Gabriel strode in, cheeks flushed, eyes alight, his happy fever causing disquiet to trickle under Daniel's skin. Gabriel stopped, expression corroding at the unfamiliar sight of father and son drinking together. He looked at Daniel and whistled through his teeth.

'Haven't you gone and made a heap of trouble?' he said. 'Runt finally finds his backbone and makes a bigger mess than my little sister mixing water in the gutter.'

'Should think you're about ready to head home, aren't you, Gabriel? You take such care of your poor mam, she'll be want-ing—' Father said.

'What mess?' Daniel's voice strident, overriding Father's.

Gabriel grabbed a chair, scraping it over the floor, sat with legs apart. 'Magistrate. Only playing at hot cockles with that girl maid of his.'

Father shifted, leaned back in his chair, stretched out a leg and brought it back in again. 'Can't be right – she's just a lass, isn't she?'

'Bonny lass, though,' Gabriel said. 'Have you seen her? I wouldn't—'

Father slammed a fist on the table. His voice was dangerously quiet when he spoke and blood began to trickle from his nose. 'Enough. You will not sit at my table in my house and talk about a young lassie like that. Understood?'

Gabriel flushed and nodded, only daring to smirk when Father lifted the tankard to drink.

'Is – is she all right, the maid?' Daniel asked. He should have stopped, could have taken her to safety.

'All right for now, but we'll only know for sure when we see if there's a babby or not come winter.'

'He's to wed her if there is,' Father said. ''Tis the only right course. And I hope you lads would never get a lassie into trouble, but I know you'd step up as men if you did.' He looked pointedly from Daniel to Gabriel.

Daniel rested his head in his hands, fingers brushing the graze above his eye, pain flaring. Good. He deserved it. Phyllis was fourteen and would be shamed and shunned if she were carrying the magistrate's child. Her tearful gaze would haunt Daniel's nights, and no less than he deserved.

He was mistaken. Daniel knew that his dreams had been spun through not with Phyllis's eyes but the raging colours of Sarah's. Against his will, the memory of her body pressed against his as they rode Bonny, the barbs and later softening of her words, had kept him awake and brought other sinful urges that he had struggled to resist.

Daniel rose and dressed, too impatient to wait for the sun to break its slumber. The air still held a chill this early, but he knew from the cloudless sky that the day would be warm. On his way to check the pea field, the air laced with smoke as the bramble and bracken roots smouldered, Gabriel grabbed him from behind and shoved him against the wall of the house. Daniel glanced past Gabriel's shoulder, relieved at least that no one witnessed his humiliation. Too exhausted to put up a pointless struggle.

'Don't think I've forgot you've stole my chance to have justice out with they devils up the hill,' Gabriel said, face so close to Daniel's that spittle splashed his cheek. 'Don't think I won't find my time. That bitch will pay.'

He left, and Daniel rested against the wall, catching his breath. The Haworths were feared, even hated, by some in the village, but he had never heard Gabriel speak against them until recently.

He brushed himself down, cleared his throat, and walked to the field in a way that he hoped showed a lack of care. He did not know how he had turned the crowd from Sarah's house once, and could not imagine doing so again. He had neither strength nor standing.

Daniel worked all day, raking the remains of the root pyre and spreading it in preparation for sowing, the scent of smoke and soil not unpleasant as he smoothed an even grey coating over the ground. His eyes stung and watered, his throat was dry and tasted of ash. Back ached, hands blistered. The discomfort should have overwhelmed him, the labour exhausted him. Yet as he worked, as he washed and ate and settled to sleep, the image of Sarah would not leave him, nor did he wish it to. As though she stood at his side throughout the day.

The knock at the door was unexpected. Daniel, Father and Gabriel had finished their morning tasks and were about to leave. They exchanged a perplexed look; they rarely received visitors and never on a Sunday morning.

On her way out anyway, Bett opened the door.

'Have you forgot it's Sunday?' they heard her ask. 'I'll be baking no bread for you today.'

''Tis not you I came to see,' a voice answered.

Bett looked at Daniel, jerked her head towards the door and left. He glanced at Father, who raised his eyebrows in a silent question, shrugged and stepped over.

Molly stood there, wringing her gloved hands. An unpleasant thought about why she was here occurred to him. He simply stood, while Father and Gabriel shuffled behind him, straining to see.

'I wanted to see you,' she said.

Neither a surprise nor welcome. Daniel gestured for her to step out with him; this was not a conversation he wanted witnessed. They walked across the field as the low strip of sunlight began to bleed into the sky. At last spring had fully arrived, warming the air and softening the tasks that filled his days.

'Are you well?' he asked. Awkward now, away from the festivities.

'Come now, Daniel, don't tease. You must know why I'm here.'

He stopped and looked at her, lifting his shoulders slightly.

'You know the tradition.' She tipped her head so that the straw hat hid her eyes. 'May Queen chooses a boy.'

'Yesterday.'

'What?'

'The day after May Day, May Queen chooses someone to court, but that was yesterday.'

'I came yesterday, I couldn't find you. Is that really all you have to say?' she asked.

Her eyes were large, she bit her thumbnail through her glove, and Daniel could not help but be moved by her uncertainty. Behind her, the trees in the orchard were sprinkled with white blossom.

'No, of course,' he said. 'I just didn't think you would choose me.'

'Well, I do.' She looked up at him. 'You're happy, aren't you?'

'I'm – grateful for the compliment, but I really think you should choose again. Someone better, someone – else.'

She laughed, stood on tiptoe and kissed his cheek. 'That's exactly why you're the right choice,' she said. 'I have to go now, I must get to church, and so must you. I will tell my father afterwards.'

And she was gone, running with one hand holding up her petticoat and the other holding down her hat, glancing once to smile at him over her shoulder. Daniel stood as the jay began to sing. His world had turned about and he had no idea how.

Father and Gabriel hurried out of the farmhouse as soon as Molly left, an enthusiasm for church never before seen in either.

'So,' Gabriel said, shouting over the distance between them, 'what did the May Queen want with you?'

The teasing tone of voice was at odds with the narrow-eyed suspicion his face wore. Father on the other hand battled to control a smirk.

'Oh she, ah, she just wanted to ask me about – about—'

The blush that poured over Daniel's face was answer enough.

Gabriel snorted. 'She's an eye on the farm, then. Why else would that pretty thing choose you for courting?'

Daniel shook his head. 'I have no idea.'

Father cleared his throat. 'Are you away to settle your mam, Gabriel?'

'Already done.'

'You're a good son.'

Daniel remembered Gabriel arriving at the farm as a boy, asking for work of any kind, and they had grown together almost as brothers, albeit disjoined ones. Father had brought him in one summer to help with the hay mowing and been impressed with his strength and determination to earn a living to take home. Claiming this boy of twelve could carry out the work of two grown men and so save him wages, Father took him on permanently. Daniel knew he only made the decision after learning of the family's plight, though.

Gabriel shrugged. 'No one else to do it.'

Father nodded. In silence, they made their way to church.

Father still revelled in the words of the King's Bible, marvelling at their beauty and clarity, but it was all Daniel had known, and was this day delivered in an especially flat tone by the parson. Impossible to concentrate. He had glimpsed Phyllis Ross as he entered, hanging her head as the crowd nudged and whispered. Only Bett and Nathaniel stopped to speak with her. Sam Finch limped in, aided by his wife, suffering with the injuries Sarah's brother had inflicted on him but days before. And Molly, sitting with her parents across the aisle.

His mind churned, and not with the pure thoughts appropriate for church. The musty scent of damp and candle wax, the light splintered into rainbows by the window, served to shame but not calm him. Daniel could distract himself with thoughts of Molly's soft-bread skin pressing into his, for sure. But every time he did, that sense of Sarah's presence returned, and with it the feeling that there was something in him only she recognised.

She was a girl like no other, whose hair danced untamed while all others' lay demurely hidden under a coif or cloth, whose eyes raged bright. One he knew he should not crave. A girl who loved her sister with the ferocity of a vixen over cubs. Who saw in him a man, with the skill to tame wildness from any creature and the courage to mark out his own path.

It was an easy life offered by Molly, if only that would satisfy. But he must have the storm. A path not just difficult. Impossible. He might as well tell Father he wished to court the mare. But he must have the eyes that truly saw him.

Resolve landed in Daniel, complete and entirely fixed, a recklessness that would once have left him afraid but today gave strength. The sermon, hymns and prayers a meaningless hum, no longer for him. He would halt this course of events. He must speak with Molly now.

Freed, the crowds spilled out across the churchyard like mice shaken from a sack. Just as Daniel spied her, Parson Walsh called them back.

'There is an announcement to be made, on a subject I would not sully God's house by mentioning in church.'

Though his voice still carried, there was a weariness to his tone. Daniel held his breath. News would now come of the aftermath of the march upon the Haworths', of Phyllis's fate.

'You know, I am sure, that Magistrate Thompson was discovered but two nights past behaving in a manner unfitting of his position, indeed unfitting for any of God's children.' He scrutinised those gathered. Startled glances and whispers passed between them. 'In my humble role I have personally spoken to those in authority and arranged for his immediate replacement.'

At this the murmurs grew louder, for Magistrate Thompson had looked away from sins of all kinds. The parson had never condoned such actions, and had taken his opportunity now to condemn the magistrate fully, shaming him by speaking truth so openly. Any other minister would concoct a story of sudden illness to explain such a departure. Daniel was sickened too, but because this was confirmation of Phyllis's suffering, and his failure to stop it at the time.

'The new man,' Parson Walsh continued, voice straining, 'travels as I speak, and shall arrive in no more than a day, God willing. He is reputed to be a character of great moral standing, and strict adherence to the law. News that brings great comfort to you all, I do not doubt.'

His expression showed he was well aware of the fear his words caused. Seemingly exhausted by this speech, he walked back into the church, ignoring those shouting questions after him. Only then did Daniel remember the urgency of his cause, and realise Molly had left.

Otherness

Every morning I tell myself I will not go to the beck. Every
afternoon I sneak away and look for the hag stone. 'Good,' I
say when it is not there. The stinging in my eyes is caused by
the breeze, nothing more.

At last I see it, dangling among the catkins from a thin strip
of cloth threaded through the hole.

'I shall not come,' I say. I take it anyway.

He waits at the riverbank, looking out over the water so that
I've the chance to watch him. The spikes of grass beneath my
feet become soft and swampy. If I were to walk in, wash away
the mark on my skin, and emerge on the other side, who
would I be? A cleaner, better version of myself. That is the
rebirth I long for.

There is nothing to this. Nothing to come of it. One evening will not break down the fragile dependence Mam has built
up between us and the village. I push away thoughts of her.
This is not a betrayal.

He turns and looks at me, though I make no sound, and waves then runs a hand through his hair. Awkward suddenly and regretting my decision to come, I walk closer. I don't understand his interest in me; we are not the same kind, the path of our lives should not meet.

His smile when I reach him and hand him the stone is so genuine it confuses me further. We're silent for a moment, then speak at the same time.

'I brought a poultice.'

'I'm so glad you're here.'

I am holding out the pot of paste, arm stiff and unnatural. 'For your ...' The words fade. I gesture to my own forehead.

He takes the pot. 'Thank you.' He sniffs it and dips a finger in.

'Camomile and thyme,' I say.

He tries to apply the cream, smearing it over his eyebrow and missing most of the cut.

I laugh, and take the pot, at ease with him now though I cannot fathom why. 'Here, let me.' Without thinking I spread the lotion over his cut as I would with Annie, fast and gentle. 'There,' I say.

'Thank you. Did you – who made this?' he asks.

'Mam.'

He nods. 'How does the cunning – what does she do?'

I try to interpret his words, listen for the suspicion in them. Think again of the fear he showed when he first knew me, of the chafe of rope against skin. Perhaps this is all a trick, enticing me to confess our guilt. This would explain his interest, but as I stand here with him I don't feel it to be true. I feel trust. I don't know why. He leans forward, anxious to hear my reply.

'Healing,' I say. Sometimes. And more, so much more – a curse if you can pay for it, or if you've hurt her. A love potion, if your chosen one does not feel as they should. A brew of poppy seeds to bring lightness to the soul and pictures to the mind that only witchcraft can conjure.

'That's quite a skill,' he says.

Yes. One that I am also born to. A thrill of both yearning and foreboding burns through me. 'Her grandmother taught her.'

'I came prepared this time,' he says. 'Come see.' He takes my hand and leads me up the bank to the trees. We're careful not to look at each other. We're careful to pretend that he has my hand only to guide me.

Under the protective branches of the alder lie his boots and hat, a folded piece of grey material, a cloth-wrapped parcel and a flint and steel. He gestures to the neat stack as though it's a pile of gold.

'See. We shall have a fire and a feast tonight.'

'A feast?' My mouth fills and I wonder what food he offers. All I've eaten today is a bowl of watery pottage, flavoured with clam and nettle.

'I brought a few bits but that's for later, let's start with the fire.'

Looking around at the fresh green shoots of grass, I doubt his ability to light them. I care more to know what food he's brought but don't want to betray my interest.

'This grass won't light,' I say.

He pulls a handful of straw from the pile of his belongings. 'I told you I came prepared.' He's so pleased with himself, I try not to be impressed and fail. The evening has cooled, the breeze chilling my arms, and a fire will be more than welcome. 'We need wood, though,' he says.

'Of course.' Does he think I've never lit a fire? 'I will find twice as much as you, twice as fast.'

'Oh really? You think so?'

'Of course.'

He pelts off into the trees at such a pace that I'm left standing, and I've given him an advantage already. I cry out, clasping my petticoat, following him.

It is not the time of year to find good sticks for fire, they are too supple and green. Still, I have a practised eye. Twigs are easy to come by and thin enough will always catch. And further in, where the branches above knot to make a roof that shields from sun and rain, I will find some old wood come down over winter. I know it.

I race around, breathless, laughing and yet deadly serious in my aim to prove myself the better. Daniel runs through the undergrowth, darts between trees, his eyes bright.

It does not take long for my arms to be filled with sticks. When I can carry no more, dropping as many as I pick up, I head back to the riverbank where he waits, a pile of wood at his feet. I cast my eye over it. He's done well, but I am the victor.

'We are evenly matched,' he says.

I am indignant. 'Nay. I have more. Let us count.'

I drop my pile next to his, but he's laughing, hands held up in a gesture of appeasement. 'No, I'm sure you're right. You win.'

He picks a leaf from my hair, and somehow steals victory from me by conceding it so easily. Crouching, he builds the thinner twigs into a frame with what I must grudgingly admit is an expert touch. I fight the urge to push him away and do it myself, just to show that I can. He strikes steel against flint, sparks hitting the straw which he coaxes into a flame and places under the sticks. The new light shows the angle of cheek and jaw.

He looks up. 'So serious,' he says.

'Did you say you brought food?' I ask. I can wait no longer.

He scrambles to his feet, runs to the trees and returns with the parcel, shoulders back and a look of pride. There's bread, the best kind, with a clean top, not the black-crusted sort from the bottom. This is a smooth, golden colour that I've never seen before. There's also butter, a luxury I've not had since we moved from the village, though the remembered taste immediately floods my mouth. Cheese, cold meat and radishes. I settle myself against a rock, facing the fire.

It's all I can do to resist grabbing a piece of everything and stuffing it into my mouth. I wipe my lips.

'Did you bring all this from home?'

'Yes.'

'They won't mind?'

He smiles. 'They won't know.'

I cannot imagine. To have so much that whole chunks of bread and cheese and meat can be taken unnoticed.

'Here,' he says, ripping the bread, dipping it into the butter and handing me some.

I hold it for a moment before tasting, trying to delay, trying not to show my hunger, my ignorance of such foods. Watch as he bites, copying his slow, casual chewing.

The taste of it, the feel in my mouth. Crunch of crust, softness of bread with the deep, earthy taste of rye and salt tang of butter. He offers me slices of meat, pieces of hard cheese, sharp radishes. I taste each one, letting the flavour spread over my tongue, brush crumbs from my lips.

'Good,' I say, covering my mouth with my hand to hide the chewing.

'I've saved the best till last.'

What could surpass this? I'm not convinced. He walks back over to the tree and returns with a smaller parcel, half-unwrapped, and sits next to me. It's some kind of pie he holds out. I recognise the pastry but not the creamy filling. There are two slices and he hands me one, saying, 'Flawn.'

I'm none the wiser.

I sniff the pie, catch him looking at me with an expression of gentle amusement, and bite in to hide my discomfort.

The flavour is like nothing I've ever tasted, sweet with a faint sense of rose, so that I close my eyes and wait for it to fade. I imagine what it must be to have a life of such ease; of a warm bed and spare clothes and a full belly. Of tastes such as this. Had I not been chosen for a different life.

'You like it?' Daniel asks.

I grunt my approval, mouth too full of another bite to speak.

'I brought something for you,' he says. 'If – you were cold before, so …'

He walks to the trees and comes back, holding a square grey cloth out to me. I sit with it in my arms, unsure what to do.

'Why do you give me this?' I ask.

'It was my mother's neckerchief,' he says, voice soft so that I can barely hear. 'We have no use for it.'

The evening darkens and flames spit into the night. All through the village people will be blowing out candles and settling to bed. No one shall disturb this peace.

'You must miss her,' I say.

He stares into the fire, light and shadow flickering over his face, and I know he sees there a life in which his mother lived. 'I didn't know her,' he says.

Not an answer, really, but I don't pursue it. 'She died when you were young?'

'She died having me.'

It's a wonder his father hasn't found another wife; he's a wealthy man, there must have been plenty to choose from.

'I remember my father.' I'm surprised to find myself mention him. He reacts as though I speak of nothing more significant than the weather.

'What was he like?'

'He was so tall. Or at least, he seemed tall but I was small at the time, so perhaps not.'

Daniel drops a branch on to the fire. I feel the flare on my face.

'He smelled of the sea. His boots were always wet and stained by the salt, he used to leave them by the door. I think I remember his boots better than his face.'

'He was a fisherman?'

I nod. 'We lived with the others by the shore. I hardly remember now.'

'I didn't know.'

The air at my back is cool, heat from the fire near-scorches my face. I shrug. 'He went out one day and didn't come back. And Mam, well she did what she could.' The memory smothers me as though I am there once again, the men and the noises they made, the coins left on the table. Mam squatting in the sea, washing and washing, face like a closed fist. The sweaty hand on my bare skin.

At first I didn't understand. She told me different stories of what it was – a special potion that made them leap like mad dogs and call out, or dance untamed until they dropped to the ground. Always, it was something that children must never see. Only later, when she warned me of men and what they want, of the results, did I realise.

I tell him nothing of this.

His gentle touch on my arm makes me start, and I realise I've been sitting with my eyes closed, fighting the memories, the cloth bundled tight in my arms. These I will never share, not with anyone. I pull myself away from the past, to the river-bank and the warmth and to him.

'Why don't you put the neckerchief on?' he asks.

He is kind to bring it, but I've never had one and am not sure how to wear it. I remember Mam's from years past, falling to points over her shift, but cannot see how to make this cloth hang that way. Reluctantly I stand, shaking it out and trying to place it over my shoulders, as I imagine it should sit, desperate not to show my ignorance. It doesn't feel right, too much at my back and too clumsily bunched at the front.

Daniel stands, giving a loud bark of laughter that sets a flush of shame running over my cheeks. 'What are you doing?' he asks.

I have never felt my otherness more keenly.

He takes it from me, folds and places it over my shoulders neatly. His arm brushes my burning cheek. The cloth is fine, and smells a little of mildew, sitting softly against me like no other clothing I own.

'There,' he says.

What must he think of me, knowing now that I am so poor I've never owned a thing so common for every village woman? So stupid I don't even know how to wear it. Hot, angry tears spill down my face, shaming me further.

I rip the neckerchief from my shoulders, throw it at his feet, and run.

'Wait,' I hear him call behind me. 'Wait, please, I don't –
what have I done?' There is desperation in his voice, but he
does not follow and I am glad of it.

Flawns and neckerchiefs and farm lads are not for me, as
Mam has always warned, and I was foolish to come. Tearing
over the scrubby ground and through the trees to the hill, I
stumble but don't stop, running so quickly that my chest burns,
taking myself away from Daniel as fast and as far as possible. I
need now to be with my own kind.

Frost Burn

Market day down by the harbour was the usual buzz of shouts and greetings, the scent of brine and salt sting of sea-whipped air. Daniel watched as Bett negotiated the price of a bundle of herring with mock disbelief, trying to put aside thoughts of Sarah. He had not dared to leave the stone these past days, knowing she would not come. He had embarrassed her, and was shamed by his own clumsiness.

'You think I came down the beck in a bubble, Hannah?' Bett said. Daniel pulled his thoughts back to what was happening in front of him. 'I can't pay that, the master's standing right here, he'll think I've lost all sense and I'll be out of work. Isn't that so, sir?'

She wore a light expression. This game was one they both enjoyed. The fisherman's wife eyed him with disdain, for what kind of master put in an appearance at market, a place only for women? He frowned and cleared his throat to rid himself of laughter. 'Seems an unreasonable high price. Would have to be taken from your pay.'

Bett shrugged at the woman, who sighed and added two extra fish. Staring past them she gasped and dropped the silvery bundle into the basket, pressing her hand to her mouth. Turning, Daniel saw a group gathered around a man who held a sobbing boy by the neck of his tunic.

Moving before he really knew why, Daniel pushed through the crowd. Many stood aside willingly. He would one day inherit the only farm in the village, after all, whatever they thought of him. He recognised the child, a boy whose father was recently lost to sea, face pale and mouth stretched wide, hanging from the fist of a man Daniel had never seen. The child's fear drove him to act, and the words were out of his mouth before thought of the consequences even occurred.

'Unhand that boy.'

The man looked Daniel up and down. 'He is a thief.'

'He is no such thing.' The boy's family now lived with his mother's sister and her husband. One small wage and many hungry mouths. 'He is on an errand for me, I forgot to give him the coins.'

A claim not supported by the fact that the child had already eaten most of the radishes he had taken and his mouth and hands were smeared with juice and mud. Nevertheless, Daniel handed a coin to the seller. He crouched before the child and gently pulled him free of the man's grip. The boy wept and gulped.

'Who are you? His father?'

'A friend to the family. Who are you, stranger?'

A cold light flared in his eyes. 'I am your magistrate, boy. I have come to introduce myself in the village. And not before time, I see. Thieves must be punished, not indulged.'

The boy wriggled free of his grip and darted away. Those gathered around whispered and jostled. He had given them even more to tattle over than usual.

'He is no thief,' he said. 'He was helping me with an errand.'

The magistrate cast his chill gaze around the crowd. 'I have observed enough to know there is much work to be done. Your ways have grown slovenly and corrupt. Do not think I cannot see what passes amongst you. Know now. It will be stopped. Those that transgress shall be punished, and I shall ensure I learn all there is to be known of this foul and wicked place. You may well look afraid. A turning of fortune was due and it arrives today.'

Daniel broke from the crowd and walked away. The magistrate remained where he stood, his anger like frost burn against Daniel's back.

'Be warned, young man,' he called. Daniel did not stop. 'I will be watching. Your insolence shall not be forgotten.'

Maggots

Annie and I sidle among the crowds down by the harbour, peering at the fishes and cockles and mussels on display. There are but a few selling radishes and baby turnips, though most will grow them in their own scrubby wind-beaten gardens and have no need to buy. Today the sea is flat and grey, appearing placid, but I know it cannot be trusted. In but a moment it may turn, and claim its next victim.

I catch an eye or two, searching out a soft-heart. Women are more likely to give but less likely to control where the coins go. Market day, when men are scarce, can be good to us. Not today. To a one, they step away, casting a disgusted look at Annie and wrinkling a nose at me.

This we're used to. But now there is a boldness in their cruelty that is new.

'Get away,' one seller yells, charging round to where we stand and shoving his face in mine. I pull Annie behind me. He shakes a fist and I do my best not to flinch, not to let the anger take me over, confirming all they think me to be. 'Away, shoo. We don't want your kind with your filth and spells.'

More gather behind him, stepping out from behind the wares they sell. Looking us up and down, whispering, curling their lips. There is an angry face wherever I glance. I hold tight to Annie.

A woman shoves me so that I almost knock Annie over. 'Should've finished the job after your brother set about Sam Finch,' she says, turning to bask in the approving nods and jeers from the others. 'Should've burned that dirty plague shack to the ground that night, and all you in it.'

I cannot find my voice, and am appalled to feel tears rise in my eyes.

'There are other nights,' the man says.

I swallow, draw myself up, willing my tears to stop. We've been hurt by villagers before. We've been sent away. But never have I been feared as I am now. Never have I looked to find a friendly face, a kindly hand to offer protection.

I spin around. A small way off I see the farm housemaid, Bett, bending over a pile of fish and arguing with the seller. Next to her stands Daniel.

The last person I want to meet. He must not see more of my humiliation.

I step back. 'Come, Annie,' I say. Feel the stalking of he that chose me, calling to the loathing in me – willing me to act. I drag myself away from the urge to do his bidding. 'We shall leave.'

The crowd simply stand silent, watching us. I pull Annie away, glancing again towards where Daniel stood. He is no longer there. We need to leave now, before there's worse trouble, but Annie taps a woman on the back and asks for a coin.

The woman lashes out and Annie sprawls on the ground.

'That was not called for,' I say, before I can stop myself, lifting her and dusting her off. She glowers at the woman, the blacksmith's wife who stands with her daughter, both in coloured petticoats, staring at us as though at maggots, with arms folded.

'Away,' she says. 'This is no place for your kind, but for those with honest earnings to spend.' She pushes Annie again. 'Shoo.'

Annie stamps her foot and it's all I can do to prevent myself from joining her. I catch my breath and calm myself.

The daughter smirks. 'Don't touch them, Mother,' she says, behind her hand but loud enough for me to hear. 'They're riddled with lice, at the least. Just look at them.'

There is a cruel joy lighting her eyes. 'Is that not the new magistrate?' she asks, head tilted towards her mother but gaze fixed on mine. Annie squirms at the strength of my grip. 'Let's call him, he shall not abide with this, shall he? Let's see his views on begging. Perhaps he may ask again of those not seen attending church.'

We are nothing more than a moment's amusement to her. I do not know how she can look upon Annie and see anything but a hungry child. I do not know how she can lack pity.

But they are both quickly turning towards a commotion on the other side of the market, hurrying to see the new entertainment. The space they leave is immediately filled with the farm housemaid, bustling in and ushering us both away.

'Leave here,' she whispers.

'But we've no—'

'Take this.' She bends and gives a coin to Annie. 'And away. No one is like to look kindly on you today.'

Annie stares at the coin, then back up at the housemaid, remembering a previous kindness from her. 'Thank you,' she says. Blinks. 'That cake was very nice, is there any cake?'

'Hush,' I say.

The woman laughs. 'Another time.' She looks at me, flapping her arms as though I'm a crow stealing her seedlings, and turns away.

I pull Annie back up the path that skirts the green and the Taylors' farm. Dare not stop by the beck and look for the hag stone. Only when we reach the foot of the hill, where our home nestles amongst the decaying remains of the hamlet, do I breathe free again.

Annie hands Mam the coin, earning leave to play. She scampers off, not to the woods today but through the empty doorway of a nearby shack. The weight of grass and ivy creeping over it have caved in the roof on one side, and bright spatterings of forget-me-nots and scarlet pimpernel burst between fallen stones. This is her favourite place to play at having her own home, creating food with mud to place on leaf-plates. Sometimes I hear her talking to the imagined friends she shares these meals with and I try not to think of what spirits Annie in her childish innocence might see, tethered still to the place they lived and died.

Mam runs a thumb over the coin, and her face softens a little. There's no better feeling than returning home with an offering for her, a coin being the best of any, though she will say she expects no less.

'Where did it come from?' she asks, as I sit at the table with John.

'The housemaid at the farm, you know her?'

'Aye,' Mam says. 'Kind soul.'

John blows dust from the wood he carves. 'Remember that time she gave Annie honey cake? She'd have flit and moved in with her, given half the chance.'

'So would I, for honey cake,' I say. 'Mam, dust know of a new magistrate arrived in the village?'

Her head snaps towards me and she clutches her chest.

'No,' she says. Not in answer to my question, but a denial, a dread, that this can be so.

She yanks out a stool and collapses on to it. All colour gone from her face.

John looks up. 'Aye. That old boater Henry Thompson got caught in the woods on May Day with his serving girl, just a young lass. New man's here, then? You always knew he was a lecherous old dog, didn't you, Mam? Always said so.'

'Gone?' Mam asks, rising again so quickly that her stool falls to the floor. 'No, no. He kept us safe, kept his distance. Could never accuse us because I knew, knew everything he was and I held my tongue, I dealt with the girls, gave them the brew free of charge, and he was safe and so were we.' She mutters the words, fast and quiet, so that I can barely grasp their meaning. My mind reels. What has she done, all this time? Served this beast to keep us safe? And what will become of us with him gone? Her footsteps quicken as she paces, agitated, breath ragged.

John catches my eye, his expression one of confusion and misgiving. 'Hush, Mam,' he says, voice gentle. 'Happen we'll be all right, just as now. Same law, another man is all.'

He doesn't understand. But I do. I close my eyes but cannot hold back the memory that is always within me.

Eleven years old and I was to be out of the house because Mam was with the men, but it was mizzling and I returned. I stood outside, soaked and shivering, building courage to defy her and step in. I can still see my own hand reaching out, pushing the door open. Can still feel that sure, sickening knowledge that whatever lay behind it was shadowed in shame. She was with one, the blanket hung in the doorway and I could hear the noises, so I stayed in the other room.

He was waiting. Bright little eyes stared at me from folds of flesh; sweat glistening, then beading, then running down the quivering jowls. He heaved to his feet, hand outstretched, and I didn't know what he meant to do, so I remained there.

Then the sound of tearing cloth as if from far away, the stench of his breath in my face. Hot, clammy palm against my skin. I can feel it now, jerk back in revulsion.

Mam behind him, arm around his neck, point of the knife digging into the doughy ripples under his chin. The only time I ever saw her driven to real violence. Red trickle that ran and pattered on the floor. Wet glisten of his lips as he prattled and begged, offered Mam whatever she asked if only she let him be. I understand now, this was my first meeting with Magistrate Thompson. And our reason for safety all this time.

Only now do I see that this encounter I had with him has sheltered us. And it is swept away with his leaving, our safety no more robust than a dwelling built of sand against the sea, licked away by a wave in a moment. We are exposed.

Without protection from a law which fears and seeks to extinguish us, without protection from the violence and hatred brewing in the village. I feel for the first time a sense of imme-diate ruin upon us. Tomorrow. Tonight.

I rest my head in my hands. Feel as though I'm falling and there will be no end to it.

'John,' Mam says, kneeling at his feet. 'Tell me all, think and tell it slow, all you know of this new man.'

John glances at me. I nod. We must know the worst of it now.

'He's come from different parts, they say, and stands by every word of law. He's a big church man and they say he sent a woman to the rope for – godless acts.' He shifts in the seat, looks again at me, expression uneasy. I press my hand to my chest, where my heart gallops.

Mam dips her head, breathes deep. When she looks up again she has almost steadied the tremble in her voice. 'Godless acts? Like those of us cunning folk?'

'No, just – witchcraft, is what they said. Spells and ...' John's voice trails off. 'Not what we do, Mam, they meant – something different.'

Mam stands, stiffly, back straight and head high. Pale, as I have never seen her before.

Meddling

Bett rolled her eyes as Daniel bumped into the doorway helping her carry the table out. The day of the spring clean, and he
was grateful to have his hands busy and his mind taxed only as
far as following Bett's instructions.

She was the beating heart of the farmhouse, her solid presence replacing that of the sour-faced nursemaid Daniel grew
up with when he was nine and Bett only thirteen. She left a
swathe of gleaming floors and scrubbed surfaces in her wake,
filling the hall with the smell of baking bread and stewing
meat.

She had brought order to the chaos that reigned their lives
and yet theirs remained a household that defied convention,
and not just for the lack of a milkmaid. Father often grumbled
that in those other village families that had housemaids, the
servant knew her place, worked in silence, greeted her master
with no more than a bobbed curtsey. He had found the only
one that confused service with advice, never fearing to express
an opinion.

'Catch hold of yourself, can't you?' she said. 'Head in the clouds today.'

Not quite in the clouds, perhaps, but halfway there at least. As far as the cursed hill. He had risen early that morning and left the stone by the river, hoping Sarah had forgiven him, and would come.

He placed the table down in the yard and glanced past Bett to see Father atop the ladder Gabriel held, dropping the rope that held a holly branch down the chimney. Daniel was not needed.

'Have you – what do you think of the new magistrate that's come?' he asked.

Bett stopped and rubbed her back. 'I'm glad to see the back of the old one.' An unfortunate turn of phrase that took Daniel to the vivid memory of what he had witnessed that night in the woods. She shook her head. 'That poor child.'

She led the way into the hall to begin removing chairs. 'Though what happened at the market …'

She lifted a chair in each hand, and Daniel did the same, following her once more into the bright yard. 'Thank God you were there and had backbone to step in.'

'Come along then, whelp,' Gabriel said, as Bett replaced him to secure the ladder while Father climbed down. 'Come join the men awhile.'

He slapped Daniel on the back, too hard so that it was all Daniel could do to keep his footing, and together they went into the hall and knelt before the fireplace. They had the job of pulling the rope until the branch came down the chimney, bringing the year's ash. Daniel tugged with all his strength, his two hands to Gabriel's one as he scratched the ghost of his pox with the other, and yet they were equal in strength. At last the holly scraped through, and a gritty cloud of soot with it.

'Have a care, lads, the whole place is filthy now,' Father barked. The spring clean always curdled his mood. 'Your mother always ran this thing so smooth. And in such good cheer.'

They stood silent, all eyes on Father. Blood trickled from his nose and he wiped it with the back of his hand, staring at the stain it left. Daniel tried to keep the pity from his eyes, for he knew Father could not abide it.

Father glared back. 'And stop scratching, Gabriel. Have you shook off this little girl's feeble curse or not?'

Gabriel removed his hand from his head, flushing. 'Aye, I've shook it off, 'tis a different itch that ails me now.'

Father snorted. Gabriel's colour deepened.

'But it vexes me, for she might pick a softer soul next time.'

Daniel shifted. Afraid now of where Gabriel's thoughts were leading. Afraid that there was truth to what he spoke.

'And that Haworth lad, he's more demon than boy anyhow. And still unpunished for what he did to Sam, and all because of your meddling.' He turned, shoving his angry face so close that Daniel flinched.

Pointedly, Bett swept at the pile of soot by Father's feet.

'Watch yourself, woman,' Father said.

The broom beat the floor with greater force, lifting clouds of soot.

'I've a mind to call some folks together, in the tavern tonight,' Gabriel said. 'And we'll end the job you stopped us from finishing last time.'

Daniel's soot-coated throat parched further. He could not speak, and yet he must, had to find a way to stop Gabriel and his vengeance on Sarah and her family. He opened his mouth. Nothing.

'Keep your head, fool,' Father said. 'Now is not the time to go causing trouble for yourself with a new magistrate looking to make his mark.'

Relief spilled through Daniel. This was an argument Gabriel would listen to.

'And you'll need to mind yourself. All this brawling in the tavern might draw his eye to you. That will be when you remember the Haworths, eh?' Father tapped his nose. 'You might need them around, so if attention's drawn to you then you can tell you've been cursed and can't be helped. New magistrate might surely want to find out more about their doings and forget yours. Eh?'

Gabriel tipped his head back and smiled. Daniel looked from one to the other, unable to believe what he heard, so strong was his horror at this plan. So strong his rage. Despite Father's temper, Daniel had always thought of him as honourable, in his way. But this. This was—

'Despicable,' he said, before realising he had spoken aloud. All three heads turned sharply to him. The scrape of the broom silenced.

'What?' Father asked. The quietness of his voice spoke of more anger than his previous shouting.

Daniel opened his mouth to apologise. And then thought again of the crowds and their flames marching to Sarah's house.

'Despicable,' he said, clearer now. 'To cover your own sins by blaming another? To shield yourself by offering up those without protection? And to scheme to do it?'

'They has protection, and it's of their own witchly making,' Gabriel said.

Daniel watched the pallor spread over Father's face, saw the set of his jaw and willed himself to stop. 'You should look to better yourself, not turn blame to another.'

It was accidental, surely, that he met Father's eyes as these last left his lips. Father's mouth gaped, his fists curled and, Daniel was sure, tears gathered as he blinked. Behind him, Bett stared, making no pretence at work now.

Before anyone could stop him, he barged past Father and out into the daylight, aware that punishment would await his return. For now, he simply needed to be away.

He made for the river, running fast. The stone still hung in the tree.

He waited anyway. She did not come.

When at last he returned, the fist caught his chin as he stepped in, spinning him so that the edge of the door cracked his cheek. Even as he sank to the ground, dizzy and sick, Daniel cursed himself. He should have been expecting this. His mind had been lost in Sarah and he had forgotten the argument waiting for him at home.

Father's breath was sour with alcohol. 'Thought you'd got away with it, did you?'

Daniel pressed his head to the cool wall, eyes squeezed shut until the room settled. Responses flashed through his mind. Sorry was the correct one.

'With what?' he asked, wiping away the blood bubbling at the corner of his mouth and drawing himself upright.

'Showing me up in front of Gabriel and Bett, insulting me and walking off. Thought you were clever, did you? Thought you'd get away with it because they were there?'

As Father bunched a fist and leaned his weight back to throw, Daniel straightened up. Standing eye to eye now.

'Do not raise your hand to me,' he said, clear and steady, as surprised as Father was by the fury rising inside him.

The moment of shock and doubt this caused in Father was enough for Daniel to step forward and push the fist to his side. Daniel leaned in until he could see the yellowed film in Father's eyes. 'Ever,' he said.

When the door swung closed behind him, Father still stood, arms hanging limp, head bowed.

A Trail in the Night

I have come at last to the beck, unable to keep away, wondering whether I will find the hag stone hanging in the tree, promising myself I will leave again either way.

It is here, and I wonder how long ago Daniel left it, whether he will still seek me out after I ran from him. I hold it now, feel it grow warm in my hand as I look out over the water.

There are footsteps behind me, too fast and light to be Daniel's, and I spin around, ready to flee. The little figure runs towards me, giggling, hair flying.

'Annie, what are you doing?'

'I followed you.'

I glance around. No sign of Daniel. 'You can't be here, go home.'

Her mouth droops and she hangs her head. 'But I want to be with you.'

I sigh. He will probably not come anyway. 'We'll go together. But don't follow—'

'Oh,' Daniel says, appearing from the trees. 'You're both here.' There is a bruise on his face. I can't ask what happened in front of Annie. He carries the neckerchief again. Bold.

'I – she just …' I shrug. Curse Annie and her sneaking.

'No matter,' he says.

'Can we find a moon fish?' Annie asks.

I pass Daniel the stone. 'No,' I say.

'A whispering shell? Please?' Knowing I am a lost cause she runs up to Daniel, tugging on his clothes and badgering about the shell. I've only ever seen her like this with John.

'She seems to think you're her brother,' I say, before I realise what meaning he might take from it. His smile caves in and he shoots me a look I cannot fathom, then turns to Annie.

'Do you know, I've made a mistake?' he says, glancing along the riverbank while she bunches his tunic in her fists and swings around. A mistake in coming, then. My stomach sickens. I'm about to yank Annie from him and take her home when he says, 'We won't find a whispering shell here, we need to go to the sea for that.'

I still myself. Annie stops swinging, keeping hold of him, biting her lip and frowning. 'I don't like the sea.'

'Then I will fetch one and bring it to you another day.'

I watch as he ruffles her hair and she stares up as though he is an angel.

'I like the woods,' she says. 'Because I was growed there.'

He glances at me. 'Grown?'

The story of how Annie came about is as much a part of the cloth that our family is stitched from as the story of how our father was taken. It has spilled from each of our mouths a hundred times and yet, as I look at the question in Daniel's eyes, I cannot speak it.

Annie has no such hesitation. She repeats the story as she's heard it, from memory and a little too fast. 'Mammy was walking in the woods one night collecting sticks for the fire and she heard a sound like a bird singing but she knew it couldn't be that because it was night so she went to the sound and she wasn't scared because it was the sweetest sound she'd ever heared and then she saw a babby and it was me. And I was lying all on the ground with the ferns under me like a mat and moss covering me like a soft green blanket and the roots of the biggest ash around me like the arms of a mammy.'

The telling of Annie's story here, away from the cocoon of our house, our family who accept it, awakens something in me. A memory, pushing at the wall of my thoughts. I look to see how Daniel is responding, but he crouches in front of Annie, face turned to hers, all solemn attention.

We have reached her favourite part and she tells it exactly as I know she will, as I've seen her do many times. She claps her hands over her mouth and laughter shoots through her fingers. 'And I was completely bare, with not even a tiniest single piece of cloth on me.'

Daniel responds as he knows he's expected to, with a grin and a widening of the eyes at this naughtiest part of her tale.

'So Mammy asked the ash if she could have me and the roots that holded me slithered right away so she knew she was allowed to and when she picked me up there was earth all in my mouth and ears from where I'd growed up from the ground like a tree does.'

The story is done. Annie beams and throws her hands down as though she has crafted and bestowed a great gift.

'What a special beginning you had,' Daniel says, his voice soft.

Annie's expression is glum. 'I know but it would've been better if I'd been growed a boy.'

I'm fighting thoughts I do not want, memories better forgotten, and I cannot respond. Daniel laughs. 'I think you were grown perfect just as you are.'

'That's what Sarah says.'

'Annie, we've to go,' I say.

Daniel stands up, looks at me quickly. There is a darkness coming over me, creeping from the very edges of my vision and laying its great, cold weight upon me. I wonder if this is how Father felt when he drowned.

'Here,' he says, holding out the neckerchief. 'You fold it like this, see?' He shows me and places it over my shoulders, pulling it tight at the front. I am aware, just, of the warmth of it against me, but too weighed by other thoughts to protest.

'But I want to stay here,' Annie says.

The memories grow stronger and I do not want to think about what they mean. Footprint of blood. Cries like a trail in the night. I wish Annie had not told the story. 'We've to go,' I say again.

Annie scowls. 'I don't want to. And you sound funny.'

In my head I hear Mam, the words she spoke that night as clear as if she stands here now, her voice sharp as the edge of John's knife.

Daniel watches me. I want to smile, but I cannot. He takes a step back. Holds himself with a deliberate steadiness that masks fear. He's waiting to see which I am, the lass who gathered wood and ate with him, or the witch with the power to curse. At this moment, I do not know.

'It's time for me to go too,' he says. Annie slumps at the shoulders and turns her big brown eyes to him. 'But next time I'll bring you a shell. Go with Sarah now.'

She trudges to me and I take her hand, pull her away. 'And tell no one of this,' I hiss. 'You should not have come. Bad girl.'

I barely hear her wails and sobs at my angry words. All I hear is Mam, those years ago. Get back to sleep, she said.

But I didn't.

Misery

Daniel had to wait until his free hours on Sunday to act on the decision he had made. He walked quickly, driven by a welcome feeling of strength. There was a storm inside him, Sarah's storm, that had come crashing through her eyes and somehow into him, changing his very make-up. Showing him that the course of events could be turned as he chose, if only he had courage enough.

He marched down the lane and across to where the blacksmith's lay, between the green and the shore. His fist on the door was firm. Molly's mother opened it, a woman with the same soft curls, now grey, escaping her coif and framing a plump, pink face. Her focus only faltered slightly on his grazed face.

'Master Taylor. How lovely to see you, come in,' she said, standing aside. This respect she showed was for his position, but not him, he knew.

Daniel forced a lightness into his voice. 'I won't, thank you, Mrs Matthews. If I could speak with Molly?'

She was already at the door, elbowing her mother out of the way. 'Daniel, I wondered when you'd call on me,' she said, giggling. She stepped out, forcing Mrs Matthews back as she shut the door on her. 'Goodbye, Mother.'

Her expression was alight with expectation and it took all Daniel's determination to hold on to the barrier of strength that allowed him to hurt her so.

'What happened to your face?' she asked.

'My father hit me.'

She blinked twice. 'Where are we going?'

He had not thought this far. His usual choice would be the river, but he could not take Molly to the place he shared with Sarah. That was part of a different life.

'The green?'

She fell into step beside him. 'My father was pleased, although of course he doesn't think that I should be the one to do the courting, he says it's not fitting. But it is the tradition, isn't it? I can't help being chosen as May Queen, can I?'

Molly stopped and looked up at him, but Daniel barely glanced at her and kept walking, nodding a greeting to the parson as he passed. She ran a few steps to catch up, linking her arm through Daniel's.

'Hello, parson,' she said. He lifted his hat and walked on.

'Of course,' Molly said, 'no wonder the magistrate chose me, he obviously has a liking for a pretty girl. Lucky I was not alone, else it would be me taken into the woods.' She shuddered, though her face was lit up. 'At least Magistrate Wright shall not allow such things.'

Again she stopped, twisting an escaped curl of hair around her finger. They had reached the green and Daniel led the way to the far edge opposite the well, sitting on the grass. He felt the curious glances of a group of women fetching water. A glimpse of the life with Molly that he was about to walk away from; though she had little in the way of dowry, he would have been the envy of every young man in the village. Molly would have been his bridge to acceptance. She pulled her petticoat up and sat beside him.

'Once everyone knows we're courting, I shall never need to worry about old goats like Magistrate Thompson.'

She reached out and placed her hand under his, arm stretched awkwardly across them both, and glanced across the green to where a group of her friends stood.

'Hello,' Molly called. The girls, who were already watching, waved and giggled.

All this Daniel saw but did not allow himself to take in. He must do this without knowing the consequences. Now.

'Molly.'

'Yes, dearest,' she said, blushing.

'I don't wish to cause you pain.'

A shadow passed over her face, but her smile stayed firm. 'Then don't.'

'This cannot be.'

'It can be. It is.'

Clouds gathered and rolled across the sky. 'There are plenty others for you to choose.'

She squeezed his hand. 'But I chose you.'

'But I do not – choose you.'

'Then why did you agree?' she asked, snatching her hand from his.

'I didn't, Molly, I tried to say but you just—'

'But why not? What's wrong with me?' Her voice was small and high, like a child's, tears falling from her pretty eyes, and his strength began to fail.

'Nothing, you're very sweet. It's just …'

There was a reason but he could not give it. Though even in his misery at inflicting misery, he pictured a new and different life for himself.

'Is this why you brought me here for all to see, to parade me?' Molly asked. 'So that my humiliation would be witnessed?'

'No, of course not.' Daniel looked over at the group of girls at the edge of the green huddled together, whispering. 'I'm sorry, I didn't think about it.'

Molly's tears fell more quickly than she could wipe them, but when she turned to him there was a hardness in her eyes that stopped his breath for a moment. 'I had thought better of you than this. Why did you not have the courage to tell me before, when we were alone? Before I spoke of it to anyone?'

Daniel shook his head. 'I'm sorry. Courage is a property I lack.'

'There we agree. I could have my father beat you to mush, you know.'

He watched a ladybird crawl over the bright petals of a buttercup, envied it the simplicity of its life. 'Then he can join forces with my own.'

Molly wiped her face one last time, shook out her shoulders. 'Take my arm and walk me home. Keeping away from them.' She nodded towards her friends. 'And I shall tell everyone that I changed my mind after all, and no one will ever think otherwise.'

'All right.'

'You know, there are plenty waiting to court me, and though none may inherit a farm, all will be more a man than you.'

Daniel took a breath, blocked the sharpness of her words, which he knew came from her pain. And were nothing he had not heard before.

As he walked with her soft arm through his, the smell of hot iron rising from her, it occurred to him that courting Molly would have been easy. He would call at her house, bring flowers tied with ribbon and take her to the fallow meadow. Being with Sarah was like winning the trust of a wild animal. She might turn on him at any moment.

In the doorway Molly unhooked her arm from his. 'You'll regret this.'

'I always regret causing hurt.'

'That isn't what I meant.'

She was gone, and so was any strength he'd mustered. Daniel walked, blindly, and found himself at the river.

So this was how it felt to say no to another person. What new man was he becoming? He had faced down his father. He had turned down Molly. All because a girl with wild hair and eyes like the sea had seen strength in him, made him believe in it too.

Even this unfamiliar, braver self had felt a spark of fear when she spoke of that Devil-incarnated-into-flesh brother of hers last time he saw her alone, when her mood clouded before she left. She was unknowable, a constant shifting of sweetness and shadow. Yet he was drawn to her.

They were a family unlike any other. Stories were told of the brother's demon powers, of him running wild in different forms and spreading curses wherever he trod. The sister, sprung magically from the ground, and he could believe that such a sprite as she would begin in that way. A benign magic, though, if magic it was, and not just a pretty tale told to comfort a lostling.

And Sarah herself. There was a promise of unknowable power about her. He knew he should keep away.

He hung the stone in the tree, and left.

A Serpent, Black and Glistening

I know from the scent of henbane rolling down the path that Seth is in the house.

'Wait here,' I say to Annie. 'I'll bring some food for you to take to the woods.'

She crosses her arms over her chest. 'I know Seth's in there. I want him to swing me.'

'Later.' I will not have her breathing in the vapours he needs to sweeten his mood when melancholy comes upon him, that if I am near I feel lingering in my throat, worming into my being and coiling a trail of madness into me. Leaving her on the path, I walk into the smoky house.

Mam sits with Seth on the floor, pressed in between the table legs and the wall, the pan of hot embers and leaves between them. His bare head is bent over it and I hear his deep, slow breathing as he takes in his comfort. Mam talks in a soft voice, soothing and praising as she would a child. I will believe all is as it appears, the stories she has told us are truth and the memories I ignore are figments from my fickle mind.

On the table lie Seth's offerings: a bowl of dried field beans and crammings. The blackened lumps scraped from the bottom of the bread oven are not the tastiest of the gifts he brings but Annie will chew on them happily enough. Would I could cover them in the butter Daniel gave me. I add the field beans to the bowl of pottage that steams in the hot ashes, so far containing only water and cabbage, and take the crammings. I pause in the doorway to look back at Mam.

'Isn't henbane for pain?' I ask, though I've seen Seth breathe it in like this many times and never has he been complaining of toothache or pangs of the joints.

The glance Mam gives me over the top of his head is a warning. 'This is pain, just of the being not the body.'

I want to argue with her. Should Seth speak of what she does there's no knowing what will become of us now the new magistrate is here He will act on the smallest evidence of witchcraft, if the stories are true.

Seth has had his fill, groaning out a long loud breath and lying back on the floor, eyes closed, arms spread wide. His sigh is one of contentment and I see his recovery quickens. He is over the worst of the sorrow. She takes the pan, dipping her own head into the fumes and breathing its treacherous scent. I leave, pulling the door closed behind me, for the effect of the vapours unnerves me and I try to keep from taking them in.

The smoke works on me already, I feel it painting the sky a heavier shade, churning the squeals of laughter I hear coming from Annie into an echoing hunting cry. She is riding on John's shoulders as he gallops to and fro across the grass. When he sees me he slides Annie to the ground, and she runs to take the crammings I hold out. I swear a serpent, black and glistening, curls itself inside John's mouth as he smiles. The smoke does its work on me.

'Aren't you just the one I'm looking for?' he says, and there is a hardness to his eyes that is a warning. He's endured some disappointment, then, some cruelty, and now turns it my way. The serpent lies in place of his tongue so I know the words that spill from there will be drops of poison I should not take in. I watch Annie dart towards the trees and wish I could follow, but I am rooted where I stand.

'You'll be wanting to know the tattle I overheard down the village today, though I've a mind not to tell you.'

'Overheard while you were crouched behind a hedge watching the lasses walk by?'

He is not to be diverted, but waits, and the serpent is a shadow behind his teeth. It mesmerises me so, I barely notice Seth stumble past us, struggling to replace his hat.

'There's all prattling of your farmer lad today.'

Mention of Daniel tears my gaze from the serpent to John's eyes, and I see from the triumph there that I've betrayed myself. He rocks back on his heels, hands behind back, chin lifted as he spins out my torment.

'What of him?' I ask, unable to bear the power of John's silence any longer. 'And how do you …?'

'Annie has spake all of moon fish and whispering shells. And you and the farmer's lad.' He waits, and every passing moment of silence torments me. 'He's only courting that pretty little blacksmith's daughter.'

These are not words, but drops of venom that fall from his invaded lips, seeping into my skin until I see nothing but Daniel and the blacksmith lass, hands entwined, heads together, lips touching, and I reach out for a wall that is not there to steady myself. How can this be true, when just the other day he left the hag stone so we might meet, and he listened with such care to Annie?

John smirks. 'Aye, thought you might care to know that,' he says. 'Only one thing he could want from the likes of you. Didn't think there was more to it, did you?'

The smoke has dazed me so, I feel no anger at myself for the tears his words bring. I look into John's face. The serpent is gone, his eyes clear and confused; regretful.

'Well,' he says. ''Tis perhaps not … I didn't mean to …' His voice breaks off and he watches me as his cheeks redden, bites on a nail, then dips his head and hurries into the house.

I am cold now from knowing and losing the comfort of Daniel's closeness. The loss weighs upon me. This is why I should not have let my life entwine with his, for that is all gone, as I should have known it would be.

I've no claim on him, have always known this. Wiping away the tears I've no right to shed, I follow John into the house, because though he's enjoyed giving me this pain and though Mam will not countenance it, I need my family now. They're all I have. I am the cunning woman's daughter, born to a fate of isolation and dark power. The kindness of a farmer's lad, and all else I might have hoped he offered, is not for me, nor ever was.

It is time to embrace my calling now, with all my being, and leave him and his kind to their lives of comfort and courting that I shall never know. There is a stirring within me, a clarity, that allows me to hear the bidding of my master as never before, and this time I do not turn away from it. For what other life is there for me?

Mam has doused the pan and smoke hangs like an apparition in the corners of the roof. I taste it still. Her eyes are black and bright, her movements heavy and fluid as they always are when she has breathed in its vapour.

She smiles at John, a serene beatific beam that sweetens and softens her. 'Oh, son. You've done well.' Her words are slow and thick. She cups his face. 'These are what I need. His punishment shall be all he deserves.' Between finger and thumb she picks something from the hand John holds out to her.

'What's that?' I ask.

'Hair,' John says.

'Whose hair?' I know, but will not accept the knowledge until I hear it from them.

'That netter's,' John says, lifting his chin. He's expecting me to argue.

Mam carefully carries the strands over to the figure that lies on the floor by the fire. She spits on the clay to soften it, kneading with her thumb, pulling a piece from the top. Looks to the floor at her side and whispers, 'We shall set you to work, shall we not?'

'Easy to sneak in and pick a few strands from their bed,' John says.

Mam hunches over the figure, muttering as she places the hair on the softened clay and moulds the spare lump back on to secure it. The result is a grotesque parody of a person, and not the first I've seen in her hands.

Yesterday I would have shaken her for this, berated her for putting John in danger, for drawing the attention of the village when they were hunting us down only nights ago. Today, I am aligned with her, and all that means. What use is there in appeasing the villagers? They will burn us anyway. I am in no mood to acquiesce.

I will embrace what I am, accept the power that lies at the heart of this family. Somehow, I shall keep Annie separate, and safe. Keep her free from the mark, from the magistrate. The rope. But I will stand with Mam, true to myself, and burn if I must. I take her hand.

'I want to try the potion.'

We stand on the hilltop, sky churning, rain droplets lacing the air, and I can taste salt on the breeze. Mam holds the bowl in both hands. The paste inside is thick and murky with a sour scent. I peer at it, heart kicking.

'You don't have to,' Mam says.

'I'm ready.'

'It's not easy. You'll be changed.' She shakes her head. ''Tis all I have to offer.'

'What do I do?'

'Dip in and spread it on your skin.'

I reach my hand over the bowl, wavering above it.

Mam touches my fingers. 'Thinly,' she says.

I scoop a handful. Cold and miry. Last chance to walk away, to fight my fate. 'Mammy?'

'Aye?'

'Stay with me?'

She kisses my cheek, mouth soft where teeth once were. I wipe the paste on my arm.

My heart is untamed, without pace, without rhythm. Breath remains my own. In. Out. Slow. Slow. I feel the air flow into me, through me, to the very tips of hair and skin and nail. Unfurling. It reaches the edges of my body and lifts me. I am light, without weight, without darkness.

The sky trickles then pours between my fingers. My hands rise of their own accord, lifting. I look up and find raindrops as big as my fist. They glide down, falling like snow, soft and slow. I catch one and it rests in my palm for a moment, smooth and cool and glossy, then bursts and splinters into droplets that sparkle. Laughter streams from me.

I turn to show Mam. She is close, I see but cannot reach her. See her speak but cannot hear the words. The space between us is small and I stretch out to her, watch my fingers touch her face but I cannot feel her. She is not really here. Nothing I see is really here.

The ground beneath my feet laps and swells, rolls and spins, gradually at first then faster and faster until the grass and sky and trees turn too quickly for me to see and finally the earth throws me off, into the sky, soaring through the air. Pitching clouds toss me between them, fat round raindrops balance and shatter on my outstretched arms.

Beyond, past the cloud and rain and sun, with my hair streaming behind and the air blasting through me, I reach night. The sound of my own breath, the beat of my eyelashes, boom and crash of my heart. Outside myself, nothing.

Then, stars. Bright, sharp specks that flare and soar through my fingers, hard and barbed, burning like an ember fallen from the grate. I open my mouth to cry out and all the searing stars are sucked into me, leaving me alight, and around me is only blackness.

In the dark I see him. At last. My new master. His eyes flaming, his mouth a depth of emptiness that I could fall into and fall forever. The fire inside me blazes and pierces. I do not want this. Do not want him. I want light and space and freedom. He opens his mouth and breathes out a hurricane of fire and smoke and soot and I am calling, screaming, begging to be delivered but I am covered with his black breath, mouth and eyes filled until I see nothing, hear nothing, not even the pull of my breathing or beat of my heart.

Splinter

Day after day Daniel went to the river, rising before dawn or sneaking from the house at night, when they all thought he slept. Still the stone hung where he had left it.

He could not think why she stayed away. He had insulted her perhaps, unwitting in his clumsiness, as before. Or she had simply changed her mind. Their time together did not mean to her what it did to him.

His appetite left him and he could not sleep. The small pleasures that had once sustained him – the baby sparrows leaping from their nests, the playful gambolling of lambs – could not touch him.

He helped Father spread manure and raked behind him as he led the oxen and plough, attached Bonny to the harrow and walked her up and down the field, May heat seeping through his tunic. The greening of the land and call of the song thrushes usually soothed his spirit at this time of year. Yet a fever lay upon him now, an unfamiliar restlessness to have his tasks done and be at the river. Every day he believed she would come. Every night she did not.

Daniel sat now with Father and Gabriel eating bread and collops under the shade of the largest oak and drinking ale. He listening to the stories Gabriel told of the village, and how all were unsettled. How all looked about with suspicion, for every man had a friend or neighbour that could tell a tale about him to interest the new magistrate.

'It's law books he recites before bed, not prayers, so they say,' Gabriel said. 'Carries that book of the King's with him like it's a Bible. There'll be floggings on the green and worse now.'

'There must be – there are those that live right and have nothing to fear, surely?' Daniel asked.

Gabriel shrugged. Flicked away a spider that crawled over his leg.

'At least you've kept your temper in check, lad, and free from trouble,' Father said.

'Aye.' Gabriel swallowed the last mouthful. 'I'm not afraid of this Wright anyhow, no matter what's the stories told about him. Should trouble come my way, I have one ready to take the blame, like you said. Eh?'

He spoke to Father but looked at Daniel. The words stuck in Daniel's throat and he choked on his food. Gabriel smirked.

Father glanced from Gabriel to Daniel and back again. 'Enough, Gabriel. Had you been brothers you couldn't have fought more. That is the last time you stir up trouble, lad,' he said, his voice low but filled with threat. 'Not one more. Or you shall be out and be damned with your sad tales of your sorry mam that needs you.'

Gabriel stood, a full head taller than Daniel and half as wide again. 'Had we been brothers all this would come to me, and far a worthier heir to it I'd have made,' he said.

Kicking his half-finished crust under the tree, Gabriel walked towards the yard. Daniel followed. But he carried Gabriel's words like a splinter under a fingernail.

No longer would he be accepting. He would not take another blow from Father, nor the constant ridicule from Gabriel. Need not live in fear of the whispers and sniggers of those in the village. Only now was he learning that his life was not set, but that it could be forged according to his own will.

He would wait a little longer for Sarah, still hopeful she would come. But if she did not appear soon, he would seek her out.

Whatever I Have Become

The body I find myself in shivers. Someone has rubbed sand into my eyes, forced it down my throat. Pain binds my head.

Cool touch on my forehead. I reach for the hand that rests there.

'All right, lass. Don't fret. You'll soon be fixed.'

It takes a will I don't know I possess to scrape my eyes open. Nothing but shadow and shape.

'Am I dying?'

'No. You are reborn.'

Makes no sense. I cannot question. Everything in me is used up keeping still. Movement causes a stream of pain, a surge of sickness. I let the darkness swallow me.

Hot fingers taffle in my hair, soft mouth at my ear. Whisper, wet and warm. 'Please get better.'

I shift, try to open my eyes. Cannot.

Sticky hand pushes hair from my head, pats my cheek.

'Wake up. I bringed something.'

I try to lift my hand and touch her. Nothing.

'Elderflower brew. I maked it myself. Open your mouth.'

The spoon rough against my lips, sweet liquid seeps in, gritty with dust and pap. Trickles down my face and pools in my neck. The hand pats my head.

'Good lass,' she says.

I am flung from sleep with my heart beating, quicker and quicker. Shaking. Skin soaked, mouth dry. I find myself on my feet, staggering as the room rolls.

Mam steps forward, catches me as I fall. 'Stop, lass, lie down.'

I fight her off, struggling, but her grip tightens. My palm lands on her cheek with a crack. She cries out and I pitch forward, free. Gulping for air, knocking into the table and tripping over John's mat, until I fall out of the door. Sea breeze lifts the hair from the back of my damp neck. Grass rough against my bare knees, threaded between fingers, soil under nails.

John walks past, carrying a bundle of wood under his arm, chewing a hunk of bread too soft to be meant for him.

'Better, then,' he says, waiting a little awkwardly. 'That's – I'm glad of it.'

'Me too.'

He offers me the last of the bread on his way in. I push it away. Mam comes and kneels in front of me, shooing Dew-Springer away and cupping my face with her coarse hand. Red finger marks on her cheek, and I remember the smack of my palm against her.

'Oh, Mammy.' I cover my mouth. 'I hit you.' Throat full with tears. 'I hurt you.'

She shakes her head, lifts me to my feet.

I hold on to her for a moment. 'I'm sorry.'

'It's all right, lass. You didn't mean it. Come in.'

Mam helps me to the table, sits me down, fills a cup with water and passes it to me. 'It'll not be long before Seth comes with buttermilk, I'll warrant,' she says. 'That'll build your strength.'

My stomach turns at the thought. But the water I drink in gulps, without pause.

She's wrong. I meant to hit her. Would that I hadn't. I was not myself. Not my old self. I was whatever I have become now. The darkness I opened up to when I used the potion streaming out of me and hurting her. I wish I'd not let my anger drive me to let it in.

The door bursts open and Annie lands in my lap. Smell of fresh air and mud. The colour in her cheek and light in her eyes make me realise how far from well I feel. I press my face into the soft flesh of her neck. She holds both her hands out of sight.

'You're up, you're better, aren't you?' She watches my face, little crease developing above her eyebrow. 'I can see you're better,' she says, uncertain.

I sit as straight as I can. 'All better. Must have been your medicine. Thank you.'

'You making tonics too now, little squirrel?' John says. 'All taking up the family trade.' His voice strains for a false lightness.

I try to stand. 'We need to search.'

'Mam did it,' Annie says. 'And John maked the circle and helped me ring the bell.'

I glance at John. He shrugs and looks away. 'Takes no time. Stops her bawking.'

'I've bringed you some things, sken,' Annie says. She holds out her hands, one clutching a muddy, discoloured metal object, the other a bunch of dandelions, brash and bright, bitter scent as she thrusts them into my face.

'It's a good piece,' she says, brushing mud-clags from metal. Her fingernails are embedded with soil. 'What is it?'

John takes it from her, feeling the weight in his hand. Turns to Mam.

'Candlestick,' she says.

John studies it, running his finger around the bowl at the bottom. Annie beams at him. 'Proper treasure, squirrel,' he says. 'Not even broke.'

He hands it back to her and she hugs it to herself, rocking it like a babby. I wonder, now, of those that owned it. An object too grand for us. Candles are a luxury I can barely remember and one Annie has never known. She will not understand what she has found. But once, this lit the evenings for someone, spilling light on to their table, guiding them to bed. A life of comfort, torn through by suffering.

I shiver. Turn to the dandelions.

'So pretty,' I say. They're flowers that lack all delicacy, though they do bring a welcome splash of colour to the house. And I will treasure any gift from Annie. 'Thank you.'

She slips from my knee and reaches for a cup to place them in. As she scoops water into it Mam snatches them from her.

'Give them back,' Annie says.

Mam turns them in her hand, tipping them upside down and splitting the stalks. 'These'll do,' she says. 'Good lass. Sap enough to add to a tincture. Cure a wart or two.' She glances to the doorway. 'Away, Dew-Springer, find one in need.'

I stifle a smile at the look of outrage on Annie's face.

She crosses her arms over her chest, glowering at Mam. 'They are not for warts. They're to be pretty. For Sarah.'

'Nonsense, child. We've no time for pretty in this house. Everything that comes through that door must have a use. The food I can buy with a coin earned curing warts will do Sarah more good than looking at these bedraggled things.'

Annie tips forward on her toes, fists clutched at her side, baring her clenched teeth and growling. Her mood sours further as Mam, John and I laugh.

'Careful, Mam, she's in the mulligrubs now,' John says.

'All right.' Mam strokes Annie's hair and passes her a single flower. 'Keep one for your sister.'

She takes it, dejected slump to her shoulders as she holds it out to me. I pull her in for a hug.

'It's lovely,' I say. 'You're lovely. Thank you.'

She sighs and scratches at the back of her hair with both hands. 'I think I've got them spiders in my head again.'

I lean back just a little.

Each day I can stand a while longer, walk a few steps further, eat a little more. This day, though, I am rooted to the mat, unable to move.

The blackness takes shape. Shadow at the edge of my eye. Swelling, shifting. An image I almost recognise that transforms again into a blur. I turn my head, trying to catch it. Nothing.

Mam senses it too. She does not ask, but I feel her eyes on me, waiting for my ability to reveal itself, for my familiar to take shape. I watch specks glide and spiral in the dribble of light falling through the roof, turn away from the shade I carry. I am feared of what I have let myself become.

Annie pulls my arm. 'Don't sit in the dark. Come to the woods with me.'

'I am the dark.'

John laughs, somewhere unseen. 'You're better looked at in the dark, at least.'

Mam frowns. 'Annie's right, that's enough. You're well now and there's work to be done.'

The shape in my eye bristles. If I stare ahead, pretend I'm not looking, it becomes clearer.

'Sarah.' She stands in front of me, hands on hips, bent so that her face is level with mine. 'Work. We need food.'

I look ahead at the golden flecks falling between us, her face a blur behind them. Annie shakes my shoulders. There are patches of light in the shadow – not a welcoming light, a flare, a blaze. Eyes.

Mam snaps her fingers.

There is more. The shadow is heavy and deep now. Searing eyes. Spines. And—

'What is it?' Mam asks. 'What can you see?'

Breath blocks my throat, the word grates out of me. 'Teeth.'

'Where?' Annie says. 'Whose teeth?'

Mam crouches in front of me, squeezed between the wall and my mat, hand on my knee. 'Don't be feared. It's your familiar.'

I've stared so long that water fills my eyes and slips down my face, I see nothing but colours before me and still the blackness at the edge, twisting, clearer with every second. It is forming, growing, spreading, and I cannot hold it back. The teeth stretch open and I smell the sour, ashy breath, feel the sting of those eyes. And hear it. The sound, deep and low, shaking me from inside.

'It is here.'

'Set it free,' Mam says.

But I cannot. Not yet. Dew-Springer is gentle, harmless. At least to us. I have conjured some foul and fearsome creature. What if it invades my whole being and warps the very nature of me? 'Can you hear it?' I ask, my voice thin as a trickle of rain.

The sound grows, I can feel it in me, hear it around me.

'Can you hear the snarling?' I ask.

I hear Mam's voice, as though over a distance. ''Tis for you alone.'

The sunbeam spiral is a haze, hidden by the tears pouring from my smarting eyes. Feared to blink, to lose this light. Breath fast and shallow, gone before I can catch it. I bunch the blanket in my fingers, grip so I will not be spun away.

I can hold out no longer. Blink.

In the moment of blackness its face is clear in front of me, great slavering dog, teeth bared, eyes scorched. Smell of burning. And the sound. Around me, inside me, shaking my bones.

Opening my eyes, I see Mam. See all that she has ever been, clear as never before, knowing my memories are truth. I beckon, and she leans in.

'I know you,' I whisper.

She laughs. 'Of course. I'm your—'

'I know what you did,' I say. 'I know where you laid them. Every one.'

The crack of her palm across my face is a blast of pain so sharp that my vision fills with lights. But I do not flinch. The dog is with me now, and its strength shall also be my own.

Unfurled

Daniel paused for a moment, catching breath, gathering courage. All around, the shadowy silhouettes of decaying shacks stood still and silent, where once there had been movement and voices. Plants sprouted through chasms like worms through eye sockets. Who knew what untethered spirits lurked here? He fought the feeling that he was not welcome. This place was not for the living. He glanced at the star-strewn sky and pressed the stone she had given him into his palm.

There were no stray strands of light falling through the gaps in the wall and roof of the Haworth shack and it occurred to him that they might be sleeping. At home the candles would be lit, Father would be sitting at the table drinking ale, thinking Daniel asleep in his bed.

Sarah had not owned a neckerchief. They would not have candles.

He almost lost his nerve, tapped lightly on the door anyway.

No answer at first, and he imagined leaving and heading to the warmth of the farm kitchen. But if he turned back now, he knew he would never come back. He must not be deterred. He beat on the door again with such force that when it swung open he almost fell into the house and the unwelcoming arms of Sarah's brother.

Daniel steadied himself, a thrill of fear coursing through him at coming face to face with the boy's black smile. An expression that was intimidating rather than friendly. The lad stepped away, looking Daniel up and down and picking his teeth with the knife he had used to slit the lamb's throat. Daniel felt himself thrown back for a moment to the fearful, paralysed state of that day. Fought it, and won.

'What do you want?' the boy asked.

'Sarah,' Daniel said. Pleased that he spoke with his new voice, the sure one, he cleared his throat and clarified. 'That is, I would like to see her.'

The brother attempted to fill the space with his spindly form, legs apart, arm stretched to doorframe. 'Surprised to hear that. What dust want with her?'

Daniel remained steadfast. 'I want to speak with her.'

The boy looked over his shoulder into the house, then stepped aside leaving just enough room for Daniel to squeeze past him, unnaturally and unpleasantly close. He was aware of the brother's eyes on him, the scrape of blade against tooth.

A smoky, ash-scented gloom inside revealed only the shapes of objects; a fire, no more than a pit on the floor. A straw mattress, three stools and a wooden table, roughly hewn, filled the first room. Furniture that was smaller and far simpler than his own, but more than he had imagined they owned. He supposed now that they had moved into the house and taken all they found in it. Those it had once belonged to were long gone. The walls were stained with soot and through the gaps in the roof and door streamed the cold night air.

In the doorway to another room stood Sarah, a blanket pulled around her, huddled with Annie and their mother. There was a wariness about them. For the first time Daniel thought how his unexpected arrival might appear threatening, ashamed that he had not been aware before.

'I'm sorry,' he said, removing his cap and clutching it in front of him. 'That must have frightened you, me knocking on the door at this time of night, especially after ...' He glanced over his shoulder at the brother, leaning against the wall and watching. Would he ever stop that infernal scraping? 'I'm sorry,' Daniel said again. No one responded.

Annie yawned and stuck her thumb in her mouth, the other hand fiddling with her tangled hair. She slumped against her mother, eyes still on Daniel. 'Did you bring my shell?' she asked.

He held out his hands in apology. 'I'll bring it next time.'

'That's what you said before,' she said, her voice thick with sleep.

'I know.'

'I knew your mam. She was a gentle soul,' the mother said, lifting Annie and carrying her into the shadow of the other room.

He looked at Sarah, waited. She pulled the blanket tight around herself. She looked weak. Was she ill? 'What do you want?'

'I—' There was too much in the way of audience here. 'Could we perhaps go for a walk?'

She gathered the blanket and stepped over to him, but the brother blocked their path.

'You'll not walk out with my sister after dark.'

'Don't be a fool, John,' Sarah said.

'But—' He glanced at Daniel, bent his head and lowered his voice. 'You're not well.'

'I'm better. Move.'

He did, and Daniel wondered which of them had the greater power. Outside the sky was clear and bright with moonlight. He replaced his cap and they walked towards the woods, Sarah silent at his side. She moved slowly, as if afraid to trip, her head bent towards the ground.

They walked only a little way in amongst the trees, stopping below the wide-spread branches of an ash. For the first time he saw the mark on her cheek.

'What happened to you?' he asked.

'Mam.'

Not the answer he had expected. Perhaps this hurt was what caused her silence. At least it had not come at the hand of someone from the village. He would take her pain a hundred times over to save her from it, felt his new fury rise against the one that struck her. Reaching out, he traced the edge of the mark gently with his thumb. She jerked her face away.

'Why have you come?' she asked.

'I left the stone. I waited for you.'

'Why?' The same hardness he had seen in Molly's eyes, though this time he did not know what he had done to deserve it.

'Because I wanted to see you. I thought you would – I thought that we were …'

She shook her head. 'I don't understand what you want from me.'

'I like you.'

She laughed, a sound strung through with bitterness. 'What can you possibly like? I've nothing, Daniel, I am nothing. You see how I live. You should not want to be with me and I cannot be with you. My life should not touch yours.'

'But it has.' The distance between them was greater than it had ever been, and he did not understand why.

'Just go back to the farm and to courting the blacksmith lass, and leave me to my own life.'

Her words like a sunbeam, throwing light on the shadows of confusion.

'What?' He laughed a little. Clearly Molly had been less than hasty to spread the news that there was no romance after all.

'No,' he said. 'That's not—' He stepped forward, serious now, took one of Sarah's hands, loosening the clutch of her fingers on the blanket so that he could ease his own in between them. She did not concede easily.

'Molly did come to my house, she chose me after being crowned May Queen but I – I said no.'

Sarah watched him with an expression that showed nothing of her feelings. His responding smile was too much, too happy he knew, but he could not contain it.

'And Sarah, I've never refused anyone anything they have asked of me in my life before, but this time I did. Because of you.'

He stepped closer to her, took both her hands in his, shook them to show the importance, the joy of what he was trying to tell her. Still her face betrayed nothing.

'And last time Father hit me, I don't even know how, I stood up and told him to stop and he did. And that's never happened before. All these years I've been afraid and now you're here and you showed me how to be strong and to be myself, but a me that I could never have been before, and that's what I want. This. That happens when we're together. And you don't – is this making any sense to you at all?'

He stopped, desperately searching her face for any indication that she understood.

'So, you're not courting the blacksmith lass?' she asked.

He laughed. 'No.'

Her expression did not change. He would need to work harder than this. 'I – how could I? There wouldn't be room.'

She frowned. 'Room? For what?'

'For anything but you.'

Her smile unfurled a little. 'All right.'

'Is that why you didn't come? Molly?'

'Aye. And because you and I, we're of different kinds. And – home.'

The anger rising in him again. 'Does she often hit you?'

'Never. This was the first time.'

'Why? Not because of this?' To be the direct cause of her suffering was more than he could bear.

'No. Because I'm starting to remember.'

He did not understand and did not feel he could ask. He had not earned knowledge of family secrets. Instead he tightened his hold on her hands. 'Don't let her do that again. Please.'

'Why not?' she asked, but this time with a slight smile. 'Because you care that I'm hurt?'

'Yes, I care that you're hurt, care that you're happy.' There was a tiny tremor that could not be hidden from her because they stood so close, hands still clasped together. 'I care for you.' Words he had said to no other, that his lips would barely form. That rang more true than any other he had spoken. 'And can I ask? Do you care for me?'

He felt the shudder in her breath, saw the darkening of her eyes. Feared for a moment that he had startled her so she would flee. Stepping away, he let his arms fall from her waist. He had been mistaken after all.

She reached out and clasped his doublet, pulling him in until his lips almost brushed hers. Silence then, just her intake of breath, the warmth of her hand on his arm, the blue of her eyes. Too close to see.

Picked Out in Starlight

As the sun rises I run, stumbling over the uneven ground, tripping over roots. My legs are weak still from the potion and shake beneath me, but I force myself to move quickly. The joy I carry will fill our whole house, chasing away our daily struggles, our fears of the new magistrate. I feel only a whisper of the dog I conjured, for now at least. There's no shadow in me today where it may hide, for I think only of Daniel and what he spoke.

'We will make our own life,' he said. 'No fists thrown.'

He pulled me to him, wrapped me in his arms, spinning a tale, a beautiful scene picked out in starlight and with as much substance, but I liked to look upon it. I did not let myself think of the battle there would be with my family, the disgust from his. Or worse, the sense I have of the ever-present master I've just pledged myself to, watching and waiting to put me to his bidding. The many warnings Mam's given of what happens to those who resist him, of what becomes of those we love. How he commanded the sea to swallow my father.

Just for that moment, I let myself believe in his stories.

'And you'll be a farmer,' I said.

'Yes, and you my wife and you shall milk the cows and bake the village bread in our oven.'

'And on May Day we'll dance together. And eat flawn.'

He said nothing, but kissed the top of my head.

This is how we stayed, until the birds broke their slumber and the sky spilled with rosy sunlight.

I yank the door open, feel rather than see my way to Annie's mat, shake the soft mound of bedding that hides my sister.

'Up,' I say. 'Up, get up, wake up.'

She wails in reply and burrows down like a mouse in hay. I laugh, kiss her cheek.

'Sleepy,' she says.

'Come on. We've to search.'

Grumbling, Annie stands, fists clenched at sides, teeth bared, trying to growl, but I laugh and then so does she.

'Stop that, little cub. You don't scare me.' I search, as always, peering into her ears, lifting her hair and examining the white gleam of skin below. She is unmarked. Of course. A light has entered our lives that changes everything. She will be there too, by the fireside Daniel and I will share.

I pull her warm, bony body to me, breathe in the woods from her hair, kiss her mud-crusted cheek.

'Why do you keep smiling like that?' she asks.

From First Light

The day had begun with Sarah in his arms and whispers of a life together. Daniel had worn a smile all day, unable to shake himself free of it as a heavy heat gathered under the grey sky and exhaustion dogged his steps, slowing him as he went about his tasks.

His fingers lost their grip on the plough, prompting curses and jeers from Gabriel. Daniel did not care. His feet slid from under him as he let out the horses and Bett was unimpressed with the grass stains left on his breeches.

'You know I hate the stench when I've to soak the linen,' she said.

'You're the heart of this family,' he said, taking her in his arms and prancing around the kitchen until she screeched and laughed. 'We're nothing without you, Betts.'

'Be off with you,' she said, freeing herself and adjusting her petticoats. 'Quick, before I remember those stains.' She shook her head. 'Too cheerful by far.'

'Nathaniel's a lucky man,' he called, dodging the cloth she whacked him with.

An unfamiliar, twitchy vitality coursed through him. He was dead tired and yet he could not have slept, thinking only of the night before. Every beautiful detail of the world was magnified: the sweetness of birdsong, the softness of the calf's eyes. Fresh leaves against weighty clouds in the sky. All was well, from first light to the evening meal.

At the dinner table Daniel gathered courage and announced to Father that he had refused Molly.

'Can't say I'm not pleased,' Father said. 'She's a pretty lass, no doubt, and you have your fun if you will, but a blacksmith's daughter? For courting?' He laughed. 'You, my only son, and her? They'd gain a whole farm, what would come to us? A new horseshoe each week? Eh?' He laughed harder, an unease spilling out, raising his eyebrows and pointing at Daniel. Pleased with this joke that Daniel did not share. 'A horseshoe, eh? For this whole farm?'

Father wiped his eyes, still chuckling. 'I'd have had to forbid it. You did right, son.'

Daniel placed his spoon on the table, the bowl of rich herring pottage untouched. A blacksmith's family would not do. What then his chance of presenting the ragged-haired daughter of a cunning woman? The daughter of a woman who had been present at his birth, his mother's death, and had been held responsible by Father all the intervening years?

Bees

Mam has sent us down to the harbour to knock on doors and sell our wares. A task I do not relish, but I was not inclined to argue, my mood still sweetened by Daniel's words.

'Get away,' the woman says, already closing her door on us. Behind her the house is small and dark, scented with fish and woodsmoke. 'I need no enchanted flowers from you.'

'Nay, it's – white heather,' I say. 'They carry their own luck.' Annie holds up the bunch of dried flowers.

'Place them on the step so they may look out over your husband while he's at sea,' I say. 'Or by the nets to bring a full catch.'

'We are protected in this house.' She points to a pattern scratched on to the wall, petal shapes in a circle. A witch mark. The first I've seen in many a year. My belly tightens. 'I need none of your spells. Your clan do nothing but harm, Gabriel has told all of what you laid upon him.'

It's all I can do to stop myself covering Annie's ears. There is a shifting in the corner of my eye. I blink it away. Now more than ever we must not be accused. She looks up at me, curious.

'It's just a lucky flower,' I say. 'We've put nowt—'

Briefly, the woman opens the door a little wider to thrust out her head. 'The new magistrate will protect we God-fearing folk and the likes of you shall be chased away. I know what you did to those poor Barton babbies, you slave of the Devil, and if you darken my step again, I shall tell Magistrate Wright every tale I've heard, you hear? Be gone.'

The door slams and Annie turns to me, frowning and still clutching the flowers. 'What does she mean? What harm have we did?'

I think of the raw patches on the farmhand's head, caused by my anger. The beating John gave Sam Finch and the clay poppet that Mam has made in his likeness. The curses she's laid on the catches, harvests and children of those that have crossed her. 'No harm,' I say.

Whatever befell the Barton children, it was not my doing, that at least I know. It was three years past and I had not begun to grow into my powers, much less tried spinning curses or uttering spells.

I close my eyes: a bitter winter, ground stinging-cold and hard beneath my feet. Annie little more than a babby, spindly and listless; I'd lain awake all night with a headache and belly-wart from my own hunger, listening to her keening. Dazed and queasy, I ventured outside, determined to beg an apple or parsnip left from autumn, that we might boil up and feed her.

The Bartons' place was the nearest, and all I had energy to reach. Standing wrapped in the blanket I'd taken from my mat, I begged the man for a coin, or if not then the smallest morsel of food for my babby sister, looking past him to a kitchen that held the warmth of the fire and the scent of dried fish. A girl not much younger than me sat at the table, bouncing a fat little babby Annie's age on her knee, rolls of flesh tucked under its chin.

He chased me from his land, waving a pitchfork above his head. I, but a lass of fourteen.

Anger rises in me now at the memory, a flicker that, should I let it, will pound through me like the sea itself, filling my thoughts with ember eyes. I breathe deep, hold fast to Annie, battle with this fury, for it has nowhere to fall.

The village lost many that winter, mostly the youngest and oldest. The Barton children among them. Annie spared, though no thanks to him. They left the village not long after.

Whatever befell them, it was not my doing.

I am no more guilty than the so-called God-fearing, according to the tales John brings of those lying with others' wives, beating their children and placing pebbles instead of coins in the collection plate. Yet they condemn us. If this is what it is to be church folk I would rather be cast out.

Growling, low and quiet, rolls through me. I could lay a curse on this woman and let her feel the cost of her cruelty, send a pestilence through her house, sink her husband to the bottom of the sea. Words sit on my tongue, never before known and perilous, tempting me. A show of my powers will turn her scorn to fear.

I teeter on the brink, caught between two lives. I can embrace he that chose me, use the gifts he gave and become, fully, my mother's daughter. I've used the potion. The power is mine. But the stories Daniel spun through the night shimmer in my mind, a life of light that leaves no place for such darkness. The sound of snarling mingles with the shifting of the sea and I am suspended in the moment before choosing which world to embrace.

With the taste of ash comes the scent of smoke and I remember a fire on the riverbank, sweet pie and the warmth of a neckerchief. I close my eyes. Step back. I don't know if I shall ever truly find a place in that world of light that others live in. But a piece of it has been offered to me, and I will take it.

'May I have one?' a soft voice asks from behind us. Turning, I see a girl, her eyes red-rimmed and her skin a sickly tone. I recognise her as one Mam trusts.

She crouches down, taking the flowers from Annie and burying her nose in them. 'Though I fear luck has already failed me,' she says, as she hands over her coin.

Annie tugs on my petticoat and I take her hand. We run from the village, happy with our success, though I cannot help but feel some disquiet. The girl Phyllis is kind and has bought our wares before. I fear something ails her.

I walk down the steep path to the shore, Annie running ahead, light and swift as a little grey cloud scudding across the sky. She has no fear. We don't often come to the sea, and when we do must find a place not favoured by others, stony and unwelcoming.

When I reach the water Annie is already returning, with her legs wet, feet speckled with sand and a heap of clams and seaweed gathered in the dripping petticoat she's clutched into a makeshift sack. She is nervous of water, especially the sea. We've seen it dip and raise itself into waves higher than houses, heard it roar like a maddened beast, seen it frozen into the sharpest teeth. Every few months it will rise and take its fill of village men. My father one of many. Even under its deceptively gentle surface today, I know there lies a great and fickle power.

Her fears have lessened, though, since Daniel took us to the beck and she is happy now to search the shore as I have shown her. Sometimes I feel she grows right before my eyes, becoming more herself with each passing day. She drops her offerings in a heap at my feet and flops down next to me. The food will be covered in sand now and need rinsing at the well as we return. On any other day I would grumble at her for this; today I barely notice.

She watches the gulls screeching and scrapping. 'I wish I was one of them,' she says. 'Then I could just dip my head in the water and find whatever food I want, and I could fly right high and see the whole of everything.'

'You don't want to be a bird, they don't have souls.' Though at least if they are born without one it's not there to be stolen, as mine was. 'You've done well, little cub. And you've been into the water too, brave lass.' I gather her into my arms, squeeze hard, laugh as her salt-stiffened hair taffles in my mouth.

She wriggles in my grasp. 'You're hurting, why are you squashing me?'

'Because you're such a good lass,' I say, releasing her but taking her face in my hands.

She leans back, frowning and eyeing me as though I've danced a jig on the table. 'Is this – are you my other sister?' she asks.

I laugh. 'What other sister?'

'That looks like Sarah but isn't.'

I ruffle her matted hair and resist the urge to hug her again. 'Of course not, nay, it's just me, as I always am.'

I pull her on to my knee, wrap my arms around her taking care not to hold too tightly, and we face the sharp sea breeze together. Her words, though spoken in childish innocence I am sure, have unsettled me. I feel light, empty. My head aches.

All familiar and no more than a lack of food, and yet I wonder. Have I become some other creature, and Annie senses the change? I cannot bring to mind now, fully, Daniel's face, or the sensation of his touch, or the words he spoke. Perhaps that was all lived by some other being, and not me at all. The other Sarah.

'We shall have a different life soon, Annie.'

She twists round to face me, picking out a hag stone and peeking through the hole. 'What different life?'

'Of a warm fire every night and a table full of food. With Daniel.' I instantly regret my words. But what harm can Annie do? If she speaks of this they will think it just another of her stories.

'I can't see the fairies,' she says, disappointed. 'I've never seed them and it's not fair, it's they that sent me to be growed in the woods and gived to you and Mammy and John.'

''Tis not we that choose the seeing, but they.'

She throws the hag stone to the ground.

'Well don't waste it,' I say. 'Bring it for Mam to sell.'

She scrabbles among the pebbles to find it again.

'Come on.' I kiss her cheek and imagine how it will feel plumped out with rich living. 'Do not speak of this, nor mention Daniel, to anyone. Understand?'

She frowns, nods, gathers the clams and seaweed back into her petticoat. 'I'll like it when my real sister comes back,' she says.

We make our way home, confident that what we bring from our day's work will please Mam. As we walk the path past the Taylors' fields my heart beats quicker and I cannot help but crane my neck over the hedge. There are only lambs, rounded out now, leaping and playing unburdened by knowledge of their fate. I lift Annie to see.

As I place her back down there's a shout behind me and hands grasp my shoulders, hard, shake them. I'm caught between fear and hope, spinning round.

John. Laughing so hard that flecks of spittle gather in the corners of his mouth.

'Goffy,' I yell. Angry with him mostly because he is not Daniel.

'There you are,' Annie says, as though we were searching for him all along. She hugs him around the waist and he ruffles her hair.

'Hello there, little squirrel.'

'This is our other sister. She looks like Sarah but she isn't.'

'That so? What were you up to, Other Sister, all night in the woods with the farmer's lad?'

'Not all night, just late. You were asleep when I came in. You all were.'

The blush on my face betrays my lie, the smirk on John's shows his disbelief.

'Go tell your pretty tales to Mam, then. She'll believe you, no doubt.'

He runs off in the direction of the village, and I fret so about what he might be doing there that I forget to wash the clams.

'What happened to these?' Mam asks, wrinkling her nose as she picks them over. She holds the stone up to the light, takes the coin, nods.

'We meant to rinse them,' I say.

'Meant to. No use.' She scoops them up, drops them into a bowl and hands it to Annie, wiping her sandy hands down her petticoat. 'Wash these at the well. Don't come back until they're clean.'

I hold my hands out before Mam's words have fixed themselves in me. Annie's eyes open out like full moons. 'Just me?' she asks. 'By my own?'

'Aye, you're old enough now. Be gone, lass, make yourself useful.'

Annie takes the bowl as though she's been handed a casket of gold and skips out of the house into the fading light. Mam and I stand, listening to the rattling of the clams and Annie's singing drifting, the table between us, each leaning against a wall. She throws me a look that makes me wary of the conversation to come, suspicious of her reason for sending Annie away, then runs to the door and pulls it open.

'Back,' she shouts. 'Back here.'

The rattle returns.

'Only go to the well if the green's empty. If there are villagers there, even ones you've seen here, leave and come home. Talk to no one. Understand?'

Mam steps in, closing the door. She presses a hand to her forehead. 'She's still innocent of their hate. I'd not have a stone thrown or a taunt spoke and steal that from her.'

I think of the ill will we've found in the village since the new magistrate is come, the venomous accusations this morning. The farmhand. But I cannot reply, for Mam is making me fearful. There's a brittleness to her movements and the way she avoids my eye. I wait, swallow down my disquiet. She is building up to something.

Taking the clay figure from by the fire, she turns and strokes it, lifts and peers at it. 'Dry,' she says. 'What should be done with it now, dust think?'

'I think we should leave be.'

'The netter should go unpunished?'

I run my hand over the table, brushing crumbs to the floor. 'He's lost some teeth, had his eye blackened.'

She places the figure on the table, looks at me until I'm forced to turn away from the crumbs and meet her gaze. 'You think you've another path now, happen?'

Her face is expressionless, voice gentle. I do not think she mocks me, but I'm not sure. I cannot reply.

'He made promises, did he? Prattled a tale of a better life?'

I say nothing but I know she can read the answer on my face. Her talk is perilous and I feel my fragile happiness under siege.

'I do believe he cares for you,' she says. The hope I want to take from her words is stolen by the pity in her eyes. 'For a lad like him to come here, to warn us of the villagers and return, just to see you. You're right to think it means something. The feelings are real. The promises are not.'

'But if the feelings are real, why can't the rest be? He wants to be with me. We will find a way.' I realise in this moment that I believe it with every part of me. When two people feel as we do, so purely and without any doubt, they can make it possible. We will make it possible.

'Oh, lass,' she says, stepping around the table, making to stroke my hair and then hesitating, hand wavering in the air. 'I wish I could tell you it were so.'

She brings her arms around her own waist, and I wonder when she was last held by flesh not of her own. She knew love once. So long ago she can't remember how it feels.

I take her hands, rub them so the truth of my feelings can be pressed into her. 'It is so, Mam. It was for you and Father. It is for me.'

'Your father was not the only son of a farmer. And I was not—'

My grip on her tightens. I do not mean to hurt her. 'Not what? What am I?'

Whatever I am, that affords me less chance of happiness than she had, she was my maker. I manage to stop myself saying it, for even now I know that whatever she has made me it was not of her own choosing.

'You are poor, lass. We have nowt to offer on your behalf. God knows, I wish it wasn't so.'

'God knows I've as much right to happiness as any.'

'God knows you were chosen by another and it is to him you must turn if you want to live.'

I drop her hands as though her flesh burns me as her words do and press my fists into my eyes. She'll not have the satisfaction of my tears. The flickering in my eye and snarling through my bones brings a feeling of such uncontrollable wildness that it scares me. I fear what I'll become when it takes me over. Already, it has caused me to pain Mam in every way possible. And this I chose, just as Daniel prepared to offer me another life. A peaceful life.

'You want something that cannot be. It pains me to tell you, but it is so. If you should try to walk a different path, with one not of us kind, you'll not escape. He will destroy the one you love so that you may be claimed back.'

I bring my fists down on the table so hard that the clay figure rattles. I will not hear her words. I have resisted my power, have caged the dog. He'll not find us. I will steer my fate, take my own life in hand, as she never did.

'You cannot remember how it feels, too much time has passed.'

A smile transforms her face, surprising me. 'I remember saying these same things to my mother. It was all not so very long ago, lass. Though sometimes it feels another life.'

She sighs, rubs the small of her back and lifts her face towards the tattered roof. 'All I want is to protect you. You put yourself in the way of pain.'

She cannot understand. Her time to protect me is gone.

'Better to embrace what lies within yourself than search for happiness in another,' she says. 'Don't be feared to discover your own power.'

'You take me for a fool, if you think this will make me reveal—' I almost say 'the dog', the words dance in my mouth like bees.

She steps forward. 'It's all right. You can tell me. Share your burden. Tell me what you've conjured. 'Tis here to protect you as you grow into your powers, nothing to fear.'

Her eyes are clear and soft, as I remember them from when I was small, those times when I ran to her for comfort, burying my face in the welcoming folds of her petticoat. When she wiped my tears and washed my scratches. Should I speak, the dog will run separate from me as Dew-Springer does and have its own will, no longer controlled by mine.

But I am weary with hiding it. Perhaps if I tell her she'll teach me to master a familiar that runs separate, and keep it under my bidding.

As I open my mouth to let the bees out I hear Annie laughing and clams rattling, and next the slam of the door and pounding of feet. Not just Annie's but Seth's too.

'Sorry, Mammy, I know you said not to talk to anyone but it was only Seth and he'd already seed me, hadn't you? So I thought—'

'Aye, right,' Mam says. 'Stop that prattling now.'

She takes the bowl of clean clams, places it in front of the clay figure, blocking it from Seth's view. And I'm saved from revealing the flicker in the corner of my eye. Exhausted, I pull out a stool, sit and lay my head on the table.

Seth stands in the doorway, beaming, clutching a pail. Another offering, no doubt, though he clearly needs no potion today. He looks from Mam to me.

'Now, then,' he says. 'What's this?'

Bewitched

When at last the day was done Daniel stood in his room, rubbing soap on to a cloth, dipping it into the bowl of water ready to wash the filth from his body. He paused to rescue a drowning spider, catching it and crouching to tip it gently into a corner of the room, watching it scurry into a hole in the wall. His skin stung when he had finished washing, but the ashy scent of the soap left him refreshed and he crawled under the blankets, relieved to rest his exhausted bones.

Sleep denied him. His mind would not let his body settle, but went over instead the events at dinner that night, hearing Father's words again and again until his head pounded. He could find no way around his plight.

The conversation about Molly had been halted by Parson Walsh arriving to collect the buttermilk they donated to the poor. For the first time, as Daniel had listened to his assurance that the family it was given to were deserving, he realised it was the Haworths. He had never truly understood the depth of Sarah's poverty.

He turned, kicked off the blankets.

If Father would despise the match with Molly then he would be filled with fury if presented with the daughter of one he loathed. They would be forced to run away. No Bett to care for them, nor even Father to advise. He and Sarah would be banished, alone in the world to make a living, build a home. He could not see a path that did not lead them to a hovel, a diet of buttermilk. He was not bold, never had been, and had never envisaged facing such a foolhardy choice.

He was but a step away from safety.

Tomorrow, he could seek her out, tell her it could not be. Undo the damage he had done, take that one step to the life expected of him. A predictable, unchanging life.

He could see this life but remained untouched by it, for he would go through the whole of it unseen. His heart thudded, his breath failed. The only way to calm himself would be to bury his face against Sarah's neck and breathe in the salt-scent of her skin, to see the turbulent blue of her eyes and hear her voice. She was both his turmoil and his comfort. And he wondered now if she had bewitched him, that he would yearn for her so, that he would act so recklessly.

His hair grew hot and damp. But even in his fear, he knew the peaceful life without her in it was not for him. He wanted what they spoke of, to share the little house with her, to dance on May Day together. He must have this life, would do whatever it took to bring it about, however afraid he was, however surprised by his ability to imagine beyond the ordinary.

Daniel turned and buried his face in his sweat-soaked pillow.

'If I am bewitched, then let it be so,' he whispered. 'If I am bewitched, let it be so.'

And to this refrain, at last, sleep crept over him.

Infused with Light

'Seth's brought us buttermilk,' Annie says.

Mam takes it from him, places the pail of white, watery slop on the table. Its sour smell begins to fill the room. 'Thank you,' she says. This time of year we can rely on a regular supply, and though its taste is not sweet, it does keep the belly filled.

'It was given freely, by those that have to those in need. The actual milk of human kindness.' He chortles at his own humour, looks around for approval. Finds none. 'But wait — why these solemn faces on such a beauty of a day?'

'Our real Sarah's went away and this one is having a new life with Daniel,' Annie says, shaking her head.

'Hush, Annie, I said it was to be our secret.'

She wipes her nose and shrugs. 'I only keep secrets for real sisters.'

'Wait, what's this?' Seth asks. 'What is all this? Springtime love blossoms?'

His smile is broad, like a child given a gift and I cannot stay solemn in the face of his joy. He will see the truth of our feelings. My blush is answer enough.

'Why, this is wonderful news. Happy news.' He beams at the stony faces of Mam and Annie. 'We celebrate, do we not, Ruth?'

'Celebrate we might, for two other people. Those who reach too far can only fall.'

'A young man from the village?' Seth asks.

'Aye, and she's set her hopes on the highest there. The family will not consent.' Mam rearranges the two bowls on the table. Picks up the clay figure and slips it on to a stool, furthest from Seth. 'Though I do believe their feelings run pure,' she says quietly, face turned away from me.

'Well, then,' Seth says. 'All cannot be lost, if the feelings are as you say. Who is the young man?'

'Daniel Taylor.' His name on my lips. Sweeter even than the flawn.

'Ah.' Seth lifts his face to the roof, considering. Praying, perhaps. I wait, impatient to hear his thoughts on Daniel. 'Well, yes I see your dilemma.' He chuckles. 'Oh my, you choose a wealthy family. The only farm in the village.'

His smile fades when he sees my expression. He clears his throat. 'Ah, but still, as your mother says, the love is there. Is it not?'

'It is.'

'I shan't never love a man,' Annie says as she peers into the buttermilk and dips her finger in.

'Good lass,' Mam says.

'When I'm growed,' Annie says, slurping around her finger, 'I'd rather be a man than love one, anyhow.'

Seth laughs. 'That will take more than prayer, little one.'

She scoops a handful of buttermilk. She has said her piece and the conversation no longer interests her.

'So you see my objection?' Mam asks. Her eyes follow movement on the floor, and I know she watches Dew-Springer, but will not speak to him while Seth is here.

'It is difficult, to be sure. The father is not one to take monetary matters lightly.'

They are all against us. Even Seth, who has been our ally all these years, gently dissuading those that have wanted to attack us in God's name.

'But you choose wisely, my dear.'

Mam snorts. 'A wealthy family?'

'But the most compassionate, the very kindest and good of heart. Of all the young men in the village, oh you have chosen the ray of light. There is hope.'

He bounces over to me, bends so our faces are level and clutches my hands. His palms are warm and wet, his eyes that look into mine so earnestly quiver. There are times of melancholy that come upon him, and times when he sees only joy, despite what may be in front of him. But his words bring my dreams alive and I choose to notice only them.

He rushes over to Mam, cloak flapping and catching on the corner of the table. 'I can help, I will intervene. If they are ardent and constant, as even you believe, then I can persuade the father. He is a man that wants to be assured of his place in heaven, for his dear wife awaits him there, and given the role bestowed on me I am the only one with the power to convince him that this is the way.'

There is a pause in which Annie burps and grimaces, and I think for a moment that she'll puke over the table. Buttermilk looks no different going in or coming out.

Mam steps back from Seth as he stands almost touching her. 'Your thoughts are no straighter than hers today,' she says. 'There are times when you see the world as more beautiful than it is. Remember. Know yourself.'

He sighs and lifts his face again. 'I see the world as God intended, touched by His hand and infused with light. And love.' He turns to me and beams.

Annie climbs down from her stool and shuffles towards me, bent a little and clutching her belly.

'This is His doing, I feel the truth of it.' Seth speaks so fast in his excitement that his words smash into each other. 'To bring together the sweetest young souls of the village and in doing so welcome a far-flung family back to the flock. And I am his instrument. I am chosen.'

He looks around at us, chest heaving, eyes bright with wonderment at this great revelation. Right now I truly believe every word he speaks. How can Mam oppose us when even God chooses us to be together?

'You carry yourself away, Seth,' Mam says.

He wags a finger at her. 'No, no, no. Recently I am struck by the goodness, the very godliness, I find in the humble village folk, the honesty and integrity.'

Mam catches my eye, and I look away, refusing to acknowledge that we know this to be untrue.

'This new magistrate brings a wave of morality and I am confident it is all we need for the village to welcome you, with warmth, without judgement.' Seth presses his hands together, smiles at us all. 'Young Gabriel, who works on Master Taylor's farm, enquired just the other day whether we might see you in church. He seems to show a care for you in particular, Sarah, and we may perhaps entreat him to speak your case with the father.'

Such ignorance. 'Oh nay, he of all—' Annie tugs on my arm and turns a miserable face to me. I sigh. 'Greed has got the better of you again, little cub.'

'She has a hunger, poor thing,' Seth says.

'Sit her down still, I don't want another tableful of her guts,' Mam says.

Annie shuffles to a stool like an old woman, removes the clay figure from the seat and places it on the table with a thump before sitting. Exposing the true depths of Mam's trade. I wonder if Seth is so sure of God's choice now. He glances at the figure, looks puzzled.

'A queer plaything. Yours, little one?'

Annie slumps forward, chin resting on the table, teeth clacking as she replies. 'Nay, it's Mammy's, for burning and sticking pins to punish the netter.'

Silence. Seth swallows and looks from the table to Mam. I lean forward. The air is suddenly tight between us. He will withdraw his offer to intervene now, I know it.

'It will surely be an advantage to you all that these two are united,' he says. 'To be accepted in the village again. To live by more fitting means. You will be protected.'

Mam says nothing, though I know as well as she there is no protection for us in the village any more.

Annie begins to whimper and gulp, and I lift her and run for the door, stepping through just before the buttermilk makes its reappearance.

The White River

Father grunted as he sat down, waiting as Bett filled a basket with a jug of ale and bread for them to take to the fields. 'Ploughing first, lad, before the day heats.'

Daniel yawned and nodded. 'Late night, was it?' Bett asked.

Father raised an eyebrow. 'Out till after dark again.'

Daniel tried to wipe the smile from his face. The beat of his days was changed, now daylight and the farm just an interlude until he was once again with her. The scent of her skin, brush of her hair against his face, taste of her lips. Evenings of fire-light and starlight. Whisper of a life together.

Bett snorted and tucked a clump of hair back into her coif. 'May is the month for it.'

Father cleared his throat. 'And check that ox, the one we thought was running lame the other day, and please God it's recovered. I can't abide the cost of a sick animal.'

'I will,' he said, passing Bett the cloth she pointed to, glad to talk of the farm once more. It suited him that they thought he was only shaking the sheets with a local lass he would soon tire of. Though he could imagine doing no such thing. The nearest he had come was the faltering initiation into the sweet pleasures of flesh that Bett had led him in many years past, and it was she who had wearied of their fumbling encounters.

With Sarah he felt their very beings had begun to meld into one. To leave her would be to rip part of himself away. And they had not even begun to explore the landscape that Bett had so willingly laid out for him.

Daniel took the basket, thanked Bett and left before they asked more of his night-time entertainments.

He led the oxen to the field, waiting as the stubborn beasts obstructed his will by stopping to eat the hedgerow. He had found none lame, at least, and was relieved to have good news for Father. There was no hurry. A scent of blossom, hay and dung sat sweet in the air and a wayward moon glimmered down from a clear sky, not ready yet to retire. The delay afforded him a moment to imagine exploring the white river of Sarah's skin hidden from sight.

'She is a lovely girl, is she not?' a voice spoke in his ear. Parson Walsh.

'I – who is?'

'The young lady that holds your heart.'

Daniel feared for a moment that the parson had an actual godly power to read his thoughts. Or perhaps he had truly lost his grip on himself and spoken aloud. He stared speechless as the oxen began to stamp their impatience.

Parson Walsh stepped closer, a hand on Daniel's shoulder. Too close, and Daniel fought the instinct to back away.

'The dear child has confided in me and I sought you out, to let you know that I am to be your saviour, channelling the light and love of the good Lord as He so wishes. I – I have been waiting on the path here.'

The words spoken too fast for Daniel to take in. Sarah had confided in the parson, yet he could not imagine how their paths would cross, never mind that she would open the secrets of her heart to him. She had never so much as mentioned him. They had not spoken of their love in the real world, nor mentioned their families. He had assumed she'd told no one.

'It is a challenging path you have chosen, no doubt, my son, but I am to intervene on your behalf and indeed on that of our dear Lord and His plan to bring together those pure in heart and welcome to the fold a family thus far cast aside.'

Daniel squinted at the parson, whose face was obscured by the sun behind him, and tried to make sense of the words he spoke. His disquiet communicated itself to the oxen. The beasts grew restless, and the parson at last stepped back.

'I—' Daniel looked about him. No one to hear. He dropped his voice nonetheless. 'Sarah has confided in you?'

Parson Walsh nodded enthusiastically. 'Indeed, and I impressed upon her, upon them all, that she has chosen a match of the most excellent qualities of kindness and purity as one can wish.' A great smile broke out on his face, and disappeared just as quickly. 'Though there are difficulties, to which I just referred and of which you are surely aware. But I shall speak to your father and we shall—'

'My father?' Daniel stepped forward, reaching a hand out as though he could physically restrain the parson. He imagined Father's fury at such a discovery, himself and Sarah cast out. Where could they go but to the Haworth hovel? Living on buttermilk with her Devil-brother. Daniel swallowed his feeling of sickness. 'No, please don't do that.'

Parson Walsh shook his head, his face a scramble of confusion. 'Then how are we to convince him of the desirability of the match?'

'I – I don't believe we can.'

No sound but the disgruntled lowing of the beasts. One of them dropped its filings right by the parson's foot, but he did not react.

'Then you are trifling with the girl? Using her for pleasures of the night only to abandon her? I had thought more—'

'No, no. I – we plan to be together. But I – I don't yet know how. We have not discussed it much.'

'You are afraid your father will not approve?' the parson asked.

A fat, slow bumblebee droned between them, settling on the pouch of a white-nettle. 'More than afraid, I am certain. My – he will not allow it.'

'But now you have me. To intervene on your behalf. To persuade. I have been chosen for this task, it is therefore impossible that I should fail.'

Bewildered as he was, Daniel understood that he must halt this plan now. 'You are very kind to take on our cause, and I cannot express my gratitude. To have an ally is unexpected,' he said, and meant it. 'But if – if I could ask you to wait a while before you approach my father? Together we will find the best way, I'm sure.'

'Of course. My enthusiasm has run me away, perhaps. I am told it does from time to time.' He laid a hand on Daniel's shoulder. 'I will let you about your tasks. Come to me if you are in need of help. And when it is time to make our approach.'

Parson Walsh stepped right in the pile of ox filth as he left, though he did not appear to notice but marched straight on without faltering. Daniel watched him for as long as he could, trying to assemble and understand what had been spoken, but the animals' needs must be seen to.

The oxen at last deposited in their field, Daniel hurried with the one Gabriel needed for harrowing, arriving hot-faced and gasping with effort. He would no doubt be in for some goading.

'All right, don't hurt yourself,' Gabriel said.

'Sorry. Delayed.'

'Aye, all right then. Shackle her up.'

Daniel worked as quickly as he could, grateful for Gabriel's cheerful mood.

'Late waking, were you?' Gabriel asked, winking.

'Ah, no, it was—'

'Too much a-bed and not enough sleep, was it?'

Daniel was horrified by Gabriel's crudeness. 'No, no, that's not ...'

Gabriel took his place on the other side of the ox's head, slapping Daniel on the back as he passed. 'No need to blush, it's the natural way of things. We both are men and the blood will fire up.' He grinned over the top of the beast. 'Who is she, then, this lass that's happy to let you dock? Not Molly after all, I hear she had a change of heart, as I knew she would.'

Daniel pulled on the ox until she moved, desperate to distract from this questioning. There was too much interest in his goings-on. He realised, heavy with disappointment, that he must keep away from the river for a few nights. They walked on at the ox's uneven pace, but Gabriel would not break off.

'Nor our Betty any more, I'm guessing, now she has a husband of her own to see to. Eh?' He craned over the ox but Daniel stared straight ahead. He was in hell. God was punishing him at last for those sinful, unwedded touches he had once shared with Bett.

Those Within

These past two nights I've looked for the stone, and found nothing. Tonight I waited as long as I dared, hoping Daniel might come anyway, but he did not and though I know his feelings are true, I begin to wonder if something has happened that keeps him away. Perhaps his courage fails. Perhaps we've been discovered.

I usually take care to avoid the tavern on my way back, for the swill-bellies coming out bring all manner of troubles, but this night am distracted and stray too close. Keeping to the shadows, I skirt the path, hoping to go unseen by the figure staggering from the door.

'You.'

The shout pulls me to a halt, chills my skin. I turn to face the farmhand, Gabriel. Look about, but no friendly face to help me. Though the only friend would be Seth, and he unlikely to be found at the tavern. I feel the shock, the fear, ripple over my features. Despise myself for showing it.

'What are you doing, eh?' he asks. 'Loitering here to bring upon me some other, stronger curse? Be warned, your filthy witchery cannot take hold, for I have shook off your sorcery and none other from your hand will have an effect.'

He saunters towards me. I resist the urge to back away, and face him. I will not falter.

In the corner of my eye I see a figure running towards us. Small and slight, but swift. Strong enough to do me harm, no doubt. I wonder, if they've drunk enough, if I can outrun them both.

The farmhand leans forward. Close enough now to smell the ale on his breath. 'Think you can hide from me? Think your home shall keep you safe? Dare to close your eyes at night and see what comes upon you. There's things unfinished between us.'

The figure is upon us, pushing me aside and standing between me and the farmhand, and only now do I realise it is John. Chest heaving, legs apart and shoulders straight, a vain attempt to appear a greater threat. They face each other. John, smaller by far and half as wide. I see his fear in the set of his jaw, smell it in his sweat. He lifts his chin and eyes the brute, nonetheless.

'Leave my sister be,' he says. Voice thin in comparison to the farmhand's, but steady.

'Think I'm afeared of you?' Gabriel attempts a sneer that does not quite convince. His sudden pallor and the widening of his eyes at the sight of John betray him.

John speaks slowly, leaving space between the words. 'Leave my sister be.'

I watch. Frightened for John, for he will easily be beaten if this comes to blows, and moved by both his fear and courage. Grateful for his protection. Angry with myself for needing it.

The farmhand watches for a moment. He looks John up and down, and I know he's considering setting about him. John holds his ground. I can barely breathe.

He laughs, an unconvincing sound. 'You all have a happy fate today, being that I am needed for my tasks in a urgent manner and may not dally here to finish with you.' As though we have not the wit to know he has no task at this time of night. He begins to step away, his eyes never leaving John's face. Daren't turn his back. 'But 'tis a delay and no more. I shall return, and do not think you have 'scaped me.'

At last he runs off, almost tripping over in his haste to leave. We watch him go.

They tell stories of John in the village. Of terrifying powers and an evil spirit. Of an ability to summon demons to carry out his work. He, they fear more than any of us. And yet he has no skills of magic. I've always envied the simplicity of his life, and he the purpose of mine.

I turn to him now. We both are breathing fast.

'John – I ...'

He nods, pats my shoulder once. Together we walk home.

We creep in as quietly as we can. The house throbs to the rhythm of Mam's snoring and Annie's snuffling sleep-breathing. It's warm in here, the air a fog of moist breath and the familiar scent of their warm bodies. My home, not the crumbling walls and drifting roof of this house, but the solid presence of those within. When I live in a new house, I will take my home with me.

We make no sound as we enter. John steps to his mat, curls under the blanket. I wonder if he is feared, shaken as I am. Turning towards my bed I almost fall backwards in surprise at seeing the little figure in the doorway.

'What have you bringed?' Annie asks, words distorted as she breathes out a yawn. Expecting that I have been with Daniel and brought back a parcel of food. How I wish it were so.

I put my finger to my lips. There is a little left from our last meeting, and I fetch the cloth from its place in the corner and lay it out. She runs and leaps over John, her bare foot just missing his head, scrambles on to a stool and leans on her elbows to inspect the food.

Her eyes are large and bright as she takes in the scraps of bread and cheese. No longer red-rimmed and sunken, no more do my hands strike bone when I search her skin every morning. She begins to look like any village child of her age. Though dirtier. And yet she is not one of them, and now, after our meeting with the farmhand, I see why Mam warns us to keep separate. I see why she says I shall never be a farmer's wife, nor Annie accepted in the village. I feel the stalking of he that claims us.

Annie picks over the food with ragged black fingers, and gathers a small pile. Elbow on table, chin in hand, legs swinging, she chews her way through, stopping only to yawn and push back the sleep-taffled mess of hair that falls over her face.

I pour her a cup of water and sit opposite. 'Steady, cub,' I say. 'It won't disappear with the sun and we don't want it going the way of the buttermilk, do we?'

She throws me a look that tells me she is unimpressed, but her mouth is saved for chewing not speaking. I sit back on my stool, try to enjoy watching her eat her fill. Try to stop wondering what kept Daniel away.

Soars too High

Daniel had rushed through his tasks, impatient to be done. After days away from Sarah, a means for them to be together had at last come to him, and he could not wait to put his plan to action.

As he ducked down now behind the hedge that lined the path out of the farm, he felt the sun warm on the back of his neck, the air sickly with the scent of pollen. He waited until he saw them. Bett usually left alone, but this evening was huddled speaking with Gabriel. Daniel shuffled as close as he could without being seen.

'… want with me?' Gabriel asked. 'I have more tasks before I may be off and eat, and I'm gut-foundered already.'

Bett was turned away from Daniel and he could not make out all she spoke. He peered through the leaves and dog roses.

'… of a brawl in the tavern,' she said.

'Well Nathaniel was mistook, it was another, for I was not even—'

'I know,' Bett's voice rose a little. '… Wright was called and now they're to be put in the stocks …' Through a gap in the bottom of the hedge Daniel watched a worm writhe on the dusty path, distracted by its discomfort. '… wanted to warn you is all, you must watch yourself and that temper now, the new magistrate is not the same as the old. There'll be no turning away.'

Daniel shifted quietly. He squinted to see Gabriel's frown become a smirk. 'I never knew you were so fond of me.'

Bett stepped back. 'There are others that rely on you, Gabriel, how will your poor mam and sister manage with you in trouble?'

'Fear not, lassie, I can care for my own affairs, no need for women to meddle.'

Bett began to walk towards where Daniel hid, leaving Gabriel to continue with his tasks. 'My part is done,' she said, pulling her neckerchief more firmly on.

Daniel reached through the hedge and lifted the worm on to the softer ground of the field, then rose to his feet. He whistled as Bett passed so as not to startle her. She turned to him with an expression of contempt, arms folded.

'What am I, a dog? Speak, don't call me to heel.'

He clambered over the hedge out on to the path, like a boy chastised. 'Sorry.'

'What is it that has you jumping out at me on my way home?' She sighed and readjusted the fit of her petticoats around her middle. 'It's this girl, isn't it? You're wanting to run off and wed?'

Taken aback, he leaped in with protest. 'No, it's not – not that, we wouldn't even know how to – no, no. Not that.'

She narrowed her eyes. 'Wouldn't put it past you, it's just the kind of half-wit notion you'd take into your head. So it's not the girl?'

'Ah well, no, yes it is the girl. Just not that.'

Her expression warmed and he was reminded for a moment of the scent of her skin in sunlight, the sight of flesh revealed little by little as she rolled down her stockings. Bett placed a hand on his shoulder, stepped closer, lowered her voice. 'You've got her belly up, haven't you? There are remedies to be had, I've heard, a brew. I know you don't like the cunning woman, but she—'

Daniel shook her hand off. 'Betts, no. Not that either, we've not—'

'Oh. A real devotion, then.' Her usual expression, that of a busy person delayed by the triflings of an imbecile, returned. 'What, then? Speed to it, I've a home to be at.'

'She – she is in need of work and—'

'I'm hardly in a position to be offering work.'

'No, I know. She is also in need of clothes.'

Bett eyed him shrewdly. 'She has no clothes?'

Behind her Gabriel returned to the yard, dragging the plough and stamping mud from his boots. He glanced in their direction, faltered a moment in his task. 'She has – not the right clothes.'

The unasked questions flowed between them. 'Poor lass,' she said.

'Yes.'

'I'll look something out tonight.'

'Thank you.' He knew he need not ask for her discretion. 'You've gathered enough, I'm sure, with Father gifting you my mother's clothes year on year, and you working since you were just a lass and now a maid of—'

She turned to him sharply. 'A what? We're all but the same age.'

He laughed. 'Well, not really, you have a few years on me and now a maid of ...' Why did he not stop speaking?

She shook her head. 'The same dolt you were at ten.'

'Sorry,' he said. 'I didn't mean to – Betts, I really didn't—'

She had gone, waving a dismissive hand to silence him.

Daniel awoke early, before the sun rose and called them all to their tasks, briefly questioning his boldness at what he had set in motion. He had asked the parson to bid Sarah meet him by the sheep field, and hurried there, hoping she would come. One look at her after days apart, the smile that lit her face as their eyes met, and he was certain of his plan once more.

He led her down the path where birds began their song in the trees that lined it and across the yard. So close to the slumbering house.

'It was well you asked Seth to pass on your instruction,' she whispered. 'He's an ally to us.'

Daniel glanced over his shoulder. No one to be seen. 'He helps your family?'

'Aye, brings the buttermilk and such. Comes to Mam sometimes, for without her cures he falls into darkness or soars too high in the light. When he's dark he feels he can do nowt, but when he's light he really believes he can change everything. For the better.'

He ushered her into the barn, filled with the scent of hay and droppings. 'And can he?'

'Perhaps.' Sarah stopped. 'Oh, it's Bonny,' she whispered, reaching a hand out to the horse, stroking her side. 'You brought me to see her?'

'No,' he said, leading her away to where the cow and oxen chewed sleepily on their hay. 'I brought you to work.'

Pippin was already beginning to call out, ready to have the weight of her milk taken from her. Sarah stepped backwards so suddenly that Daniel's arm was almost wrenched off.

'Why is he bawking?'

'Why – what? It's just – needs milking, that's all.'

'He's much bigger close to.'

'She,' Daniel said. 'And she's soft as butter. Pippin's much sweeter than Bonny and you're not afraid of her. Come on. I'm right here.'

'Does she bite?'

Daniel laughed. 'Bite? She's a cow. Not unless you're a clump of grass. Now, take that pail and put it under her, then fetch that stool.'

'Why?' Sarah asked, pulling the pail away from the wall and darting under the cow, dropping it into place so quickly that it fell on to its side.

'You'll need to know how to work the farm. Won't you?' He could not tell her the whole plan until Bett had played her part.

She looked up at him. 'Yes.'

'So. Again. Stay calm.'

'All right,' she said. 'Aye.' Took a slow breath in, edged towards Pippin, righted the pail. Turned to him with a look of triumph.

'Good,' he said. 'Excellent. Now, sit.'

He crouched behind her as she sat on the stool, took her hands in his, showed her how to bring the milk down.

★

Daniel finished the day's work and hurried back in time to eat with Father. Bett gave him a slight nod as he walked in and quickly, before the confidence this gave him faded, before he thought again of the perils of his plan, he sat at the table, cleared his throat.

'I am going to find a milkmaid,' he said. Cut up the collops and eggs and took a bite, all without looking to see Father's reaction. The sound of Bett calling her goodbyes as she left filled the gap.

'Milkmaids cost,' Father said at last. A predictable response and one Daniel had prepared for. It was not that Father was without the money to pay a dairymaid. He was just unwilling to spend it.

'I'm a man. Your only son. There's better work for me to do.'

Father chewed, swallowed, wiped his mouth with the back of his hand. 'And where do you plan to find her?'

'The mop.'

'Not for another few weeks.'

'I will manage until then.'

Father grunted, and spoke not another word that night.

Daniel ate his fill, and sat back, content. A milkmaid would bring less in the way of dowry than even a blacksmith's daughter. Father would not be pleased.

But it was not unknown for romance to blossom between farmer's son and dairymaid. And should Father learn of such a thing, should he believe Sarah might be left in some kind of trouble, he would insist they wed, however much the match disappointed him. As long as he did not discover who she truly was.

Sea and Leather and Fish

Bett's house is as ours would be, had it not stood abandoned all
those years, had we means and time to show it the same care.
Two rooms, the first with table and chairs, fire glowing in
grate, water pail standing in corner, pans hung on wall, nets
draped from beams. There's a smell of hot water and woodsmoke,
and underneath that, faintly, fish. She takes a candle to the fire,
lights it and shields it with her hand as she carries it over.

An unfamiliar and none-too-pleasant scent of burning tal-
low fills the room, a slow-flickering, warm light I've not seen
before throws a small illuminated pool across the table. The
house is not large but neat, the tabletop gleaming and empty,
the floor clear and clean. No ash-fall around the fire, no mould
on the wall, no draught whispering through the roof.

I'm still a little unnerved. Daniel had not told me the housemaid would be there when we met this evening and I stepped
back when I saw her, my belly tightening. Still, she did not
look unfriendly, a woman of rolling roundness, apple-cheeked
and ample-stomached, holding a bundle of cloth.

She eyed me up and down and turned to Daniel with an exasperated expression. 'Not here. I can't just give them to her, would you know how to place a coif without help?'

'Well, what then?' he asked.

This conversing about me as though I was a sick beast on the farm was new, unwelcome. 'Tell me what's happening,' I said, loudly, and they both turned to me at once. 'Do not speak and concoct plans without my knowing, I am not one of your horses, I will have some sway over my own life. Why do I need a coif? What have you both decided is happening to me?' I glared at them, and then added as an afterthought, 'And Mam has worn such things, we were not always as you see us now.'

Bett raised her eyebrows. 'Picked a fiery one.'

'Sorry,' Daniel said. 'I – I'm a fool.'

'As we've already agreed,' I said, and caught sight of Bett hiding a smile.

'The farm is in need of a dairymaid and I thought, you have a natural ability with animals and I can teach you the right skills, I will present you to Father in this part and it will begin your work as farmer's wife.' He flashed a look at Bett as she turned sharply to stare at him, blushed.

'But – will your father have me?' I met his eye, challenged him to be truthful. This was no time for stories.

He did not fail me. 'If you are dressed as any other girl, and if I say you were found at the mop, then yes. He will not have the curiosity to question. I am certain. Yes.'

'All right,' I said, hiding my excitement, not wishing him to think he had triumphed completely, riled as I was that he planned it so without me.

I stood as tall as I could, trying to show myself to be more than my ragged outer to this housemaid woman. 'Then I thank you for these,' I said, indicating the bundle. 'And as I shall soon be earning a wage, I'll pay you what I owe for them when I can.'

'As you wish,' she said, sparing my dignity.

Daniel turned to me, pleased with himself, and I could not help but give him the smile he craved. Bett coughed and looked away. Under the hedge something shuffled, and I glanced quick to see a hare, no doubt this time, bounding away, and I wondered if it was Dew-Springer, running back to tell all to Mam.

'Well, this fool, as it turns out we are all three agreed upon, did not inform me as to his plot either, but simply instructed I bring these,' she said. A look passed between them that I did not understand, though I felt Daniel had been reprimanded. 'Your mam is able, I know, but I have time. What do you think to us going to my house and trying them out? Then if they don't fit I can find others.'

So here I am in Bett's tidy little house, watching her unwrap her neckerchief, remove her hat and hang both on a nail in the back of the door. Order, where I'm used to chaos. Her hair is light, unruly curls bursting free from her coif.

'Right,' she says, wiping her hands down her apron. She turns to the fire, throws on two logs from the neat pile in the corner and rattles at the grate with the poker. I stand, awkward without a task. She looks at me over her shoulder and waves her hand at the table.

'Sit,' she says, and I do.

'Did you not think to leave the farmhouse when you married?' I ask.

She snorts. 'How could I? No other would keep order over that shambles as I do.' Her tone softens. 'And besides, 'tis like family, in its way. I'll stay, until I have my own.' She glances heavenward and quickly presses her hands together. 'God willing, I pray.'

The sea beats against the beach, wind shaking the front door on its hinges. We lived in one of these cottages once, and I remember more strongly than ever the sight of my father's salt-stained boots, warped into the shape of his feet, drying by the door; the smell of sea and leather and fish he carried with him.

'My father was a fisherman,' I say. I don't know why.

Bett sits at the table, opposite me. 'Oh?'

'Once. We lived down here.'

She nods.

'It was a long time ago.' I don't know why I started this conversation, don't know what I expect of this stranger. Unperturbed, she begins to sort through the bundle of clothes she placed on the table, shaking out and holding up a petticoat, looking from it to me with her eyes narrowed.

She sniffs. 'You're a spindly one. This is the smallest I could find, we should be able to tie it tight enough.'

She stands up, lights a rush, holds it and the bundle out to me. I don't know what I'm expected to do.

'Well, go on then,' she says, flapping a hand towards the door to the other room. 'Try them on, come back and I'll help you with the coif.'

I take the clothes from her. 'Thank you. Aye, I will. All right.'

She looks at me as though I'm the village goffy, and I hurry through the door. In the half-light I hear a scuttle and flurry of small creatures taking refuge as I enter. One mat fills most of the space, blanket neatly spread over it. There is a chest squeezed in by the wall and I place the rush on it, laying out the clothes.

The petticoat is not so different from my own, though this is thick and warm, smooth at the edges and without a thin patch to be seen. Such material is unfamiliar and a little prickly in my hand.

Leaving my own rags in a shameful pile on the floor, I sit on the mat and pull the stockings on, wriggle my toes now encased in cloth, feel the material rest right against the skin of my legs. Imagine myself a farmer's wife, and that wearing these clothes is as unremarkable a feeling for me as it is for any other village woman. Pull on the shift, too large so the cuffs fall almost to my fingers. Then the stays, stiffened with reeds. A memory I didn't know I had of Mam putting hers on comes to me, and I manage to tie the laces well enough. I reach for the petticoat, forced by the stays to bend awkwardly, feeling already more like a village woman simply because of the way I must hold myself now. Warm and thicker than I'm used to, the petticoat falls to my ankle. Wide at the waist, but no matter, I bunch it and tie the belt fast. Next, waistcoat and apron. So many clothes. More than Mam and I own between us. I'm glad Bett agreed that I may pay her.

I feel no longer myself. Held tall by the stays and layers covering every part of my body, I cannot imagine running along the riverbank or bending to lift Annie as I'm used to, nor ever feeling the wind from the sea cut through to my skin again. These clothes hide me, and I wonder if they are disguise enough to fool the one that chose me. Yet I'm shy to show myself. Sitting on the mat, in the rushlight, I listen to the chewing of mice and wonder what Annie, Mam and John are doing now, what they would make of me could they see. I want the life these clothes fit, but fear it will keep me apart from theirs.

The sound of knocking makes me jump. 'Come along, then. Show yourself,' Bett says.

I open the door and step through before allowing myself time to doubt. She holds the candle up, moving it so the light falls from my neck to my ankles.

'Good, yes, you look a proper little lady. Well, excepting that.' She waves a hand at my head. 'Sit down.'

I take a seat at her table, and Bett combs my hair. She works silently, more gentle than I expect, holding clumps near the top and tugging below her hand. The comb is wooden, and she uses the wide-toothed side so it does not catch. There's a strange comfort in being cared for this way. She pulls my hair from my face, winds and pins it at my neck, and stands back, hands on hips.

'Nearly there,' she says. She pours water into a bowl and brings a rag, dipping it in and wiping my face and the back of my neck. The water is cold and the cloth rough, but I close my eyes and make no sound. She takes each of my hands, washing the back, turning them and washing the palm, pressing the rag under my fingernails and scrubbing.

'And now,' she says, 'a woman's secret.'

She fetches from the shelf a small pot of pink powder that carries a scent of rose, dips in her finger and pats a little on each of my cheeks.

She lays the coif on the table. Plain linen, shaped to cover forehead and ear. Just as she wears, just as every village woman wears. Seeing it here, a memory of Mam removing one and placing it down like this flickers.

'Go on,' Bett says.

I put it on. Laughing, she shakes her head, pulls it down harder at the back, tighter over my forehead, tucking in any loose strands of hair. She steps away, arms crossed. I watch her, uneasy as the cloth presses against my head.

'Now we're there,' she says. 'No, wait. Shoes.'

She takes the candle into the other room, leaving me at the table. The room quiet and lit by the lilting flames from the fire, the sound of gently crackling wood and the distant rolling of waves, nothing more. Calm.

Returning, she wipes dust off a pair of brown leather shoes. 'Old,' she says. 'Sorry.'

I had shoes as a child, I remember looking down at the shiny toes. Cannot recall the feel of them now.

She kneels, placing them in front of me, and I push my feet in. Too big, but once she's laced them they fit a little better. Enough to stay on my feet, at least.

Bett sits back. 'Walk,' she says.

I stand. The weight unbalances me. I lift my foot, too high. Take a step, too far.

Bett laughs. 'Keep going. Practice is all you need.'

I walk around the room, steps too large, too slow, as though I am wading through water.

'You look like a duck,' she says.

'I can't do it,' I say. Feel like crying but laughter comes instead.

She wipes her eyes, hiccups down mirth, smiles encouragingly. 'Yes, you can. Keep at it.'

Around and around I go, past fire, bedroom, front door, pans on the wall. At last my steps are smaller, swifter.

'There,' she says. 'Perfect.'

I stand for a moment, dizzy from my travels around the room, from the twist of events that have led me to be in this stranger's house, wearing her clothes. She begins to busy herself with food preparation, and I fetch my own clothes from the bedroom. I dawdle, unsure whether to change back into them.

Bett wipes her hands down her apron, brushes an escaped strand of hair from her face. 'Leave them on,' she says. 'Show him.'

In the doorway I turn to her, this woman I don't know, who has dressed and washed me and spoken with me as one of her own. 'I don't know how to—'

She cuts me off. 'No need. You're buying some bits of clothes from me, is all.'

I nod, as grateful for the words as the clothes.

'Your mam helped us once,' she says. 'When we were first wed and Nathaniel's nets were empty as often as not. She placed a charm on the boat and told us which parts of the sea were more generous. We've not gone hungry a day since.'

Walking away, shoes scuffing and scraping along the ground, I hear her call after me.

'Walk, don't waddle.'

Peddled a Dream

She stood at the riverbank, the woman, looking out over the water as the sun set, and he knew it was Sarah. The way her chin tilted, the straightness of her back. His mother's neckerchief wrapped around her shoulders. He knew it but did not feel it.

He took her hand, turned her to face him. Still the same narrow fingers in his own, still the same turbulent eyes looking out from under the coif. Larger, they seemed, skin more pale and clear with her hair pulled away. The nape of her neck exposed now, a whisper of dark hair grazing the skin there. He knew the feel of it, and it was for him alone. He resented the gaze of others on this part of her.

She was still Sarah, still his, but as she would have been. The Sarah of another life. He longed, briefly, to see her in rags again, hair wild and raging in the wind. To put stop to this brave and treacherous plan.

He smiled, taking both her hands and spreading her arms wide, looked her up and down.

'Beautiful,' he said. 'Yes. They will all be charmed.'

'Will they know it's me?'

'No. Only I will.'

As they spoke, walked and ate bread spread thick with butter, she became more herself to him. She wearing the costume with more comfort, he seeing her through it. She looked now like any village girl. But she could never be.

'Have you shown your family?' he asked, reaching past the edge of the coif to stroke her cheek.

'Not yet.'

'They will like it,' he said. And then, unsure, 'Do you think they will like it?'

She looked beyond him, to the river slipping past. 'I think so. I don't know. Nay, perhaps not.'

'They want you to be happy?'

'Aye. But perhaps they'll think me – a different Sarah.'

'But you're not.' He reached in past the linen that framed her face, found her lips. 'You're the same Sarah.'

'Aye,' she said. She did not sound certain. 'This will – it'll protect them too. Yes? I'm not beginning a new life and leaving them in the old.'

'Of course.'

'Because – because I'll be paid? Even so, I can feed them, but how will they be safe? From the village, from the new …?'

Truthfully, he had thought little beyond bringing Sarah to him. But he spoke as sure as he could. 'With your wages they will not need to sell charms, or any other thing that might bring trouble.' He reached in, brushed her cheek with his thumb. 'You can take them food, still. More, even. They will be safe.'

'Yes,' she said. But still she frowned, and bit on her lip.

★

As Bett prepared the food basket the next morning she looked at Daniel as though she'd like to prepare him for the spit.

'I'll send this with the young master while you're off to your work,' she said. Dismissed, Father and Gabriel left.

'You – it looks like you're about to slice me and feed me to the pigs,' Daniel said. Tried a laugh that came out too thin and that he regretted immediately.

She scrubbed the table so hard that her arms shook.

'You do not like Sarah?' he asked. A guess, for she gave him no hint of how he had offended.

'I like her well enough.' She wrung out the rag, dipped it back in the pail and resumed wiping the already gleaming table. 'I didn't know it was she you had chosen when I agreed to pass on the clothes.'

'You would not have helped us?'

She turned, folding her wet arms across her chest. 'I'm not sure there is any helping you.'

He shifted, swallowed. 'Not – not so. I have spoken to Father, he is expecting a dairymaid. Sarah has a natural sense with animals. I will teach her the rest. And now she has the right clothes. For which I thank you.'

'She is not another broken beast you can fix and house in the barn.'

'I am well aware.' His breath was coming fast and sharp. He had not expected this.

Bett dropped the rag into the pail and reached for her broom, yanking chairs out from the table to better reach the floor. 'And when you cannot save her—'

'I can.'

'What's to become of her? Farmer's wife? You know that can never come about. How can you even think to bring her here, knowing what your father feels about the family? The very one that laid the curse on Gabriel.'

'I thought you didn't believe that?'

She batted him away as she tackled the floor by the door, shrugging. 'I – who knows that she didn't curse him, even with no more than cow pox? If I had the skill, I'd do it myself. Besides, he believes it and so does your father. You'll be lucky if either of you ends the year under his roof. You've peddled a dream you cannot deliver, and having dreamed it she'll be worse off without it. Poor lass. You'd have better left well alone.'

'I could not,' he said. His voice quieter than he intended. 'I could not leave her alone.'

She sighed, scratched under her coif, shook her head. 'Then you're a bigger fool than any of us knew.'

Daniel worked with a fury, labouring until his limbs burned, until his breath scratched in his chest and a mallet of pain struck his skull. Fool, he may be. Bewitched, even. But he would not give up.

Father was expecting a milkmaid. Sarah had a natural skill. He would teach her the rest.

He allowed no other thoughts to contaminate his belief that this would come about.

Quiver Through my Blood

The whistle is loud and sharp. Unnerving, slicing through the night air. The type of which I've heard before from village boys, sometimes men, meant to show a woman she will not escape unnoticed.

A figure walks above me, down the hill, a solid shadow against the starry sky. I cannot see the face but no matter, I know from the way he walks, swing of shoulder and sway of step, that it's John. Fear turns to irritation.

'Look at this,' he says as he nears. 'What're you dressed as?'

I lift my chin. 'I've new clothes.'

I am not the only one. He wears a tunic I don't recognise, too large, hanging to his knees and with a piece ripped off at the bottom. A donation from Seth, perhaps. I hope.

'I'll not ask what you did to earn them,' he says.

'I'm to have work. I'll pay for them.'

He laughs. 'There's no one in this village will send work our way. No matter how your flitter-mouse dresses you up.'

He moves to walk off but I catch his arm and turn him. His expression so angry it stops my breath. 'What?' he asks.

'Things will be better, John. There'll be work for us. For you.'

He shakes himself free. 'Aye, and we'll wake every morning to find bread growing from an enchanted tree in the garden, and pretty village girls'll stand in line to court me.' He catches my eye, yearning and pain there. Looks down at the ground he scuffs with his foot. 'Well. Until then.' He waves and runs off down the hill.

'Where are you going?' I call.

He turns, running backwards as he faces me, shrugs. 'You've your night amusements,' he shouts. 'I've mine.'

He runs on, leaving me to wonder. I pull the coif from my head, shake out my hair, trudge back to the house.

Morning comes and Annie, sleepy and tousle-headed, picks over the remains of the food, poking her grimy fingers into the butter and licking it off. Her skin is unmarked, her belly full and so I can sit easy. She swings her legs, plays with the clay figure of the netter, walking it up and down the table, stroking the strands of hair and whispering to it. There is a scrap of cloth on it now, though I don't care to think how it came to be here. Grotesque. This is the closest she has to a plaything.

'I miss the real Sarah, when's she coming back?' she asks. 'You smile too much. And you sing, she doesn't sing.'

'I'm the same Sarah. They're just clothes.' I take the coif from where it lies on the table, pull it on to her head. Too big, it falls almost to her nose. She tilts her chin back and peers at me. 'See?' I say. 'You're still you with it on.'

Yet the sight of her in it sends a quiver through my blood. In the coif I see how she would look as a village girl. As another Annie. I pull it off her.

Mam returns from wetting down the ash pile, shaking out her petticoat and brushing mud off her feet. So far she hasn't commented on the clothes, but her gaze slides to the coif as she passes. She stabs at the fire.

'Where's John?' I ask. His mat still empty on the floor.

Mam busies herself adding wood to embers. 'He'll be back soon.'

Annie quietly places the clay man down on the table, clambers from her stool and stands as if petrified, eyes on Mam's back.

'On an errand for you?' I ask.

'Finding diversion. He's as much right as you.'

No more comfort than John himself gave me. Annie tiptoes to the door, lifting her feet high, holding her wide-spread fingers out in front of her. I cover my mouth to smother laughter.

'Where dust think you're going, little lass?' Mam asks, without even moving from the fire to look at us.

Annie stops, slumps and sighs. Face a picture of tragedy. 'To the woods,' she says, voice slack with defeat. 'There's a tiny babby fox, it hasn't growed like the others, it's too small, I want to feed it.'

Mam turns, hands on hips. 'Feed it what? We've nowt to spare for foxes, however stunted.'

Annie reaches into her sleeve and pulls out a desiccated shrew. We watch it swing from the tail she grips in her grubby fingers, and Mam stifles a smile.

'All right,' she says. 'We'll afford your fox that. But later, we all have work to do first.'

I cannot help but protest. 'But Mam, we've food, let's keep away from the village awhile. They look upon us with only spite now, and it's not safe to—'

'We cannot live on the crumbs from your honey-sop's table, and we mustn't come to rely on them, for who knows when that well will dry. You and Annie can go beg a coin or two, for as you say, without protection from old Thompson we cannot be selling cures and curses. Can we?'

She pauses as we shake our heads.

'Change into your own clothes, where did this get-up come from anyway?' she says.

At last the acknowledgement I've been waiting for. 'They came from a friend in the village.'

Mam snorts. 'There is no friend to us in the village.'

'They're for the other sister,' Annie says.

Mam's skin becomes pale and thin as a shell. She glances around the room, fearful. 'What?' she asks, running over to Annie, crouching before her and grasping her arms, shaking her. 'What other sister do you speak of? What do you see?'

Annie wipes her nose and glances at me in confusion.

'She means me,' I say. 'She thinks I'm changed.'

'She looks like Sarah but she isn't,' Annie says. 'Dust see, Mammy?'

Mam slumps to her knees, head bowed, and Annie bends down, stroking her hair and peering at her with worried little eyes.

'What did you think?' I ask. I can hardly speak now. 'That she sees the spirits of her dead sisters? That past deeds stalk these rooms in a form only Annie can see?'

Mam covers her face with her hands, shoulders beginning to shudder. Her grief is silent for the sake of Annie, perhaps for me too, and I wish I could snag my words from the air and swallow them again.

'Are you sick, Mammy?' Annie whispers. 'Did you have greed with the buttermilk too?'

I gather my own clothes, step towards the other room. As I pass her, Mam shoots out a hand and grasps my ankle. A burst of fear in me.

'My only wish,' she says, looking up through the straggled hair that sticks to her wet face, 'is that you will never suffer to know what makes a woman act as I did.'

The rap on the door is loud, even; three slow knocks. A man clears his throat on the other side. Not a voice I recognise. Mam rises to her feet, finger to her lips and eyes weighted with warning, indicates that Annie and I should go.

I guide Annie into the shadows of the room we sleep in. As an afterthought I take the clay figure from the table and hide it in the cloth of my petticoat. Annie looks up at me, opens her mouth but I stop her words with my hand.

The knock comes again, louder, faster this time. Mam glances over her shoulder to check we're out of sight, straightens her hair as best she can and pulls the door open.

I point to the mat but Annie shakes her head, remaining clasped to my waist, huddled by the wall, peering through the doorway. From here I can just see Mam's back and the tip of a hat and toe of a polished shoe, now sprinkled with dust. A blast of fresh air dashes in from the open door, reaching my face. Annie buries her head into my clothes.

The hat moves as our visitor eyes Mam up and down. I hear the voice, clipped and sharp as though each word is a separate stone laid out without touching the next. Mam tries to close the door and a gloved hand pushes it back, the gleaming shoes step in. He strides around the room, hat tilted as he regards the pocked beams and rotting roof.

Annie tightens her grip on my petticoat, lifts her face to look at me. A pale smudge in the gloom. I point again to the mat and this time she creeps over and climbs in, pulling the covers over her head.

He lifts the coif I left on the table, holding it as he turns to Mam, fingering the edge. 'Who owns this property?' he asks.

Mam hesitates for a moment. 'It's – unwanted,' she says.

'But not unowned.'

'We'd a dwelling in the village before, my husband was a fisherman, but when he died we moved here.' There is a tremble in Mam's voice that makes me want to weep. Or sink my teeth into the no-doubt soft flesh this man hides under his rich clothing.

'No one objects,' Mam says. 'There was plague here, they say it's cursed, no one wanted—'

'Cursed?' He places the coif carefully back on the table, using both hands. 'By whom?'

'I – it's just what they say.'

He walks slowly around the room. Stops to inspect the shoes I've left by the wall. 'And how do you make your living?'

'I do what I can. People come to me if they're sick.'

Reaching the doorway to our room, he steps in and looks around. Says nothing when he sees me huddled against the wall, just touches his hat. Turns his back, strides to the door and stops.

'One of the cunning folk, are you?' he asks.

Mam does not reply. He casts a look around the room again. 'I see no evidence of faith here. You attend church?'

Mam hangs her head. Nods. My heart quickens and I will it to quiet for fear he will hear.

'These cunning practices, there can be – evil in them. Can there not?'

His gaze lands sharp on Mam. ''Tis just the use of plants, knowing which ones heal,' she says. 'Nowt more.'

'I have heard otherwise. There is a bleeding through, from cunning folk to witch folk. From plants to potions, from cures to curses. A calling on the evil spirits that lurk, and using them for your own devices.'

'Oh nay, sir,' Mam says. Her voice earnest and soft. 'I'd never use such – practices, as you say. I know only of herbs and healing.'

His arm remains outstretched, holding the door ajar. He makes no move to leave. 'A godless knowledge, nevertheless. I am sure even so simple parts as these have heard tell of the King's concerns over such things? What happens to those that are found practising?'

There is silence as his words fall. We know of what he speaks.

'There's no such thing here,' Mam says. I hear her voice strain. 'You've nowt to fear.'

'Indeed, no,' he says. 'For my conscience is clear.' He touches his hat again. 'Wright is the name. I shall return.'

At last he steps through and the door closes with a dull thud. Mam sinks on to a stool. Annie throws the covers back, leaps from the mat and runs to her. Mam holds her tight, raising a finger to her lips to warn us to keep quiet. We wait, silent, until we are sure he's gone.

'He could have taken his hat off,' she says.

'Hardly the worst of his behaviour,' I say.

'But still.' She strokes Annie's hair, staring at the floor. 'Ah, Dew-Springer. This is more than even you can protect us from.'

I remain in the doorway, throat so full of questions they cannot fight their way out. Still hiding the poppet in my petticoat and thankful that I had the foresight to take it. It would have been all the evidence he needed to have us sent to the assizes.

John's singing alerts us to his return, a lilting tale of a witch turned hare that should, were it sung with any skill, melt the heart and strike the soul. A poor choice. Mangled by John's caterwauling, his once-sweet voice now cracking and lurching from a deep rumble to a sudden screech.

He bursts through the door, banging into the table and laughing, hiccupping. Hair falling over his face and carrying a stench of ale I've never smelled on him before. Clutched in his arms a pile of clothes that he waves at us as he did the lamb.

Mam runs out and casts her eye over the hill, then returns and slams the door, bolts it. Annie sits at the table, chin in hand, thumb in mouth, her legs swinging. Observing, untroubled. She knows nothing of drink or its effects, and I am glad for her innocence.

'Where did these come from?' I ask, though there can only be one answer.

'Stole,' John says, proudly, as though he has achieved a great feat. Once again he has risked his neck, risked us all. Now more than ever, we are vulnerable to the anger of the villagers. The protection we once had is gone, that much is clear. Reassuring anger blocks any pity. My fingers twitch for the feel of his face.

'Quietly, I said, lad, unseen if you must at all,' Mam says. 'Not to be thieving and supping in full view of the whole village, and bawling your way here with an armful of their wares. I told you of the new magistrate, of how we must go with care.' She bends over, presses a hand to her side.

John falls on to a stool, almost missing it, beams at her as though she has poured praise on him.

Annie's thumb pops out of her mouth and she looks from John to me, laughing. 'He's gone funny.'

Mam snatches the clothes, the boots flying to the ground, shakes them in his face. He tries to catch them, too slow, chuckles.

'What is all this?' she asks. 'What half-thought notion are you concocting now?'

He waves an arm at me, belches, blinks from under hair. 'Good enough for her, why not me?'

'You plan on wedding a farmer too?' Mam asks.

He wags a finger at her, shakes his head. 'No, no, no.' He leans forward on the stool, too far, rights himself. Annie giggles. 'Work,' he says.

Mam sits at the table, fingering the clothes. 'You've been given work?'

'Nay, but I shall. I'll put on the –' he flaps his hand at the clothes '– those. And I'll walk the village and I shall be given work and I'll take it, any work, whatever they offer. Like Sarah said. There'll be work for me.'

He sits back, triumphant, as Mam turns accusing eyes my way.

'You filled his head with this?' she asks.

'Nay, I didn't mean—'

She leans over John, shakes the clothes in his face. 'And did you think, fool of a lad, that you could stand in their thefted clothes and be offered work? With no skill to offer?'

'Then what's to become of me?' he yells. 'That I'll have nowt, be nowt. Thieving because there'll never be work for me, starving and watching you all wither when I am the man, I should be providing?'

Tears pour down his face, and he squeezes his eyes with finger and thumb. Annie creeps over, solemn now, and climbs on to his knee, arms around his neck, and he clings to her as though she is driftwood and he is drowning. Sobs shudder out of him. Try as I might to hold on to my anger, pity overwhelms it. I look at him and see my little brother, in despair, nothing more.

I crouch by his side, rub his heaving shoulder. 'It's all right, John,' I say. 'It will be better. It will be better for us all. Together. Soon.'

I believe it because I must. I will live and work as dairymaid, and my wage shall protect them. We will have a better life. Together.

Mam gives him the clothes, and he holds them to his face with his free hand like a babby does a blanket. She kneels, arms around us all, stroking any head she can find. No one moves.

This Bitter Seed

At last the day of the mop came. A fat and generous sun rose.

Daniel gathered what he needed and made to leave.

'Have all you need, son?' Father asked, rising from his seat. 'Know what you're looking for?'

Daniel tore his thoughts away from Gabriel, who sat at the table with one heavy finger trapping a spider by the leg while he slowly stripped it of the others. 'What? Yes.' He took out the full purse and shook it.

'Don't be distracted by a pretty face or—' Father made the shape of a woman's body in the air with his hands. Daniel coughed and looked away. The spider struggled to escape, remaining legs scrabbling and slipping on the table. 'Nothing wrong with a good, stout dairymaid. See how well our Bett has done us.'

Bett frowned and shook her head.

'I'll remember,' he said, trying to step through the door. Anxious to leave, for this new life to begin.

'And go gentle with the ale, you know what it's like at the mop, and the horse and cart doesn't drive so well when you've a bellyful.'

'Of course.' Though in fact he had only been to the mop once as a boy and knew little of it, just the stories told in the village of drinking and violence.

'Here,' Bett said, handing him a cloth filled with food. He waved his thanks, but she had already turned to Gabriel. 'Can't you leave that poor creature be, you brute?'

Gabriel looked up but kept his hold on the spider. 'It has no feelings, what does it matter?'

'Has more feelings than you,' Bett said, but under her breath, head bowed as she concentrated on placing a jug of ale in a basket.

Daniel hesitated in the doorway. He needed to be gone, or Sarah would be left waiting. But Bett's stand held him here.

'Can't you – surely you needn't be so cruel?' An appeal to Gabriel's charity that he knew was a mistake even as he spoke the words.

Gabriel glowered. 'What do you know? You, with all this?' He waved his free hand around the room. 'And you, with your husband warming your bed every night? What do you know about me?' He rose from his chair, at last releasing the spider and allowing its hobbling escape. 'Mam sickens, though I do all I can to care for her. And they, down there –' he waved a hand at the doorway '– they's all saying I'm a thief, things gone missing each night and Sam Finch saying he's had clothes stole and I see the way they're looking at me, and that new magistrate will have any thief dangling from the Hanging Tree. I hear the whispers but if there's thieving happening it's not me, and if they's planning on telling the magistrate I'll let another take the blame, like you said to, I'll gather a horde and we'll—'

'Enough, Gabriel,' Father said.

Daniel clenched a fist and bit down on his tongue to prevent himself raging at Gabriel and his stupidity, or Father for sowing this bitter seed in Gabriel's mind.

'There's no one here calling you a thief or anything else besides. Is there?' Father asked. He looked around at Daniel and Bett, who both shook their heads. A bully and a brute Daniel knew him to be, but not a thief. He must leave, before anger took hold.

'There,' Father said. 'See?'

Gabriel took his seat again, staring at the table and flicking crumbs on to the floor.

'I'll be off, then,' Daniel said. The only response came from Bett, catching his eye and giving a small nod. He stepped out into the warmth, the sound of the blackbird and scent of new grass. Soothed by the promise of what was to come. He broke into a run, changing path as he spied the parson loitering once again by the sheep field, waiting for him no doubt. He had not time for such blusterings today.

Blur and Shiver

It is another world. A world of enchantments and delights that souls such as mine were never meant to discover. Crowds of people as I've never dreamed. Children running, laughing, fingers and faces sticky with remnants of sweet treats. I walk among them, waiting for someone to see past these clothes, to point and taunt, to throw a stone.

Scents of ale and cooking meat mingle with those of so many bodies close together on a hot day. The air rings with the shouts of those selling their skills: girls carrying mops or pails, boys with crooks or a wisp of straw.

Daniel is at my side again, having paid a coin to stable Bonny and the cart for the day. He takes another from his purse, holds it in front of me, grins.

'Young lass,' he says. 'I wish to purchase your services as dairymaid, for which I offer this token payment as binding of our understanding, that you return with me to Taylors' farm and agree to work as such for a year to the day. If you find this arrangement to your satisfaction?'

I laugh, take the coin from him, drop a little curtsey. 'I do.'
I hold the coin, warm and gritty in my hand, unsure whether
it's actually mine. 'Is this how it's really done?'

'It is,' he says. 'The payment is yours now and a token of the
agreement on both parts.'

'Oh. Well, thank you.' I look around at the rise and fall of
the colourful crowds. 'Then should we go back?'

'Oh no,' he says. 'We've only just arrived. Besides, I need to
search more thoroughly. I may yet find a better milkmaid than
you. I may leave you here and take another back with me
instead.'

I skip ahead of him, waving the coin. 'Too late – the agreement's been made on both parts.'

'So it has. And what are you planning to buy? Shall we walk
about the stalls?'

I feel my eyes widen and see Daniel's smile in response.

He takes my hand. 'Come,' he says. 'Stay with me. And stop
waving that around, this place is full of pickpockets.'

I hide the coin in my closed fist, glance over my shoulder.
Though I know too well how hunger can tempt a body to
theft, we strive to live on the side of right, and I would not
have my first earnings taken from me.

Stalls line the edges of the marketplace, and it's here that the
smells of food come from, the shouts of the stallholders adver-
tising their wares. A small man, no taller than I, dressed in
clothes made of bright rags and with his head bare and garish
hat laid on the grass at his feet, throws and catches coloured
wooden skittles.

I pull Daniel towards a stand where jewellery is laid out –
fine rings gleaming in the sun, bands of polished stones and
wooden pendants carved into the shape of flowers or animals.

Leather purses and pouches. The village women wear such things sometimes but there's nothing like this in our house. Mam once wore a thin wedding band, but she sold it to a pedlar in exchange for a worn petticoat each for me and her, and a little food besides.

The woman at the stall watches us as we admire her wares. 'Trinket for your pretty lass, sir?' she asks.

'I've my own money,' I say. Honestly earned. At least, it will be.

'What better to spend your wage on?' she says. 'A bracelet, perhaps, for your sweet wrist?'

There's something about her gentle persistence, the toughened and chapped fingers that hold out the trinkets to me, that reminds me of Mam.

I pick out a polished leather case, perfect for John's knife, and pendant in the shape of a fox's head, the wood smooth under my finger, a light brown that is almost the right colour. 'Look at this,' I say, holding it out to Daniel.

'You like it?' he asks.

'Annie will love it, she spends all day scampering around the woods looking for spadgers and foxes and squirrels.'

He smiles. 'Anything else?'

I look again, head bowed over the frivolous objects laid out, fingers gliding over cool metal and hard stone. There's another pendant, it looks like a hare, the ears too large to be a rabbit, that I'm drawn to again and again. I feel the woman's eyes on me, feel she can read who this gift would be for, why the hare calls to me.

'She's a beauty, is she not?' she says. Her voice soft, sibilant. Like Mam's.

'Aye.' I take the pendant she holds out to me, staring so hard at the little hare that it seems to blur and shiver in my fingers, and I feel the spirit of Dew-Springer in it.

'A special animal, the hare. You could make no better choice.'

The heat of the day dries my mouth and soaks the back of my neck, makes my head feel as though it's about to float from my shoulders. In my palm the hare twitches and blinks.

The woman leans towards me, whispers. 'It is the right choice for her. The perfect gift.'

I look up at her so suddenly that the sky tilts to the side, the grass slides up towards me.

'Steady,' Daniel says, arm around my shoulder. 'You all right?'

I force myself to focus on his face. Shake my head a little. No whispers of mysterious understandings can be heard when he is here. 'Aye. I lost my balance.'

'All right.' He rubs my arm. 'Ox roast next, I think. You need to eat, yes? Shall you take these?'

I glance at the woman and her toothless smile. The fox and the hare, now perfectly still, a carved wooden pendant, no more. Yet I cannot leave without it. 'Please,' I say. Keep my voice light to show her this is nothing more to me than a pretty trinket.

'I want to take something home for them,' I say to Daniel. 'Something they'd never have.'

I wait in the cart, skin smarting from the day's sun.

Daniel returns at last from whatever business he left to take care of. He looks pleased with himself.

'Here,' he says, climbing up on to the cart and handing me a small parcel.

'What is it?'

'Something you would never have.'

I unwrap it and find a bracelet from the woman's stall, the stones small and glossy, all colours from so pale as to be almost translucent to the darkness of Bonny's shining coat. So pretty. I am torn between knowing what the selling of it would buy for my family, and wanting just one thing for myself. The stones are hard and cool against my skin as he rolls it on to my wrist and I expect it to feel unnatural, but it rests there comfortably, as though I was born to wear such things.

'For our new life,' he says.

'Thank you.'

I cradle the gifts in my hand, the smooth pendants, the hard leather case. Bonny stamps and the cart rocks. Daniel waits. Tonight I will not fall asleep to the sound of Annie's steady breathing, tomorrow will not wake to hear Mam rattling the embers. Will not keep check of John's wanderings.

Daniel places his hand over mine. 'You wish you were going home? There's still time,' he says gently. 'You can change your mind. I'll tell Father I could find no one suitable. He will be glad to save the money.'

I look to the hare, see if he'll give me an answer. He remains a piece of wood. 'When will I see them?'

'Sundays. After milking.'

Today is Tuesday. I cannot imagine the sun rising on Annie four times without me there to search her skin, though Mam has promised to do it in my place.

'But I will find a way for you to go more often,' he says.

'All right,' I say.

'Yes? You want to come?'

'Aye.' I blink away tears. I will be a milkmaid. Live on the farm, with Daniel and his father, earn my wage and bring it to my family. See them only on Sundays.

Daniel leans in, so close that I smell the straw scent of his skin. His lips, when they reach me, are warm and soft. There's nothing in the world but this.

He breaks off but remains close, head dipped against mine, breath on my cheek.

'Go then, why do you tarry?' I say. 'It's turning cold.'

Wavering Light

Bett came to greet them, dressed in her hat and neckerchief, ready for home.

'Well,' she said. 'You look born to those clothes now.'

'No more waddling,' Sarah said.

Bett's eyes flickered with amusement. Daniel walked around to lift Sarah to the ground but she had already jumped.

Bett stepped closer, glanced at him and then Sarah. 'I put another petticoat on your bed. Spare is good to have.'

'Thank you,' Sarah said. 'When I can I'll—'

Bett shook her head, scowling a little. 'No. It's a welcome gift. Nowt special. Do the same for any new milkmaid.'

They all knew that any other milkmaid would bring her own spare clothes. Daniel felt a brief urge to kiss her, though she would not approve, and thanked God that Father had seen fit to gift Bett so many of his mother's clothes. Her generosity would not leave her short.

'Well, I can't be dawdling here all night,' she said. 'In you go.'

Inside both fire and candles were lit, there was a smell of cooked meat and the dinner plates had been washed and cleared away. Father sat at the table with his ale and Gabriel stood in his cap, ready to leave. Daniel looked around, trying to see as for the first time. It was welcoming, as new homes go. Sarah stood in the doorway, her face cast into shadow so that he could not see her expression. Daniel swallowed and steadied himself. There was no turning back now.

'Step in, lass,' Father said in a voice so soft Daniel barely recognised it. 'Strange feeling to start anew, I know, but this is your home now. Do not be shy.'

Sarah stepped in, smiled at them. 'Thank you.'

Daniel waited for a shout of recognition to come. The moment stretched endlessly. He kept his eyes on her, and saw just a girl, a milkmaid, no different from any other but that he knew the chaos of light and dark that stormed through her, and had been drawn into it. Bett's warning spun through his mind. He had brought Sarah to the home of her enemy, and placed her in a worse situation than before. They would know her now, and all would be undone.

He waited. Nothing.

Gabriel cleared his throat, removed his hat and turned it in his hands. 'You are welcome to be here,' he said, glancing at Father's amused expression and raised eyebrows. 'Though it's not for me to say so, not being my home to offer.' Head down, he stepped towards the door. 'Lovely to have you here, miss. Meaning that, you are needed. By the cows.' He stopped in front of Sarah, blushing, peering at her face. 'Wait, we have not – have our paths crossed?'

Daniel's heart beat faster. Sarah stiffened, glancing at him. He laughed, as convincing as he could. 'Not – not possible, how could it be so?'

'Out, Gabriel,' Father said. 'Be off home.'

Gabriel shook his head and replaced his hat. 'Aye. Senseless notion. I'll be saying good evening.' He hurried out into the night.

'Well,' Father said. 'You must be hungry and tired. There's food saved and my son will show you to your room.' He emptied his tankard, placed it on the table and swallowed a belch. 'I shall be off to the tavern.'

Just he and Sarah, then, standing in the wavering light of the fire, listening to it snap, waiting as the sound of Father's footsteps receded. Sarah put her hands over her mouth, stifling laughter, and ran to him.

'Oh, I thought they'd know me,' she said.

'To them you will only ever be a dairymaid from another village.' His words were more confident than his spirit. Still, he willed this to be so, with all his being. All their plans depended on it. He removed her coif, pulled her hair from the pins until it fell over her shoulders as he had seen so often before. 'But not to me,' he said. 'Not me.'

Full-Moon Eyes

A new life, a new skin. Perhaps.

In the light of the candle I unlace the stays and strip off my shift with shaking hands, turn my side to the flame, lift the flesh as much as I can to be sure, scrutinise it.

The mark remains.

I look again, again. Run my fingers over the skin, though it's always been smooth, the stain just for the eyes.

Still marked, still chosen. I press back tears with my fists, hold at bay the flicker at the corner of my vision. I don't know why I thought that a different house, a new outfit would wash this fate from me. Relief and disappointment mingle. I must manage my powers with care, must ensure that the dog does not overwhelm and expose me as imposter.

I am still chosen, and I don't know how long my master will let me hide here before taking me over, even against my will. He may yet take Annie. I press my hands to my eyes but cannot force away the image of her little arm bearing his mark, of the magistrate casting his cold eye upon it and dragging her, them all, to the assizes. And after that … I beat my forehead with my fists, driving out thoughts of the rope.

Snarling shudders my bones. If so much as a whisper of harm strays their way I shall bear all the dark power I can muster down upon those responsible. Any that speaks of my family to Magistrate Wright shall suffer my wrath.

The gentle tap on the door can only be Daniel's. I pull my shift back on, lace the stays and call for him to enter.

'So,' he says softly. 'Do you like it?'

I look around the room that once was Bett's and now is mine. The same size as the one Annie, Mam and I sleep in, with a mat in the centre, a neatly folded petticoat lying on top of the thick blanket. Annie will be cold tonight without me there to warm her.

'It's lovely,' I say.

'It's small,' he says.

'Big enough for me.'

He sees through me. 'I think – you miss home, don't you?' he asks. 'Tomorrow you will go to them. There will be time, I'll make sure.'

'Thank you.'

He takes me in his arms. 'I'm happy you're here.'

'I'm happy to be here,' I say. And at this moment it's almost entirely true.

The bed is a large stack of hay tied together, it's thicker than I am used to and the blanket warmer. I am under the same roof as Daniel. I should sleep like an angel, but I cannot.

At home Sleep sails in on the sounds of Annie's steady breathing, even John's night-time snorts. Here there's only silence and she has no means to enter. I lie in my comfortable bed, relieved when sunlight fingers through the window and I may rise to be about my work.

Shift, stays, petticoat, shoes. The stays feel unnatural and stiff, the petticoat is bunched at the waist. Three attempts to pin my hair and it begins to loosen and fall already. Pull the coif on to my head, trying to feel the position that Bett set it in.

In the hall there hangs a round, polished plate. The house is silent yet and I allow myself to stop there. The girl stares back with large, blue eyes, face exposed by the pulling away of hair. Like any other village girl. More serious, perhaps. I wonder what she would think of me, had she been born to this.

Daniel's chin appears at her shoulder, his lips touch her cheek. She smiles, and is me again.

'Shall I come with you?' he asks. 'Help on your first day?'

'I can manage. Have you no task of your own, idle?'

'Yes,' he says, laughing. 'Though it's dung spreading and now I regret passing milking to you.'

'Too late. You must away to your dung and leave me be. I am very busy about my work.'

The sound of footsteps and Mr Taylor coughing the night's phlegm from his throat approaches.

'Yes, miss,' Daniel says, winking. 'Then I shall see you tonight, when we are done.'

The beasts seem larger now I'm alone with them; the horses baring their great teeth, the oxen cracking their horns. Even gentle Pippin, with her eyes like deep pools, seems bigger and clumsier.

I take a breath, smooth down my petticoat. I am Sarah, the dairymaid. Reaching for the stool and pail, I settle myself, set to my task. Soon enough, though once I almost slip from my seat and once Pippin prances and almost spills the milk, the bucket is filled and my first task complete. I would skip to the dairy were I not so weighed down by the results of my efforts.

I swing the linen parcel at my side, walk as fast as I can up the hill, though the rub of these shoes and warmth of my clothes hinder me. News of my day, my new life, brims, waiting to burst from me.

My timing is good, they're all sitting around the table, though it's sparsely covered. I've eaten more food today than they have to share between them.

Annie jumps up, runs to me and throws her arms around my waist, buries her head in my petticoat.

'All right, little cub,' I say, crouching so that I'm face to face with her. 'What news today?'

'Seth comed, he didn't need a cure but brought buttermilk and crammings, and he swinged me round and round and round.'

'Until the buttermilk and crammings returned,' John says.

'And the babby spadgers are learning to fly,' she says, skipping back to the table.

I follow her, placing down the parcel and unpacking the food. 'That's sweet,' I say.

Mam presses her toothless mouth to my cheek.

'See you've come just in time to eat our food,' John says, grinning.

'I brought my share.'

'Well,' Annie says, reaching across the table for a chunk of bread. 'It is sweet for the foxes when the birds learn to fly because they eat the ones that have fallen.' She takes a huge bite, pushes the mat of hair from her face, continues talking around the food bulging in her cheek. 'And today the one flapped and called, even while it was in the fox's teeth.' She uses both hands to shove the remaining bread into her already-full mouth, says something that I think is, 'And the mammy bird flapped around it and called and called.' Impossible to be sure, muffled as her words are.

She continues to chew, swallows, picks her teeth, oblivious to our stares. 'Can I have the cheese?' she asks, and I push it down the table to her.

When the meal is done I bring the gifts from my pocket, hesitant now to pass them out, as though I somehow set myself above them in doing so. Annie cups both her hands to take the pendant, full-moon eyes and mouth opened.

'It's so pretty,' she says.

'Here.' I place it around her neck. 'Like this.'

She dips her head, lifting the little fox to look at it. 'I'll wear it always and forever, and never not once take it off.'

John whistles through his teeth as I pass him the case, turns it in his hand. ''Tis not such a bad thing to have a worker in the family after all, then, even though it cannot be me.'

'Cannot yet be you,' I say.

He snorts in reply, reaches for his knife and slips it into the case. I can smell the leather from across the table.

It is Mam I'm most feared to pass my gift to, knowing her demand that all coming through the door must have a use. Here am I presenting a trinket.

She swallows as she takes the necklace, peering down at it in her rough palm. 'Oh, lass,' she says at last. 'You should not have wasted your earnings on an old crone like me.'

'No crone. Just my mam.'

She pats my cheek and I long to take her hand and keep it there always. 'It's beautiful,' she says, putting the necklace on. 'I shall wear it day and night and it will be like carrying you with me.'

I nod, embrace her. 'Has he been back?' I whisper. 'Wright?'

She shakes her head. 'Nay but – the stories I hear. The things they're saying he …' She catches sight of Annie watching and swallows her words.

'All will be well,' I say, though fear sickens me so, I can barely speak.

Mam smooths her hair. 'Aye. Now. Tell all of your new life.'

Gifts given and tales of the luxuries of life on the farm shared, I help Mam with her work. We crush dried camomile leaves and prepare a brew, for though Alice Turner has been released by the sprite that tormented her, she still suffers with wild thoughts and frequent fears, Mam says. As we stand together stirring leaves and water in the pot over the fire, I can let myself imagine for a moment that I did not leave, that tonight I'll lie with Annie curled at my side again.

But the light fades, and I know I must go. Annie and I take ash from the fire, sprinkle a ring around her mat, then I stand her by the open door to search her skin. Mam assures me she's done it, but I must see for myself.

She hops from foot to foot, hugging her skinny body. 'Too cold,' she says. 'Tarry till morning, look then.'

'I can't, Annie,' I say, prising her arms from her chest so I can turn them and search the underside.

'Why not?'

'I've to live at the farm now, remember?'

She is still, wet brown eyes turned to me so that I can barely look at her. 'But, why?'

'So that I can work, and bring you food. So that we may all have a better life.'

She crosses her arms, stamps a filthy foot. 'How is it better if you're not here?'

I pull her to me but she resists. 'Who will keep me safe?' she asks.

I swallow back tears, force my voice to come calm and steady. 'Mam will search for marks, John will ring the bell. You'll be safe.'

She does not meet my eye, nor even lift her face to look at me. Tears drip from her chin and leave little splashes on the dusty floor, and if each one were a drop of molten iron on my skin they could not pain me more.

I cannot stay. Mam holds me, cups my face, gives the same smile I gave to Annie. 'Proud of you, lass.' Even John pats my shoulder.

I kneel in front of Annie, take her in my arms. 'Farewell, little cub. I'll see you again very soon.'

She turns away and I leave, each step another pain to my heart.

I'm halfway down the hill when I hear the call. The wind thins and steals her voice, but I hear my name nonetheless, know it's her. She flies towards me, so fast that if I were not here to catch her she would run on forever.

She lands against me, thumping the air from my chest, almost knocking us both to the ground. I sink to the grass, holding on to her as though she'll float away if I let go. Her arms are tight around my neck, fingers taffled into the hair that has fallen loose from my coif, and I tell myself that it is for us both, for us all, that I must leave.

The Darkness that Broods

'Wickedness,' Magistrate Wright said. 'Buried in the very breast of this community, a viper deep in the heart of you.'

Every face turned to him, every breath held. He did not bellow, but the steady authority of his voice, the lance of his gaze entranced them all. A small man, thin-faced and spotless amongst the dust and hay of the barn, the weathered faces and ever-present odour of fish in the crowd before him. Magistrate Thompson, gluttonous in every way, had been replaced by a being different from him in all aspects. There had been rumours of his interests in the flesh, but only when the village caught him with Phyllis were they moved to act. Even now, many preferred the appetites of the old magistrate to the rigour of the new.

Daniel leaned against the wall, present in body but removed in spirit. He lost himself in thoughts of the white skin that ran below Sarah's shift, to the place where he had dared lay his hand only over her clothes. Of the wildness in her, the parts of her spirit she kept from him that he could never truly know, that both thrilled and disturbed him.

As if in reply to his sinful thoughts, when Daniel at last focused his eyes they fell upon Parson Walsh, standing at the edge of the crowd by the door. Quiet now, in contrast to his gregarious behaviour at the beginning of the evening, the minister's face was crumpled and he wrung his hands.

Daniel glanced at the magistrate.

'Papists,' he said. 'Hidden from sight, continuing with their rituals of abomination behind closed doors, but there are those among you who know of such happenings.' He paused long enough for his audience to begin shuffling and examining their hands under his accusing stare. 'And innocent you may be, and godly you may be in your own practices, but if you turn a blind eye to the work of the Devil through your neighbour then you are as sinful as he. And I in my duties to God and King and country must smoke out these traitors and bring them to justice, and you in yours must aid me.'

Daniel leaned forward a little, his stomach turning at each word, watching the furtive glances pass between those who called each other friend. Sam Finch, sunken-eyed and grey-skinned, stood a way apart from the fisherman Turner. Still, each let his eye slide to the other every so often, laden with guilt and suspicion.

'And worse than this: witchcraft. Suspicious happenings, with a want of any natural explanation. Beware the darkness that broods amongst you. Light your candles at night, leave a jar to ward off evil at your doors. If you do not turn this malevolence away then you invite it in. Come instead to me, the instrument of right, and light, the very means by which the King asserts his will to you.'

A movement at the open doorway, barely there but he saw because he waited for it, knew it to be Sarah passing on her return from the secret visit to her family. He slipped round the side of the barn, at the edge of the crowd who all were intent upon the words of the magistrate.

'Evil can bear the face of neighbour, friend, even family, those we trust, those we love,' he was saying. 'Look about you with sharp eyes. Those that hide wickedness become wicked. I call upon you to speak your suspicions in clear and honest voice and I will act. The only way to protect the innocent is to punish the guilty.'

Daniel had reached the door and already in his mind he and Sarah were at the river, her skin spilling warm beneath his hands. He made to step free of the barn and the foul words within, but these last held him. He had not attended when the brawling men were put in the stocks. Still, Gabriel's description of how folk had jeered, hurling rotten cabbage and stones, had been unavoidable.

'That lad Joshua fell to snivelling and calling out for his mammy by the end,' he had said as they shovelled dung. 'Little runt.'

'Poor lad,' Daniel said.

Gabriel snorted. 'It's well you're hid away from the village here, you're too soft for the lives of ordinary folk. There's a demon loose down there, one of they devils, I don't doubt, and each night changing form to a different animal, and bringing terrible fate to any it choose, and Sam and Nelly more than any, they's saying. He's not fit to work, even now.' He had stopped to wipe his brow. 'You should take more thought, all in the village is using witch marks and jars. Happen you'll need protection here too.'

Daniel had not dwelt on his words, convincing himself they were rooted in no more than Gabriel's hatred of the Haworths. But seeing the dread and suspicion the magistrate stirred tonight unnerved him. He felt more keenly the danger of his plan; should Sarah be exposed, the village would certainly condemn her as a witch, believing she had tricked them all.

Behind him, a shout of 'papist' rose, and the responding cry of fear and denial had him turning to see some scuffling. He did not recognise those involved.

At the edge of his eye that movement came again, the quiet shift of cloth at the doorway of the farmhouse. He hesitated, caught between his desire to protect, and the need to see Sarah. Parson Walsh hurried past, to where the commotion continued. One man, moving to protect the innocent.

Streak of Silt

I run along the edge of the water, laughing at the chill on my bare feet and legs. Daniel chases after, lifts and spins me round so that my toes make a circle of ripples.

He sets me down and I stand calf-deep, the bottom of my petticoat floating.

'Oh, look what you've done.' I strike his arm. 'I'm wet.'

'You're standing in the river, did you suppose you'd stay dry?'

'I held my clothes up, this is your doing, and on purpose, I think.'

'I beg your forgiveness, lady,' he says, smiling. 'If that is your wish, so be it.'

He kneels at my feet, gasping as the water hits his waist, and gathers my dripping petticoat, holds it up to me. Places his free hand on my bare leg, at the back of my knee. Turns his face up to me, and I look down at him, feel his touch warm through the cold water, calloused hand against smooth skin. We stay silent a moment.

I laugh. Take the wet cloth from him, slap his shoulder with it. Shaking just a little. 'Goffy,' I say.

'What?'

'You know – goffy. You're puddled.' He looks at me blankly. 'A fool,' I say.

'As I believe you've mentioned before.' He stands. 'You are in danger of repeating yourself.'

'Nay, you're the one in danger, for all this cheek.'

'I shall happily take the risk,' he says. Steps forward, arms around my waist, lips on mine. Body pressed against me, and he kisses me until I cannot breathe and no longer wish to, if only this can continue, and the blood races through me, warming my skin and beating through my head and I long to lie on the bank, pull him to me.

Sun rises and calls me from a content, comfortable sleep. I lace the stays and quickly tie the belt around my petticoat. Hold the pins in my teeth, twist hair into place and fasten it with a blind but expert hand, position the coif.

There is more to my life as dairymaid than I first thought; not just milking but also helping Bett with any work she chooses, from herding the geese to washing laundry in the beck. I relish each one, hoarding every new skill. Daniel has taught me to ride Bonny, even to swim, though I dare not go in deep. It is more than I ever imagined.

At meals I don't wait for invitation, but fill my bowl with pottage, so much richer than at home, and eat as the others do. As much as I desire, more than I need. A marvel to me, still.

'You're filling out,' Gabriel says as he waits in the doorway for Daniel to collect their basket of food. 'See how your cheeks have plumped.'

I glance at him, do not respond. Can barely disguise my aversion.

Mr Taylor snorts. 'That's not the kind of comment to appeal to a young lass.'

Gabriel looks confused, but perseveres. ''Tis a fine thing. Sign of a healthy girl, good appetite, ruddy cheeks.'

'Thank you,' I say. Glance at Daniel, but he's looking at Gabriel, frowning.

'So my mam says, anyway.' Gabriel's face is the colour of the turnip we ate last night.

'Does she?'

'Yes, the poor old crab. I shall never be free to leave her, as you have.' He laughs, and I know it's meant as a clumsy jest, but I'm assaulted with yearning for Mam, Annie and John, so strongly that I feel it ripple across my face.

'I'm sure Sarah misses her family,' Daniel says. 'And they her.' I smile, comforted not only by his words but also, to my shame, by Gabriel's miserable silence as he stares down at his hands.

'Well,' Mr Taylor says. 'Miss you they might, but they'll be glad of your wages when the year comes to an end.' Blood trickles from his nose.

'Oh,' I say. 'I can cure you of that.'

All heads turn to me and I remember, too late, that I am dairymaid not cunning folk here. Mr Taylor wipes his nose, but it continues to bleed.

'I – I saw it done, once. Far away in my own – in the parts where I dwelled.' I should stop, but it's too late. My knowledge is spoken. And even now, despite danger of discovery, there is pride in sharing it.

I gently tip his head forward, catch the drops of blood in my cupped hand. He is silent, doing my bidding. Gabriel gives an uncertain laugh. 'Well, lassie, how come you by such skills? It's almost like you're—'

Disquiet makes me short-tempered. 'I told you, I saw – I remember how it was done.' I look straight at Daniel. He sits pale and wide-eyed. Feared, and I know why, but I cannot stop now. 'Fetch me the shovel.'

He nods and together we kneel by the fire. He holds the shovel, I drip the blood into it. 'Hold it over the flame,' I say.

He does my bidding, though the shovel trembles in his grip. Soon the drops are dried to dust. Casting my eyes about, I spy Bett's goose-feather duster.

I catch Gabriel's eye and nod to it. 'Pluck me one of those.'

He laughs, glances from me to Mr Taylor, who simply shrugs. 'Aye, aye, all right,' Gabriel says, bringing me a feather. With care, as I've seen Mam do, I brush the dust on to the feather and, as Mr Taylor leans down when I bid him, blow it into his nose.

'There,' I say. 'You'll be cured while the first task's done.'

I look around at them. All three stare at me. Gabriel and Mr Taylor with bemusement, Daniel with something verging on terror.

'I – at least, that's how I think it was done. I saw it once.'

Mr Taylor reaches for his hat. 'Aye, well. Thank you, lass. But now, let's about our day.'

I hurry out, before Daniel can take me aside and question me. Happy to help Bett with the cheese. Gabriel runs to catch up with me before I can reach the dairy.

'That were a good trick,' he says.

'No trick. I saw it done.'

'I – I did not mean to offend,' he says. 'Before, when we were—'

'I know you did it without thought to.'

He takes off his cap and turns it in his hands, looking at me with a worried expression. I wish I could curse him again, to be away from here and never return. Drawing myself up I lift my chin, meet his eye, hoping he'll lose his nerve. Just as I faced him the day he hit me.

'Well, I – wait …' He stoops to peer at my face, narrows his eyes. 'Sometimes I could almost think that … We do not – know each other?'

His words thrill through me, a warning, and I fight the urge to leave. I should have stopped myself from curing Mr Taylor. 'How could we?'

He continues to squint at me. 'You almost make me think of—'

A flare inside me. The scent of ash, the flash of ember eyes. I should act the demure girl he thinks me to be, but I cannot. I know him; his cruelty, his vanity. The anger caged within me scratches to be released. He, who thought me unworthy of his scraps when in my rags and simpers at me now I appear respectable. I will not grant him the power to destroy me by letting my rage give me away. I hold the dog in check, a task more difficult each time it rises. Force myself to tip my head, smile at him.

He laughs, waves a hand. 'Of course, it could not be. You are a innocent and she were a—' He glances in the direction of the hill. 'Well. I shall not blemish your ear by speaking what she were.'

I shake my head a little as though confused and he backs away, waving his cap at me before replacing it. Hatred beats through me and I swallow the snarl in my throat, furious at myself for displaying such coyness in the face of his question-ing, furious at him for forcing it upon me.

Willing him away will not do. He is too close to knowing me and destroying all Daniel and I dream of. I need a more lasting plan, a permanent absence. I have the knowledge and skill to bring it about.

I will gather all I need later.

When at last I reach the cool of the dairy, Bett is unim-pressed. 'Where've you been at?'

I shrug. She has already prepared today's milk, and I hold the muslin so that she can pour it through, separating the curds and whey. I turn my head against the bitter stink, then hang the parcel and take down the curds from yesterday.

'You can manage this?' Bett asks.

'Aye.' I line the cheese press with muslin and put the curds in, squeezing out the last of the whey. Bett eyes me but says nothing, and so we work in silence as she wipes and turns the older cheeses, and I lean with my full weight, imagining it is Gabriel's head I press down upon.

A stain circles Annie's face, a ring of grime where the cloth Mam uses to wipe her does not reach, like the streak of silt left on the beach when the tide goes out. Her hair is damp and her cheeks pink from scrubbing; the fox necklace sits on top of her clothes. This has been done for my benefit. As though I am no longer part of the family, but a visitor.

She reaches her arms around me nonetheless, though not before rummaging through the food I've brought and taking the whispering shell Daniel found and sent for her. She turns it in her hands, holds it to her ear, mouth falling open in won-der. She's grown thinner again in the weeks I've been living

away, I'm feared to embrace her in case she breaks in my arms.
I need to come more often. To feed her. To keep my place in
their lives, as daughter, sister. To keep the dog at bay. Visitor I
am not and shall not be.

Mam too looks drawn and thin, though the weather warms
and there should be food enough to be found. There's something in the glittering intensity of her quick-flitting gaze, her
sinister whispers to Dew-Springer, that troubles me. I fear
Magistrate Wright has returned, but daren't ask in front of
Annie.

'You're busy with tonics, Mam?' I ask, sitting at the table
while Annie settles on my lap and takes another portion of
food. She smells of mud and fresh air. The house seems small,
drab and decayed. Fragile, leaning on the keck as it does. I am
used now to solid, straight walls. 'Many calling for an amatory
in summer, isn't it?'

'Happen they've all no need of my amatory, but let nature
do as it will. Like you.' She makes to sit with us, stands again,
turns her back and pokes at the dead fire. 'There's no appetite
for us wares in the village, the new magistrate has them all
feared to call upon me. Not one has asked for an enchantment
on the crops, as usually they would this time of year.'

I can hold my tongue no longer. 'He hasn't returned?'

She shakes her head. 'Bides his time. Waiting for good reason, happen.'

I pray she doesn't give him one. Does not walk the village
selling curses. Does not send John on missions of revenge upon
the netter. Open my mouth to say so, to brave the sharpness of
her reply.

'I'll give you more food,' I say. Cannot bring myself to challenge her on this day I feel myself a stranger here, this day I

remain plagued by Gabriel's questioning and the darkness it conjured in me.

'We've no need,' Mam says, without turning.

Annie almost chokes on the mouthful she's chewing, her eyes rounded with indignation. 'But – Mammy, we do, we do have need, Sarah. You'll not stop bringing food, will you?'

'Nay, of course not, cub,' I say, laughing. 'I'll have you stout and round so that you'll not even fit through the door.' I tickle her bony ribs and she squirms, giggles. Gone is the little fold of fat that had grown under her chin. 'Won't you have some, Mam?' I ask.

She stiffens, straightens. Wipes hair from her face and turns towards us. 'Perhaps just a mite.'

Sitting at the table, she pulls a small piece of bread from the loaf and places it in her mouth. In amongst the ashes behind her lies a patch that's discoloured. Burned and crumbled clay. I look around for the likeness of the netter, find nothing.

'Where's John?' I ask.

'In the village,' Annie says.

'Fetching water,' Mam adds quickly, though the pail sits in the corner behind her.

'Nay,' Annie says, frowning. 'In the village you said, sorting things out, is what you said.'

I understand immediately what this means. Once again Mam's fury at one that has hurt her own sends her spinning, embracing a path of revenge that threatens those she means to protect.

Annie turns to me, oblivious to the glare Mam gives her. 'I've to heft the water now I'm big, but only I've to wait for night, Mam says it's not safe in the daytime.'

One winter I pulled icicles from the roof and ate them until my belly stung and my mouth was numb. I've the same feeling now, looking at Mam's fevered eyes, thinking of what John is about in the village this moment, of Annie's spindly arms heaving the pail of water. Of the talk I hear from women washing their laundry in the beck with me, of witchcraft and evil acts they fear. Of how Magistrate Wright even questioned fisherman Shaw and his wife about Papism.

'Today I shall do it,' I say, walking past Mam to fetch the bucket.

I feel Mam's gaze on me all the way to the well, as though she's attached one of her seeing eyes to my back.

Still, I pause to gather the flowers I need, with their white blooms and mouse-like scent. The farmhand shall not go unpunished.

At the farmhouse I lie sleepless in my bed, as Gabriel's words spin through me, as I remember Annie's newly-cleaned face. As the dog purrs at my back, inviting me to embrace it. I am a Haworth and always shall be, no matter my clothes nor where I lay my head. Family, not visitor. I wish for a moment that Gabriel had known me earlier, that he could understand the girl he so admires now is the same one he despised and ridiculed before. My desire for his suffering outweighs even my fear of discovery, and the dog drives me on.

Silently, I rise and take the flowers, creep to the kitchen. The house creaks around me. No one stirs.

The stench is musty and sour as I crush them in a bowl, mix them to a paste. My heart patters and stutters, in time with the prowling of the dog. It will be easy. I shall lace his food. Or pierce a wild strawberry and smear the potion within, then offer it and he'll take it gladly. And he shall know me for who I really am, the respect he shows me as dairymaid shall be shown to my true self, before the end. And never shall he scorn me or my family again.

It's not a potion I've used before, nor even one I've seen Mam make, but she has told me of it should I have desperate need and I know the effect it will have. She has taught me well. He shall suffer spasms and his limbs shall set until he cannot move. Before long his breath will be stopped forever.

I hold the bowl, stare down at the potion I can barely see past the hackles and teeth and burning eyes that obscure my vision, that fill my mind and beat through my body. I stand this way as my feet numb on the cold floor, as my fingers stiffen from hours of gripping, and the dog, little by little, recedes until I'm free. I stand all night.

The sun has almost risen when at last I step outside, tip the paste away and wipe down the bowl. Return to my room and dress; pin my hair, place my coif, pull on my stockings. Wear once more the costume that hides me, and keeps me safe.

Turning of the Air

It was sheep-washing day. Daniel shivered with cold, despite the warmth of the June sun on the back of his neck, soaked as he was from standing in the river. His hands were red-raw and aching from hours of washing and gripping struggling, water-logged sheep. The buzz and bite of insects was ceaseless.

Released by Gabriel's need to take a piss, Daniel staggered to the bank and gulped down some of the posset Bett always prepared for this task, the milk still warm, the ale and spice spreading much-needed heat. His shoulders ached from the constant bending and the skin on his hands was loose and wrinkled.

'Ah, there's the lad himself,' Gabriel said, though they had worked together all morning, slapping Daniel on the back. Too hard, voice straining to achieve jollity.

It was not the words but the false tone that stopped Daniel mid-swallow. He shaded his eyes to see Gabriel's face, twisted into an unaccustomed smile.

'You – you're wanting to carry on?' he asked.

'I ah – no, no. Just thinking we can speak a little.' Gabriel cleared his throat, glanced to the sky and then back again. 'Man to man, like.'

Nothing in Daniel's experience of Gabriel had prepared him for such words. He adjusted his expression from astonishment to mild interest.

'I stopped to take the posset,' he said.

Gabriel nodded. 'I will join you.'

Blinking in the shade, they sat under a tree, each looking carefully at his own flagon. Only the faint sound of the sheep chewing as they dried in the sun.

'Still tupping that lass, are ye?' Gabriel asked at last.

Daniel met his eye, said nothing. God had intended this soul to inhabit a boar or bull, surely. He was not fit to carry the body of a man.

Under the steadiness of Daniel's stare Gabriel flushed, took a gulp of drink and wiped his mouth. Belched quietly. Jiggled his right leg.

Daniel drank his fill of the posset, stood and brushed down his breeches.

'Dairymaid's a pretty little bantam,' Gabriel said.

Daniel stopped. He felt the ground shift beneath him.

'The – Sarah?'

'Aye. There's something about her.'

Daniel's breath stuck in his throat like straw and he remembered how Gabriel had felt he recognised Sarah when she first came to the farm. Did he know?

Gabriel downed his drink, placed the flagon back. 'Think she'd look at the likes of me?'

Daniel waited, taking in the words, letting his mind catch up with their meaning. Was this a trick? There was an uncomfortable sincerity in Gabriel's expression. He spoke the truth, Daniel knew it, though he hardly dared to trust it.

There was such naked yearning in Gabriel's eyes that Daniel was moved to pity. Even now.

'I've had lasses before,' Gabriel said, lifting his chin, 'many a time, I'm no innocent.'

'I – I do not doubt it.'

'But now I'm thought to take a wife.'

Daniel shook out his shoulders, cleared his throat, relieved.

'I know my way around the cockles, I'll not be asking a whelp like you about that,' Gabriel said, leaning forward, hands clenched. 'Not be asking any man about that.'

Daniel quelled the image this brought to his mind. Gabriel was sweating, face the colour of a setting sun. Daniel could see that each word pained him like a hot ember on the tongue. Yet he persevered. 'I've seen you with her,' he said.

Daniel waited to hear what Gabriel said next before refuting this. Still on edge. Watched the oldest ewe, the one destined for the midsummer feast, shake herself free of water and close her eyes against the sun.

'Talking. She smiles when you speak with her. She never smiles at me. I need to know what to say.'

He looked at Daniel, waited, daring him to mock.

'I'm sure you have no need of my help,' he said carefully.

Gabriel scowled and waved away a cloud of midges. 'I've just asked for it.'

'She is a modest girl,' Daniel said. 'Reserved. She would need approaching gently.'

'Quiet, like?'

'Yes. Like an unknown animal.'

Gabriel thumped one of his fists lightly on the ground. 'All right, then. I can do that.'

He rose and bent to place his lips by Daniel's ear.

'You'll speak of this to no one.'

It was not a request.

Daniel remained standing, watching Gabriel haul another sheep to the water. He did not know why his advice had been truthful. Because he was certain of Sarah's loathing for Gabriel, perhaps, or relief that they remained undiscovered. Or because he simply could do no other.

The magistrate's shoes tapped as he walked across the yard to the house. The cleanest the farm had ever seen, and Daniel did not know how he avoided the dust and dung that covered the ground. He was silent as he entered the kitchen, lifting his eyes to search the corners for cobwebs, running his finger along the wall, where Bett scowled.

'Won't you take a seat?' Father asked. 'There's plenty food left if you're hungry.'

'I shall not, thank you.'

'Then how can we help you, Magistrate Wright? Are you in need of another meeting?'

'It may well come to that,' he said. 'For there is disturbing news from the village and I am concerned regarding a family there, the Shaws? You know of them?'

Father rose. 'He's a fisherman, is he not? He seems an honest—'

The magistrate lifted a hand, silencing him. 'I do not need the man's history, I am wondering if you see them at church, that is all.'

Daniel opened his mouth, about to defend the Shaws, but as he thought, he could not recall having seen them in church. His instinct to protect was silenced by his fear of speaking untruths where God was concerned.

'I have heard tell they were not present even for the Easter service? They held their own – celebration?' The magistrate's gaze bore down.

Gabriel began to shake his head, but Father threw him a warning glance. 'I'm sure they were – I couldn't rightly say,' Father said. 'Perhaps the parson …?'

'Parson Walsh has been less forthcoming than I had hoped. There is also another matter you may know of. Concerning the netter.' He strode around the room, turning the pans that hung on the wall, peering into the trough. Bett folded her arms and glared at him.

'S–Sam Finch?' The brute who had lost a tooth to Sarah's brother's fist. Unease flickered.

'Indeed. A sad spate of ill events have befallen him – his entirety of food souring while he was about prayer at church last Sunday, the sufferings of he and his wife with sickness and inflaming of the skin – that cannot be laid down to poor luck. There is an evil hand at work, I fear, and I know that Master Gabriel here spoke of a bad grace towards him by a certain family in the past?'

He spoke of fear and yet it was something else that Daniel saw in him: appetite.

'Aye,' Gabriel said, standing so quickly that his chair scraped along the floor. 'Aye, I can help you out there for certain, there's a bad blood flowing towards the Finches from that family up the cursed hill.'

'Just – only one incident,' Daniel said, before Gabriel had even reached the end of the last word. He laughed, trying to show how trifling an occurrence it had been. He was met with silence. 'No more than a squabble, surely?'

Gabriel snorted. 'Happen it was more a attempt at murder by that Devil-boy.'

Daniel kept his eye on the magistrate. Surely a gleam of elation in his eye at the word Devil. He stepped to the fire, glanced into the pot that hung above it, stirring the contents and lifting the spoon to his nose. He grimaced. Daniel did not dare look to see Bett's reaction.

'You distort it, Gabriel,' he said. Gabriel looked at him in surprise, and anger.

'Yes, and you're not so slow to use your own fists when provoked,' Bett said.

Again Daniel felt the most extraordinary urge to kiss her.

Father snapped his fingers and pointed. 'You overstep, lass. Be gone to your own hearth and return tomorrow with a sweeter tongue.'

For a moment Daniel thought she might argue, but she merely walked to fetch her neckerchief and left. The magistrate stepped aside as she passed, as though she carried some contamination.

'I apologise,' Father said. 'She has been with us a long time, sometimes I think she supposes to be more daughter than housemaid.'

'You have been too lax with her, perhaps,' the magistrate said. 'This has indeed been of use. There is a turning of the air, a wickedness riding in on the breeze, that you would do well to prepare for, I fear.'

Again that word, though he betrayed nothing of the sort.

He turned to the door, and then back, as though with an afterthought. 'Oh, I hear you have a new dairymaid not from these parts.'

Daniel's heart gave a sharp kick and he could not be sure he did not cry out aloud.

'I should like to meet her.'

'She has retired to her room,' Father said.

'Nevertheless.'

Daniel began to rise, praying that Sarah had not left to visit her family, but Father said, 'Gabriel, bring Sarah to join us.'

Gabriel was gone before Daniel could speak.

'Ah,' the magistrate said as Sarah appeared. He took her arm and led her to the light spilled by the fire, fingered the edge of her coif, tipped her chin to inspect her face, lifted her petticoat just a little and peered at the tips of her shoes. Her trembling showed in her clothes but she kept her expression obstinately calm.

Gabriel stepped forward, then checked himself. Father glanced at Daniel, gave a frown and slight shrug.

'I see,' the magistrate said, turning to Father. 'You are satisfied with this one?'

'Oh, indeed,' Father said. 'A good little worker.' He smiled at Sarah, though she did not return it, just slid her wide eyes to him.

'Very well,' the magistrate said. 'Then I shall leave you for now. Remember, light your candles. I see you have no witch jar yet. Do not tarry.'

The door had barely closed when Father gave a loud burst of laughter, looking at each of them in turn.

'Well, I've never seen the like. Poor little lassie, I would not have batted an eye had he opened your mouth and counted the teeth.'

'Had he laid another finger on you I'd have split his face,' Gabriel said.

Sarah smiled at Father, ignored Gabriel.

'Should you like to return to your room?' Daniel asked.

He stood, placed a hand on the small of her back and led her away. Still shaking.

Garlanded with Leaf and Flower

Not yet light when I'm woken by a fist hammering on my door. For a moment I think I'm at home, with Annie by my side, and fear the crowd has come to attack. A dream of Magistrate Wright, leaning down and whispering that he knows my real name, clings to my mind.

At the edge of my eye, shadow flickers. I try to swallow the taste of ash, cannot rid myself of the sight of the dog's eyes. Words fall from my lips in a whisper, unknown yet familiar, a call upon dark forces to bring suffering to the one that threatens us. I cannot stop. The power I've embraced seethes through me, beyond my will or bidding, bringing with it both exhilaration and terror.

The rap on the door comes again, thrusting me back to the world around me, releasing me from the grip of darkness. Bett pokes her head into my room.

'Up, lassie, work to be done.'

Then she's gone. Scrambling into my clothes, remembering the warm, dry touch of the magistrate's hand, I follow the sounds of her raking the ashes and thudding pots on to the table.

'Busy, busy, busy,' Bett sings as she heats water and surveys the carnival of food – two legs of mutton, bread, elderflowers, milk, cream and cheese. This would feed my family for months.

'The best night of the year, and the busiest day to prepare. Never before have I had another pair of hands to help me out.' She frowns when she catches me hiding a yawn. 'And not much use your hands will be if your head's still a-bed – wake up, lass, get yourself to the garden.'

And so begins a day like I've never known. First I pick gooseberries, whitecurrants and apothecary roses. The petals are used for salads and rosewater, but I keep back a few to give to Mam, for those that may need the spirits brightened.

Bett keeps me busy with chopping, boiling, stirring, pouring, as well as my own tasks of milking, turning and wiping the cheese, collecting eggs. All the while she is full of instruction, giddy with anticipation. I'm grateful for the work, to fill my mind and steady my hands.

'What happens at the festival?' I ask, adding gooseberries to the pot where one of the mutton legs cooks. The scent of herbs and meat so rich that I want to take the spoon and have at it.

She turns from stirring the sops in wine. 'It'll be a rampage not a festival, if we don't have this fare prepared in time.'

I can almost taste the food already. This mutton will be cooked until it falls from the bone. I lick my lips.

'But midsummer's the best night, with the fire and everyone comes, and all the feasting and dancing and wine.' Bett looks over her shoulder, wipes her red face. 'You will think you've been swept to heaven, and to have made the food and see the whole village enjoy it – worth every drop of sweat.'

She presses her hand to her back and groans. I glance around. We're alone.

'There's nowt so healing as the midsummer sun,' I say. 'Away outside and close your eyes, turn until the sun falls upon the part that ails you. You'll be cured while the sun sets.'

She scratches under her coif, frowning. 'I've no time for healing now, too busy for midsummer sun. On with your tasks. Too much tattling.'

Then, with her back now turned and just as I'm raising the spoon to my lip, 'And don't eat it.'

We work all day and at last, as shadows lengthen and sunlight ripens, the food is ready. Bett and I begin to carry it to the fallow field where the men are laying out the fire, sleeves rolled up and hair damp with sweat.

Daniel winks at me and heat rises in my face. Even now, though I see him daily, though our plans of a life together are set. The days of standing in the sun washing and shearing sheep have browned him, blue eyes bright against burnished skin.

Bett clears her throat and looks away. 'Enough time for that later – set to it, lass.'

I keep to the edge of the crowd as the magistrate holds the flame. He watches it intently, and I think he would not be inclined to notice me at this moment, but after his inspection I take extra care. I wear no coif but the white campion Bett twined in my hair and my new clothes still disguise me. But is it a mistake to put myself in the way of others? The cunning woman's daughter has no place here.

He puts the flame to the wood and it begins to blaze and spark. A cry goes up from the villagers, the fiddlers play and there is some jostling around the food and ale. Boys jump through the fire's cleansing smoke. I watch the children, garlanded with leaf and flower, dancing hand in hand, running and laughing, sitting in the grass with their shoes off, eating food by the handful.

One day this will be Annie. Next year, perhaps. I'll dress her in ribbons and plait her hair and she shall play with her friends rather than the spirits lurking in the plague hamlet. So long as she remains unmarked, her unblemished skin is proof of her innocence. We're done hiding her from the lascivious eye of the last magistrate, but must now protect her from a whole new cruelty.

Bett presses a small cup of wine into my hand. It is not my first. She wears buttercups around a straw hat and clasps the arm of a tall man.

'Your food is fit after all, so you have earned a drink.' She looks up to the man, who raises his eyebrows at me. 'You should have seen the mess she made.'

He laughs. 'I pity you, lass, for she's a hard taskmaster. As I know to my cost.'

'Oh, and there was I thinking I was your love,' Bett says.

'You are, heart-root.' He dips his head to kiss her cheek.

Bett away from the farm is sweeter, softer. This I already know, but seeing her with her husband is like seeing a thistle transformed to a daisy.

She looks at me. 'Sorry. A glass or two of cider and he thinks we're still courting.'

The wine is sharp and slightly spiced in my mouth, warm in my stomach. 'I'm so happy.'

'All right, go steady with that, will you?'

Nathaniel tugs gently on Bett's arm, leading her towards the circle of dancers. She pulls against him for a moment, clasps my hand and squeezes it.

'Enjoy yourself, lassie. But remember not to bring attention on yourself, aye? Keep yourself quiet, stay at the edge of the crowd. Should anyone know you, they'll accuse you of trickery and worse.'

I understand her words. Wine prevents me from feeling them.

The jig the fiddlers play is fast and though I'm sure I cannot dance my body sways and feet pat in time to the music. It brings delight but also something more – a memory of John's sweet voice when he was a lad, a sudden yearning to see him here, carefree and dancing. Never have we been part of such a joyful gathering. I watch as all laugh and talk and dance. All except Phyllis Ross, who stands by the food, watching, keeping space between herself and all that come near her.

I know it was she Magistrate Thompson took in the woods, the story was whispered to me the first time I joined the women washing clothes. She seems but a slip of a lass. I've tried to protest her innocence, as much as a newcomer can, but none will listen.

Across the crowd I look for Daniel, who of all in the village will surely offer her a kind word, but once more find myself facing Gabriel.

'Oh, I brought you wine,' he says, holding out the cup as if to prove the truth of his words. It looks absurdly small clasped in his great, meaty fist.

'I've some already.'

'Yes, I see.'

I look past him. Somewhere nearby is Daniel.

He clears his throat, stands awkwardly holding the wine and his cider. 'You are a timid lass,' he says.

'I am not.'

'No, no, not timid, I misspoke. I mean, that is, you are – a innocent.'

He calls me whore when in my rags, innocent when dressed like any other girl. 'Really you do not know me so well as to pronounce my character,' I say.

'But I should like to.'

'Why?'

He shifts his weight, goes to lift his cap and spills wine down his tunic, curses quietly. Sweat balls and trickles down his cheek. He squints into the setting sun, then back at me. Clears his throat again. 'I have not the pretty words you deserve, but to see you there all the time, with those eyes and your—' He gestures towards me, spilling more wine. 'And I a farm worker and you a dairymaid, it's clear that …'

His voice peters out. Were it not for the taste of his thumb still on my tongue, his fist on my cheek, I might pity his stumbling advances. I stare him down, made bold by wine and anger, until he hangs his head and I've the satisfaction of watching colour spread over his face.

Past him I see Daniel, and call out to him. He glances at Gabriel, hesitates, then walks over.

Gabriel looks at me miserably, and walks away. I am filled with momentary pity, and must remind myself of the brute he is.

'Shall you dance?' Daniel asks.

'Oh I – don't know that I can.'

He takes my empty drink, throws it to the grass and pulls me, laughing and protesting, to the circle by the fire. And I am moving, my head filled with music. The warmth of flames on my face, the voices of those around me. Daniel's hand in mine. We dance on and on, until we can barely breathe.

If only my family could be part of this. If only the fear of discovery did not lurk in the shadows. Then I would have crossed the river, to become the new Sarah.

As the music slows, so do we. Daniel leans so close I feel his lips against my neck. 'Come with me,' he whispers.

We break away as the music begins again, run from the light and the faces towards the darkness that hides us. His hand in mine. Once, I turn back to see if anyone watches. Gabriel looks towards us but he's talking to the blacksmith's daughter and I don't think he notices us leave.

Other lovers will be in the woods, but I know already where he's taking me. We've barely reached the riverbank when we stumble to a stop, hands still clasped. The air is cooler here and I feel the heat of his skin, step closer.

His chest heaves from dancing and running. He lifts a strand of my hair, entwined with flowers, shakes his head a little. 'You look beautiful tonight. You're always beautiful.'

He presses his lips to my own, tasting of ale and the sweet pudding I made earlier, and he kisses me so that I feel he will not ever stop. I don't ever want to stop.

The ground rough beneath me, the river babbling in the night. And us. Nothing more. I want this, I know I want it with every part of me, only here and only him. Daniel pushing my petticoat higher. My breath coming faster. Yet my hands shake as I unlace his tunic, I'm clumsy, tangle the ties. He breaks off, looks down at the mess I'm making, laughs.

'Here, let me,' he says, sitting back, unpicking the knots. 'There.' He strokes my face. 'Are you happy?'

'So happy.'

His smile fades and he drops his head. I know why. I sit up, place my hand on his tunic. 'Are you not?' I ask.

'No, I am.' He laughs a little. 'I couldn't be more – it's you, and you're so beautiful. It's just, I – we are not yet wed and – to sin this way.'

I should free him, cover myself, catch my breath and walk away. But I cannot. The yearning is too great to let him go so easily. 'We shall be married,' I say. 'We'll have our house and you shall farm and we will have that life, Daniel. God knows that we shall.'

'And you will bake the bread.'

'And we'll dance and –'

We speak together, laughing. '– and eat flawn.'

I lie back down. He follows. 'God knows we shall be wed,' he says.

'Then it's not such a sin,' I say. Though really, just now, I don't care if it is.

Crisp and Brittle

As Father drank ale at the table, Daniel made an excuse and stole into his room. Stepping lightly, straining to listen for footsteps. His mother's nightshift lying on the bed, worn thin in patches where Father had rubbed it between finger and thumb, held it to his nose and wept into it, like a child with a blanket. She had been gone twenty-two years. There could be no trace of her left in it, yet he would not relinquish her shift, nor her place to another.

Daniel took the key, as he had once before, turned it and winced at the creak of old leather as he lifted the lid. The ring, he knew, was tied by a ribbon threaded through the lace of her wedding gloves. He felt no guilt. It was to come to him, Father had told him so on his sixteenth birthday. Soaked with ale and tears, he had opened the trunk and shown Daniel the ring, promised that were he to find a girl worthy, one that he could love as Father had loved, he was free to offer it to her.

Daniel knew that he had.

All day he had carried a soft-spun happiness, for what he had spent each waking and dreaming moment imagining had come, and they were together, and always would be. He had been woken by the chill of fine rain but cared not, for he was with Sarah, and there could be no sweeter start to the day.

She had sat forward, hand clutched to her side, back turned to him as she reached for her clothes.

He placed his hand on hers. 'Show me.'

Her fingers had loosened just enough for him to lift them. The mark she hid was dark red, as big as his thumbnail, flat against her white skin.

'Is that it?' he'd asked. 'It – it's just a birthmark, it's nothing.'

'The mark doesn't trouble me,' she said. Tears standing in her eyes. He had not seen her like this. 'But what it means.'

He took her hands, pulled her to him, kissed her. 'There is no meaning to it. I've seen the like on calves and pups and piglets. Just a mark on your skin.'

She had given a smile he wished he could believe. 'Aye, you're right. I'm sure you're right.'

When they parted, he had felt the strip of his skin where they touched was peeled off and taken with her.

In the yard Gabriel had grabbed him by the tunic and hauled him to the shelter of the orchard.

'You took her away,' he said, flicking a chunk of damp hair from his eyes. 'Didn't you? The dairymaid, and you knew I'd my eye on her, I was just warming her up and you took her away.'

'She – you walked away, you were done.'

Gabriel brought his face in close. 'If she was not lying under me in the woods, I was not done.'

A brutal image had entered Daniel's mind and would not be gone, no matter how he pressed his eyelids together and concentrated on the drip of water through leaves.

'Were she not such a innocent and you not such a whelp, I'd be thinking it was she you were tupping through the night.'

Daniel had forced out an unconvincing laugh. Breathed in the scent of air washed clean. 'Enough trouble to manage one girl, and the talk of sweethearts and what's to come, eh?' He slapped Gabriel on the arm. 'Couldn't begin to take on another. Eh?'

The frown had lifted slowly from Gabriel's features.

'And, as you say,' he ploughed on, rain seeping through his tunic, 'she is not the kind to go lying in the woods with no promise made, I think.'

'Not with the likes of you, anyhow,' Gabriel said, shrugging. 'Still, you took her from me. So if you're wanting to know who I lay with last night, it was your little blacksmith girl. Split her like a gutted fish, and she was begging me not to stop.'

Daniel had stared, sickened.

He shook his head now, freeing himself of the memory. Calmly, carefully he took out a petticoat and apron from the trunk until he found the wedding gloves. Faded and smelling of dust and mildew, crisp and brittle so that he feared they might crumble in his fingers, he lifted them and worked on the knot in the ribbon. Wondered at the woman who had worn them, who had never held him as a babe or washed the dirt from his knees.

At last he freed the ring. A simple gold band. Tiny, so that he could barely make out the words engraved on the inside: *Love me and leave me not*. He brought to mind Sarah's small hands, her narrow, chapped fingers; he was sure it would fit.

Trinket

I am breathless when I reach the house, having marched up the hill as fast as I can, preparing what to say to Mam. How she'll respond I cannot guess – with kindness or anger, depending on her mood. I've no choice but to face either.

Bitter scent of henbane lingers as I step in. Seth has been, once again in need of Mam's offerings. I pick my time well; he is gone when I arrive, Annie in the woods and John away, though when I ask where, Mam just shrugs and replies that he's busy. I have not time for the flare of fear this would usually spark in me.

Her gaze alights on the ring glinting on my finger as soon as I step in, and she grabs my hand, examines it.

'What's this trinket?' she asks.

'No trinket, Mam.' Sweat prickles my skin. I don't know why. This is proof I was right and she wrong. Her eyes take in my face like birds scratching for scraps.

'Are you telling me there's been a wedding?'

'Not yet,' I say.

She drops my hand. "Tis just a trinket, then.'

'We will be married,' I say. The truth of it chimes through my voice.

She looks at me, eyes narrowed. 'Got yourself in trouble, haven't you, lassie?'

I ignore the heat creeping over my cheeks. 'No trouble.'

She watches me. I wait, fiddle with the cloth of my petticoat, stones at my wrist, ring on my finger.

'At least, I don't think there'll be trouble,' I say. 'We've only just—'

She steps forward, jerks her arms out, so suddenly and with such force that I flinch.

'Well, don't stand there gormless, lass,' she says. 'You know where the parsley and tearthumb are kept. I'll set the water on.'

The brew is one I've not tasted before. An underlying bitterness, tongue scorched as I swallow. We sit at the table, and were it another drink we could be just mother and daughter, sharing stories of nothing.

'When will you know?' she asks.

I think. 'While the next full moon.'

'You'd best take some with you. But just know, it will fail, in the end. This won't always keep you safe.' She clasps the hare pendant in her hand, rubs her thumb over the smooth wood.

I swallow the last mouthful, grimacing at the grainy sourness. Nod. But I can only hope it keeps me safe long enough. We've discovered a new way of living and there's no undoing it now.

She reaches across the table, places her hand on my arm. 'Whatever happens, this is where you dwell. Always. You know that, don't you?'

I put the cup down, glad now I've drunk its contents for I could not swallow another thing, my throat is full. Grasp her hands. 'I know, Mam.'

She squeezes my fingers, gives her head a little shake. 'Well, now. Tell me of the fine life you have there, eh? I want to hear all—'

The door opens and Annie tears in, launching herself on to Mam's lap, sobbing. We glance at each other over her head. An orphaned fox cub or some suchlike, I expect. I hope.

Eventually, her words become clear, though sodden with grief.

'The lassie,' she says. 'The lassie's dangling in the woods.'

We run silently, the three of us. Annie leading the way, faster than I've ever seen her, pulling Mam by the hand.

The feet are level with my knees. Not so far from the ground that kept her safe.

Around her neck, and tied to the branch above, a strip of cloth torn from a sheet. Staring blankly down at us her bloated, blackened face. Tongue swollen like a rotting fish.

Hers was not a quick death. Not merciful. She will have swung and choked before life drained away, with not even a kind soul to pull on her legs and break her neck.

Tear tracks still, on those bruised cheeks.

Mam moves slowly, weighed by the horror of what we have just seen. She wraps the neckerchief around me, as though I were a child, and presses the package of petals into my hand. Cups my face and kisses my cheek.

'Tell only one you trust,' she says. 'Say nowt of us, we cannot be tied to this. And let it be known another discovered her, not you. You mustn't be found out now.'

I embrace her briefly and bend to Annie. She's folded herself in Mam's petticoat, sucking her thumb. Small, brown eyes peer out at me.

I kiss her cheek. A little plumper than before.

'Mammy will keep you safe,' I say. 'The lassie's resting now.'

'Poor thing,' Mam says as I straighten up. 'Her soul will tread that wood with the others.'

He is stabling the animals and I am grateful, for there's no other here I must put on an act for. One look at my face and he frowns, steps forward and takes me in his arms.

'Phyllis,' I say. 'Phyllis hanged herself in the woods.'

Crescent of the Whole

Daniel counted the tolls of the passing bell. Six for a woman, and then one for each year Phyllis lived. Fourteen.

They always offered the horse and cart for funerals, and so here he stood once again, looking into the faces of the bewildered and sorrow-stricken. Phyllis's mother leaned forward, grasped his hand. So close, he could count the new furrows and contours marking her in the days since her daughter's death.

'She did not give herself to him, you know. She was not willing,' she said.

The sight of Phyllis's tearful face that night in the woods would plague him always. 'I know.'

She stepped closer, cold hands gripping his. Tears flooded and fell. 'It was when the second bleed didn't come,' she said. He could not tell if she nodded, or simply shook so violently in her grief.

'Mary,' Phyllis's father called, frowning. He strode over, took her by the arm and led her away. He looked over his shoulder at Daniel. 'She's mad with the loss of her,' he said. 'Speaks not a word of sense.'

Daniel took his place in the line of villagers that would follow the cart to the graveyard. Glad of the darkness to hide him, glad of the candle to protect from returning spirits. Glancing back he found Sarah, part of the procession for the first time, coif bright in the moonlight, Bett at her side.

It was not usual to retire to the barn after a burial.

There were no biscuits offered, no wine, only a gathering of the sober and sorrowful. Magistrate Wright's suggestion. He resumed his position from the last gathering, standing high and precarious on a sheaf at the front of the crowd.

'It is a sad event that brings us here,' he said. 'The tragic perishing of a young spirit, and one that is a great loss to her family, to the village.' Sobbing from Phyllis's family. 'But we must not turn blind to the unsavoury happenings that played a part in this, brought about by her own female failing and womanly wantonness.'

Daniel's breath caught in his throat. He waited as the magistrate looked around. Though every person in the village knew Phyllis's death was chosen, and unnatural in every way, the story that had been told to and accepted by Parson Walsh was of a calamitous accident. His voice had cracked with sorrow during the service. He would, surely, deafen his ears to any contradiction even, Daniel hoped, from the mouth of the law itself.

'All you who are parents, all you who have standing in this village, the duty is yours to lead the way, to light the path of purity with your own model. I see the wickedness that shrouds you, lurking like a fog. Your catches will dry and your children starve at the evil hand you invite in.'

Daniel shifted, kept his eye on Sarah. Could see nothing of her face. He longed to be at the river with her in his arms, on a day just past, when Phyllis was still living and he not sullied by the guilt and despair of her death. Only Sarah could reach him now, for he was in a well of misery. He began to sidle round the edge of the crowd. To stand near her would be enough.

'Our young are weak,' the magistrate continued. 'Our women are weak, they have not the strength of spirit to resist the workings of the Devil. Blighted by feebleness and an existing stain of the soul, they are willing prey for the forces of evil. We must protect them from their own base urges.'

There was shifting, murmuring amongst the villagers. Daniel made his way past, slowly.

'You must be vigilant.' The voice rose. 'Observe your womenfolk for wantonness above their usual failing, watch for the meeting of covens without a man to give spiritual strength. You must keep an attentive eye for secret knowledge of herb-use, the mark of the Devil upon the skin, for these are the signs of wickedness.'

Daniel walked faster. The words moved like a poisoned vapour, slowly intoxicating the crowd, until it had them shuffling and shouting. He thought of Sarah's mother and her herb remedies, the whispers he had heard of worse, and had no doubt he was not the only one. Some courageous female voices dissented.

'I warn you now,' the magistrate shouted above the rabble, 'these women are among you, breeding like maggots. And they wish harm upon you in every way.'

He saw her head turn. Looking for him, and he not yet with her. Behind her now, an arm's reach away.

'I question why,' the magistrate bellowed, 'I do not see witch jars outside your houses, I do not see lights in windows at night and witch marks on your walls. I question if you are not warding off this evil, then who amongst you invite it in? My studies into the papist abomination you hold in the breast of this village are almost complete. Those guilty will stand before God and my judgement, and for the sake of your souls, no mercy shall be shown. Now is your chance to show your innocence, come to me with what you know, or stand tainted with those that sin.'

Daniel pressed through, reached out his hand, fingers grazing her shoulder. She turned to him abruptly, eyes dark with fear and fury.

Bett leaned back. 'Get her away,' she said softly. He saw her squeeze Sarah's hand, then release it.

There was scuffling in the corner where Phyllis's family sat, then the anguished crying out of a woman and a male roar of pain.

Daniel took Sarah's hand, caring not for the eyes around them, and led her quickly towards the door.

The crowd swelled and surged as Phyllis's father lunged forward, and those nearby held him back.

'My daughter was not wanton. And no witch,' he yelled. 'Hear me?'

Daniel and Sarah recoiled to avoid his flailing fists and wild eyes. The open door just a few steps away.

Phyllis's father pushed through the crowd. 'She was an innocent that fell prey to—'

Daniel did not wait to hear more. He dragged Sarah through to the cool night air, passing the parson as he slumped against the wall by the door, head dropped.

'I have to get to Mam,' Sarah said, as soon as they were safely outside.

'I know.'

They made their way back to the house, loitering in the shadows and speaking in whispers.

'But – but she's a cunning woman, every person has turned to her at some time for a, a salve or remedy. Only healing and herb-knowledge.'

Even as he said the words he knew they were but a crescent of the whole, the other truth lying in unspoken shadow. The Haworth hag, up the cursed hill in the old plague village, with her brood of wild Devil-brats. Stories of crops dying if you crossed her, of starvation and suffering and maladies afflicting your children. Spells to wipe out your foe for the price of a coin. Sarah's cursing of Gabriel. The demon seen in the village.

'You know they all carry guilt of one kind or another,' she said. 'Every woman washing clothes at the beck tells of who lies with another's husband, or which man beat his wife and then claimed she'd become possessed by a sprite and flung herself into the walls. They're feared and they'll hand her over to cover their own sins as sure as they beg her for cures and then spit at her on their way to church.'

The tap on his shoulder caused him to cry out. There had been no warning footsteps.

'I'm sorry, my son,' Parson Walsh said, hands lifted by way of apology. 'I did not intend to startle, but I must speak with you both urgently.'

Sarah clasped his arm. 'Seth, will you go to Mam? Please? Warn her?'

'I will, rest assured.' He patted her hand. 'But I'm sorry to say I was mistaken in my confidence and now I have churned you both into the befouled workings of my mind. I have failed to convince Magistrate Wright of the Shaws' innocence and I realise now the staggering arrogance of my belief that I would be chosen to bring your families together.'

This was unexpected. Daniel glanced at Sarah for explanation, but she looked upon the parson with pity.

'You strove only to help,' she said.

'You are in a precarious position of my making. Why the Lord has burdened me with this corrupted soul I shall never know.' His voice dropped so quiet that Daniel could hardly hear. 'Though I do endeavour to bear it.' The parson bent his head and wiped his eyes. 'Oh, had I but counselled you with more caution.'

'You weren't to know,' Sarah said.

He shook his head and spoke at pace, barely drawing breath. 'You must see that now you cannot be wed, you cannot be discovered, Sarah, in such times as are coming. Magistrate Wright has spoken with me of his past achievements, as he sees them, of hunting down papists and witches, condemning them on no more than a mark on the skin and the word of a neighbour.' He leaned in, whispered. 'Should he learn who you are, I fear you will be condemned for bewitching young Daniel here.'

Daniel felt something run through her, though she made no sound.

'But we are already wed, as good as, we have pledged to God and He knows it,' he said. 'I gave my mother's ring.'

He heard voices from the barn, rising in a growing tide of anger and fear, an uproar that made the hairs on his arms rise.

Seth's whisper quickened. 'And God I am sure sees the purity of your feelings, but you must concede now that those marvels you dreamed cannot be.' He took a breath and said, 'You must part.'

Daniel reached for Sarah, and she for him, as she spoke. 'We shall not.'

'They will not discover her,' Daniel said.

'Eventually, they will. Someone will, and this venomous talk destroys any hope we had that your union be accepted.'

Daniel could not catch his breath. 'We cannot part.'

'You must.'

'Nay,' Sarah said.

They stood together, joined by hand and in purpose. Daniel's heart kicked, his breath came fast and thin. He was afraid as he had never been, and sure as he had never been.

The villagers began to pour out. Parson Walsh started and was gone into the darkness, leaving them silent, and bound together.

Sewn

I lie a-bed, awake. Weeping hot, angry tears into the thick straw mattress and cotton sheet. Tonight more than any I am feared to my belly that my master will seek out Daniel and take him from me. Remove me from this new life and this house. I feel him so strongly, calling me to whisper a curse upon the hate-filled magistrate, and I long to, I imagine him cowering in fear before me, but I dread to let this power consume me. I must battle the shadow in my eye.

When at last I sleep, I dream of Annie, standing white and still, thicket of twig-filled hair and scraped, muddy knees. Whispered words spool out of her, fine and silver as spider's web, and surround me until I am caught in their gossamer threads. I cannot move, cannot speak, cannot see, but I know she is gone and ever will be, and all because I stood and let it be so.

As I wake I hear through the floorboards Daniel persuade his father that I'm stricken with grief at Phyllis's death. Mr Taylor is fond of me, I am a good dairymaid, and so looks with a soft eye and grants me leave for some hours of the afternoon.

First I must help Bett with the laundry, and we carry the basket of clothes and sheets to the beck. A task I usually like, but am not eager to be in the company of village women today.

The lye we've soaked the linen in stings my eyes as I wade into the water and dunk the clothes, then beat them against the rocks with the washing-beetle. Satisfying work. Today Bett minds my mood, and does not chat or laugh and splash me as she usually does but instead watches the children playing at the bank with the same expression Annie wears when she sees someone eating cake. Still, I cannot avoid hearing the other women talking about Phyllis, and how they had always known she had badness in her, and no wonder she would come to such an end.

I slam the clothes with extra force, splashing the woman next to me, not one I have seen here before but one who sometimes came to Mam for a salve to soothe the skin. I turn away.

'Sorry.'

'No matter.' She stares at me. 'You know I – have we met elsewhere?'

I bend to inspect the clothes, heart beating a little faster. 'No.'

'Yes I – can't place, and yet I know you from somewhere, I'm sure.'

Bett steps between us. 'Ah, she's that kind of a face, everyone feels she's a life-friend when in fact they've just met.' She pats my arm, turning me gently towards the bank. 'Isn't that so?'

I try to laugh. 'Yes.'

'See, there we are. That's all it is. How's that son of yours, still a wild one?'

The woman laughs, and I wish I could thank Bett, but she waves me away. 'You begone,' she calls. 'I can wring these myself and I know you've that task to be about.'

I walk through the village to see the aftermath of the magistrate's words for myself. And it is plain. On every step sits a witch jar, in every window a cross fashioned from driftwood or corn. Many a wall bears a newly-hewn pattern. There's a hush I've never known, I can hear each of my shoes hit the ground. No lingering on the street to exchange news, no wandering by the harbour to flirt. Into this quiet falls another set of footsteps, quick and light.

I see a furtive figure, crouched and swift-running from the direction of the netter's house, glancing side to side. The way he moves, bent and unlike a man, I can see why a fearful mind would think him a demon. Barely there, but I see him. I know him. John.

I turn and head towards home, not daring to call to him, though I wish to. Whatever John is about cannot be good, and can only invite danger after last night's meeting. I'll have it out with Mam as soon as I see her. Hurrying up the hill, caring not to protect my white stockings from the dust as I lift my petticoat and march on. Mouth dry and brow damp with exertion but I do not stop. I pray they are there, that Seth had the goodwill to rouse them from their beds last night with warnings of the bitter words flying about the village.

Outside the door I pause, even now, to twist the ring on my finger. As though I carry Daniel with me this way, though I only dare wear it on visits home lest his father see and discover us. Watch my own hand reach out, metal glinting in sunlight, push the door open. The moment, the last unknowing one before I find which of them awaits inside and if all is well, stretches out unbearably.

'Mam,' I call before my feet are even in, before I can see anything of the dimness inside. 'Mam, tell me you're all safe there's talk in the village, and I've just seen John—'

She appears in front of me, says softly, 'I did not expect you now.'

I throw my arms around her, chin on her shoulder as I stare into the shadows for Annie and John, for perhaps he's reached home before me.

A woman sits at our table.

I am fixed, holding on to Mam. I know who this is that watches me as I, Sarah the farm dairymaid, embrace my mother, the cunning woman from the cursed hill, but am unable to understand her presence here.

Her soft-edged beauty is out of place against the battered furniture, grimy walls and cobweb-strewn corners. Her skin too bright, her round eyes too light. Though I note, as I grow used to the gloom, she carries a haunted look I've not seen on her before. Of course. Only the troubled call upon this dwelling.

She looks from the ring I wear to my face under the coif that is my disguise, and I see she understands all.

'You,' she says, the word floating from her cracked lips like a feather.

Mam eases out of my clasp and steps to the table. 'Drink up,' she says.

The girl lifts the cup and swallows down the brew. I cannot see from here, but I know well enough the scent.

She meets my eye again as she finishes.

'Parsley and tearthumb,' I say.

There is nothing more to be spoken. Each looking at the other, knowing the one thing we would strive to keep hidden is revealed.

Mam takes the cup from her, holds out her hand for the coin in return.

I remain by the door as Molly stands and straightens her petticoats. Walks past me without a word, without a glance, just the brushing of fine cloth against my arm and the faint scent of hot metal.

Annie and John don't return home. Mam assures me they're both in the woods, and when I tell her I saw John in the village she claims I'm mistaken, that I saw another lad and imagined my brother. She swears it so, I'm almost convinced. She busies herself over the fire.

I tell her all. How with just the prattling of one tongue her work will have her condemned and swaying from the Hanging Tree. To continue with balms and poultices if she must, but on no account to stray into enchantments and curses.

'You tell me nowt that Seth did not say last night, and nowt that has not always been the case,' she says.

'It's not the same, now. Magistrate Thompson is gone and they're feared, I've seen the change. They're angry. You've no hold over this Wright. You mustn't give him any chance to hurt you. Any of you.'

She pats my hand. 'Don't fret, lass. I know how to keep them safe.'

At last I must leave, without knowing the comfort of holding Annie, without seeing her sweet, unmarked skin. Hearing nothing to assure me that Mam understands.

Heavily I walk, from a home no longer a home, to a home not yet one.

Daniel waits at the path by the sheep field. A risk, but I'm glad to see him. He takes me in his arms and, just for a moment, I let myself breathe in his scent of sunlight and hay, and be comforted.

'It feels everything we've built is about to be swept away,' I say. 'Should they discover who I am we'll be forced to part. And worse, they will hurt you.'

'We will not part,' he says. 'We are bound now.' He releases me, taking my hands in his. 'There is another way.'

I know his mind, for the same thought is in mine. 'To leave?'

'Yes. Leave and find work.'

I long for it so, but the thought of Mam, John and Annie left here is too much to bear. To go without them is not possible. 'But – I can't. My family ...'

He hesitates just a beat. 'They shall come. Yes. We'll find work and then call for them. And one day, in the end, we shall have our own little house. You will bake the bread.'

'And we'll eat flawn,' I say.

Even now, in the face of desperation, we laugh. He pulls me to him, kisses the top of my head. 'You would run away with the flawn itself, I am surplus.'

I shrug.

'Oh,' he says. 'Do not deny it.'

'I – nay, of course.'

He shakes his head, smiling. 'You lingered too long, I know the truth of it now.'

For a moment the thought of the fire and the flawn, the thought of this life with him, feels real. Hope soars in me. 'Where can we go?' I ask.

He sighs, spreads his arms. 'I don't know. We both have skills, we can find work. We cannot wait for the mop, we shall have to travel and seek. Take whatever work and lodging we may find.'

'You'll lose the farm.'

'Matters not.'

'And your family?'

He shakes his head.

'This is our plan?' I ask.

He bends to kiss me. 'This is our plan. But first, we must be wed.'

I have not set foot in church before. Colourful splinters of light fall from the window behind him and splash on to the dusty floor, and I struggle to focus on Seth. There is a scent I recognise from the farm as candle wax and, though the sun shines outside, a chill seeping from wall and ground.

'We will not part,' Daniel says, glancing at me.

'Would I could persuade you otherwise,' Seth says, slowly, as though each word is a boulder of great weight heaved from within. He holds a leather-bound book, which I know must be the Bible.

'You cannot,' I say. 'But you can help us still, if you're willing.'

Seth chews his lip. 'If there is any way to make amends for the hurts I've caused by encouraging your feelings and putting you in danger, then—'

'We're leaving this place,' I say.

'And we must be wed,' Daniel says.

Seth looks upon our clasped hands. 'Where shall you go?'

'We don't know yet,' I say.

He walks to a raised area at the front of the church and climbs the wooden steps. 'Then I may be able to help a little, and perhaps do some small good after all. It will not be easy, but I see you are determined.' He lays out his Bible, turning the pages until he finds the one he's looking for. Daniel meets my eye. It is all I can do to stop myself screaming at Seth to continue.

'I know of a family,' he says, 'far from here, that might help. Farmers, they have suffered dreadfully with the loss of their children, and I in my humble way comforted them. Perhaps, if I entreat on your part, they will allow you to work their land and share their home, echoing as it does with vanished joys.'

Daniel's grip on my hand tightens. 'Parson, we would be so grateful.'

Seth gives a brief smile. 'Then I shall send word today. Bide just a little time, I shall inform you as soon as I receive reply. And you shall be husband and wife before you go.'

Outside, Daniel glances around to make sure no one sees, pulls me into his arms and swings me until my shoes lift free of the grass.

I hold on to my coif, laughing. 'What?'

'We shall be together. It will happen – the house, the farm.' He runs his finger down the centre of my face gently: forehead, nose, lips. 'Husband and wife.'

★

No word of Molly passes my lips, nor ever shall. For the balance of all things lies in this, that her secrets remain sewn into my mouth unspoken and so then mine shall lie buried in her breast also. Never shall we call ourselves friends, but we are bound by the frailty we have each shown the other today.

Innocence

The hay rattle was bleached dry and thin, ready to cut, and so the endless toil of August began. Rising at dawn and working till dusk, straw hat little protection from the callous sun that left Daniel's arms and the back of his neck raw as he bent and swung the scythe all day. The constant itch of sweat, dust and insect bites. He thought often of the new life that was to begin, trying to imagine what it would be to live and work elsewhere, to leave all he had known. Sometimes in trepidation, sometimes excitement. Soon, he would rest each night in the arms of his wife. They counted the days in secret smiles and stolen glances, waiting for word from Parson Walsh.

He returned at last, hot, exhausted and dirty from the field. On the doorstep stood a jar.

He recognised it, but asked all the same. Opened his mouth. Waited for his voice to come. 'What's this?'

Father cleared his throat, met Daniel's eye. Stamped the dust from his boots before entering. 'You know what it is.'

'Why do we need a witch jar? There's no – we are none of us cursed.'

'To ward off those that are coming.'

Daniel stooped to remove his boots. 'We needed no such protection before.'

'There was no such wickedness in the air before. Happen the magistrate warns us rightly, we should fear these spirits, son. We know the truth that Phyllis gave in to the mischief that tempted her, and so she's lost. Now Sam Finch fails – cursed by the Devil-boy up the hill, some say. You know that young Robinson lad was out in the woods when he should have been helping with the catch last week and his father fit to beat him until the boy told of a demon in the shape of a hare that tempted him away and swore to lay a curse upon the family if he disobeyed?'

Daniel looked out at the endless spill of trees and fields, the blinking of the first stars. Put his hand to his pocket, where he carried the stone Sarah had given him, and wondered how strong was the protection it brought. 'I hadn't heard,' he said.

'Aye, well, you must keep your ear to the ground now, son. Listen out for whispers of what takes place. The boy's family took him straight to tell all to Magistrate Wright and he is keeping record of any such happenings to better hunt down the evil that breeds here. Papists and witchery. What should become of us if we fall victim to a curse? Hay harvest fails, we lose the livestock come winter and we starve. I must protect the farm and all that work it as best I can.'

A moment of silence.

'I thought witch jars are strongest when buried? Or – or burned?' Daniel asked.

Father opened the door. 'This one is strongest here. Where the magistrate can see it and be assured of our innocence.'

Flesh Will Pay

The door opens and Bett throws something on to my bed, tearing me from imaginings of life as Daniel's wife. Of the life that's soon to be mine.

'What's this?' I ask.

'Sunday best.'

'For what?'

'For God.'

I sit up, pulling the blanket to my chest. 'Church isn't for me,' I say.

'It is now. Magistrate's on the lookout.'

'But none questions that I go to my own church of a Sunday …'

'They will now. Show your face with the rest of the village.'

She leaves, door swinging closed behind her, and I take a better look at what she has given me. A coif, not much different to the one I already own, but for the holly leaves embroidered on in black thread, silky under my fingers. Such beauty as I never dreamed of possessing.

Gabriel walks beside me all the way, too close so that I can smell his skin in the hot air.

'Stay next to me, lass,' he says. 'For once I saw that witch-girl and her Devil-sister from the plague hill lingering here ready to curse any passing, like she did to me, though I am strong enough to withstand it. I shall keep you safe.'

Shadow bristles in my eye. I wish now Mam had not given him the salve to cure his pox. He would not be so bold, then. I breathe deep, bite the inside of my cheek to bring me back to myself, before my fury takes hold and the dog overpowers me.

My laughter is spiked with hate. 'I hardly need protection from a lass and a child.'

'These aren't no ordinary ones, but riddled with hellish magic and ready to harm any person on their way to church. Have you seen her, that witch? Wild hair, and those eyes, nowt earthly about her.'

Growl shudders my bones. I bite down harder, and blood fills my mouth. I stop and look him in the eye. 'Happen they ask for nowt more than a kindness.'

His head jerks towards me, eyes narrow as he studies my face. My heart lurches and I know I shouldn't have spoken those same words Annie used that day. I should drop my eye so he cannot recognise the wildness that flickers there, but can no longer bring myself to cower before this brute.

He shakes his shoulders out, laughs. 'Ah, you're such a inno-cent, you just cannot fathom their true nature. And you'll never have to, for none such evil will touch you, I'll make certain of it. I've a mind to walk up the cursed hill and take her to the magistrate myself, watch her dangle from the rope.'

I walk ahead, fighting to control the snarling that overcomes me, the blaze that flares whenever I close my eyes. My head aches by the time we reach the church. Framed by a bright, blue sky and nestling behind a great oak. The sight gives me an unexpected and welcome sense of calm, quieting the fury in me.

The top of the wall is lined with the heads of some creature I do not recognise, carved in stone, with a wide-open mouth and hair surrounding the face. To instil fear, perhaps, at the masterful beings God has at his command, yet I feel nothing but peace, and am glad to step into the hushed gloom. Chase the turmoil from me. Stop the power taking me over.

At first I keep my eyes on those around, lest my true master seek me out in disguise. I recognise most faces; Molly Matthews sits across the aisle, with her parents. Still sickly and red-eyed. I wonder if the parsley brew has played its part. In front of us is Nelly Finch, her clothes loose and face lost its softness since last I saw her. Sam is not here. Phyllis's mother sits at the back, hands clasped on her knee.

I watch the feet walking down the aisle, for I know should he come for me that would be the only part he could not change. And he may not have me, not now, when I can almost reach out and touch my new life with Daniel. When to be exposed would be to call down disaster upon all I love. Shoes peeking from petticoats, boots under breeches and socks. No hoof. Nothing that makes me think all is not what it seems.

At last I lift my eyes. Seth takes his place, and though I've seen him in robes and hat before, he seems now unlike the man I know. He speaks of love and trust, of withholding judgement and obedience to God. I try to catch his eye, search for any hopeful sign that he has good news for us. His words are slow and flat, I see the effort it takes for him to pass them through his lips.

He will be at Mam's after this.

I try to join in with the prayers I've never heard, sing the hymns I don't know. Kneel, stand and sit when others do and, when the service is done, follow everyone out into the dazzling sunlight.

In hopes of catching Seth, I linger, but Bett takes my arm and drags me to a quiet corner of the graveyard. I stumble as I try to keep pace with her.

'It's well you brought me,' I say. 'I'd no idea it would be so—'

'Hush, lass. You make a show of yourself, babbling on as though you've never stepped inside church before.' She bends her head close to mine. 'The talk is all of Sam Finch.'

My happiness floats away into the warm air, leaving me chilled under the beating August sun.

'What do you know of it?' she asks, glancing past me to the crowd gathered near the path. I turn. No one approaches.

'I know nowt,' I say.

'You know that there have been troubles for him, a series of luckless happenings, and now he is suffering with the flux.'

'Well, aye, I knew that—'

'And you know that three times now who has been seen running from the house but your brother?' Her words a near-silent hiss. Behind her a spadger sits in the branches of a tree and chirps, and I long to listen only to its song and keep her words from my ears.

She stops, hands on hips, scrutinising my face. Her chest rises and falls quickly.

'Sarah?'

'I know nowt of it.' Though even as I say the words I think of the crumbled clay image of Sam Finch, of the mysterious business John's been about. I knew it was he I saw in the village. I swallow but the bitter taste in my mouth returns.

Bett breathes out heavily, purses her lips and turns her face up to the sky. 'They say he's dying.'

'I'm sorry.'

'If they are about some wickedness, your brother or your mam, you must make them stop. This place is changed. If Sam dies, they'll gather together and punish those they blame. I've heard talk of a plan to march with torches to the house again. I have begged Nathaniel to calm them and he does what he can, but he is just one voice. And the next they look for shall be you, folks have started asking why we've not seen you beg— out with your sister of late. Understand?'

I do.

Bett gasps and presses her hand to her mouth, looking past where we shelter from view under the trees. I turn to see a woman, caught in the clutches of the magistrate.

'Please,' she cries. 'Please, sir, I beg you, show mercy.'

Magistrate Wright grips her arm, and uses the other to fend off a man attempting to pull her free. 'The time for mercy is passed,' he says. 'Your sins have caught up to you.'

'Please,' the man says. 'We are honest people. God-fearing.'

A crowd gathers around them, standing a little back, watching silently. Bett and I do not move. 'The Shaws,' she says. Her face has paled to the colour of milk.

'What have they done?' I ask.

'Papists,' she says.

'Your trickery has failed,' the magistrate shouts. 'Time is come to face the truth and away to the assizes. Where were you on Good Friday? Not here, the God-fearing folk of this village tell me, but about your own heathen rituals. There is witchery here.'

Mrs Shaw sobs and shakes her head. 'No, sir, as God is my witness, you have it wrong. I am no such—'

A boy in the crowd points at her and shouts. ''Tis she, the one I saw turned to a hare that day, the one that tricked me away.'

The ground tilts beneath me and I reach for Bett. She clasps my arm. This mention of the hare is too close to Dew-Springer for me to ignore.

Mrs Shaw's eyes roll towards the child, mouth agape. 'No,' she implores. 'The lad's mistaken, it was not me, as the Lord is—'

There are shouts now from the crowd, accusations of her sorcery and evil doings. Mr Shaw tries again to reach her, muttering about God and prayer in a torrent of words that I know shan't save either of them.

'My will is that you be hanged for your sins,' Magistrate Wright says. 'And no doubt God shall ensure it is so.'

She screams at his words, collapses to the ground, sobbing, almost taking the magistrate down with her. He turns a furious glare on those gathered. 'Are you all also sinners, that stand by and allow the witch and papist to escape? Take hold this man and assist me in escorting them away.'

I grip Bett's hand. 'But – they're in church. How can they be ...?'

She shakes her head. 'In church today. Never before.'

I watch, I do nothing as they're hauled away, she limp and silent now, her shoes leaving a trail on the dusty path. Gabriel helps the magistrate, his meaty hand clasped around Mr Shaw's arm. I search for Daniel. No sign of him, nor Seth either. Magistrate Wright picked his time well.

'Will they really be hanged?' I ask.

Bett wipes her eyes. 'That is the punishment.'

I cast my eyes over the crowd that lingers. Women who help me wash clothes in the beck, who ask after me when they come to bake their bread in the farm oven. Those same that have pushed me away, thrown stones and pulled my hair when, in my other life, I dared ask for a coin.

My mind is playing tricks; it seems now that every face turns to me with suspicion. With recognition. And my fate, should I be discovered, is clearer than ever.

The closer I am to the hill, the more I feel its shadow.

I'm surprised there's no scent of henbane from the house, and disappointed, for I'm desperate to hear good news from Seth.

Annie runs from the door before I reach it.

'I heard you,' she says. 'John said Seth was come but I knowed it was you.'

She is warm and soft in my arms. Grown, surely, since last I saw her. I hold tight, breathe in the scent of earth and trees from her taffled hair.

She frees herself from my grip, pulls at my petticoat, searches behind my back. Steps away, hands on hips, frowning. 'Where's the food?'

The pack lies neatly tied, hidden behind my bed. In my haste I came straight from church. I pinch my own arm, hard.

It's not been so long since I lived here that I've forgotten how much that food is needed.

I drop to my knees, take her hands. 'I'm sorry, Annie. I forgot. I'll bring it in the week.'

She pulls away, chews her nail, deciding what she feels about this betrayal. Fingers the embroidery on my coif. 'All right. I'm going to fetch something for you now.'

She scampers off in the direction of the woods.

Mam is stirring nettle soup, her back to me. 'John thought you were Seth,' she says, without turning.

'I saw him this morning,' I say. 'He'll be here.'

'Knew as much,' John says. He sits at the table, whittling a stick. 'Struck by the melancholy last I saw him.'

'And where was that? When you were about your wickedness in the village?'

The accusation is out too soon, and not in the persuasive manner I planned. Neither of them move or speak, until Mam turns, wipes her hands on her petticoat and steps to embrace me. Her face is red and swollen, a deep scratch running under her left eye.

'What happened?' I ask.

She glances past me to John. Waves a hand in dismissal. 'Oh, a woman in the village. Swears I've cursed her belly to be barren. Dew-Springer was about an errand and not there to warn me.'

John snorts. 'The reason her belly shan't bear fruit is more caused by the tastes of her husband than any curse, I've heard. Prefers to lie with his own kind.'

'Oh, Mam. Have you used a salve?'

'Of course, lass, don't fret. Nowt we've not faced before.'

She steps back and looks me up and down. Not so different from Annie's inspection earlier.

'I forgot the food,' I say. 'Sorry.'

'Bring us nowt but your interference, then,' John says.

'Because I'm feared for you, there's talk in the village and I saw you—'

He stands, stick dropping to the floor, but he keeps hold of the knife. 'Easy for you, in your new clothes. You're a village lass now, you've forgot what we must do to live.'

'Whatever you've set upon Sam Finch you must call off. If he dies they'll turn on you. They'll come for you, all of you. Annie too, and a scratched face shall be the least of it. Even today the magistrate's had a man and his wife dragged away, for less than this. You must listen to me, Mam.'

'He hurt my flesh,' she says. 'His flesh will pay. It's as simple as that.' She glances at the floor by her feet. 'That's right, little one. You understand, and you've your role to play.'

'But, Mam—'

Her eyes like needles. I daren't argue. Despair has me pressing tears away. Pain beats in my head, a darkness that I only hope I can hold back, tame and quieten.

The door behind me opens and Mam gasps. 'Out,' she says. 'Get them out.'

Annie stands on the threshold, holding a cluster of scarlet flax and cow parsley. The smile on her face, as though it's jewels she offers, falls and she glances down at the flowers, frowning.

'Get them away,' Mam says. Pushes past me and bears down on Annie, snatching the flowers from her and throwing them through the air and down the hill as far as she can. Annie stamps her foot, clenches her fists and bares her teeth, growling. Tears seep from her eyes and trickle down her cheeks. John laughs.

'They were for Sarah,' she shouts. 'They were pretty.'

I take her in my arms but she shakes me off.

Mam leans against the door, panting, pressing her palm to her side. 'Thought I'd brought you up to know better than that, lass.'

John keeps his head bowed as he whittles the stick. 'Never put red and white flowers together,' he says.

Annie looks up at me, her eyes awash. I stroke her hair. 'Brings death to the dwelling,' I say.

What He Had Seen

There was no news from the parson when Daniel spoke with him after church, though he expected word any moment. The waiting was unbearable, and Daniel woke each morning, well before dawn and wrung through by terrible dreams, praying that it would be the day their new life could begin. Under Magistrate Wright's influence this place had become one of fear and suspicion. The danger of discovery was greater with every day that passed, and he dared not think of what would befall them then.

At last summer was nearing its end, and its tyrannical grip on his time. The wheat was now golden and brittle, giving a rich, dusty scent. It was ready to be cut, tied into stooks and stored. The stubble had dried and was harvested. Long days of labour and thin nourishment of bread and butter in the field were done. A goose had been slaughtered to celebrate and Bett and Sarah had cooked up a feast.

On this first free night Sarah and Daniel at last had some time together, the air was warm and the riverbank empty.

Sarah had taken no persuading to set foot in the water. She shed each layer and ran to immerse herself before her beauty was too long displayed. He hurried to follow, cursing as his eager fingers tangled laces, as he tripped on the uneven surface, and longing for the day soon to come, when their love need not be hidden.

The cry came from the riverbank as they swam, and they both turned to see who it came from.

Daniel squinted into the sun, feet reaching for the muddy bed as he shaded his eyes. Surely, he was mistaken. Surely, he had misheard.

'Witch,' it came again, a shriek that could not be ignored, no matter how the wind snatched it.

The figure stood at the river's edge. They were so entranced, they had not noticed. Had not cared to.

Sarah's arms reached pale under the rippling surface, her body a white blur that wavered below. Dappled sunlight lit her face. She kicked her way over to him, silver droplets of water falling from her lifted arms.

'What's this?' she asked. 'Happen a visitor.'

Her voice was light, but her eyes hard, snapping a fire he had only ever seen when she felt Annie to be threatened. He was distracted still by the desire to slip his arms around her, bring her body to his own. She turned from him, glaring towards the bank.

He peered into the sunlight again. 'I – I think it's—'

'Molly,' she said.

It was, as he already knew, Molly Matthews stepping over rocks, closer and closer to the river's edge until she was in danger of soaking her shoes, screaming into the wind. 'You have bewitched him. Stolen and bewitched him. I will tell them all.'

How did she come to be there? How did she know who Sarah was? His thoughts tumbled in a panicked cascade – what she would do next, what would happen to Sarah as a result. And to himself.

'Do not be afraid,' he said, though his own voice shook. 'I shall talk to her.'

'It's she that should be feared,' Sarah said, a cold flame in her eyes.

She swam as far as she could towards the bank, then stood, rising naked from the river right in front of where Molly stood, water pouring in rivulets from her slick, dark hair. She raised a hand and pointed a finger. Molly was silenced.

'You dare to call me witch. You, who knows I see the truth of what you are,' she said.

Molly whimpered and gathered her petticoats to her. Daniel, afraid to show himself to a person other than Sarah, stayed where he was and called for her to stop. She did not.

'You took him,' Molly shouted, words broken by sobs. 'Used your sorcery and took him from me. If it had been him, all would be well. What am I to do?'

'Swallow your foul words and never let them pass your lips again. Else your tongue shall blister and weep,' Sarah said. 'Each word shall transform into a bat, flying from your mouth and turning its teeth to you, filling you with the wickedness and pain you seek to inflict on me.'

Molly screwed her petticoats up in her hands, face crumpled like a little child's, body bent like an old maid's. 'I am already filled with it,' she screamed. 'There is none to help me now.'

Sarah stepped forward, arm still outstretched, and Molly backed away, tears flooding, mouth gaping in fear.

'Sarah,' he shouted. 'Stop.'

She took another step, standing but an arm's length from Molly. 'Blood shall seep from your poisoned flesh, pool at your feet, pour from your fingers.'

Her voice was lower, slower than he had ever heard it. As though another spoke through her. And the words, more vile than he had ever thought to hear from her, such foulness he could not believe she harboured within. Sunlight glinted upon the water until it was all he could see, each breath sharper, faster. He washed his face, blinked, forced himself to stay aware, that he might know what was happening.

'Leave her,' he called, his voice breaking. But she was unreachable. No longer the Sarah he knew, but a being unknowable and powerful. In this moment she was everything the villagers feared the family to be.

'And all that you touch, all that you love, shall be infected,' Sarah said.

Molly sobbed, made to run, but Sarah reached out and held her arm fast, spun her round. Standing tall over the cowering girl, she took Molly's chin in her hand, tipped her face and brought her own close.

'Heed. My. Words.'

She released her hold and Molly ran, tripping over a branch and falling, catching her head on a rock. He heard the crack from where he stood in the water. She lay unmoving for a moment and Daniel waded to the bank, scrambling into his breeches. He glanced at Sarah. She stood, watching. Where Molly lay a red stain spread slowly over the ground.

She was moving before he reached her, holding her head and groaning, whimpering at the sight of blood when she brought her hand away.

'You saw,' she said, voice high as she clinged to him. 'She moved the branch to trip me, it wasn't there before, she used her witchcraft to do it. You saw, didn't you, Daniel?'

Daniel looked from Molly, to the branch, to Sarah. Her face showed no trace of what she felt. Had the branch been there? He could not say. He did not know what he had seen.

'I – I think it, it must have been an accident,' he said, hearing the doubt in his own voice.

'She put it there.' Molly's voice rose to scream. 'I would not have run into it, I looked, the ground was clear. She moved it, to punish me. You know what they say of the Haworths, how they steal your children and boil their bones to make potions.'

Daniel helped her to her feet, glancing once again at Sarah. She stood as she was, did not take her eyes from them. 'I think perhaps that's just – '

'She has you bewitched,' Molly said again. 'She's used her powers on you. You know it was the mam that conjured the storm and drowned their father, think what will become of you. Come back to yourself, Daniel. Please. Come with me.'

She reached up unsteadily, balancing on her toes and pressing her hands against him. Kissed him on the lips. He shook his head, and she ran off.

Daniel waited until Molly had gone, then made his way to Sarah. Turned her, afraid to see her face for fear it was transformed to that of the foul creature that had spoken through her, but it remained her own. White with cold, eyes wide and barren, but still Sarah.

'What have you done?'

Her empty eyes met his. 'It came,' she said calmly. 'It was here but it didn't take me over, I shared myself with it. I chose.'

'I – what came? You're not—'

'The dog. It was here and I chose to let it be. It is part of me. But not how I thought.'

He looked into her face, tried to see her as he always had. Tried to banish the mounting whispers of doubt.

Spike of Hope

Seth is a weighty burden, leaning on me as he does, but one I'm happy to carry. It is to him I owe all the happiness that begins now.

I had walked up the hill to the scent of henbane lacing the wind, and pushed the door open to see him splayed on his back, arms wide.

Though I dared not tell Mam, the talk's been of Sam Finch's recovery this past week. I knew in my heart it was not my appeal but Annie's bringing of a death portent that made her leave off whatever curses or poisons she had been laying on him. I was still grateful. A mite less feared for them, for now at least.

Less feared about everything, for I felt a steady strength coursing through me, remembering how I opened myself to the power of the dog when I cursed Molly. I had begun to tame it, learned to use it for my bidding. And the terror in her eyes assured me that she would speak no more dangerous words about me.

Seth lifted his head, blinked. 'Little one, this is fortuitous.' The words drawn out, as though torn from him, and slightly slurred. 'I have need to speak with you.'

My belly tightened, and I left off dreaming of my newly-conquered powers to focus on what was happening right before me. Seth had news and I prayed it be good.

He sighed, reached inside himself and dredged each word out at an agonising pace. 'I have heard from the family we spoke of. They would be grateful for the labour, and could offer board, food and a small wage in repayment.'

I gasped air into my burning chest.

He slumped his head down on his arms again. 'I shall marry you tomorrow.'

I rushed to Mam, threw my arms around her. 'Oh, Mammy. It's happening, it's really going to happen.'

She held me fast. 'You shall be saved.'

'We all shall. Though we must leave, Daniel has sworn we'll send for you as soon as we're able.'

Mam's face closed, a shield against hope. 'That one of my childer should have such a life is more than I dreamed.'

'We'll send for you, Mam. And you shall come.'

The words run through my mind still as we walk down the hill, his arm over my shoulder and the full weight of him leaning in to me, and I twist the ring around my finger. The smile remains on my lips, even as Seth talks in a constant, low murmur. I catch little, only half-listening.

'The village is a good journey away, far enough that none may know your family,' he says. I shift the weight of where he leans higher on to my shoulder. The back of my neck sore and dry from the sun. 'Past Middon, you must go, you know of it?'

I nod, lick my dry lips.

'Past Middon, through Aldmore and then it is a way, a long way, with always the sea at your left, and then you shall reach a place called Blackop and, though the name be dark, it is a place of fish, fields and furrows and the people are good and honest to a one.'

I tighten my hold on Seth's waist, though the heat of him is almost more than I can bear on such a day. A figure stands at the foot of the hill. A man. It appears he looks this way. He doesn't move.

'They shall make you welcome, to a one, to a one, and the Wilsons are the best of all. Such good souls and so beset with grief.'

I keep my eye on the man standing below. It is not Daniel. This man leans back, swinging a stick like a child.

'Tomorrow nightfall, you come to me, and we shall have you wed and gone before sunrise.'

'Thank you, Seth,' I say, breathless from the heat and walk and heaviness of him. 'We owe you everything.'

Seth stops, so abruptly that I almost trip. He holds his finger up as though considering the direction of the wind.

'I fear I must puke,' he says, and falls to his knees.

The figure walks towards us, and I towards him. It's not long before I know him. Gabriel.

He whistles through his teeth, stands still. Regards me, and stabs the ground with the stick. He has sharpened the end.

I glance back at Seth, on hands and knees, retching. That Gabriel knows who I am matters not, for tomorrow I shall be gone.

I face him, silent. No point attempting to lay a curse, it will take more than a pointed finger and some words of magic to fright him.

'So, Molly spoke right after all,' he says. 'You are none but that witch-whore, disguised as a sweet, comely lass.'

The story fits together in my mind like pieces of a broken branch, entwined to leave no space for doubt.

'The brew didn't work, did it?' I ask.

'What?'

'She carries your babe.'

He moves closer, but a step away from me now, tall and wide as a wall. I stand my ground, staring up at him. Seth groans behind me.

'You planted it in her belly with some witchery, for all I know.'

'I'll stake it was you did that, Gabriel.'

'Dare you speak my name?'

His hand flies out, dropping the stick at his feet, and I flinch, despite determination to stand firm. He grabs my coif and throws it to the ground, rips the pins from my hair so it falls down my neck and over my shoulder. Slowly, he wraps it round his hand, brings it up and caresses his cheek, dips his nose and breathes in, eyes closed. I am brought closer to him as he winds my hair around his fist.

'Leave me be,' I say.

'Long, I have dreamed of this,' he says, voice softer than I've ever heard. 'To know the look of it about your shoulder, to know the feel and scent.'

I try to keep my breathing slow and steady. Fail. This moment, when happiness rests within reach, he dares touch me, forces fear upon me.

'Get your hands off,' I say.

His eyes snap open, grip tightens on my hair. I wince.

'No matter, for I see you with a clear eye now. Did you lay a spell on me, that I would see you as other? I have shook it off, witch.'

He winds my hair tighter, tighter, reeling me in close, my body pulled next to his, head tipped up to him. I feel the pounding of his heart against my shoulder, the fast rise and fall of his chest. I would have to rip the hair from my head to escape. At the corner of my eye I see the shape of Seth, on hands and knees, body wracked as he heaves. He turns to us, and I pray that he keeps away, protects himself.

'I would not waste my time with the likes of you,' I say.

'I see you now,' he says. 'Ugly. Only your sorcery could make me want to wed you, give myself to you. Touch you.'

He runs his thumb over my lips, head bent close to mine, breath hot on my face.

'You got a ugly little mouth, lass. You little whore, it wasn't you, never you, the one I loved, the one I wanted. Not this mouth.'

He forces his thumb between my lips. I struggle to free myself.

'Not this hair.'

Twists and yanks. A blaze of pain in my scalp and I cry out. Heart thundering now.

'Not this body.'

Hand on my skin, forcing under my shift and closing hard around my breast. Face so close to mine now, the breath from every word hitting my cheek.

'Was never love,' he says, 'but trickery, a mockery of my feelings, but I see you now, I see you, you ugly little bitch.'

His lips on mine, tongue forcing into my mouth, invading, hands yanking hair and pounding skin. I pull away as hard as I can, but he is too strong, too determined. Try to cry out but my mouth is full of him and I have no voice. Heart thudding, I struggle, fight, but nothing happens. Taste of him, and of my own tears. I pull away and away, must free myself. Cannot. I am trapped.

'Gabriel.'

The voice is loud, sure and slow. Seems to come from above, and we are both jolted out of the moment. Gabriel loosens his grip and I run free, wiping my mouth and aiming a sharp kick at his shin on the way. More grateful for the shoes than I've ever been. He yelps and staggers, glaring at me.

'Whore,' he says.

'Brute.'

I hate now as I've never hated, with every part of mind and body. For forcing his touch upon me. For laying this fear on me, leaving me shaking and weak and taking refuge at Seth's side. I hate him enough to embrace my powers, to release the dog just so I can watch it rip his throat out and soak this desecrated ground with his blood. Enough to become what I fear and lose all I hope for.

Seth lays a hand on my arm. He stands tall, face calm and commanding, though I see the pallor of his skin, catch a whiff of puke about him.

'You leave her be,' he says to Gabriel.

'But, parson, you don't know—'

'We are all children of God, and you are to leave this one be. Always.'

'No, she isn't what she appears, you've been—'

Seth turns to me, speaks softly. 'Go, now.'

I shake my head.

'Go,' he says. Drops his head lower to look me in the eye. 'Go to your love, share your news.'

I glance at Gabriel. He listens to every word, frowning.

'No,' I say.

'Begin the new path,' Seth says. 'I will calm the seas here, and see you both tomorrow night.'

I back away a few steps, then run to him again, kiss his cheek before turning and fleeing the hillside. The words that begin to pour from Gabriel's mouth follow on the wind.

Witch. Whore. Slave of the Devil. Sorceress. Rising in volume and venom with each one.

I run from them. Run to Daniel. To our new life.

The Very Brink

They stood. Daniel and Father in the silent kitchen, looking about at the cold fire and empty table.

The sleepless night of excitement at what was to come and heartache for what he must leave had left Daniel exhausted, and filled with uneasy vigour.

Father looked at him, shrugged in an open-armed gesture of defeat.

'Gabriel, I can understand,' he said. 'Bellyful of ale last night left him sore-headed and lazy, or he's found a fray on the way in and delayed himself. But Bett – never been away a day, has she?'

Daniel shook his head. 'Not one, but for the day she wed. And that they should both be gone—'

Father pulled on his beard. 'Strange.'

They glanced around again, as though the absent persons might crawl out from under the table and confess some jest.

'Little lassie will be milking, of course,' Father said.

'As ever.' Daniel tried to keep his voice dispassionate. He had not seen Sarah this morning, could only hope that she was about her tasks as always. 'Do you—'

The door swung open and Bett staggered through, panting and pressing a hand to her side.

'Oh,' she said, leaning against the wall. 'Oh, news from the village, the most fearful news, and though I pray God it's not true, but I have heard from many.'

'News of what?' Father asked.

She heaved herself from the wall and lurched towards Daniel, taking his hands. 'You must come, for what they're saying it's – you must quiet them.'

'What news?' he asked.

'Of the parson,' she said.

Daniel ran as never before, outstripping both Father and Bett.

The happiness and fearful hope that had filled him through the night, knowing that he would end this day Sarah's husband and at the very brink of a life of his own making, felt still within reach. The tale Bett had been told would prove false. A mistake; so great an evil could not have taken place. He would find all calm, all as it was and should be. And he and Sarah would say their quiet farewells, and begin along their own path.

He heard the shouts and wails before he came upon the crowd gathered at the foot of the cursed hill, standing a small distance from the figure on the ground. Desperate, he flung aside any that stood in his way, until he looked upon the dreadful sight himself.

The parson lay on his back, arms outstretched and feet together, a grotesque imitation of Christ on the cross. Pinned to the ground by a stake through the chest, grass below him darkened by black wings of blood. His face waxy and white, mouth gaping, eyes open and blank. Hat nowhere to be seen. His wispy hair shifting in the breeze in a cruel replica of life.

Daniel refused to believe what he saw, looked again and could not deny. Gasped for air and found none. Fell to his knees and reached to stroke the parson, to ease pain or give comfort, but found only the chill of death beneath his touch. A sound he did not recognise came from his own mouth, an expression of grief and anger that could not be articulated. The knees of his breeches stained with blood.

Hands gripped his shoulders, lifted him to his feet and turned him. He leaned for a moment in Bett's sturdy embrace.

'He – he is a good man,' Daniel said. 'Godly. How can this be?'

Bett nodded. 'I know. And you are stricken, as are we all, but you must come back to yourself now. Blame is being laid and it falls close to your heart.'

Daniel took in her tear-tracked face, let her words seep into him. Heard the voices around him, smelled metal soaked into sod.

One voice rose above all, leading until others followed. Gabriel.

'Plain as day who's the culprit. Only one family lives just outside our reach. Only one family would do this to a church man. It's that witch-girl from up the hill, with her curses and sorcery.'

Daniel looked around, as the crowd bayed its agreement. No familiar face to reason with, no one in a position to make them listen, and Sarah accused. He thanked God they would not know where to find her. It had always been the parson that

Daniel turned to for a calming voice in situations such as these. Long gone was a magistrate who could be called upon to exercise fair judgement.

'Surely this is no witchcraft?' he shouted out, desperate to stall them. 'This was an attack of force, we can see what killed him, there is no spell or curse here.'

'Who else would kill a man of God?' Gabriel said.

Daniel could not answer.

'Look at the way he's laid out,' a voice came from the crowd. 'A mockery of the church itself, of all the man stood for. It can only be those heathens.'

'Still, my son speaks some wisdom,' Father called. Daniel was grateful for this calmer, stronger voice of support. 'No girl would have the strength for—' He waved his hand towards the brutal scene laid out before them. 'By my reckoning, it must be the son.'

Daniel's heart jolted so hard that he gasped.

'The boy has strength and fury enough, we've seen it before, and he has a demon in his power, the one seen running from Sam's house. It's him that's done this wickedness. Who else could it be?'

'Aye, and I've been telling you all these weeks past, was not I but him that thefted your belongings,' Gabriel put in. 'You see he is guilty of that and much worse now.'

Daniel ran, let their voices fade behind him, let the pounding of his blood drown out his own doubts. Knew only that he must reach Sarah. Did not let himself think of the question he could not answer.

Who else would kill a man of God?

★

She walked along the path, sun at her back, her expression calm. If he knew some spell, some word of magic to stop her at this moment, before all she loved and hoped for was swept away, he would barter his soul and save her the pain to come.

'There you are,' she said as she neared him. Glanced over her shoulder at the clear path. 'Husband.'

She reached her arms around his neck. His heart broke for her fleeting happiness.

'I came back to the house and no one was there, what's happening?' she asked.

Still he could not bring himself to speak.

She frowned. 'What? What is it?' Looked him up and down. 'Is that blood?'

'When you saw your family yesterday,' he said, 'was your brother there? Did you see him?'

He tried to stop her. Tried to reason, to persuade her that she should hide. She ripped off her coif, picked up her petticoat and ran. He followed.

Bett met them at the foot of the hill. 'I'm sorry,' she said. 'I tried to stop them, or make them wait for the magistrate at least, but—' She shook her head.

'They're at the house?' Sarah asked.

'On the way, yes. Sorry.'

Sarah ran on, pausing when she came upon the parson. So intent on exacting revenge on his behalf, they had all abandoned him to his indignity. Sarah gasped, bent to place a kiss on his forehead.

'I'm sorry,' she whispered.

Daniel took her in his arms and shared her misery. She stood a moment, face pressed against his tunic.

'It's all gone,' she said. 'Everything just gone.'

He kissed the top of her head. 'I know.'

'And now they blame my family.' She pushed him away, staggering towards the Haworth shack with tears pouring down her face.

The crowd was already at the house. Some had collected weapons: sticks, knives, ropes, torches. Gabriel had a pitchfork.

Hackles

They have ripped him from his bed, I see by the way his blanket is flung aside. Four men to carry him, one grasping each limb. He twists in their arms, eyes rolling, face the colour of wood-ash.

Just a lad. Frightened lad. I don't know why they cannot see that's all he is.

'Mam,' he calls. 'Mam, make them stop.'

She runs from man to man, pulling on their arms and weeping. 'Leave him be, what dust want with my son?'

Annie in the corner of the other room, kneading her petticoat. Tears dripping into her stretched mouth as she wails and sobs, as I've not seen her do since she was tiny.

I run to her, lift her. She shows no sign of knowing me. Allows me to pick her up without speaking or putting her arms around me. My neck soaked with her tears.

Daniel stands in the doorway, staring helpless as the men struggle to carry John's thrashing body outside, as they throw

Mam off. He looks at me, eyes huge against the sickly shade of his skin. Feared.

I run to him, force Annie into his arms.

'Take her,' I say.

His arms close around her, he strokes the hair from her wet face. 'Come with us,' he says.

I shake my head. Cannot.

'Sarah—'

'Go.'

He nods.

The men carrying John, the crowd that follows and Mam as she drags against them are all outside the door now. I am sick with fear, sick with seeing John's fear.

'Please,' he shouts. 'Let me be. Please.'

There are whoops and jeers from the crowd. People I saw at church, women who chat and laugh at the market, who have come to Mam for cures many a time. Gabriel at the head of them, pitchfork held aloft.

I run after, pull with all my strength at those holding John, try to prise their fingers away.

'Stop,' I say. 'Please, he's just a lad, he's done nowt.' Earn a stinging slap to the face that sends me crashing to the ground. Stand again, beg again, try again to free him.

I don't look down the hill to see Daniel make his escape with Annie. He will keep her safe.

They surround us and those holding John's legs release him, stand him up. He struggles, but they hold him fast. He sobs, calls for Mam.

'He's just a lad,' I shout. 'Let him be.'

'This is no lad, but demon in the flesh,' Gabriel says.

'Please,' John says. Holds himself up straight, breathes deep and I see him try to stay calm, keep reason, despite the trembling that quivers his whole body. 'Please, this is a mistake. I don't know what you think I've done, but 'tis no more than try and fail to earn honest living. And any here look into your soul and find pity, offer me a chance and I will prove decent. As God is witness.'

'Why did you kill the parson?' Gabriel asks.

And I hate. The flicker comes to my eye, the shudder to my bones, and I welcome it.

John stumbles back, as if the words knock him. 'What? Seth? I never touched him,' he says. Taunts from the crowd. John looks around, eyes wild. 'Please, I never would. He's good to us. Please. Let me go.'

'Was not John that killed Seth and you know it, you carry that guilt yourself, murderer,' I shout.

Gabriel turns to the crowd, laughs. 'Oh, the witch-sister would lay blame on me for the killing of a church man, lain out in mockery of Christ and right where these Satan-slaves dwell.'

I launch myself at him, am held back and look to find it's Bett that pins me. 'I'm sorry,' she says, soft in my ear. 'I cannot let you sacrifice yourself, even for this.'

There is a crescendo of sound, from outside and inside myself. Mam wailing, John begging, the roaring voices around. The growling, growling till it thunders through my bones and I don't know how Bett has strength to hold me.

Gabriel strikes the first blow. Pitchfork to chest, and John falls. Cries out. Sobs and clutches his wound. Calls for Mam.

I scream his name into the din. Pull against Bett's arms.

After that, too many to see. Beasts, hollering and beating, each taking a turn, each calling the others on. Weapons, fists and feet. I cannot see John beneath them, cannot hear his cries over theirs. Mam is held back by village women who once were her friends. Bett keeps hold of me, arms around me, head resting against mine as she weeps.

'I'm sorry,' she says. 'Close your eyes, don't look. Oh God, what's become of us?'

I blink and the eyes are there, glowing embers. The snarling shakes me from inside. Hackles rise. I feel it, the dog. It is me, I am it.

Silence spreads from the centre. John's stillness infects them. One by one they fall quiet, step back. Eyes downcast at the tangled, bloodied mass that was once my brother. Soundlessly sucking on their bleeding knuckles, wiping their stained weapons.

'My son,' Mam cries. 'Oh, my boy. My son, my son.'

The only sound.

She is released and crawls over to John, cradles his head, kisses his hair.

'Wake up,' she whispers. 'Open your eyes, lad.' Strokes his face again, again. 'Not so bad. Just a little hurt. Waken.' Her hair parts at the neck and her mark shows clear for all to see.

'Dear God,' Bett says, weeping. 'What have we done?'

Hands fall to sides, limp. Not one can meet another's gaze. I watch with ember eyes, claws break through my fingertips. Snarling shakes the bones of me.

Only Gabriel looks about, eyes bright, face flushed. He stabs the pitchfork into the ground and is upon me in two steps, grabbing my arm and hauling me from Bett's grip as she yells at him to stop.

'And what of this one, that tricked and mocked us? Bewitched us into trusting her, putting her to work and homing her, and all the while she was the Devil's own?'

His words are met with silence, turned backs and averted eyes.

'You see what she is now,' he says. 'No dairymaid, but the Haworth witch-whore.'

'Leave be, Gabriel,' Mr Taylor says. A web of blood drapes across his knuckles.

'Enough done today.'

I struggle but cannot free myself from the grasp of Gabriel's meaty fingers. Cast my eyes down and see claws, run my tongue over fangs. 'You see what I am?' I scream. 'Then look upon me some more, for this is nowt to what will be. I shall haunt your waking and sleeping hours all, until you see nowt but his face, hear nowt but his cries, and you shall know your own hand in the evil done here. I wed myself to any being that will make it so. And I shall spill the blood of each and every one of you while this day is done.'

I sink my teeth into Gabriel's hand and he lets go with a cry, releasing me to fall upon the others. Tear at skin until my nails are thick with it and warm blood tracks my fingers. Dig into eyes, rip hair out by the handful.

'A curse upon you all,' I scream. 'Your every child shall wither and die before you.'

They fall back as I bear down upon them, whimpering and raising their hands as though the heat of hell itself burns through me.

'Pestilence shall pass from house to house until you all have suffered as he.'

They turn, cowards, and flee to their solid walls, thinking they shall keep me out.

'And at the end,' I yell at their retreating backs, 'the hands of my brother, pouring his own blood, shall reach up from the earth and draw you into it.'

They are gone.

Nothing else to see. I am forced to look upon John's pulped and twisted body. Mam hunched over him, her tears falling on to his face as she holds him to her. Oblivious to all else.

Bett, with her hands clasped together as though she prays, steps towards me.

'Oh, Sarah.' She reaches a hand out, slowly, as though I might break or burst into flame. 'I'm sorry, I'm so sorry. What can I do?'

'You can leave.'

'I want to help.'

I kneel by Mam, put my arm around her heaving shoulder, look upon John's face.

'Your kind have done enough,' I say, and after a little time hear footsteps as she does my bidding.

His skin is split, lips and cheeks swollen and misshapen. But still so much himself that I know his spirit remained his own till the end. A quiet about his closed eyes and softened mouth so that I could almost, even now, believe he is but sleeping.

Mam is wrapped in grief, and no use at all. I drag John back to the house, a long and painful process that smashes him against roots and stones. I know he's past reach, yet I fear to hurt him. Twice he slips from my grip and his head falls to the ground. Mam follows, wringing her hands and weeping.

I wash him as best I can and lay him behind the house, where the earth is soft and looked upon by the empty windows of our home. Mam kneels at his side, resting her cheek against his and whispering a mother's love into his deafened ear.

Later I shall bury him. If it takes all night to scratch a grave with my bare fingers.

His Own Hand

Annie's tears had stopped. She sat on the riverbank next to him, pulling her hair over her face and whispering. He could not hear what she said. Did not know what to do.

'Shall we look for moon fish?' he asked. Hoping she could not hear the strain in his voice.

She spread her fingers and yanked them through her hair, tugging at the tangles until clumps broke off and gathered in her hand. Whispered.

He opened his mouth to tell her all would be well, but could not bring himself to. All he thought he knew of the world was lost and he could not grasp his place in it, much less offer Annie a comforting account. He should have kept Sarah away, protected the brother. Spoken out and spoken louder. Yet here he hid on the riverbank, grateful for Annie as his justification and ashamed of his gratitude.

The whispering slid from her mouth, entwined itself around him and slithered through his blood. She was but a child, an innocent surely that was caught in terror. Still, he had the sense that some incantation fell from her lips. He wished and feared to hear the words. Could no longer tell what was real, the life he had built with Sarah or the stories of the family. The image of Sarah, so unlike the girl he knew, so filled with power, cursing Molly, stuck in his mind.

Gabriel's question was one he could not answer – who else, but the devil-brother, would kill a man of God? And now even the child whispered words that were surely laden with sinister magic.

'Have you stolen a waif?'

The voice, unexpected, stunned him. Molly flopped down next to him and peered at Annie with undisguised disgust. A thin red mark, almost healed, scored her forehead. The little girl whispered and added to the pile of hair that gathered at her bare feet.

'She looks infested,' Molly said.

He was thrown back for a moment to the day he helped Sarah wash Annie's hair. Were you stealing her? she'd asked. Assailed by grief, he could only look silently at Molly. Her face was drawn and red around the eyes.

'Where on earth did you find her?' she asked.

'Have you not heard?' he said.

'I've heard no village tattle, for I was here searching for stones to weight me down and sink me to the bottom of the water.'

Clouds gathered heavy and low, rolling in a mist from the water. 'There's been a terrible – wait, what? You were looking for what?'

She glanced at him and then away, tears welling in the green pools of her eyes. 'I was too faint-hearted. Filled my hands with stones and stood at the edge of the river until I gave up and threw them all in the water instead. I will find an easier way.'

She gave an odd, hiccupping laugh and wiped her eyes but the tears kept coming.

'But – why?' he asked.

'I'm too shamed to say.'

Quiet then, just the wash of the river, the first splashes of rain on the ground and the incessant slip of Annie's whispered words. He heard them now, though they made no sense. 'He's been. He's been. I have the mark.' Repeated over and over.

'Whatever it is, it cannot be so bad,' he said.

'You're kind. It should have been you, if it had been you then all would be well, but you chose another. And I was angry and he said he loved me, though I knew he spoke false, but I wanted it to be, just wanted someone to and – it was only once. But now he will not—'

She lay her head on her arms and sobbed. Daniel worked on the riddle of her words and saw the labour of his own hand in the hopelessness she now found herself in. How could he, so feeble that he walked the earth without leaving a print upon it, make such an impact as to cause this much pain? He had made a wrong choice at every turn; abandoning Molly, failing to come to Phyllis's aid. His weakness all that left a mark on those he touched.

'I even tried a brew, but it didn't work,' Molly said. 'Did she put an enchantment on you, the witch-girl? To make you love her?'

She looked to him, wiping the tears from her cheeks, sniffing.

He meant to answer no, meant to tell her Sarah was not as they all thought. But the child's whispered words still swirled around him. The evidence of the brother's vicious temper and black heart, the demon he summoned to carry out his ill deeds, still confronting Daniel each time he closed his eyes and saw Parson Walsh's body. And was the scar that Molly bore testament after all to Sarah using her power to move the branch and trip her?

His own words spun through his head. If I am bewitched, then let it be so.

Even when he was lost in love for her, he knew it. She had preyed upon his fragile soul, used sinister forces to conjure his affections, and he had allowed her to.

The scream came from behind, and he and Molly both jumped up. Only Annie remained oblivious, whispering and gathering a soft pile of hair at her feet.

'You,' Sarah yelled.

She bore down upon them, a black mass of blazing fury against the rain. Molly turned and fled, but Sarah soon pounced upon her, shook her like an animal does its prey. Molly fell to her knees.

'Stop,' she said, weeping. 'Please, I'm sorry.'

'You.' Sarah's voice a low growl. 'You told Gabriel. Didn't you?' She grasped Molly's hair and shook her again. 'Didn't you?'

Molly sobbed. 'You took them both,' she said. 'You didn't even want Gabriel, but you still bewitched him just to take him from me. I'm sorry, please don't curse me.'

Sarah pulled Molly's face close to her own, hissed the words. 'You told Gabriel and he killed Seth. And John was blamed and now he is dead, do you understand? He is dead, because you told.'

Daniel reached out, to stay Sarah's anger, to protect Molly. To grasp the meaning. John was dead, and he felt the horror that was Sarah's, but a part of him breathed deeper, surer, because the Devil-boy could no longer reach him.

'I do curse you,' Sarah said. 'I curse the babe in your belly to split you open and send you to hell on its way out, curse it to a life that carries all the pain caused by both its father and mother.'

Molly wailed and begged to be spared. Sarah released her grip, and Molly stumbled to her feet, staggered away.

Daniel stood, watched her go. Turned back to Sarah. Both soaked now. Could think of nothing to say. Nothing to do. How could she know of Molly's plight? He was afraid of this unearthly ability to see what was hidden.

'John is dead,' she said, her voice flat now after the fury it had been filled with.

'Yes. I'm sorry.'

'Thank you for taking Annie.'

'She's—' He gestured to show the state of the child, still pulling her hair, though the whispering had stopped.

Sarah nodded. 'I'll bring her now.'

She did not move.

'Sarah?'

'Aye?'

'When you visited your family yesterday, was he there? Your brother?'

She gave him a look dark with loathing. 'No. But it was Gabriel killed Seth, not John.'

'Gabriel? He's a brute, but even he wouldn't kill a man of God. And in such a way—'

'It was Gabriel.'

She walked to Annie, crouched and gently pushed the hair from her face, kissed her cheek and gathered her into her arms.

He watched, torn by grief for the life they had planned, for the person he had thought she was. Even now, he would choose to let her bewitch him and believe in that life. 'We should have been wed tonight,' he said.

Sarah lifted Annie on to her hip and stepped past him. Her hair had fallen loose and the petticoat Bett had given her was ripped and stained, clinging wet to her legs as she walked. She looked like Sarah as he had first seen her, but more – a deadened form of herself, the storm she carried slowed and cold.

'Aye,' she said, as she walked away.

Take Any Day

Annie does not speak. She does not let me go, clinging with arms around my shoulders and legs around my waist, and I'm grateful for her warmth. With her held against me, the snarling subsides. Her face is buried against my neck, no tears now.

She does not ask of John, and I do not tell her.

The house is in shadow and Mam at last left John's side, but lies curled in his bed, his blanket held to her face.

'Do you remember,' Mam says, 'when he fell from one of the Taylors' apple trees? Clean white his face went, and his ankle turned black, but he still ran all the way home. Loved apples so much, he didn't drop a single one. And when he was younger and his father still alive, he couldn't reach to climb the gate to the lamb field. He'd wriggle underneath and I'd scold for the stains on his breeches. I'll have that day.'

Her breath shudders.

'I'll have those days. Oh, I will live those days, any of those days, over and again. I'll take any, with him thieving and cursing, lazing in his bed, I will take any day but this, not this, I don't want this, I cannot live this day.'

Her pain fills the house. I close my eyes against it, stop my ears to it. I don't have room for my own grief. The village will turn upon us now, and I don't know how to protect Annie. If we run our troubles will follow, for there's no place that will see a bedraggled group of desperate women and not cry witch.

I hold her in my arms, little lass. Wild creature that grips tree bark with her toes to climb all the faster, watches and learns about any small animal she can find. Clenches her fists and growls in anger. Brings flowers as a gift and wishes to grow into a man.

I pull her close to me. Shall never let go.

The finding of Annie comes to me now, as if I lived it yesterday. A cold, clear memory as sharp as a knife edge.

In the years when the men came. I lay in the same place I lie now, watched as Mam winced and groaned and clutched her swollen belly. She bent down, brushed hair from my cheek.

'Don't fret, lass,' she said. 'I swallowed a stone, is all. I must bury it in the woods. Stay here and watch your brother. I'll be back while morning.'

It was not the first stone she had swallowed and buried.

I waited through the night, peering through the lashes of half-closed eyes when she crept back in at dawn. Footprint of blood on the floor as she passed me.

'Get back to sleep,' she said, and crawled to her bed.

I went to look for the stone.

The sound was thin, a desperate bleating, wrapped like a ribbon through the trees, leading me to the place I found her. Scrawny little babe, kicking her tiny feet and reaching her tiny arms from under the tree where she lay.

I could not leave her.

'Look, Mammy,' I called when I brought her home. 'Look what I found growing in the woods.'

Mam wrapped her in a cloth and held her to her breast. Smiled and wept. Cradled her and whispered of love.

That was the day she showed me my mark, told me what it meant. No men came after that.

When all is quiet I creep from bed and out to the moonlit night. Fury and fear burn through me as I dig down again and again, the snarling strengthening my bones, driving me on. I've been grateful today to have this creature conjured from the blackest parts of me, giving me strength, doing my bidding. It is tamed now, tethered to my will. On and on I work. The pain in my exhausted arms and broken skin on my hands cannot stop me.

His is a shallow resting place, unmarked and less than he deserves, but he sleeps in it as sunlight breaks across the sky.

I lay myself down over his blanket of earth, nourish it with my tears.

Darkening

Milk threatened to slop out as Daniel walked, bucket pulling on his arm. Gabriel, on his way to the house, whistled and chuckled as he passed.

'Back in your rightful place, Danny. No little witch-whore shall take the women's work from you.'

Words like a pitchfork to the chest. Daniel walked on. In the two days since Parson Walsh was killed, Gabriel's mood had soared. He laughed, told jokes and stories of women that Daniel hoped were not true, slapped him on the back. There was an edge to his good humour, a constant flicker to the eye and twitch of the hand.

No one had spoken of the parson. Or Sarah. Until now. It was as though she were dead, and all he had felt gone with her. The love they shared, the life they dreamed, all a figment she had conjured and planted in him.

When she tried in vain to protect her brother and then unleashed her fury upon the villagers, everyone knew that their dairymaid had been none other than the Haworth girl.

Including Father. Daniel had expected to find himself banished for bringing her under their roof, but there had been no mention of her. It was well, though, that Sarah stayed away. Gabriel's blood still burned for revenge, and Father's pity would not extend to the cunning woman's daughter. And Daniel feared what punishment she would call down upon those that murdered her brother.

Each night he dreamed of the storm in her eyes.

There was a held-breath silence in the kitchen as he entered. Magistrate Wright walked the edges of the room as Father, Gabriel and Bett sat awkwardly at the table. Father glanced his way. The first time he had met Daniel's eye in two days, and his pain and shame were clear to see.

'Yours is an unexpected response to tragic news, and yet one that has greeted me wherever I have shared it,' the magistrate said. 'No shock or grief. Hardly surprise, even.'

Gabriel shook out his shoulders. 'Not much to surprise us, living as we do with that family of heathens up the hill.'

The magistrate stopped, looked down at the tips of his gleaming shoes, nodded slowly. 'Interesting you should say so, given the location of the body and the, ah – position. I would have expected such an act to be brought to my attention much sooner. Hard to believe no one knew.'

Daniel closed his eyes and willed the image of Parson Walsh away. Breathed slow and deep. He could not hear the magistrate's words over the beating of his own blood.

'We do not,' Father was saying, rising to his feet and indicating the door. 'But if any of us hears anything we'll be sure and tell you.'

The magistrate touched his hat and allowed himself to be ushered out. Father collapsed back into his seat, shaking, head in hands. Blood seeping from his nose and dripping on to the table.

'Oh, this is a bad business, the worst I've known in all my years,' he said.

'We should tell him it was the witch family, we know it sure as day, and he'll be wanting to put the law to work,' Gabriel said.

'Has your thirst for blood not been quenched, Gabriel?' Bett asked. 'You've had revenge on the lad.' She swallowed, steadied her voice. 'He has paid, if he was indeed the black soul and commander of demons we feared. But the mother and sisters, what do we really know of sorcery in them? The conjuring of enchantments and cures and giving you the cow pox is far from murdering the parson.'

Daniel glanced at Bett. Even now, as she defended Sarah and her family, she confirmed his fear that Sarah did indeed possess powers of witchcraft, and had used them to create a phantom love. He blinked back the sting of tears. Bett was free to believe in the innocent version of Sarah she had known. But he had seen her cursing Molly, the fury and power rushing through her, and the memory sat in him like a chip of ice, numbing him to all that was once good. He knew what Bett did not.

'She's right,' Father said. 'Enough done there. The sight of his mother in such grief – it were almost enough to persuade she feels it like any other. To make me think she perhaps did all she could to save your mother, as she claimed.'

Bett pushed her chair back and walked out. The men glanced at each other. There were no words with the power to express what had been done, and the feelings of each at the role he had played.

Gabriel shrugged. 'I can hold my tongue. He'll know soon enough, anyway.'

Father ran his hands over his face, again and again. Fingers shaking, tears in his eyes.

'Work,' he said. Voice strangled, as though shame squeezed around his throat. 'Farm cannot wait, tasks to be done and we have been delayed by events too much.' He rose and walked to the door. 'About it, lads.'

Daniel made to follow, but Gabriel stood and blocked his path, a great mass darkening the doorway.

'Don't blame yourself,' he said. 'She had me fooled awhile there too.'

Daniel shifted. Gabriel reached his arm to the doorframe.

'I – I don't grasp your—'

'Did you think your courting was stealthy? She did not hide it from me. There must have been some spell upon us to see a beauty in her that was not there. Even I, that's laid with so many girls, when she pushed herself against me I was taken in, so how were you, with only our Betts to compare with, supposed to see the trickery?'

'Pushed against you?' The smile upon Gabriel's lips surely, Daniel hoped, showed there was no truth to his words.

The smile lifted on one side. 'Aye, a time or two, though soon enough I saw through her sorcery and was disgusted by her. Ugly, underneath the spell, she is.' He bent his head low to reach Daniel's, eyes level. Voice lowered. 'Did you see how ugly she was?'

Daniel saw the turbulent blue eyes, soft curved lips and smooth river of skin. Remembered laughter strung through the air like stars in the night. Longed with every part of himself to believe in their love, yearned for it to be true.

He saw her pressed against Gabriel.

A wash of heat ran through him. Foolish, he had been. Weak in his need to be seen for his true self, loved. Nothing about her had been as it appeared – her innocence of spirit, her loyalty to him. All conjured.

She had understood his frailty and appeared to him that day, with Bonny, made him see in her everything he yearned for. Entranced him to give himself and turn away from all he knew. And all the while her mother worked fatal magic on Sam and the brother commanded his demon to slaughter the parson. Her own acts of vile magic, the cursing of Gabriel and the moving of the branch to trip Molly, were even seen by his own eyes. Some part of him had known all along that she was not as he thought, that there was truth to the stories about her. The only time in his life he did not listen to the voice of doubt was the one time he should have.

None of it was true. The strength she saw in him. The bond between them, the life they planned.

Wild, beautiful witch. She had devised all.

Gabriel laughed, slapped Daniel on the shoulder. 'You should revel in the turn of events, Danny. You've been saved a fate as witch-husband.'

The laughter weakened his stance, and Daniel was able to push him aside and pass into the bright outdoors. Only from Gabriel's mouth could fall the suggestion that he revel in these, the worst of times. Through the cloth of his breeches he felt the stone that he still carried in his pocket. Unable, yet, to let it go.

Daniel worked as never before, until his hands bled and his tunic was soaked through and melded to his back. He watched young rabbits capering at the edge of the field, a sight that would once have soothed him. Still he could not quiet his mind.

He had crashed through the past months, destroying all he touched and leaving a trail of devastation. Planning to abandon his family and inheritance, involving the parson in a scheme that left him murdered, turning his back on Phyllis and then Molly, leaving her prey to Gabriel's appetites and moral destitution. Taken in by the worst evil, willingly.

He scythed and weeded and ploughed and sowed. Still his boisterous mind persisted.

At the end of the day, faint with exhaustion, he had decided upon a path that would ease his conscience.

With Bett and Gabriel at last gone to their own homes the kitchen was quiet.

'I must speak with you,' Daniel said.

Father raised an eyebrow and drank from his flagon. Daniel sat. No anticipation this time, no fear, just a flat determination to say what he had to. To put right the one thing it was in his power to.

Now. Before he was once again seduced by Sarah's bewitchment.

'I must confess that, though you forbade my courting Molly Matthews, I have continued.'

The flagon stopped on its way to Father's lips. 'I thought you refused her?'

'I – yes, I did but then she persisted and I was—'

Father nodded. 'I see.'

'I have lain with her.'

'Oh.'

'And she is—'

'Oh, no.'

'Yes.'

Daniel waited in the silence as Father took in the news. Once he would have feared an explosion of anger, a beating even. No longer. The fire crackled behind him.

'I gather there are remedies for such a—'

'They have been tried,' Daniel said.

'Oh. And no success?'

Daniel shook his head. Father swallowed the last of his ale, wiped his mouth with the back of his hand. Sighed. Stretched out a leg, brought it in again.

'You have disappointed me, son.'

Daniel focused on the groove of the wooden table. 'Myself also.'

'You know where your mother's ring is kept.'

'Yes.'

''Tis not as I had hoped,' Father said.

'Nor I.'

'But you love her? Son? To put you both at risk of this? You care for her as I cared for your mother, the ring will find its rightful place?'

Daniel hesitated. Molly was sweet, and silly, and manipulative, and frail.

The feelings he had known and called love were not real. Were not even his own. He knew nothing of it.

'Yes,' he said.

★

Sarah's room was as she left it. Blankets pulled neatly over the bed, clothes folded in a corner. Beneath them, he knew, the ring. Hidden, until the day they escaped and she could wear it freely. Never now to be.

Deceived into giving it, he was free to take it back.

Still the scent of her suspended in the air.

Within a Curse's Reach

Bett has brought food, wrapped in a cloth just as I used to on Sundays. Bread, butter, cheese, collops, salad leaves and a pail of milk.

'Eat,' she says, taking my shoulders and guiding me to the table. She glances at Annie, standing in the doorway, one foot tucked behind her knee. 'And you,' Bett says.

Annie looks at me. 'Aye,' I say, and she sidles to me, settles on a stool and nibbles on a piece of bread.

Bett looks at Mam, curled in John's bed, stroking his blanket and whispering. Says nothing.

'I'm so sorry,' she says. 'About what happened, Sarah, so sorry I couldn't stop it. I didn't know what to do, I wanted to go to the magistrate but Nathaniel said it would be worse for you.'

'Nathaniel's right.'

She sighs, pleats her apron. 'You could leave, you're a dairy-maid, go to the next mop and find a new place.'

'What of Annie and Mam? I cannot go to a mop with them. If three women such as we arrived in any village, you know what everyone would think.'

Bett hangs her head, nods.

'There's nowhere to go, the three of us, that will not end the same way as here.'

Bett puffs out an angry breath. 'It cannot be so. I will not have it. There must be something to be done, something I can do.'

I think, briefly, of the small pile of belongings I left at the farm and dare not go back to retrieve. My clothes. Bracelet. The ring Daniel gave me. 'Thank you for the food,' I say.

'Something more than food.'

The words come out, unbidden, each ripping a piece of me away as I speak it. 'You can take Annie.'

They both start. Bett stares at Annie, Annie stares at me, stops chewing, though her mouth bulges with food.

Bett gives a thin laugh. 'I – no, you've lost all—'

Annie spits her mouthful on to the table, clenches her fists, glares at Bett and growls.

'Take her, keep her safe. You yearn to mother, and she is in need.' I wipe her mouth with my hand, frowning. 'And she is usually much more appealing than this,' I say.

'No, she – they all know her anyway, it would not work.' Her eyes burn bright as she looks at Annie. She pictures being her mother, I know.

I lift Annie, carry her around the table and try to put her into Bett's arms. 'Take her,' I say.

Annie wails and clings to me, gnashes her teeth at Bett. All this while Mam whispers, so overwhelmed by the loss of one child she doesn't note the losing of another.

'Take her,' I say, pushing Annie towards her. 'Keep her safe.'

Annie screams and weeps. 'No,' she shouts. 'Sarah, no.' Her arms are tight round my neck, legs clamped around my waist, gripping with fingers and toes. I feel the sobs shudder through her body, the tears warm on my neck and can't hold back my own.

Bett steps away, shakes her head. Tears in her eyes too.

'I cannot. She needs you.'

As Annie holds on to me I know I can't part from her, even to save her. I sink on to a stool, press my face against her shoulder.

'All right,' I whisper. 'It's all right. You stay with me.'

Bett clears her throat, gives a sharp nod. Bats her hand across her eyes. 'Good, then. I shall bring food. But, Sarah, think of leaving. The magistrate goes from house to house, asking about Parson Walsh's – asking about Satan and witchcraft. I fear for you.'

She reaches into her petticoat and takes out her purse. Pulls from it a comb, made of bone. One I've seen many times before.

I press my hand to my mouth. 'How did you …?'

Her voice is soft. 'I saw him sneak out of the house with it that day. Saw it in your room later. I thought you might—'

I take it from her. Can say nothing in response, my throat too full to speak.

When she's gone, Annie slides from my lap, stands with fists clenched, glaring through a pile of hair. 'You gived me away,' she shouts, and runs to flop on to her mat.

I sit at the table, turning the comb in my hand. Remembering. I had been at the beck. After he'd shown us the moon fish. Before May Day. Before he'd ever been to this house. Air laced with the scent of mud.

'I thought I might find you here,' he had said. 'Not that I was looking for you. I like the river, I'm here very often. Well, not very often but—'

I watched the blush spread over his cheeks, smothering the freckles. Couldn't make sense of him. He puffed out a long, slow breath, rocked back on his heels and looked up at the sky.

'No sister with you today?' he asked. He sounded as though someone squeezed the air from him.

'Are you all right?'

He had laughed. 'Good question.'

I turned back to the water. Felt him move from foot to foot, lift his cap and run his hand through his hair, clear his throat.

'Have you been in?' I asked. 'Properly – over your head?'

'Oh yes. It's lovely on a hot day. But I know you don't like the water.'

He turned to me and smiled, too much. Spreading. My own face did the same, I didn't know why. I felt the warmth of him next to me, breathed in his scent of hay and horses.

'Oh,' he said, a note of surprise in his tone that didn't convince. 'I have something for you.' He held out the comb, a thing of beauty such as I'd hardly seen, and certainly never owned. 'It was my mother's. I thought – for your sister. To help with the, er—'

He had waved his hand over his head to indicate Annie's lops.

I studied his gift, running my fingers over the curved edges, the points of the teeth. When I looked up he was walking away, already disappearing into the cluster of trees.

Holding the comb now, that day feels so far away. Part of another life, that happened to another lass. I hold it in both hands, press it to me, just once. Place it on the table. Sigh, pour milk into a cup and lift it to Mam's lips. She does not look at me.

★

At first I think dawn is peeking through the gaps in wall and roof. The light is not constant, nor gradually growing stronger as it should, but laps against the house.

Something has come, and I don't know what. I stand in front of the door, watching the brightness slip and pulse through the spaces between planks of wood.

There's a cough outside.

Before I can waver, I yank the door open. No man will hold me imprisoned by terror in my home.

Were it not a threat, the sight would be beautiful.

A splash of yellow lights in the night, in a half-circle around the front of the house, seeming to float, though I know they're held by unseen hands. A few steps away, for those carrying them are too feared to come within a curse's reach of us. There are so many. Every person in the village must be here. I wonder which light is held by Daniel.

I stand in the doorway while Annie sleeps, while Mam whispers and weeps, watching the fearful, flickering beauty in the darkness.

The Stars Above

It was a mistake to come to the river. Like pressing a finger into an open wound.

He touched the places they had been. Here, they had searched for wood, here lit the fire. Lain together for the first time. There, they had swum. Here, he had given her the ring. He longed for all that he had believed to be truth, fumed at his own frailty in falling prey to her. Took the stone she had given him from his pocket, thought perhaps to hang it on the tree and see if she might come.

This was his farewell. He would not return.

At last, the moon clear above him and knowing he would begin work in but a few hours, he pocketed the stone and turned back towards home. Walked fast, until the bodily pain of trying to catch and keep breath was almost enough to distract from all else.

He had refused to join the witch walk of the previous night, his reputation for cowardice serving him well. Instead he had taken the ring, sought out Molly while the men lit candles and made their way up the cursed hill.

'What brings you here so late?' she had asked, stepping into the night.

'Marry me.'

Even in the darkness he could see the black blot of her open mouth.

'Were I free to refuse, I would,' she had said. 'Not because I do not wish to be your wife, but because you ask out of kindness and not love.'

'Kindness is as strong a beginning for marriage as any. And perhaps there is a form of love.'

She had looked out across the quiet sea. 'If there was love, you would know it.'

He shook his head. 'I don't think so.'

They stood side by side, watching the black lilting waves.

'Thank you,' she said, kissing his cheek.

Her footsteps were soft behind him. The ring still warm in his palm. He had not been able to part with it, in the end. Could conceive of it resting on no other finger but Sarah's, even now.

So today he and Molly had stood, awkward in their Sunday best, in Magistrate Wright's sparse room, an unlit fire laid in the grate, a Bible and a copy of the King's *Demonology* on the desk.

The magistrate held steepled fingers to his lips. 'The replacement minister is on his way and should be arriving any day. Once he has settled I'm sure a wedding can be arranged. In the meantime, I have other pressing matters to attend to. I would be grateful if such frivolities as weddings could be dealt with elsewhere.'

Daniel cleared his throat. 'I'm afraid there is some urgency—'

The magistrate had turned his cold, comprehending glance to where Molly's gloved hand lay on her belly. 'Ah,' he said. 'I thought it was an unusual match. I am unused to such – rural customs.'

Daniel had flushed with a shame he did not own.

'I am sure the new minister will be delighted to arrange such a happy occasion at the very moment of his arrival, and I shall inform him of his duty to do so.'

He stood, indicating the door.

'May – can I ask,' Daniel said, 'how your studies into the parson's death progress?'

Silence for a moment.

'I am all but certain I have discovered those responsible. I never rush such matters. The more thorough my examinations, the more sure that just punishment is carried out.'

The air had thickened around him and Daniel allowed Molly to thread her arm through his and lead him to the door.

'It's odd,' Magistrate Wright had said from behind. 'I must have been mistaken, but from my previous observations I would have supposed it to be the dairymaid that had taken your fancy.'

He had sealed his own fate. Not one filled with light as he had dreamed of with Sarah, but one that might atone for the pain he had unwittingly caused. Perhaps he could discard the shame that weighed so heavy.

His night visit to the river had left him walking home just as the tavern emptied. Someone whistled, hiccupped and then laughed. Daniel sighed, and turned to face his tormentor. Gabriel.

'Been taking a drink, I see,' he said.

Gabriel swayed before him, smirked. 'Oh, do you, you see, do you? I've been where the men go, milksop.'

Daniel made to leave, but Gabriel caught his shoulder, shook it. Breath sour with ale. 'Hear you'll be cleaning up my filings, Danny.'

'If you mean your cowardice in abandoning Molly, yes I shall step in where you had not the backbone.'

'Dare a snivelling shrew like you call me coward?' Gabriel's voice rose, but he was so unstable on his feet that Daniel had no fear. Were he to raise a fist he would likely fall to the ground. 'Take care yet, for the last to offend my honour came badly out of it.'

'I am in no mood to hear of your brawls.'

Gabriel bent forward, leaning on Daniel's shoulder with such unsteady weight that he almost fell. 'And of this one you nor no one ever shall, for another has took the blame and can speak of it no more.'

'Well, that's not – wait, taken blame for what? Who has?'

Gabriel smirked. 'Do not cross me. For I can do as I please and a ready-made villain shall bear the guilt and no one shall question.'

Daniel dared not breathe, dared not move. He must do nothing now to bring Gabriel to the ground beneath his feet, the stars above his head, and the truth he was about to utter. His heart drummed. He must know, and feared to know, what would be said next.

'If I can stake out a church man and not be found, then there is nowt beyond me.'

Daniel staggered. 'You?' he said, voice cracked. 'You killed the parson?'

Gabriel smiled.

'But – surely not.' Daniel's mind raced, understanding then denying what he had been told. 'Even you would not – you could not ...'

Gabriel stepped towards him, lurching to the side and righting himself. He scrabbled at the pocket of his breeches. 'You think I have not the courage? I am not man enough?'

Man, enough. Brute, enough. But not the demon it would take to commit such an act. Surely.

'Then what do you think of this?'

Daniel could not at first comprehend Gabriel's meaning, could not recognise the piece of black cloth that was waved in his face. Soft. Bloodstained.

He could barely speak the words. 'The parson's hat.'

Gabriel sneered, fumbling to place it back in his pocket. 'Aye. And I keep it about me all the while, so I may have a reminder that I do whatever I please.'

Gabriel. Not Sarah's brother. No demon.

She had told him as much. He had not stopped to listen.

'And you said she pressed against you, was that—?'

'Oh, yes. I pressed her against me, I laid my lips on hers. Felt her.' He made a drunken attempt to mime his actions.

Daniel swallowed, swallowed again. Mouth still full.

'Oh, she squeaked and struggled a bit but she wanted it, the little whore, I was not the first to make his mark, eh? Only because the parson saw did she protest, and I was forced to stop. But I made him pay.'

Daniel's jaw clenched.

No demon. No enchantment. She had not betrayed him.

He was a bigger, weaker fool than he had known.

'We should have been wed,' he said.

Gabriel swayed. 'What?'

'We would have been wed, and away by now. In another life. The life we said, it was real, we would be living it now.'

'What?'

Fury as he had never known surged through him. 'You took it away. You took it all away.'

As Gabriel opened his mouth to speak again, Daniel gave way to his anger, shoved him off his unsteady feet and sent him tumbling to the ground.

Tomorrow, he would visit Magistrate Wright. Tell all he had seen and heard. Gabriel would be found with his own guilt carried in his pocket.

Daniel turned back towards the river. Didn't know why.

Breadcrumb

I watch the lights gather into a line and weave their way down the hill.

John's blanket has fallen to the floor, and I pull it back over Mam as she sleeps, curled on her side like a child, and crawl at last to my bed, as dawn begins to make itself known. The ring of ash is unbroken around the mat. Sleep overcomes me at last.

I jerk awake, dazed from the first full sleep for days, feared that something dreadful has happened in the time that's passed.

'Annie,' I call. 'Annie, come here, where are you?'

Rise from the bed, not yet fully woken, stagger with the blanket wrapped around me to the door. Annie is at the table, spooning milk into Mam's mouth as she sits on a stool, empty stare seeing another, happier day perhaps.

Annie's eyes small and brown like a spadger's behind her mop of hair. 'What are you shouting for?' she asks.

'I didn't know where you were. I was worried.'

'You stayed in bed all day. Mammy was hungry.'

I look at Mam. Older and younger than I've ever seen her, her eyes hollow, face sagging and hanging in heavy lines, she opens her mouth obediently as Annie waves the dripping spoon in front of her.

'You're such a good lass,' I say, sitting next to Annie and putting my arm around her shoulder.

She wriggles from my grasp, spilling the milk down Mam's chin. 'Then why did you give me away?'

'I'd never choose to be away from you.'

'You gived me to that lady.'

'I'm sorry. I thought you might be better with her. Happier.'

'But you're my sister.'

'I know. I'm sorry.'

I pull her on to my lap. She resists at first, then turns in towards me.

I am feared, breathing in the scent of Annie that no longer carries traces of fresh air or trees or mud, but just decay. We wait, and I lose track of time, of days, and for what? For them to return with weapons instead of candles? For the magistrate to take us to the assizes and we languish until the noose?

If only Annie can be saved, that will be enough. She is so small. They'll know she is innocent, surely.

I carry her over to the door, open it, though night has fallen and there is only moonlight to see by.

'What are you doing?' she asks.

'We've to search.'

She tries to break free from my grip, struggles so that I am forced to tighten my hold. 'Nay,' she says. 'I don't want to, leave me be, let go.'

'Annie, stop. Don't be silly, we've always done it. Let me look.'

'Nay,' she shouts, sobbing. 'I don't want you to see.'

I let go. She stands, covering her face with her hands, tears dripping through her fingers.

My worst fear come about. I can barely speak. Gently, I pull her hands from her face, crouch so I am level with her. 'Show me.'

She rolls up her sleeve, crying, shows me the underside of her arm, just above the wrist. And I see the mark. Flat and dark, hardly bigger than a breadcrumb.

Enough to condemn her should the magistrate come looking.

'He's been, hasn't he?' she asks, turning her tear-sodden face to me.

I smile. Steady my voice. 'Oh, this? Nay, that's not him. That's nowt. I've seen the like on calves and pups and piglets, at the farm.'

She dries her face, gulps. 'Really?'

'Oh, aye.' I take her in my arms. She wipes her nose on my shift. 'Silly me, I thought he'd been.' Laughs through tears, her eyes both hopeful and fearful.

I will not see her hunted down. Will not see her taken by the magistrate. Darkness has closed in on us so completely that there is only one choice left to me.

'Let's go to the beck,' I say. 'Find a moon fish.'

She glances out of the door, uncertain. 'It's dark.'

'Aye. They're moon fish. That's when they come out.'

'All right.'

'Say farewell.'

Annie walks over, puts her arms round Mam, and Mam strokes her hair. As though she knows. I kiss her soft, sunken cheek.

'Goodbye, Mammy,' Annie says.

Mam turns her watery eyes to me, says nothing.

The beck is dark and deep, slow today. I take Annie's hand, walk her in.

'It's cold,' she says. 'I don't like it.'

'Just a little further.'

The freezing water is past my knees, up to Annie's chest. She gasps and clings to me.

'Where are the moon fish?' she says.

'Underneath.'

'We're going under?'

I force myself to smile down at her. 'Aye.'

'I won't like it.'

'Aye, you will. I'll be there.'

She starts to cry. 'I want to go home.'

She scrabbles at my legs, climbing up me, and I lift her on to my hip. Wade deeper, deeper until weeds taffle round my legs and the water reaches our chins.

'I'm feared,' she says. 'I don't like it, I want to go home.'

'It's all right.' I try to stop my teeth chattering. 'We're going to see the moon fish.'

She is sobbing now, shaking. 'I don't want to.'

'Just be brave a while,' I say. 'And then it'll be so beautiful, we'll be under and it'll be filled with sparkling fishes.' I spit water from my mouth. 'Not long now.'

Two more steps, and the riverbed falls away. I kick my feet into nothing. Annie's scream bubbles through the water that closes over our heads.

A sour, cold mouthful. Eyes stinging, chest burning. I hold tight to Annie as she struggles. Open my eyes and see her through the water, pale face, brown eyes, hair spreading. Little fox pendant rising between us.

I'm sorry, I say, but there is no space for the words. I just want you to be safe.

I watch her until the blackness closes in.

See the Storm

He looked out from the cover of the trees. Thought perhaps, with witchly power, she had sensed his longing and regret, appeared to him when he most yearned for her.

He did not understand what she was doing until it was almost too late. Waded and splashed through the water, fully clothed, boots still on, breath knocked out of him. Gasping, coughing, spitting. An undignified rescuer.

Reached for the sister first, knew it was what Sarah would want. She was so small and light. A tiny dark shadow, unmoving under the surface. Threw her on to the bank and staggered back for Sarah.

Don't let her be dead. Please don't let her be dead.

Dragged her by her clothes, lurched up the bank and fell, dropping her on the mud. The little girl was on her hands and knees, gasping and crying. Sarah began to cough as soon as she hit the ground. He crawled over, cradled her head, pushed the soaking hair away from her face. Waited to see the storm when she opened her eyes.

'I'm sorry,' he whispered. 'I'm so sorry.'

What Remains

I know I am not dead. I'm too cold and sore. My chest hurts and I'm chilled to the bone.

'Annie.' I try to shout but it comes out as a croak.

She crawls over and climbs on to my lap. I wrap my arms around her. Both shivering. 'I don't want to see the moon fish,' she says.

'All right.'

'I'm sorry,' Daniel says. 'I'm so sorry. I know it was Gabriel.'

I nod. He knows it, and I'm glad, but that will not help us. I cannot face the water again. He hasn't saved us, but taken our last escape.

'What will you do?' he asks.

'This was our only path.'

'No.' He shakes his head. 'No, it cannot be. I will not have it so.'

Just as Bett said. He can do no more than she. I hold Annie close.

'I should have believed you all along,' he says. 'Stood by you. Married you and gone away, like we said.'

'You couldn't. Seth was dead before we had the chance.'

'I will wish it always.'

I stare out over Annie's head. Dare not wish it, even. That life so far out of reach now. All I wish for is to save Annie from the magistrate, and I have failed.

He stands abruptly, pulls me to my feet. 'Go,' he says. 'Return in dry clothes, bring your mother and all you can carry. Come back here, wait for me. I shall not fail again.'

'Where are we going?' Annie asks, over and over.

'Away,' is all I can answer.

She is dressed in rags, but they're dry at least, grasping the whispering shell. Her most precious possession. I check her arms, her legs, the underside of her feet and between her fingers, looking for injuries from the beck. Scratches, bruises, but nothing that will last. I wrap a blanket around her. Change into my old clothes, the ones from before the mop.

Mam sits on the stool where we left her. I kneel at her feet, take her face in my hands. She looks at me, but I see no recognition there.

'Mam,' I say. 'Come with me.'

She looks towards John's bed.

I shake my head. 'I'm sorry. He's gone. Annie and I remain. You must come with us now.'

I ease her to her feet. She barely weighs more than Annie. I place a blanket around her shoulders and guide her. Our route veiled by night. One step. Another. Another. Annie takes her hand, walks with us.

Ours will be a slow journey.

★

Daniel waits on the riverbank. Annie has grown tired and I carry her, supporting Mam with my free arm. He runs, takes Annie from me.

'Here,' he says. Leads the way, and we follow.

On the path, tucked beneath an oak, stands Bonny, shackled to the Taylors' cart. Daniel lifts Annie and helps me to guide Mam in. She looks at him as she steps up.

'She was a good woman, your mother,' she says. 'The sweetest ever I knew. She gave you her spirit.'

Daniel swallows. 'Thank you.'

Annie curls under the blanket, thumb in mouth and head on Mam's knee, closes her eyes. Mam strokes her hair. 'There, there,' Mam whispers. 'Sweet babby.'

'Food,' Daniel says, indicating three cloth parcels. 'And the last of my mother's clothes.'

Peeking from the knot of one of the bundles is my bracelet, gleaming in the moonlight. The comb I clutch in my hand. I look at him. Tears stand in his eyes.

'You remember the name of the family the parson was sending us to?' he asks.

I nod.

'You remember the name of the village? The way?'

'Aye. But they're expecting a farmer's wife.'

He opens his palm, and there sits his mother's ring. Takes my hand, places it on my finger. 'Farmer's widow,' he says, voice shaking. He takes a shuddering breath, tips his face to the sky. A tear falls down each cheek. 'I would give anything to join you, but I cannot. There will be blood on my hands if I do. Molly is—'

'The brew didn't work.'

'I promised myself as husband to keep her from finishing her life. I'm sorry. I thought that—'

I taste my own tears. Look down at the ring. The gentle warmth that his presence brings will be lost forever, leaving me to face an unknown path alone.

Cold, the darkness that stirs in me now. He is to be Molly's husband, and I a widow. The flare of the dog's eyes is a white flame, the growl shuddering through me spiked with frost. I cannot see his face beyond the shadows of my fury.

I could let this creature take me over. One last time. Could wish upon him all the pain I feel at this moment, equal in depth to the joy we shared.

Mam's voice is dry and brittle, barely breaking through to me. 'They will always find a way to leave,' she says. 'I told you he takes them. The men we love.'

All that she feels for my father races through me, and is met by my own thoughts of Daniel. Love, rotted to bitterness. I blink, breathe. Tear myself free of it. I will not let myself hate him. I will not become Mam.

'Tell them you are a widow,' he says. 'And brought your mother and sister out of desperation.'

He helps me on to the horse, places the reins in my hand. From his pocket he takes the hag stone, unties the strip of cloth and fastens it around my wrist.

'For protection,' he says, voice cracking. 'Go, before light comes.'

'Daniel?'

'Yes?'

'Thank you.'

He shakes his head. 'I wish—'

'I know.'

I flick the reins and click my tongue as he taught me. Bonny walks on, and the cart rattles and jolts into movement.

'Sarah,' he calls. 'Sarah, wait.'

I stop the horse, wait for him to catch up.

'Tell them you're a widow because you are one,' he says. 'This body shall work and eat and sleep until God chooses other. But the part of me you brought to life goes with you.'

I lean down, press my lips against his for the last time.

He stays on the roadside and watches. Whenever I turn back I see him, until the path itself is obscured by hills and trees.

I hear Annie's steady sucking on her thumb behind me, Mam murmuring sweet words of love. What remains of my family. And I, Sarah, daughter and sister, dairymaid and widow, shall lead them past Middon, through Aldmore to Blackop.

I do not know if Dew-Springer rides with us. My own familiar, the creature born of my anger, is carried in me, unseen, and always shall be, for I choose a different life. Never shall it run separate, never shall it be named. And never in command of me, but I over it, to give strength when needed.

I look to a path obscured by shadow, so that what lies ahead remains unknowable. But the sun will rise, and when it does our new home shall be waiting. The darkness has dropped away again, and we travel from death, towards life. A life I will make with the chance Daniel has given us and my own honest labours. A life where Annie is fed, and free. No more shall I search her skin, no more shall she be the urchin from the cursed hill, feared and forsaken, but simply the dairymaid's sister, and will know herself only as this. Soon all memory of the life we leave behind will be washed from her.

But not me. I shall remember him always.

At last I am the other Sarah. I have crossed the river.

Acknowledgements

Writing this novel has taken a village, not least the one I grew up in, a community far kinder than the one in this book.

Huge thanks to everyone at Solihull Writers' Workshop, who nurtured my fledgling words, especially the Pub Club: Carla, Cheryl, Deb, Den, Pete E, Pete H, Ray and Sarah, for constant talent, wisdom and friendship.

Thank you to Richard Beard, Rena Brannan, Ian Marchant and everyone at the National Academy of Writing, where I learned the art of editing. To Lorraine Blencoe, Sofie Baekdal Brauner and Susan Haniford for years of friendship and inspiration.

I owe a huge debt of gratitude to the brilliant and generous Marian Keyes, who sponsored my scholarship place on the Curtis Brown Creative course. To Lisa O'Donnell, whose guidance was invaluable, the writers and friends I met on the course, and to everyone at Curtis Brown Creative.

Thank you to the excellent beta readers who helped me make this a better book, Kate Mascarenhas and Laura Tisdall.

I will be forever grateful to the dream team, Lucy Morris and Charlotte Cray, for their wisdom, passion and sheer hard work. I am still pinching myself. To Jodi Fabbri, Sarah Harvey, Luke Speed, Anna Weguelin, Isabelle Ralphs, Natalia Cacciatore, Hope Butler and Kate McQuaid for their enthusiastic support for the book, and to Glenn O'Neill for designing a cover more beautiful than I could have dreamed.

I am so blessed to be part of a big, happy family that find humour in everything and bring so much joy. I'm especially grateful to my late dad for passing his eccentricity on to me, and to my lovely mum who has offered support in every possible way.

Much love to my crazy, clever, compassionate children, Zoë and Ed, who amaze me every day.

And to Pete, whose talent never fails to inspire and whose support never wavers.